11-21-92

To Dale

May success
be your constant
companion

Best Wishes

Clifton J Busso

BREAKTHRU

BREAKTHRU

Clifton Brusso

VANTAGE PRESS
New York • Los Angeles

Published by Vantage Press, Inc.
516 West 34th Street, New York, New York 10001

Manufactured in the United States of America
ISBN: 0-533-08817-8

Library of Congress Catalog Card No.: 89-90469

2 3 4 5 6 7 8 9 0

CONTENTS

ACKNOWLEDGMENT

I would like to express my thanks to a very special unnamed friend who renewed my interest in writing and without whose encouragement this book would not have been possible. I also thank my family, especially my daughters, Courtney, for her time in editing, and Robin, for her contribution. A special thanks also to my friends who have read the book and encouraged me to publish it, especially Joanne Thomas, who painted the portrait for the cover.

PROLOGUE

Peter's story really began during his formative years, when as a dyslexic child he suffered the insidious label of stupid. His supposedly educated teachers in succession improperly tagged him with this sobriquet and influenced his fellow students and family to share their views, to his detriment.

The image created by this misinterpretation of his behavior was, unfortunately, ultimately accepted by him. The resulting feelings of utter emptiness rankled him clear through to his very bones, chilling him even during hot summer days. Loneliness, like his shadow, was his constant companion, changing his demeanor and causing him to shy away from life itself.

With no understanding and few friends, he turned inward. This left him with but one real ray of light: his brother, John. He was the ultimate reason for Peter's existence and the only one he could turn to in times of need or sharing his innermost feelings. That is, until now. . . .

BREAKTHRU

Chapter 1

PETER

THE door shot open wide, slamming against the siding on the front porch with such force it threatened to separate from its hinges. Peter, fear imprinted across his face, catapulted through the doorway and rocketed across the ten-foot porch floor, landing on the edge of the top step. One more desperate leap vaulted him over the thirteen steps to the sidewalk. His feet struck with sickening force, casting him to the cement in a crumpled heap. He sprang to his feet but, too late. His father pounced upon him like a tiger on a monkey.

He caught Peter by the back of his shirt collar, lifting upward. The sound of his ripping shirt screeched in his ears.

"You no-good, son-of-a-bitch! I'll teach you! You'll never lie to me again or I'll break every bone in your body!" his father yelled in an ear-shattering volley.

Twisting and ducking, Peter attempted to break free as he felt his father's work boot ram deep into his rear.

Suddenly, he felt his body being jerked, then twisted around to face his father. Immediately he felt a sharp jab in his guts. Pain surged up into his brain. Unexpectedly he felt his father's hairy, muscular arm wrap itself around his neck and tighten against his Adam's apple, pulling him off balance backward. Choking and sputtering, Peter attempted to pull it loose, only to feel the pressure increase. Unable to breathe, his eyes darkened, his body went limp, and he slumped to the pavement.

Lying in a heap on the sidewalk, carefully he opened his eyes as he slowly recovered. Coughing and sputtering, he was greeted by the sight of his red-faced father squatting over him. Still sputtering, Peter attempted to speak, but no words would pass through his spasmodic throat.

"You goddamned bastard! Admit you did it or I'll make meat pie out of your face!" his father howled, his menacing eyes fixed on Peter.

1

"But, Pa," Peter started to protest and quickly realized it was useless. Tears of pain filling his eyes, he knew he had no choice. Falsely he admitted, "I did it."

With a sudden jab in the direction of the porch, his father directed him, "You're grounded indefinitely! Get your ass in the house and up to your room! By God, you're going to straighten out or you'll only live long enough to regret it!"

Fearfully, Peter pushed his painfully aching body up from the cement, got to his feet, and without saying a word, headed for the house. He wanted to explain. He desperately wanted his father to know the truth. To believe HIM for a change, but it was always the same. *He's too stone-headed to hear my side. He won't listen to me,* he thought, while torrents of anger built up, eating away at his guts. Powerful feelings of resentment and hatred coursed through his veins. Dejected, he climbed the steps and headed for his room. He could hear the thumping feet of his father's heavy boots following close behind.

"You shit-head! I don't care if you never get out, this time!" his father threatened.

Peter knew the inevitable. Physical pain soon became secondary. A strong feeling of enclosure tightened his neck muscles, his guts drew up into knots as he thought about being locked in again. Mucus in his nostrils dried. His head began to feel as though it were being pressed in an ever-closing vise. The thought of confinement crowded his brain.

A desperate feeling of intense despair flooded his mind and drained his resistance. His situation seemed entirely hopeless.

Dragging his feet, slowly Peter moved into his gloomy bedroom and headed for the bed. He was entirely unsurprised when the door slammed shut and was locked tight with a sharp snap of the key in the lock. "Now stay there and rot!" his father growled, moving away from the door.

Peter, his face dug into the pillow, listened to the diminishing footsteps on the bare wooden stairway. *Will it ever end? Will I ever be able to stand up to him?* he wondered. It seemed he had no choice but to accept the inevitable punishments. *Someday I'll show him. He'll be sorry when he finds out that he's been wrong about me,* Peter told himself as he wept silently into the pillow. Oh, how he wished he had the courage to leave and never return. Desolation and an empty feeling of constriction once more became his companions. "No one cares about me, anymore." He remorsefully wept aloud.

The following day was shimmeringly beautiful. The sun's rays sparkled and danced through the multicolored leaves of the soft maple trees. But Peter didn't seem to notice as he crossed the city park on his way to Mather High School. Reaching the fountain, he hardly noticed the gray squirrel perched on top, licking the drops as they fell from the leaking spout. Blowing through the branches of the trees, a slight warm breeze purred pleasingly, but Peter's thoughts chilled his body. A few whirlwillies in their tornadolike manner appeared and then disappeared just as quickly, picking up bits of paper and spewing them helter-skelter in his path. His thoughts were intense, and his life seemed helplessly complicated.

Peter's mind came to rest on his brother, John. *Why has he changed so much toward me? We used to be so close. When I got into scrapes, he always looked after me, especially at home. He wouldn't go anywhere without asking me.* These thoughts rolled around in his brain as he moved along listlessly, in the general direction of the school.

"Hi, Pete!" He heard someone, and the sound was behind him to his right.

Recognizing her voice, he turned and as she approached, called back to her, "What's happening, Maggie?"

He looked at her. Her bright smiling eyes made him feel good inside.

She called to him. "Saw you walking by yourself, kicking at the ground and thought maybe something was bothering you."

He let her catch up with him before answering. "Naw, there's nothing bothering me." He lied because he didn't want to involve her or anyone in his problems. He knew he had to work them out himself.

She stopped beside him. Her face became stern, and she turned and faced him saying, "I know it's none of my business, but there are some times I think I just don't know you—you've been so moody lately. What's up? Do you want to talk about it?" Her eyes pierced his, hoping for an explanation.

"Everything's fine. No problem," he lied again, not wanting his situation to affect their friendship. He didn't want to have to explain what he himself didn't understand. Purposely he changed the subject, saying, "Say, how'd you like to skip school and go skinny-dipping over at the Mill Pond?"

"Peter Dunn! That's not something you ask a girl, especially a nice girl like me!"

Looking downward, then back up at Maggie, he reacted to her expression of astonishment. "Just kidding, you know that I respect you. I just wanted to see your beautiful brown eyes flash, as your red hair reacts to me. . . . But I forgot, red's the danger sign! . . . I'll have to try to behave myself. I don't want you to get down on me too." He paused and thought a moment. "But seriously, I've been thinking of skipping today. That stuff they give you doesn't turn me on one iota." Then,

3

smiling widely and with a lilting glance at Maggie, he added, "But you do!"

She looked to one side, then squinting her eyes and shaking her head, she responded, "I don't get you. One minute you're down and the next you're flirting with me!"

Peter had known Maggie O'Neil for many years in school. They had been dating each other for some time, but recently it seemed to Maggie their seeing each other had become less frequent.

She was the daughter of Irish settlers who had lived in the area on the outskirts of the city. They had been farmers, but when her father was killed in a freak accident by their tractor, her mother moved them into Boston proper. It was then that Maggie and Peter were able to spend time together after school. She was becoming irritated by the fact that she would not see him, except in school, for weeks at a time, but he would offer no reason.

This morning Maggie looked stunning in her colorful light blue frocked skirt with flowers sprinkled here and there. She wore a sweater she had knitted, which was a dark blue with white bands around the wrists. She stood out in sharp contrast to Peter, with his long black unkempt hair blowing in the breeze. He wore faded jeans and a flannel shirt that seemed to rebel, just as he. The corner hung out of his pants in the back, and the rolled-up sleeves showed tears where the elbows should be.

By now they had left the park and were heading toward the school.

"Will I see you tonight?" she asked, knowing full well that if he said no, there would be no explanation.

"Can't say," he replied. "If I skip today, I'll be in trouble if my dad finds out." He hadn't meant to mention trouble or his father to her. He wanted their friendship to be good, to be different from the rest of his life. She was to him an island of refuge in the stormy sea that his life was fast becoming.

With her face reflecting concern, she asked, "Peter, is there something that's happening that I should know about? That you haven't wanted to talk to me about?"

"Don't be dippy," he quipped. "There's nothing wrong. It's just that school is starting to give me claustrophobia. Sometimes, when I'm sitting in class, I feel like I'm suffocating inside. My nose gets dry, and I can't breathe. Also, elevators are starting to bother me. I get uptight inside them."

"Oh, Peter! I'm so sorry!" She queried, "Why didn't you tell me? We can walk the stairs or use the escalators from now on."

The tone of concern in her voice caused Peter to turn and take her by the shoulders. Then, while looking deep into her eyes, he was momentarily quiet. He wanted to share his thoughts with her, but he resisted.

Instead, he said, "It's no problem really, just sometimes. Don't worry about it. Really, don't look that way. I'm all right. . . . It's just that I don't want to go to school today. I'd rather spend it with you . . . but I don't want to get you into trouble, so just forget it! You go on in! . . . I'll see you around!"

He suddenly bolted down the street.

"No! Wait! Peter, come back! Talk to me! Don't go!" she called to him excitedly.

Maggie couldn't concentrate on her schoolwork. Her thoughts were constantly drifting back to Peter, wondering what was really bothering him. She had seen changes coming over him, but though she didn't understand, she knew they were affecting his life. What bothered her the most was that these changes were also keeping them apart. Time they could be sharing together, she was alone. Becoming more helpless in reaching him, she found herself constantly pressing him to explain and yet she didn't want to have him think of her as a nag.

She missed the closeness they had once shared. And a hopeless feeling of despair ate at her insides as she tried to concentrate on her studies. Questions raced through her mind. *Is it me? Is our relationship bothering him? Is it a fear of being tied down to me that's giving him closed-in feelings?* These thoughts and more darted through her mind. Swelling up into a sick feeling, they reached deep into her soul.

Ending her first class, she headed to the bathroom for relief. *How can I survive today feeling this way?* she wondered. Regret at not having skipped this one day and gone with Peter, as he had wanted, kept surfacing and she detested the accompanying feelings.

Bending over the bowl and feeling the end of the urging, then wiping her mouth with a string of paper from the roll, she stood upright and straightened her clothing. Visualizing through watery eyes, she recalled the good times she'd had with Peter. Her mind's eye changed perspective as she thought about how they hadn't been together after school for a long time. She murmured to herself, "I really miss him. All that precious time is lost forever."

Feeling too sick to return to class, but not wanting to be excused in case Peter decided to return after all, left her confused. She realized that if he did return and she missed him, she knew she would surely feel worse when she found out. *If only I had taken him seriously about skipping, maybe he wouldn't have left so upset.* She seriously questioned her decision.

Maggie's day passed in torment. She knew that Peter had grown deep within her feelings. Feelings that she took to be feelings that she had not dared to mention to him.

5

Worst of all were her own feelings of guilt that she'd felt helpless to resolve. Sneaking time to be with Peter, knowing of her mother's total dislike of him, also kept gnawing at her guts. She knew she had to resolve the situation before it affected her sanity.

Walking listlessly from the restroom, she considered her options: *Breaking off with Peter . . . but I know I couldn't stand that; standing up to Mom and dating Peter openly . . . but she can be mean and vicious when she's crossed and I couldn't live that way.*

Maggie had been hesitant about taking Peter home to meet her mother, because of her mother's Puritan approach to life. It was only recently that she'd had the courage. It was then her mother had told Maggie afterward that Peter was a "smart-aleck." She had added, "He's going to get into big trouble some day, and I don't want you to be with him when it happens."

Maggie struggled through the day with questions that brought more questions and left her even more confused.

Approachng the outside door, she pushed her way along with the boisterous mob that developed at the end of the day. Looking at the steps as she descended, she decided not to hassle Peter with questions about his actions when next she saw him.

Deep in thought and pondering much, she heard a noise and at her shoulder, she felt a touch, light at first, but then firm with a suddenness that twirled her around.

Immediately she recognized Peter—with that pleased smirk on his face. Her large brown eyes ablaze, Maggie blurted out, "Peter! You scared me! Don't you ever do that again!"

Sporting a big shit-eating grin from ear to ear, he answered, "Wanted to see you before I go home!"

She shot questions at him. "Where did you go? What did you do today? Why didn't you come back when I called you, as you ran off?"

Hurriedly he replied, "No time to tell you now, Mag. . . . Gotta get right home. . . . Don't tell anyone I bummed one. Tomorrow morning before school, I'll meet you in the park where I saw you this morning. I'll explain everything then."

Maggie wrinkled her nose defiantly. "I'll think about it. . . . I might, but only if you promise we can have some time together, so we can talk." Although she'd told herself she wouldn't even think her mother could be right, Maggie couldn't help asking, "Are you up to something you don't want me to know about? You're not getting into trouble, are you?"

"I'll tell you everything tomorrow. Be there!" he called back to her over his shoulder as he ran off. Then he pleaded, "Please."

Chapter 2

AN UNUSUAL SURPRISE

Peter arrived at the park early, so as not to miss seeing Maggie on her way to school. As he waited, he wondered how much he should tell her. Should he reveal his innermost thoughts? Feelings he wondered if she also shared? Because he'd remembered the look on Maggie's mother's face, he hadn't been able to show Maggie he loved her. Thus, he'd avoided the embarrassment of a situation where his feelings might not be returned. The thought of rejection was too much for him to take.

Peter stood leaning against a tree, absorbed in thought. Glancing up, he realized Maggie was standing in front of him.

"Hi, Pete." She frowned as she spoke. "Aren't you going to say something? You're in a dream world again. Didn't you see me come up?" she asked inquisitively.

Their eyes met. "Hi, Mag! Yeah, I guess I was lost in thought. . . . I want to be with you so we can be able to talk again, the way we used to." He paused, then added, "I want to SPEND TODAY WITH YOU— ALONE!"

Seeing the questioning look in her eyes, he pleaded, "Please, don't say no!" Then he followed with, "I'll explain it all to you, what's been on my mind for a long time, but I couldn't talk about to anyone—even to you."

"I do want to talk to you. But skipping school? I don't know." She looked directly at Peter. Knowing she wanted to be with him, she was in a quandary as to what she should do. Missing school was against her principles. She recalled her misery of the previous day and looked at the ground without responding.

"Please, only this one time!"

She looked to one side, then into his eyes. Seeing earnestness in his burning look, she hesitated before responding. "I've never skipped before. My mom would be furious if she found out, which she's liable to. Sissie might notice that I'm not there and tell her." Unconsciously she twisted her fingers together. "You know how she loves to get me into trouble."

Peter's grin disappeared and his face muscles tightened. "That's part of my problem. My older brother, John, has been acting kind of strange for a long time now and has been getting me into trouble with my parents. Sissie's younger than you and maybe she's jealous, but John and I used to be real close. Now he's turned on me." Then, establishing eye contact with Maggie, Peter pleaded, "Come on, Mag. Please, skip school today. It's just like a big prison, and anyway they won't miss you. . . . Let's spend today together. It'll be fun. I know a place where some of the guys hang out. We could go there."

Frowning, her eyes glazed over in thought. Then, she answered, "I don't know. . . . I could get into a lot of trouble. My mother doesn't like you. If she finds out, there'll be hell to pay."

Maggie saw anxiety growing in Peter's eyes.

He took her by the shoulders, pleading, "Please, say you will! It'll be great! I never knew this place existed. Jaako brought me there yesterday. I was really bummed out, but when we got there, it was so peaceful—like another world."

She looked away from his intense, piercing eyes. His incessant voice rocked her mind like thunder. She looked back into his eyes. "YOU'LL HAVE TO DECIDE QUICKLY BECAUSE SCHOOL'LL BE STARTING IN A COUPLE OF MINUTES. You won't be able to change your mind once you're inside."

Seeing his face muscles wrapped tightly against his cheekbones as he begged her made the decision more difficult. She stood quietly, simply gazing forward, with a serious look extending across the garden of freckles on her face. She wanted to go with him, but she knew the possible consequences could be a disaster.

Reflecting her perplexed feelings, her eyes were partially closed as she glanced around to see if anyone was watching her and Peter talking. Seeing no one, she spoke hesitatingly, "Okay, I really want to be with you. I suppose missing one day won't hurt, but you've got to promise me you won't skip school anymore, if I go with you."

"That would be easy if it didn't give me such a feeling of being boxed in, but I will honestly try," he assured her. Then, catching her arm, he gave it a tug. "Quick! We've got to get out of here fast before anyone sees us leaving." Rushing her, he grabbed her hand and began sprinting with her in tow.

Peter led her to the south side of the park, near several storage buildings. Rounding a corner he pulled up short.

"Get on!" he commanded as he seated himself on a waiting motor-cycle.

Showing displeasure on her stern face, she grilled him. "Where did you get this? You didn't steal it, did you? I'll never speak to you again if you did!"

He smiled slyly. "Don't be silly. I've never stolen anything in my life. Jaako loaned it to me for the day, while he's in school."

Having relaxed but still feeling hesitant about getting on, Maggie questioned, "Do you know how to ride good enough with both of us on it?"

His body surging with excitement, Peter answered, "NO PROBLEM. Jaako's let me ride it many times out in the boonies. It's a dirt bike and really easy to handle."

Maggie looked at him without moving.

Rushing her, he shouted, "Come on! Get on so we can get out of here."

She stammered, "I—I've never ridden before." Inside she wasn't sure she wanted to either. She had heard of them referred to as murder-cycles. Finally she asked, "What do I do? What if I do the wrong thing and we crash?"

Anxious to get started and trying to set aside her doubt, he encouraged her. "It won't happen! Do exactly as I do. When I lean, you do the same. Always lean into the corners—don't try to fight them by sitting upright. The bike might feel like it's going to slide sideways, but it won't." He caught her hand and pulled her slightly toward him. "Now get on behind me, and let's get going."

"Don't be reckless and get us killed," she pleaded while sliding her leg over the bike and pulling herself into position onto the seat.

He instructed her, while pointing to the foot rests, "Sit close to me. Put your arms around my waist and your feet on those two pegs down there."

Peter started the engine, and they moved out rapidly. He took the back streets to the expressway heading west. Having traveled a dozen miles, they cut off onto a side road that led to a bike trail, then up a steep grade.

As they climbed Maggie felt the wind take her breath. She called forward, "Be careful."

Holding tightly onto Peter, Maggie was trying hard not to slide off, over the back.

Feeling her grip tighten around his chest, he yelled back to her, "Just a little farther and it levels off."

When they reached the top, he turned the bike off the trail and shut off the motor.

"Well, how did you like it?" he asked, as she dismounted.

Her body thrilling to the new experience, she exclaimed, "Exciting! . . . I'd like to get one someday, if I could learn to ride it!" Then she added, "You took that hill like it was nothing! You sure know how to handle that bike!"

Kicking the stand down and sliding his leg over the seat, he answered, "Thanks, but it wasn't difficult. I like to ride these dirt trails better than the highways."

He set his helmet onto the seat and looked at Maggie. "You know, I could teach you to ride one. If you can ride a bicycle, this isn't much different."

She set her helmet beside his, shook out her shoulder-length hair, and walked to the top of a small rise. Peter followed.

Her head had become sweaty in the helmet, and the light breeze lifted her hair, tossing it around. She noticed how good it felt. She turned to look at Peter who was right behind her. She smiled and said, "Having the wind blowing in my face is like nothing else I've ever known . . . sort of the way a bird must feel, soaring through the air. In a way it made me feel like a bird—I just love it!"

Waving her hand across her front, indicating the expansive area, she changed the subject. "It's such a beautiful view from up here."

Looking to her right and pointing across the valley that stretched out before her, she exclaimed, "Look, Pete! There's one of those mile-long trains winding through the mountains over there! It looks like a huge snake, twisting like that!"

Peter looked out across the distant hilltops that lay at the bottom of the mountains across the valley. He grinned, then professed, "Sure is. I told you it was great up here, but that's nothing compared with what it's like up the trail a-ways."

He continued with, "I thought we'd stop here awhile before going on, so we can have a chance to sit and talk."

Maggie's attention was elsewhere. She noted with interest, "A flock of ducks from that pond below are coming right toward us. I'll bet they fly directly overhead."

Peter watched them change direction and fly off to his right. He commented, "This place is filled with wildlife. That's one reason I like it here so much."

Facing out toward the valley, Maggie invited, "Come sit by me."

Peter sat close to her on the rock. Looking at him, she said, "I know you've told me it was peaceful here, but I didn't believe it could be so beautiful. The quiet is so relaxing compared to the city."

10

"You're right. I wish I'd known about it a long time ago."

A quiet, peaceful feeling settled over Maggie. She took Peter's hand and gave it a slight squeeze. "I don't get away from the city much. This reminds me of when I lived on a farm. You could hear the cowbells at night and on warm evenings the bullfrogs' croaking was so restful. Sometimes they'd croak all night long, and I'd lie awake listening to them and dreaming of what I'd be when I grew up."

Maggie felt Peter's body move closer to hers, which added to her pleasure. She paused a moment, then added, "I've always dreamed of performing on stage."

Peter glanced at her and noticed a warmth in her eyes as she continued, "It would be great to be an accomplished actress. Being out in front of a lot of people is scary though, . . . but making them happy and enjoying what you're doing is important, too." Then turning and looking directly into his eyes, she queried, "Pete, have you ever had dreams of what you want to be? What do you want to do with your life?"

He tried to avoid the feelings of bitterness that began forming in him, but they took control of his mind. "Right now, I'd like to be through with school and get away from here! It's driving me batty! Half of those teachers are jerks. Nothing worth knowing is taught in class. They just give out homework and expect you to stay up all night doing it, so they can give you more the next day. I think they enjoy making our lives miserable."

He felt downtrodden and wanted to shake the feeling. He finally had a chance to be with his girl and didn't want the anguish these feelings brought. He put his arm around her shoulders and said, "Let's talk about something else."

"What do you want to talk about?" Maggie asked him. Having looked away she turned back and looked into his troubled eyes. She could see that something was on his mind and hurting him deep inside. She tried to encourage him to share his thoughts with her. "I don't want to talk about school anymore, either, but yesterday you said it gives you claustrophobia."

"I can't really explain it, but it's like the walls are closing in on me so bad sometimes that I can barely stand it. I can't concentrate, either. I just sit there, trying to fight the feelings. I've had it a long time now, but it's getting worse. Out here I feel so free that I don't ever want to go back. I know I promised you I would try and because I promised, I'll do it for you."

A deep sympathy for him swelled inside of her entire being. "Oh, Peter, I'm so sorry that you have those feelings. Why didn't you tell me. . . . Since yesterday I've been worried sick about you."

11

Noticing he was fighting back tears, she turned away.

She paused for Peter to speak, but hearing nothing, she continued. "Have you had these feelings long? How did they start? I mean, was there something that caused them?"

Wet spots formed in the corners of his eyes. He took a deep breath. Summoning up courage to be open with her, he replied, "I get locked in my room when I'm grounded. In there, I think I'll go out of my mind." He looked down. "When I was younger, it was because I wouldn't eat. But, then it wasn't too bad, since my older brother, John, would smuggle food up to me. I'd live in a pretend world when I was there."

After pausing a long moment and clasping his hands tightly together, he continued, "John was good to me then. . . . I don't know what changed him toward me." He looked off across the valley, thinking of reasons, but he was at a loss to understand it himself. He wondered how he could explain it to her. Finally he continued, "That's another thing that's getting to me. For the past year now, he's been screwed up. He steals money from my parents, and they blame me . . . especially my Dad. He whips me and locks me in. Then he'll say something like 'Penance cleanses the soul.'"

His shoulders slumped and his arms hung limp. "The other day he accused me of taking money from his wallet and chased me around the back yard. When he got right up behind me, I crouched down and he toppled over me. I was scared out of my mind he'd catch me. I jumped up and ran into the house. He almost caught me as I darted around the furniture, so I ran out the front door. I fell at the bottom of the steps, and he was on me like shit on toilet paper. He 's grounded me after school again, indefinitely."

Maggie felt a flood of compassion invade her mind. "Oh, Peter, I feel so bad for you." Her eyes expressed the compassion she felt for him. "Did you hurt yourself?"

"Not too bad. He punched me a bit and that hurt."

Peter looked at her through blurred eyes. He took several deep breaths, looked at the ground, and said, "I think John is on drugs, but I really don't know. He acts so weird sometimes. I just can't believe the way he is now." He paused again, sighed, shook his head, then continued. "My parents think the sun rises and sets on him, so I end up getting the blame."

Maggie lifted Peter's chin with her hand and looked into his sorrowful face. She leaned forward and kissed first one eye, then the other.

He picked his shoulders up and brought his limp dangling arms up onto his knees. Then, looking at Maggie, he leaned over and put his arms around her. He pulled her close to him and looked into her eyes.

He could see real concern dwelling in them. He remembered the last time they'd been together alone. He'd missed holding her like he was now. Feelings of love began welling up inside of him as he bent forward to her waiting lips. As they touched, he lost his balance and sliding sideways, they rolled to the ground. Maggie let out a cry as her elbow scraped the jagged corner of a rock.

Recovering quickly and fearing she'd injured herself, he checked to see what had happened to her. A small amount of blood oozed from her red, roughened skin. Fortunately, the thickened area prevented it from being torn open.

After catching his breath, he rolled her onto her side and kissed the sore. "A kiss to make it better," he whispered.

Lying beside Maggie, Peter leaned over and kissed her lips. She responded by putting her arms around his neck, pulling him to her.

Peter apologized, "I'm really sorry for being such a klutz. I'm glad you weren't hurt really bad."

"No problem," she responded with what she'd heard him say so many times.

He kissed her wound once more and then her lips. They laughed about the incident, and he helped her back onto the rock. Feeling good inside about Peter having opened up with her, she put her arms around him and gave him a long and sensuous kiss.

With the tension diminished, Peter continued explaining to Maggie what had been upsetting him at home. "I've been grounded this past year so much it's driving me out of my mind, being in that hell-hole of a room." He felt good talking with Maggie. Finally being able to explain his mysterious behavior to her made him feel good, and he knew she understood. He continued, "Now that I'm here with you, I don't want to leave. I don't want to have to go back ever, but I don't have anywhere else to go." He sighed remorsefully.

She felt a deep compassion for him. "Why didn't you tell me this before? Then I would have understood. I thought you didn't care about me and didn't want me with you." She paused, lowered her eyes, and finished with, "Maybe you had another girlfriend . . . I didn't know what to think. I didn't understand . . . I'm so glad we've had a chance to talk about it now. It makes me feel much better to know it wasn't something I did."

Peter squeezed her to him. "I didn't want you to worry about me. It's my problem and I didn't want to get you involved in it. You mean too much to me to have you burdened with my troubles."

She smiled at him. "Don't be silly. You know that I care for you and because I care, I want to share this with you."

Peter noticed how the deep brown in her eyes had widened into large circles. With renewed feeling, he continued, "I'm glad someone cares. I've been feeling 'who cares'? What's the difference what I do? I'm going to get blamed for it anyway." Pausing, relaxing his arm on her shoulders, he continued, "It's just that I can't take being locked in my room anymore. . . . The guys've been wanting me to do things they do, but I couldn't take going to jail. . . . I'd commit suicide first. . . . Just the thought of being locked up makes me feel uptight inside."

Maggie became concerned. "What kind of things do they do?" she asked in puzzlement.

"Picking up things at the stores sometimes. Sort of stuff like that. You know, little things. It's that sometimes I feel 'What's the use?' " He paused, then added, "I wouldn't do that kind of thing, though."

"Oh, Peter! How horrible this must be for you! Is there anything I can do?"

"I don't want this to affect you. I didn't tell you because I didn't want you to worry about it. Anyway, as soon as I'm able to, I'm going to leave this area for good." Then, still looking at Maggie, he finished, "I'd like you to come with me."

"I don't want to lose you, but I have another year of school to finish before I can go anywhere. Besides I would be a burden to you until you got a job somewhere. If you do go, you could get yourself established and then send for me. I'D COME THEN!"

Peter turned away from Maggie and stared out into the clouds on the horizon. "Maybe it's just a dream. . . . I'm sorry that I'm ruining your day with my problems. I had hoped this would be a happy time for us. When I was locked in my room and nothing to do but think, I wanted to be with you so badly that I could taste it. You were on my mind constantly." He turned back and looked into Maggie's eyes. "I'm crazy about you, Mag. I really miss you when we're not together. I need a friend like you. We've been seeing each other for a long time now, and I don't have anyone else I feel close to—or who even cares." He looked beyond her, then back at her and went on. "I've never had any real girlfriends 'til I met you, Maggie."

She felt helpless. She watched as tears swelled up in his eyes. Wanting to tell him that she loved him and to help him, she didn't know how he'd react. She wanted to say "I love you, Peter," but she couldn't. Instead she said, "I want this to be a happy day, also. I've missed you, too. I'd like to have a lot of time to share with you. I enjoy being with you and want us to be together as much as possible."

She looked toward the woods, then back at him. "It can't be all bad, Peter. There must be some happy times at home, for you. Maybe if you went to your father and talked with him, you could make him understand what he's doing to you," she suggested consolingly.

Looking back at the ground and rubbing his moist hand along his pants leg, Peter sat quietly without responding. Then looking up and slowly turning to face Maggie, he explained, "No . . . I've tried to, several times a while back, but he said I was just making excuses and wouldn't listen. He always thinks he's right. He's like that with my mom, too. He's just an old bull-headed German who won't listen to anyone. . . . I'll be all right now. . . . Let's go up to the shack. I want to show you something up there that's really unusual."

"Maybe if I talked to him. It wouldn't hurt to try," she ventured.

Peter got up and walked to the bike with Maggie following him. "No, he wouldn't listen to you, either. He'd really think I was hiding something then. . . . Let's forget about it. Come on. Get on and let's get going," he urged as he started up the bike.

The trail was narrow as it curved between large boulders and through dense thickets. The ride was rough, and Maggie realized with relief they were lucky that Peter had become a good bike rider. After they crossed a shallow stream, the trail widened out onto an area where there were huge limestone rock formations, some of them towering thirty feet into the air like malformed giants. Trees grew here and there, clinging fragilely to the sides, with their roots tangled in the rocks. Maggie stretched her neck to see around Peter and wondered how any vegetation could survive on such a barren area. She called out to him, "Those trees amaze me the way they fight to survive! If they can do it for so many years, we should be able to help ourselves, too!"

He yelled back, "It does say something for the will to live! . . . There's the shack over to your right."

Feeling relieved, she shouted back to him, "Good. My butt is paining me!"

As Peter guided the bike alongside the other cycles near the side of an old, half-dismantled, one-story building, he said to Maggie, "It's an old mill of some sort. Jaako told me this part was once a tool shed."

"It's sure different from what I'd expected," Maggie whispered as they entered a large one-room area and looked around.

On the wall to their right were bunk beds built of cedar poles. They had been stripped bare and had hearts and names carved into them. Burlap bags a few inches thick were spread over boards for mattresses. A large spool, discarded by a power company, provided a table, while a bench and several straight-backed chairs completed the set.

Pages from *Playboy, Playgirl*, and other choice magazines were pieced together to cover most of the walls. Drawn on barnboard in colored chalks was a mural of a woman in a squatting position, naked from the waist down. In her right hand, she held a roll of toilet paper. In her other, a length dangled behind her.

As Maggie's eyes came to rest on it, she flushed and began to wonder what she'd gotten herself into. But she decided not to say anything about it to Peter.

"Hi, Pete. Who've you got with you?" one of the boys called out.

"I brought my girl. This is Maggie O'Neil." Indicating the boy who had spoken, Peter introduced him, "That's Jack Kilner."

"Good know'n ya. Welcome to the den of evil," Jack said. Then he introduced his friends. "Meet the rest here, Ron Savoy, Terrin Blow, and Tammy Jones."

"Hi," they said in unison.

Maggie acknowledged them by waving her hand, and Peter nodded his head.

Jack appeared to be much older than Peter. The question of how Peter knew him popped into Maggie's head, but she didn't ask it.

He handed Peter a piece of meat, which was stuck on the end of a hunting knife. "Here, try some of this."

Peter accepted it and after the first bite, he realized he'd never eaten anything quite like it before. "Tastes different." He offered it to Maggie, "Want some?"

"What is it?" she questioned.

"Skunk!" one of the girls teased. Then she couldn't hold back her laugh, as she watched the expressions change on Maggie and Peter's faces.

Maggie turned down the offer. "No way."

"Terrin's a real vixen." Jack said, then he clarified. "That's venison. . . . You know, white-tailed deer." Then, glancing across the room, he admitted, "Guess I forgot to introduce Millie. Sorry." He offered his apology. "That's Millie Miller in the brown blouse." He pointed to a teenage blond girl sitting on the edge of the table.

"Hi," Peter said and Maggie smiled.

"About the meat. We shot it this morning out in back. Course, it's out of season, but it always tastes better when it's poached," Ron commented.

"Who did the decorating?" Peter inquired.

"It's a contribution of many. Terrin did the drawing. . . . It was Ron's idea," John answered and Millie cut in with, "Yeah, we had Tammy pose for it. Can't you tell by the fat ass? We disguised the face to protect the guilty. Anyway, we got the best part of her there."

Millie ducked quickly as the remaining soup Tammy had in her cup flew at her.

16

Losing her balance, Millie fell from the table, landing against Ron's shoulder as he pushed his chair sideways to avoid the soup.

They both fell to the floor in a tangled heap. Tammy shouted at Millie, "Your face and my ass make a good match."

Having recovered, Millie challenged, "I'll beat your ass, bitch," as she leaped toward Tammy.

"Settle down now!" Jack shouted as he caught Millie by the shoulders and held her back and cautioned, "Fight nice. We've got guests and we don't want to give them a bad impression."

"I'll get you for this," Millie promised while rubbing her butt.

"You and whose army?" Tammy retorted.

"Shut your face," Millie warned.

Looking at Maggie, Terrin explained apologetically, "Don't pay attention to them. They get carried away sometimes. I'm sorry you had to see them at their worst."

Maggie was stunned, but she tried not to show it. She had never expected anything like this and had only wanted to have a quiet day, expecting to be alone with Peter. Now she was regretting having missed school.

"Don't worry about it. It doesn't bother me any," Maggie lied.

Peter and Maggie stayed for a few minutes, talking to the others. Then, turning to Peter, Maggie mentioned, "It's getting warm in here. Can we go outside for a while?"

"Sure, babe." Then to the others, Peter said, "We're going out to catch some rays. See you all later."

Outside the sun was shining brightly through patches of clouds as it warmed the day. The sudden change from the dim room to the bright sun caused Maggie to squint at first. After adjusting her eyes, she suggested to Peter, "Let's take a walk and absorb some of this beautiful day. It's too nice to be inside and besides, I wanted to spend the day alone with you."

"Sounds great to me," he agreed, then said, "I'm sorry about what happened in there. If I'd have known they were like that, I wouldn't have taken you in there."

She passed it off with a shrug of her shoulders. "It's no big deal."

To their right were the remains of a demolished brick building with a partial wall remaining. Next to this stood a huge smokestack that towered above the trees. Piles of rubble from destroyed buildings was scattered around the area, attesting to the immense size the mill had once been.

As they walked slowly toward the piles, Peter put his arm around

Maggie and gave her a squeeze. He looked at her and said, "I wanted to be alone with you today, too. When I brought you up here, I thought we'd be the only ones here because it's a school day. We could have gone somewhere else, but this place is so special I knew you'd like it, too. I wanted this day to be an especially enjoyable time for us to share. I'm really sorry it turned out this way."

Maggie looked at Peter and believing him to be sincere, she said, "You don't have to apologize. It wasn't your fault. You had no way of knowing what was going to happen."

Watching the ground as they walked, she tried to be careful of the clutter underfoot. As they joined hands, Maggie looked up at Peter, saying, "Let's just forget about what happened and enjoy ourselves."

He smiled and answered, "Right on, babe."

His smile broadened and he announced, "I have a surprise for you."

This aroused her curiosity. "What kind of surprise? There doesn't seem to be anything here but these old ruins."

"You'll see. It's just ahead."

While climbing over a pile of loose bricks, Maggie lost her footing and toppled sideways, but Peter steadied her quickly.

"Have to be careful. Don't want anything to happen to you, do we? . . . Did you hurt yourself?"

"No. I'm fine. Just a bit clumsy, though," she answered laughing.

Approaching the smokestack, Maggie pointed to a large hole near the base that was rounded at the top. "What's that for? It's kind of odd-shaped, isn't it?"

Peter turned to her. "I don't really know. I suppose that's where it was attached to the furnace. . . . Let's go inside."

She fretted. "It might be dirty. We could get all black with soot."

"I've been in there already. The weather's cleaned it."

Maggie couldn't imagine Peter wanting her to go into it. She couldn't help but wonder what kind of surprise this could be.

Once inside he said, "Look up—it's like a long tunnel to heaven. . . . Yesterday, I just stood here for a long time imagining someone was going to shoot me straight into heaven through it. Just like when they shoot a clown from a cannon in the circus. It gave me a weird feeling."

"Oh look, Peter! There are a lot of small birds at the top."

"They're swallows. They were there yesterday, and I imagined they were angels waiting for me. I was so sick inside I felt like dying. To me life wasn't worth living anymore. It was as if I would float right up with them, if I did die."

Still looking up at the birds circling, Maggie began getting the feeling of being lifted upward. Her mind felt the sensations of slowly turning in circles and rising to the top.

"This IS a RUSH!" she exclaimed, while absorbing the feeling for a few moments. Then, turning to look at Peter, she asked, "What's the ladder for?"

"You climb it first, then tell me what you think," he coaxed her.

The ladder was about six feet long and stood leaning against the inside wall. At the top of it was a small hole through the bricks.

Still feeling weightless, Maggie had difficulty getting started up.

"Go ahead and climb it. I promise it'll be worth it."

Regaining her bearings, she climbed to the hole. Looking through it, she was amazed at what she saw.

"It's so beautiful. Is there some way we can get down there?"

Far below, a stream meandered through a valley filled with farming country. A hayfield, a few cornfields, and acres of golden grain captivated her view. In the center was a farmhouse and a red barn with cattle and chickens. In a pasture, a black stallion with a white patch across its face, grazed lazily on the long green grasses. A log rail fence separated it from the cattle. "Great place to build a castle," she called down.

"I thought that too," he answered. Pausing, then feeling confident, he added, "I think we can get down through the trees along the edge to the right. I haven't tried it, but we can take a look."

Outside in back of the smokestack, the ground fell off sharply. They couldn't see where the drop-off started because of the thick underbrush that obscured their view. Walking carefully through the thicket, Peter came upon the edge abruptly.

"Let's walk the edge and see if there is a way we can get down." He cautioned her, "Be careful and stay back a little so that you don't slip and fall over the edge—it's a long ways down."

Peter took her hand and guided her through the trees. The brush was thick in spots and tore at their arms, making it difficult to walk.

"That looks like it might be a trail up ahead." Peter nodded as they came to a thinner area. Then he questioned optimistically, "Maybe it will go all the way down?"

The trail had a steep incline and wound snakelike through the brush and rocks. There were many bad spots where the rains had washed away parts of the footing. Peter walked ahead, kicking footholds in the loose earth to make it easier for Maggie to follow. Slowly, they picked their way down and finally reached a plateau, which was still some twenty feet above the valley. The view was good, and Peter stopped to allow Maggie a chance to rest.

Sitting together on a fallen log back from the edge, Maggie was mesmerized by the tranquility of what lay before them. She felt a tinge of guilt as she thought of how she had believed Peter had known there would be people at the shack. She realized that questioning his intentions of wanting to be alone with her was not fair to him.

Getting up, she moved behind him and leaning forward, she put her hands onto his shoulders. Rubbing gently, she massaged his neck and upper back. "You could hypnotize me that way. OOOh—it feels sooo goooood. No one's ever done that for me before."

"Like it, eh? Maybe I'd better stop then or you'll have me doing it for you all the the time," she teased.

"Love it. Don't stop yet."

He changed the subject. "You know how we were talking when we stopped before we reached the shack?"

Maggie nodded her head as she continued to massage his neck. Not seeing her acknowledge his question, he turned slightly and asked, "Did you hear what I said?" When she confirmed she had, he continued. "It was good to be able to talk to you about my feelings. Now, it's like a heavy weight has been lifted from my entire body. I've wanted to tell you why I couldn't be with you, so many times before this, but I just couldn't bring myself to and have you worrying about me."

Maggie moved back to the log beside him, and he turned toward her and said, "I've always wanted to be with you. So many times I'd sit alone in my room, fighting the feelings of confinement. Thinking of you was the only thing that helped me control it. . . . You're the best thing that's ever happened to me, Maggie." Then tenderly he said to her, "I love you."

Maggie was surprised. She had known that he cared for her a lot, although he'd never talked about his feelings to her before today. Hearing him tell her this now sent shivers throughout her entire body. It was what she'd wanted to hear for a long time. Yet, she didn't know how to respond now that it had actually happened.

She looked at him intensely for long moments. Then, putting her arms around his neck, she kissed him lightly on the lips. As he reacted to her embrace, she leaned forward and with strong emotions building within her, she gave him a long and meaningful kiss.

Maggie had never before kissed him with such intensity. Peter felt a mixture of pleasure and desire. He'd had flings with girls before meeting Maggie that had ended in sex, but he knew this was different. He hadn't loved any of those girls and after he'd derived the pleasure of the sex, he was left with feelings of emptiness inside.

Fighting back desires of wanting to go all the way with her was difficult for Peter, but somehow he managed to hold them in tow. Knowing Maggie was different from the others, he wanted it to be special for them when they made love for the first time together.

Ending their kiss of passion, Peter whispered to Maggie, "I've wanted to tell you for a long time that I love you, but I couldn't. Sometimes, when I've tried to tell you, I'd get so messed up inside that I couldn't let you know my true feelings. I didn't know how you felt about me either, and that made it even more difficult. Now that I've had a chance to share my inner thoughts with you, I guess it was easier, but I still wasn't sure how you'd react to hearing it."

"You're a good person, Peter, and I really have enjoyed the times we were together. I know you've had a very hard time in your life and that it's been especially hard with no one to talk to about it. I know also that it must have been hard for you to tell me. I'm so happy that you've opened up to me, now." Momentarily, Maggie searched deep into his eyes, then she said, "I love you, too, Peter. My feelings have grown stronger for you each time we're together. I've tried to hide them, not wanting you to think I was fast or forward."

"I could never think that of you. You've been so quiet and reserved when you're with me. You're a living angel right here on earth. That's the way I've thought of you." He paused. Then pulling her to him, he kissed her again. There was no emptiness in him now. His longings were finally realized by the pleasure of having her love fill his heart.

Peter stretched himself out onto the grass in front of the log and invited Maggie to join him. He put his arm around her as she lay beside him, and she laid her head onto his shoulder. Wrapping both arms around her, he held her tight to him. "You don't know the gnawing that's been going on inside of me. Sometimes it felt like my guts were being torn apart. Now, just knowing that you share my love gives me the courage to go on."

Feeling a little guilty, he said, "It bothers me, though, that you had to miss school just to be with me. But it looked like there was no other way for us to be together." Then, pausing and showing concern, he added, "I hope you don't get into trouble over it."

Maggie felt peaceful inside being with Peter, like this. Feeling his heart beat against her breast excited her. She was silent momentarily before speaking. "I'm not going to worry about it. I'm so happy that we can be together now. . . . I want to be with you forever."

Lying in his arms like this had been an unfulfilled longing that was finally being realized. She knew that she didn't want to be without him anymore. She whispered, "We can take care of each other. I don't even care if my mother finds out that I missed school. It's worth anything she could do to me, just to have this precious time with you. Being together like this makes everything all right." Twisting her head to look at Peter, she continued, "We've been missing out on a lot of enjoyment not being able to be share our time together. I don't want it to be that way anymore. Somehow we've got to find a way to be together." Maggie paused. Then, as an afterthought, she added, "I'm sorry, Peter, that I thought you didn't care to be with me. I've missed having your company and didn't know the reason you couldn't. Now that I know, I'll never doubt you again."

She whispered in his ear, "I do love you, Peter—I have for a long time."

Chapter 3

UNEXPECTED CIRCUMSTANCES

Maggie's mother, Desney, a woman with a six-foot stature, dwarfed her two daughters, Rebecca (Sissie), who stood five-foot-four inches and Maggie, who was a mere five-foot-two inches tall. The girls took after their father, who was slight of build, while their mother's large frame supported two hundred pounds plus.

Sitting in the living-room chair, which gave her a view of the entrance door, Desney waited for Maggie to return home, while giving the appearance of reading a newspaper.

Not seeing her mother at first, Maggie pushed the front door open and walked in.

Springing forth from her chair and looking disheveled in her loose-fitting, light-blue-flowered house dress, Maggie's mother charged toward her. "What's the meaning of this?" she demanded.

"Of what? I'm just a little bit late, Mom!" Maggie explained, trying to appear innocent.

"Your not being in school and now getting home at this hour," Desney yelled, not caring if the people in the other half of their duplex could hear.

Maggie lied while trying to appear calm. "I WAS in school. I suppose Sissie's trying to get me into trouble, again. Anyway, I was only talking with Peter in the park and lost track of time. That's all."

Desney's face muscles drew tight. With her eyes bulging while holding her white lips tight to her teeth, she shouted, "I knew that boy had something to do with this! . . . When Sissie told me you weren't in school, I figured that Dunn boy was behind it! Don't you lie to me about it! Sissie doesn't lie to me! What she told me is the truth! Admit you spent the day with him or I'll beat it out of you!" she persisted threateningly, while holding her hand menacingly ready to strike.

"Ma! I'm not lying! Sissie isn't telling you the truth. You always believe her and not me. I WAS THERE—she JUST DIDN'T SEE ME, that's all."

Desney's face, white with anger, yelled, "If you're lying to me, I'll tan your hide and you'll never go out of the house after school again! . . . NOT EVER! I won't take your lying to me, and you know it. I can check with the school tomorrow!"

Maggie's eyes glared her resistance. "Go ahead and check if you don't believe me!"

"I will!" her mother raged with determination.

Calming herself down somewhat, Maggie held up her hands. "Mom, please calm down now. I'm sorry I'm late. I won't do that again. Maybe Sissie didn't see me there . . . but I was, honest."

Turning and walking away, her mother started to climb the stairs. Glaring back at Maggie, she proclaimed in a more controlled manner, "I'll let you off this time, but don't you ever see that Dunn boy again! Do you hear me! . . . NOT EVER!"

Maggie knew she should have been home earlier, but the time had passed so quickly and against her better judgment, she had allowed Peter to convince her that one more hour would be all right. Besides, she had reasoned, they hadn't been able to be together in a long while and had so much to talk about.

Maggie didn't see Peter the next morning on her way to school, and it bothered her. Although this wasn't unusual, it made her wonder if he would be keeping his promise. Anxiety swept through her as she searched the halls for him.

Trying to avoid being seen with Peter, so that Sissie won't tell Mother, will be an ordeal, Maggie was thinking, when she heard him talking with his friends behind her. Turning around and smiling, she waited for him.

Raising his eyes up from the floor as he walked, he caught sight of her. His face lit up. His eyes brightened. "Hi, Mag."

Happy to see him, Maggie blurted out, "I'm so glad you came, Peter!"

Separating from his friends, he walked alongside of her. "Hope you didn't get bagged for yesterday."

"I did. I felt like I was chewed up and spit back out. Sissie told my mother that I wasn't in school. I know my mom means well. She never had a chance to get an education herself. She's a clerk at the supermarket and tries hard to provide for us. It means a lot to her that I graduate with good grades," Maggie explained as they walked. "It's her temper. She flies off quickly, and it takes a long time for her to calm back down."

Maggie reached over and took Peter's hand. "She's been depressed a lot lately, too. I don't know what that's about, 'cause she won't talk

24

about it. . . . I really shouldn't have skipped." She stopped Peter, looked at him, and with a slight frown, she added, "She knows I was with you and doesn't want me to see you anymore, either."

Peter became concerned. "I don't want to stop seeing you. You'll be seventeen in a few months. Then she won't be able to tell you what to do."

As they began walking again, she answered, "She will as long as I live at home. And, I've got to finish school, so I have to live there until then. But, that's not it. I don't want to hurt her, and I want to be with you. . . . So what do I do?" she asked him, as they approached his first classroom door.

"Don't look so down. We'll figure it out. Now don't worry. Everything will work out all right," he tried to reassure her, as he entered his classroom. "See you at the break."

Maggie couldn't stop worrying. The problems on her mind were all-consuming, as she walked toward her classroom.

When the class was over, she headed listlessly toward Peter's classroom. Upon seeing him emerge, she walked over to him and asked, "How was class? Did you get that enclosed feeling, at all?"

"I was thinking about us and what we talked about yesterday, so it wasn't too bad. But, it started coming on toward the end. When I keep my mind busy, I'm not aware of it," he said as he guided her into the hallway that led to the gym.

He continued, "I'm concerned about us and how we can be together without you getting into trouble because of it. I thought about it a lot in class. The more I think about it, the more uncertain I am as to what we should do."

They stoped near the entrance to the new gym, which was still under construction. A few other students had already gathered there.

As Maggie and Peter continued talking, a teacher appeared at the far end of the gym floor. One of the boys, seeing him, whispered to the others in the group, "Here comes a teacher. Get rid of the cigarettes.

Those who were smoking threw them up onto a small ledge that had not yet been sealed in and hurried away. Peter and Maggie were alone when the teacher approached, but they were so engrossed in their conversation they didn't hear him.

"Better get to class or you'll be tardy," he warned them.

Back in class, Maggie found it difficult to concentrate. The last class was nearing its end when the fire alarm sounded. The suddenness of the bell brought Maggie back to reality. *It's another drill*, she thought as she joined the others in filing out of the building.

Once outside, she heard fire trucks off in the distance and searched the crowd of students, hoping to spot Peter.

The principal made an announcement from the steps of the school, but Maggie was too far away to hear what he'd said. Looking to her right, she saw smoke and flames billowing out through an open window of the gym.

"My God!" she exclaimed half to herself, "the school's on fire!"

The students were leaving as Maggie sought out Peter. Seeing him near the park, she called out, "Peter! Wait for me!"

Running to him, she blurted out excitedly, "I don't believe this! The school is burning! They haven't even finished building it, and it's burning up! . . . I was daydreaming about us in class when the alarm rang! I thought it was a fire drill! . . . When I got outside, I couldn't believe my eyes. It was on fire!"

Peter glanced at the burning school and said questioningly, "I wonder how it started? Maybe . . . the construction workers got careless."

Maggie looked at Peter and said, "Mom won't believe me when I tell her that I'm home because the school is on fire."

He took her hands as they began to leave the school grounds. "She'll have to believe you. It'll be on the radio and TV. Before you go home and tell her though, let's spend some time together. How'd you like a soda?"

"I'd love one!" she replied enthusiastically.

Peter was in his room that evening when there was a knock on the front door. His mother, Delmar, answered it, talked with the person standing there, then called up the stairwell. "Peter, the police are here. They want to talk with you. Something about the school fire."

While descending the stairs, Peter's thoughts ran through his mind. He wondered, *What do they want me for? I don't know anything that would have to do with the fire.* As he turned the corner at the landing, he could see two men. The closest one to the stairs wore an unbuttoned light tan trenchcoat. He could make out the light blue tie and gray suit he wore underneath. *Must be a detective*, he thought.

Peter felt nervous. He could see only the head of the second man who stood to the rear, near the door.

Upon seeing Peter, the taller man in front, his face lacking expression, asked, "Are you Peter Dunn?"

"Yes. Why do you want to see me? I don't know anything about the fire."

"My name is Detective Sergeant Ronald Blake. This is Officer Grandstead. We'd like to ask you a few questions about the school fire. First, Officer Grandstead will read you your rights."

"Is he being accused of it?" Peter's mother, Delmar, interrupted

26

excitedly. "My son has never been in trouble with the police."

Stone-faced, Sergeant Blake turned to her and explained, "We only want to ask him a few questions. He was seen in the gym area with a few others between classes this morning and was identified by one of the teachers. The others left quickly and he wasn't sure who they were, but your son was there with a female student when he approached. He didn't know who the girl was. . . . No charges have been filed. At this point we only want the names of the other students and any information your son might have, which will help in the investigation. First we must read him his rights." Then, turning to his partner, he instructed, "Go ahead with it."

When the officer had finished, Detective Blake, in a fatherly tone, asked Peter, "Do you want to answer the questions now or do you want a lawyer present?"

Delmar interrupted him in a controlled voice. "We're poor people. We can't afford a lawyer and never had to have one before. We are law-abiding citizens."

"Yes, we know, Mrs. Dunn," he assured her and was about to address Peter, when he was interrupted again.

"My son has nothing to hide. Go ahead, Peter. Tell them what they want to know. Do you know who did it? Tell them if you do."

Peter relaxed a little as he spoke. "Sure, I was near the gym this morning. Maggie and I were talking when Mr. Gregor came over. I wasn't paying much attention to anything but Maggie. I don't remember who else was there. . . . Is that where the fire started?" he asked in wonderment.

Ignoring his question, the officer continued, "You're sure you don't remember anyone there with matches or cigarettes?"

Peter shook his head, indicating he knew nothing about it.

"What about someone who might want to light a fire? Do you know anyone who would want to see the school burned?"

"No, I don't. I can't imagine why anyone would do it," he answered, still feeling a little nervous.

Looking toward his mother, anticipating possible disapproval, he added, "My girlfriend, Maggie, might remember something. You can ask her."

"What's her last name?" the shorter officer, who had been quiet until now, asked as he stepped forward holding a notebook and pen.

"O'Neil. Margaret O'Neil."

"Know her address and phone number?"

"It's 3845 Agate Avenue, and her phone number is 555–4365."

"That'll be all for now. We may be back. Thank you for your assistance," the detective said, as he replaced the black cap he'd held while talking and then, turning toward the door, they left.

"Your father will be upset when he finds out that the police were here. You know how he feels about our reputation in the neighborhood. . . . It'll be best if you try to avoid a situation."

Still upset from being questioned and knowing his mother was right about his father's anger upon finding out what had occurred, Peter felt an uneasiness surge up into his guts. He attempted to assure his mother of his innocence.

"I didn't do anything wrong, Ma. We were just talking near the gym. Maggie'll tell you the same thing. . . . You haven't met her yet, but I know you'll like her. She's been a good friend to me."

"All right. I believe you." Then looking at Peter with interest, she asked, "What does she look like? . . . Is she older than you?"

"No, Ma, she's not older than me! She's about eight months younger. . . . She's a really nice girl. Kind of short with reddish-brown hair. I've known her a long time, and we get along good," he explained, feeling relieved in believing his mother was apparently receptive to his having a girlfriend.

Broaching a smile, she told Peter, "You go back upstairs now. When your father comes home, I'll explain to him about the police being here for information."

Peter's mother was an excitable woman, who held a sensible head on her shoulders. Had she been married to another man, Peter often thought, she would have had a much better life. She would try to intercede for him when his father came down too hard, only to be turned on herself. This would send her recoiling back into silence. Acting like a tyrant was the manner in which Peter's father, Adolph, attempted to dominate the world he was constantly at odds with. It wasn't that he was entirely mean, but his insistence on everything being his way made him difficult to be with.

Raised by his parents in postwar Germany, Peter's father had learned frugality, which he brought with him when he emigrated to the United States in 1951 at the age of nineteen. Peter's brother, John, was an exception to his father's wrath, being the first born and three years older than Peter, which gave him privileged status. This was not to say that he was exempt from criticism, but whenever Peter was present, the rage would inevitably transfer to him.

Peter was awakened late that night. He sprang upright in bed at the first sound of his father's voice. Through blurred eyes he saw him standing in the doorway.

"What's this business with the police all about?" he questioned angrily.

"Nothing, Dad. They were trying to find some of the guys they think may have set fire to the school. I couldn't tell them anything, 'cause I didn't know who any of them were."

"You'd better not have anything to do with it!" he shouted, then finished with, "You DAMN WELL will regret it if you did!"

Turning, he stalked from Peter's bedroom, slamming the door behind him.

The following day, when Maggie returned from the public library, her mother met her at the door.

"Mag, a Detective Sargeant Blake from the Police Department was here. He wants you to call him at the police station. He said he thinks you might know who set the school on fire. . . . Do you know anything about it?" she asked. Her face drew tight. "I have a feeling it was that Dunn boy you've been hanging around with. I wouldn't put it past him to do something like that. He's no good, through and through."

Maggie's voice became protective, "Oh, Mom! I know you don't like Peter, but he's not that kind of person. He wouldn't do anything wrong. I know him too well to believe something like that about him. . . . I don't have any idea why the police might think I know something about the fire. I was as surprised as anyone about it. I thought it was just another fire drill—'til we got outside and I saw smoke and fire coming out of the windows."

"I believe you didn't have anything to do with it, but if you know anything about it, you'd better tell them what you know."

"If I knew anything, I would. I don't have the slightest notion why they think I might know something," Maggie stated. Her face was covered by a puzzled expression.

Maggie turned and walked toward the phone, "I'll call them right away."

After hanging up the phone, she called to her mother. "They want me to come down to the police station. I'll be right back. See you later."

Maggie had not seen Peter for three days since the fire and felt uptight inside, wondering why he hadn't gotten in touch with her. She'd walked by his home a few times, hoping to see him in the yard, but she was disappointed in not seeing any sign of him. She was sure they'd become much closer after spending the day at the shack. Now she tried to avoid the feeling of doubt that was beginning to come over her.

Since no decision had been made as to where they would be attending school, their days were free for the time being and she wanted to spend time with Peter. She had even tried to call a number of times, but she

29

was met with either no answer or the line remained busy for long periods. Each day without hearing from him frustrated her more deeply.

On the morning of the fourth day after the fire, Maggie met her friend Mary Schultz at the Edgewood Shopping Mall.

Mary greeted her cheerfully, "Hi, Maggie."

A smile crossed Maggie's face as she responded, "Hi, Mary. Sure is a nice day."

"Just great."

They walked along the midway toward the Giant Restaurant. Unaware of Maggie's close relationship with Peter, Mary casually inquired, "Say, did you hear about Peter Dunn?"

Maggie's ears perked up quickly, and her face muscles tightened. Looking at Mary, she tilted her head to one side and blurted out, "What about him? I haven't seen him for a few days and have been wondering about him."

"I heard that the police are holding him. They've charged him with setting the fire at school, and he's in jail."

Maggie stopped walking. Her face turned ashen white, and she half-shouted out, "I don't believe that!"

Mary hadn't expected Maggie to react in this way. She became concerned and explained, "I heard it on the radio this morning. Everyone knows."

Maggie's breath came quickly as she became defensive. "It wasn't him! He would never do anything like that! The police came to see me the day after the fire! Peter had told them he didn't know anything about it! They wanted to know who else was at the gym that morning, when Peter and I were there talking! They knew we were there because a gym teacher had recognized him and told them about it!"

Mary became upset. "You don't have to shout at me!"

Maggie calmed down somewhat. "I'm sorry, Mary. I didn't realize that I was. But it makes me so mad. I told them the same thing Peter must have, that we were talking and that's all! We weren't paying much attention to the others who were there, but I remembered Bell Brown was with her boyfriend, Rick. I told the police that, but I don't think they had anything to do with it, either." She breathed easier. "Why would anyone want to purposely burn it? It doesn't make any sense to me."

Mary explained, "I knew you and Peter had gone out together a few times, so I figured if you didn't know, I'd better tell you."

"I haven't heard the radio or TV today, so I didn't know 'til now. I'm glad you told me."

Feeling hyper inside, Maggie declared with determination, "I've got to go down there and see him! They've made a mistake, and I can prove it. I'll testify to that!"

Her stomach muscles churned her food to liquid. She couldn't contain herself. "I feel that I should go to the station right now . . . I wonder why his parents haven't gotten him released by now. If he's been there since Wednesday, he's probably climbing the walls. He can't stand being cooped up like that," she said to Mary and followed with, "I hope you don't mind. I know that we planned this a couple of days ago and I wanted to look around with you, but this is upsetting me. I won't be good company anyway, with this on my mind."

Attempting to be helpful, Mary suggested, "I understand, Maggie, but maybe if we get something quick to eat, we can talk about it. You might remember something else that could be important. We're already at the restaurant, and you do need to eat in case you don't get a chance later. Besides, maybe there is someone else who's always in trouble with the teachers, like Bill Gretts, who did it. Do you remember if he was there when you and Peter were talking?"

Maggie made a quick trip through her memory banks. "I don't remember seeing him there, but then I don't remember much. We were so absorbed in talking. I hardly knew anyone else was there. I was too interested in what Peter and I were talking about." She paused and started walking again before agreeing. "Maybe you're right. I should eat something. A few minutes won't change anything, and I'll probably feel better." Then, as they turned into the restaurant, she continued with, "I am a bit hungry."

"Is my Uncle Mike in?" Maggie asked Jean Murphy, his receptionist.

Looking up, Jean smiled when she recognized Maggie. "Hi, Maggie. Yes, he's here, but he has someone in with him. Why don't you sit and wait awhile? I'm sure he won't be long . . . How are your mother and sister?"

"Thank you," said Maggie as she walked to a chair. She added, "Oh, they're just fine. . . . I hope he doesn't take too long. I have somewhere else to go."

They were interrupted by the intercom. "Jean, can you come in here, please?"

"Yes, Mr. O'Neil. I'll be right there," Jean answered. Then, turning to Maggie, she mentioned, "I'll tell him you're waiting to see him."

Maggie had changed her mind about going directly to see Peter. Instead she'd decided that it would be better to talk with her uncle, who was a defense lawyer. She believed that he might be able to advise her as to what she could tell Peter, in case he didn't have his own lawyer.

She found it difficult to constrain her feelings of anxiety while she waited in her uncle's office.

A short while later, Jean returned. "I told him you're here. It'll only be a few more minutes."

Having returned to her desk, she looked at Maggie and asked, "Isn't this beautiful weather we're having?"

Forcing her mind to respond, Maggie answered, "Yes. It is very nice today."

"Were you attending the school that burned?"

Trying not to appear impatient, Maggie replied, "Yes, I was. They haven't decided where they're going to send us, yet."

"That was a terrible thing that happened. A new school and all. I've heard they have a boy they say started it. . . . What some kids won't do for a thrill these days," Jean stated matter of factly.

This casual remark ground at Maggie's insides. Instinctively she felt compelled to defend Peter. "It wasn't him!" she responded sharply.

"I'm sorry, Maggie. I didn't know that you knew him."

The fire that had ignited in Maggie, ebbed slowly. She stated, "Yes, I know him. I was with him when someone else lit it on fire."

"Did you tell that to the police?"

"Yes, I told them everything I knew. Peter did, too. Apparently they didn't believe us."

"And that's why you want to see your uncle, isn't it?" Jean asked in an understanding tone.

"Yes." Maggie hadn't wanted to discuss this with her uncle's secretary. Not that Jean was a gossip, but she'd hoped to keep her mother from finding out that she was trying to help Peter. And she wasn't sure she could trust Jean to not repeat what she knew.

"My mother would be upset if she knew I was here. Please don't tell her," Maggie requested.

"I won't tell a soul," Jean assured her.

Her uncle's office door opened, and he emerged talking with a young blond woman. Seeing Maggie, he turned to her and said, "Hi, Mag. What brings you indoors on such a nice day?" Then, not waiting for an answer, he turned back to the young woman and said, "I'll take care of those things for you and get back to you sometime next week."

When he'd finished, he turned back to Maggie. Noticing the look on her face, he asked, "What's troubling my favorite girl?"

"Can we talk about it in your office?"

"That bad, eh? We certainly can," he agreed, and extended his arm, indicating she should precede him. Once inside, he closed the door and asked, "What's this big problem you have that's made your face so scrunched up?"

Maggie had been more like a daughter to Mike O'Neil since the death of her father, but now she found it difficult to ask for his help. Twisting her fingers into knots, she looked at the floor, not sure how to express herself. Finally, after an uncomfortable minute of silence, she looked up at him and said, "I don't know if I should ask for your help, but I don't know who else to turn to."

"I've never seen you this way before, so it must be something awfully important. Why don't you just tell me what's bothering you? Then we can decide if I can be of any assistance."

"All right. Uncle Mike. I hope you will help. You have always been good to me, and I hate to have to ask you for anything. . . . It's not really for myself, either. I have a friend who has been falsely accused of setting fire to our school."

"I've heard that they have a boy by the name of Peter Dunn in custody. Someone reported having seen him at the scene."

"But they have it all wrong! I was there, too, and they haven't put me in jail!" Maggie blurted out, unable to control the anger she'd been holding inside.

"Why don't you start from the beginning and tell me everything you know about what happened?" He encouraged her with a smile.

After explaining the circumstances of the fire as she knew them, Maggie concluded with, "He can't stand to be confined! He's probably half out of his mind right now!"

"I can understand how important this is to you. I'll go right over to the police station and talk with him. If he's still there, I'll try to have him released on bond. From what you tell me, he probably doesn't have his own attorney, so he may have a court-appointed one. If it's agreeable with him, I'll represent him. You can be assured that I'll do what I can for him."

"I don't want my mother to know that I asked you to do this for me," Maggie said, her face showing apprehension. "She doesn't like him. I know that she thinks he's guilty, but she doesn't know him like I do. He is really a very good person."

He walked over to Maggie and put his arm around her shoulders. "I believe you. You've always had a good head on your shoulders, and I trust your judgment."

"I'll never be able to thank you enough for doing this for Peter. I just know that he'll die in prison if they succeed in blaming him for the fire."

"We'll do whatever we can to prove what you've told me is true. Right now I should get over to see about having him released."

As they walked out of his office, Maggie asked, "Can I go with you? I want to see him."

Allowing her to proceed him out of the door, he agreed. "You're darn tootin', you can."

When they arrived at the police station, Mr. O'Neil went in to talk with the captain, while Maggie stayed in the waiting room. After a few minutes, he came out. "They've transferred him to the county jail this morning. Captain MacIntyre wasn't sure if they'd appointed an attorney for him, yet."

"I'm so worried about him. I know what he's going through. Please, let's hurry," Maggie requested.

Maggie's uncle posted Peter's cash bond, but Peter's father refused to be responsible for him, so he was released under Mr. O'Neil's custody.

Standing on the lawn of the county jail, Maggie's Uncle Mike smiled as he spoke to her and Peter. "It's such a beautiful afternoon. Why don't you and Peter spend it together? I'm sure he'll appreciate the fresh air. Besides, you've probably got a lot to talk about." He paused, looking at them both, then said to Peter, "There'll be a preliminary hearing tomorrow. You'll have to be there. . . . It's at four in the afternoon, so why don't you two come by my office right after lunch . . . say around one . . . and we can get all of the facts then."

Peter was grateful and tried to show Mr. O'Neil his appreciation, "I'll be there! You can depend on that! I just don't know how to thank you enough for getting me out! . . . I thought I was going to go out of my tree in there," he said, looking very haggard. "I tried to sleep the time away as much as I could, but last night there was some woman screeching most of the night, so I didn't get much rest."

Maggie looked at Peter. "You do look very tired, Pete. Maybe you should go home and sleep for a while. I can see you later this evening."

Peter looked down along his nose then back at Maggie. "My parents don't want me around anymore. My mother only came to visit me once to tell me that my dad had washed his hands of me and didn't want to see me if I got out."

Mr. O'Neil became concerned. "I'm really sorry to hear that, Peter."

"See, what did I tell you about his parents? They blamed him for everything," Maggie told him. Then, turning to Peter, she said, "They've never given you a chance. Uncle Mike will help you. You don't have to ask them for anything, anymore."

"Yes, Peter. Don't worry. I believe what you and Maggie have told me. We'll take it one step at a time. . . . I have to leave now, so I'll see you tomorrow in my office."

"We'll be there," Maggie reassured him. "And thank you again, Uncle Mike. I do really appreciate everything. . . . Good-bye," she said and stood on her toes to kiss him on the cheek, before he turned and walked toward the courthouse entrance.

Maggie turned to Peter as they started walking down the jail steps. "Remember that place you took me to? It was so peaceful there. . . . Do you think we could go there for a while today? . . . You could rest and we would have a chance to be alone and talk."

Peter's eyes lit up. "That sounds great! God, I've been cooped up so long, I thought I'd never get out! I can hardly believe that I'm free now!" He turned to look at Maggie, a flush of coloring beginning to brighten his ashen face. "I'll call Jaako and see if he'll let me use his cycle!"

They walked to a phone booth, and Peter placed his call. Maggie heard a swallow calling nearby and looked up just in time to see it swoop down underneath the eaves of the courthouse across the street. As she watched it, she noticed a group of nests strung out under the eaves of the building, with many birds flying in and out. Speaking out loud to them, she said, "I know that your life isn't easy, but you don't have to deal with people. They can be so ignorant at times, when it's someone else whose life is at stake. . . . Even people you care about can do things to you in the name of love. It makes you wonder what love really is. . . . You're so lucky. . . . Sometimes I wish that I could fly like you, high above all of the problems of this world."

Not hearing Peter come up behind her, she was startled when he asked, "Who're you talking to, Mag?"

"I was sort of daydreaming and thinking out loud. Those birds look so contented up there. I wish we didn't have any problems and could be like them and just fly away from all of this." She paused and looked at Peter.

His eyes twinkled softly. "I'd be right there with you, babe, if it were possible."

"Did you get ahold of Jaako?" she asked.

"Sure enough did. He told me I could use it anytime I want. He said he'll ride over to Marge's Subshop, down the block from here. You can wait there while I drive him home. That won't take long and we can have the rest of the afternoon to ourselves up at the shack."

As they walked over to Marge's, Maggie said, "I was so upset when I found out they were blaming you for the fire that I didn't know what to do to help you. I felt like going to the police station and screaming at them about how stupid they are. . . . I don't get upset very easily, but look out when I get my dander up!"

Peter's eyes twinkled and he said, "You ARE a beautiful person, Mag. I believe you would have. . . . I really appreciate you getting your uncle to help me."

"That was the only thing I could think of doing to get you out."

"I don't know what I'd have done if your Uncle Mike didn't help me. You're lucky to have an uncle like him. I don't have anyone but you who really cares if I live or die," Peter said to her remorsefully.

She looked at his long face and smiled. "Don't look so down. It isn't the end of the world." Then she changed the subject. "Uncle Mike has always been good to me, but I wasn't sure he would help you. . . . He doesn't know you like I do." She turned and gave him a pecking kiss as they walked. "You know that I more than care for you. I love you with all my heart, body, and soul, forever and ever!" she exclaimed and took hold of his shoulder and stopped him. She threw her arms around him and gave him a long and sensuous kiss.

Then she looked at him. "Pete, I know that I told you this when they let you out, but I want you to know how much I've missed you. I'll always love you. You're what I want in this life."

"I know that, babe. I missed you, too. Thinking of you was all that got me through the days. I know we'll always be together."

They'd started walking hand in hand when she asked, "How long were you in there?"

"They picked me up three days ago. But it felt like a million years! You know how being enclosed is difficult for me. Well, that small cell made me think that if I had to stay in there, I would be better off dead."

Concern flushed Maggie's face, and her eyebrows drew down into a frown. "You must never think that way. . . . If I had known about it sooner, you wouldn't have had to stay that long."

Peter stopped her, his eyes contacting hers. "I know that. . . . No matter what happens, always remember that I love you."

He took Maggie's hand, and they started walking again. "Mag, I know that we'll be together forever. I can feel it in my heart. Nothing will ever separate us. When this is over, I'm going to finish school and get a job so I can have my own place. You can finish, too and then we can get married, move away from here, and have a family." He paused, then asked, "Would you like that?"

"Like it! I'd love it! Being with you and having a family is all that I've been dreaming about since you first told me you loved me!" She paused, then asked, "Are you proposing to me?"

Pulling her to him and looking deep into her eyes, he answered shyly, "Yes, I am. . . . I promise you I'll be good to you, and I'll treat our kids a hell of a lot different than my parents treated me."

Later that day, the temperature had climbed to the mid-eighties. Maggie and Peter were in the shack and had changed to lighter clothing.

As they stepped out, a cycle drove up. Peter recognized the driver as a friend from school. Walking over, he greeted him, "Hi, Jerry. Looks like you had the same idea. Too nice a day to waste in town, isn't it?"

"Sure is," Jerry returned as he waited for the girl riding with him to dismount. Not knowing either of them, Maggie stood back a few feet. Looking from them toward Maggie and then back, Peter introduced them. "Jerry, I want you to meet my girl, Maggie."

Stepping forward, Maggie extended her hand. "Hi, Jerry. Nice meeting you." Then turning to the girl, hand outstretched, she said, "I'm Maggie O'Neil."

"Hi, Maggie, I'm Mikkie Ballantini. Pleased to meet you. . . . Guys are like that. They take women for granted. They'd never think of introducing us," she kidded.

"Sorry. . . . I assumed you knew each other from school," Jerry responded.

"See what I mean," said Mikkie.

"Just like women, fussing over little things," Jerry quipped.

Peter took Maggie's hand and as they started walking from the shack, he said, "We're going down to the point that overlooks the valley."

Jerry answered, "We're thinking of going all the way down to the waterfalls, near the Natural Wall."

Peter and Maggie's faces showed their surprise. "I didn't know there was a waterfall here. That sounds like a neat place," Peter said. Then, turning to Maggie, he asked her, "Want to go down to the falls, Mag?"

She was quiet a moment. Wanting to be alone with Peter, she replied, "Why don't we go to the lookout point first? It's so peaceful and quiet there. . . . We can go to the waterfall later."

"That sounds good to me," Peter agreed.

They all walked together as far as the plateau, which stretched along the side of the cliff for a distance of about five hundred feet, most of which was clear of brush. Peter turned to Jerry. "Why don't you give me the directions down and we'll see you both later?"

"Sure," Jerry agreed. Then, pointing down the plateau to his right, he instructed, "There's a trail down where the level area narrows. Some places get bad from washouts, so be careful. At the bottom the trail forks. The one to the left goes to the Natural Wall, the one to the right leads to the stream. Follow the one to the stream about a quarter mile. . . . You'll like it there. You'll hear the roar of the falls. You can't miss it. . . . We'll see you later, then."

"Right on. See you both later," Peter answered.

Maggie and Peter watched them as they took up a slow run, weaving through the short brush. Mikkie's long brown hair, highlighted by the sun, flowed in the breeze as she trailed along behind Jerry.

Maggie sat on a log and looked out over the valley. Patting beside her leg, she invited, "Come sit by me."

After waiting a moment, she turned around in wonderment that Peter hadn't joined her. To her amazement, he was nowhere in sight. Puzzled, she stood up to look for him. Off in the distance, Jerry and Mikkie disappeared out of sight, but there was no sign of Peter.

"Pete! Where are you?" she called out frantically.

From the woods, he reponded. "Be right there, babe."

A few minutes later, he appeared on the trail. Upset, she demanded, "Where did you go?"

Sheepishly, he replied, "I had to tap a kidney."

"Why didn't you say something to me before you left?"

Peter tried to excuse his actions. "I guess I was embarrassed. I know that I should have. . . . You were so busy looking out over the valley that I thought I'd be back before you noticed I'd left."

Her anger dissipated and as she sat back down onto the log, she invited, "Come and sit with me."

Peter joined her. As he moved closer to her, Maggie looked at him and began expressing her concerns. "Peter, I want to be able to spend time with you, but I know I'm going to get ragged on by my mom if I do. I don't like to upset her either, so I don't know what to do. I've thought about it, and there just doesn't seem to be an answer. I really wish she liked you."

"I do too, Mag. I've been thinking about it, too. . . . All I know is that I want to be with you. You're all I have in this world that means anything to me."

She took hold of his hand and put it around her shoulders. While snuggling up to him and becoming dreamy-eyed, she said, "You mean the world to me, too. I can't wait until we get married and can really start our lives together." She paused then added, "You've never told me what you wanted to be when you were young."

"When I was real young, I wanted to be a pilot, but that was only a dream. When I got into grade school, I learned about reality. Everyone was down on me. They convinced me that I was stupid."

Turning to look into his eyes, she inquired, "What do you mean, Peter? What happened to make you think that?"

"Well, it started with my third-grade teacher. She was an old-maid spinster who would say things like"—he wrinkled his nose and scrunched his face to demonstrate how he viewed her, then still repeating what she'd said, he continued—'Everyone in the class did good today except Peter.' Or, she'd call on me to answer a question and before I had a chance to answer it, she'd say, 'I don't know why I called on him. He doesn't know it anyway.' Then she'd ask someone else. She was always calling me stupid or dumb. The other kids called me retard and things like that. I admit that I did have a problem reading and that didn't help any." He looked across the valley.

"I started to believe she was right. . . . I was stupid and I began to accept it." He paused and then looking back at Maggie, he added, "I guess I figured if they all thought I was stupid, they must be right. . . . I did daydream in school a lot though—about how some day I'd show them all they were wrong."

"Oh, Peter! I'm sorry to hear that you were treated that way. You're not stupid in any way."

"I now know that I'm not, but I believed then that I was. That old bat told my fourth-grade teacher that I wouldn't try to learn anything, so she never called on me to answer questions, either. She flunked me in the fourth grade, even though I'd started to do a lot better than in the third. My mother tried to have me passed. She even brought my test papers into the teacher. The teacher's excuse was that my only friend in the class flunked and I should, too, so that way we would be together."

"I can't believe that they could be allowed to do such a thing and ruin your life like that. It's the height of stupidity, if you ask me," Maggie exclaimed as the sorrow she felt for Peter swept through her. With these feelings of caring welling up within her, she put her arms around his neck and kissed him long and with deep feeling. He responded by gently passing his hands over her body as they kissed.

"I love you. I really love you," she whispered as her eyes turned dreamy, and she kissed him with short, pecking kisses on his face.

Peter gently eased himself from the log to the ground while slowly pulling Maggie down on top of him. Extending his arms into a bearhug, he tightened them around her and kissed her on the neck, then on her earlobes. She pushed away slightly. "That tickles," she said, chuckling under her breath.

Paying no heed to her resistance, he nuzzled his nose into her neck under her chin. "Grrrrrgggrrrr," he purred as he moved his head around playfully. He then continued to move up the side of her neck and snuggled his face into the hair behind her ear. Maggie wriggled and tried to pull her head backward.

"Stop it!" she commanded, as she giggled.

"I could eat you all up!" he said teasingly, wrestling with her as their excitement mounted.

"Stop it now, before you make me want to do something we shouldn't!" she demanded, still giggling.

Peter continued to nuzzle her neck and kiss behind her ears. Then kissing and nuzzling her neck, he moved slowly to her waiting lips and kissed her. Rolling his body to one side, he cupped one of her firm, warm breasts, gently kneading it. Releasing her luscious lips, he pulled back slightly and breathed deeply. Then, looking into her sparkling brown eyes, he whispered, "Feeling like making love is all right when two people love each other. I've wanted to make love to you for a long time now."

"Not here, Peter. They might come back and see us doing it."

High on emotions, he moaned, "Don't you want to feel what it's like to know each other in that way?"

"I've had fantasies about it," she whispered. Refusing his request to demonstrate his love in the ultimate way was hard for her to do. Feeling the same desires and seeing the longing in his eyes made it even more difficult. She knew it wasn't lust, but true love that dwelled in him.

"We can do it when we can be sure we're alone. This is the first time for me, and I want everything to be right when we do it. . . . I'd be so embarrassed if someone saw us," she said to him, hoping he would understand.

Seeing the disappointment in his eyes, she offered, "I'm sorry, Peter, but I want to be able to give myself to you completely with no worries."

With concern for her feelings, Peter's urge began to wane and he agreed. "It will be such a wonderful experience that I wouldn't want anything to ruin it for you, babe."

Feeling more at ease, she said, "We'll have a lifetime to share our love. We can put off some pleasure now. . . . The anticipation will make it that much better when we do."

His eyes twinkling, he pulled her to him and kissed her tenderly.

Shifting herself so as to be able to look into his eyes, then snuggling up to him, she whispered, "I just want you to hold me, now. . . . I want to feel your body close to me."

Lovingly brushing back his hair, she kissed him and whispered, "I don't want to put you off, Peter, but, when the time is right, I'll know the pleasure of making love with you." Pulling him to her, she kissed him long and with a deep feeling of love and gratitude.

They lay on the grass, warmed by the bright sun, talking and spontaneously kissing from time to time. They became oblivious to the cares of the day as they found pleasure in being able to share time together. Time she'd longed for but couldn't have before.

Looking back at the top of the embankment, Peter pointed up. "The swallows are still using the smokestack for a home. . . . This is such a beautiful place to be. . . . Wouldn't it be wonderful to have a home built right up there where the point juts out?" he commented, then added kiddingly, "But, we'd have to tie the kids up with long ropes to keep them from falling over the edge."

Beaming from ear to ear, she answered, "Sure. . . . Then I'd tie you up, too, and never let you get out of my sight."

"That'd be great." He paused and looked back at Maggie, before continuing. "All kidding aside, someday when we have the money, let's come back here and build a beautiful home up there," he suggested. Then he followed with, "We could put a large deck across the front, with sliding doors leading into the living room. It would have large windows across the front, too."

Becoming excited by the idea, she exclaimed, "I'm with you on that!" Then she added, "I'd like the dining room overlooking the valley. That way we'd be able to have this view while we're eating.

"Pete," Maggie said, turning to look at him, "I wish we could have it all right now. . . . I know that we can't, but it's such a beautiful place that I wouldn't mind spending the rest of my life living right here with you," she said wishfully.

Believing they'd bring their dream to reality as soon as they became financially able, he said with determination, "I promise you that someday, we will live here and raise our family."

"We'll be so happy, then! I just know it! Nothing would make me happier. I don't want anything else in the whole wide world!" Maggie exclaimed. She threw her arms around Peter's neck and kissed him.

Her thoughts turned to the realization that being with Peter was the only way her life would have real meaning. Suddenly, she felt a tinge of guilt sweep over her as she remembered having refused his desires, earlier. Looking at the ground, she admitted, "I'm really sorry that I couldn't let you make love to me."

"No problem, Loves. When we do, it'll be twice as good, you'll see."

"But I really wanted to. I just couldn't."

"I understand. Don't let it bother your pretty head anymore."

"Okay. . . . You're so kind and understanding, Peter. Sometimes, I love you so much it hurts."

An insecure part of Maggie suddenly surfaced. "Pete."

Feeling her body become slightly tense, Peter responded, "Yes, beautiful."

"You'll never leave me, will you?" she questioned.

"You worry too much, Loves. 'Course I won't ever leave you," he reassured her.

The sun was hanging low in the southern sky, across the valley by now. Maggie suggested, "I'd like to see the waterfall now, before it gets too late."

41

Getting to his feet, then grabbing Maggie's outstretched hand, Peter pulled her to her feet as he agreed. "It'll start cooling off soon. I guess we'd better go if we want to see it today."

They walked along the edge of the wooded bank until the trail narrowed. Dropping down steeply, it was covered with loose rocks and gravel. Peter went ahead to find the most secure areas. Halfway down, Maggie lost her footing and started sliding sideways toward a sharp dropoff. "Peter, help me! I'm falling!" she yelled frantically.

Loose gravel kicked up a small avalanche ahead of her as she slid toward the edge. Grasping out wildly and scrambling to gain footing, instinctively she clutched at anything within reach.

Peter, hearing her cry out, turned in time to see her catch hold of a small, twisted, dry tree that jutted out from the bank.

Hurrying back, he carefully worked his way down to where she stood, breathlessly clinging to the scrub tree, afraid to move.

"Are you all right?" he asked breathlessly. She nodded her head.

Grasping hold of a sturdy tree branch, he extended his hand out to her and called out, "Give me your hand."

Whimpering like a young child and on the verge of crying, she released one hand and reached up to grasp his. He pulled her upward. Her feet dug into the loose soil, casting it over the edge of the embankment. Carefully they worked their way back to the trail, where they paused to catch their breath.

Once they were back to a secure area, still shaking, Peter said excitedly, "That was too close! I was afraid I was going to lose you!"

Breathing deeply, she sputtered, "I—I thought I was a goner!" Sitting down to remove her shoes and shake out the dirt, Maggie continued, "I don't know how I could be so careless! My foot just slid right out from under me!"

After a brief rest and deciding it would be safer, he ushered her ahead of him. Holding her hand he helped her the remaining way down.

When they'd reached the bottom, he put his arms around her and held her body tight against his. She shivered from pent-up anxiety.

After a few moments, he released her and she commented, "I guess it takes a mule to walk that trail, not a jackass like me."

"Don't say things like that. It was my fault. I should have seen that spot was dangerous and helped you across it," he admitted.

When they reached the point where the trail divided, they saw Jerry and Mikkie were just coming back along the one that led to the Natural Wall.

"Hi," Mikkie called out. "We're heading back."

"So soon?" Peter asked.

"She has to get home," Jerry answered for her.

"How is your day going?" Mikkie inquired.

Maggie answered, "This is such a beautiful place. We're enjoying every minute of it."

"It is, isn't it?" Mikkie agreed. Then she said as they started up the trail, "Catch you later."

"Right," Peter agreed.

As Maggie and Peter approached the waterfall, the sound of thundering water reached them. Through the trees they could see the sunlight reflecting off the foamy crest in sparkling rays. "Look, Peter, there it is!" Maggie pointed upward as she called his attention to it.

Unexpectedly, she bolted out ahead of him, running at full tilt. Peter sprinted after her. Catching up quickly, he reached out and grasped her by the shoulder. She stopped and spun around with a broad smile across her face. Stopping short to avoid bumping into her, playfully he threw his arms around her to pull her to him. Maggie giggled and started to squirm, then suddenly went limp. Her smile vanished, her eyes closed, her face became flaccid, and her body went limp.

Fear grabbed at Peter's guts. He'd heard of insulin shock and diabetic coma. His immediate thought was, *Maybe she's diabetic and is dying.*

Gently, he eased her to the ground. Not knowing whether to go for help or wait to see if she would come out of it, he decided on the latter and gently patted her face, trying to revive her. His mind raced. *God, don't let her die! . . . Maybe mouth-to-mouth resuscitation will revive her*! he thought as he bent over her. He placed his thumb on her eyelid and opened one eye. Without warning, she threw her arms around his neck and gave one quick pull.

Not anticipating the suddenness of her attack, he lost his balance and sprawled halfway across her body. A surge of relief that she was all right and just being playful, quickly replaced his fear. "You bugger! You scared the living shit right out of me! I thought you were dying!" he exclaimed and planted a firm lip-lock on her lips before she had a chance to respond.

Releasing her lips and with an impish look, he said, "You sure can be unpredictable. I've never seen that in you before."

"I try to be." Maggie grinned. "It's no fun being too serious all the time. Besides, I wanted to see how you'd react if you thought something terrible had happened to me."

Giving her a serious look, Peter said, "I like to have fun, too, but don't ever do that to me again. I was scared shitless that I was losing you. My heart jumped right up into my mouth when I saw you go limp."

Wrinkling her nose, she questioned, "You called me a bugger. I've never heard that word before. What does it mean?"

"That's what people in Mongolia call each other when they're in love," he kidded her.

"It is not. . . . You're putting me on. . . . Really, what does it mean?"

"It's just a term that I've heard. I've been told that it's what they call a person who goes out at night looking for bugs."

"That doesn't sound too bad. I'll accept that explanation. . . . I don't think it's appropriate to call me that, but, considering that you were emotionally distressed, I'll forgive you."

She pulled him to her and kissed him full-mouthed. He felt her lips warm and tender as they passed tightly against his. Maggie squirmed to one side slightly to get more comfortable and felt Peter's hand lightly touch the tip of her breast. In reflex action she reached out and grasped it lightly. She threw her head back slightly to toss the hair from over her eye and with softening eyes, she looked deep into Peter's. Her emotions aroused, her heart beating rapidly, Maggie released his hand and whispered, "I know you want to make love to me, and I want you to, but I'm a little afraid."

"It's all right, Maggie. Relax, no one will see us, now," he tried to reassure her.

Slowly he moved his hand along the length of her body, tantalizing her senses.

"Okay. But, I've never done this before, so be patient with me."

Feeling her heartbeat thundering against his chest, he kissed her softly and whispered back, "I understand, babe. It's just that I want you to know my deep love for you by becoming a part of you."

Maggie felt his hand moving softly down her body, sending slight shivering emotions through her entire being. When he reached her shorts, she did not stop him. Her blood burned her face as it flushed from the heat of her mounting passion. Suddenly, she became aware of Peter's fingers sliding into her two orifices simultaneously. Stiffening her body and responding to his unwanted attempt, she quickly stated, "No. Don't, Peter! I'm not a bowling ball!"

He immediately withdrew his finger, leaned over, and looked into her eyes, as he breathed his apology. "I'm sorry, Maggie. I wanted it to feel good to you. I thought it would, that way."

Maggie responded by moving close to him, her body becoming totally relaxed. Previously unknown feelings crept up her spine, spreading to every fiber, entrancing her mind and body. Her voice quivered with sensations. "Beee gentle with me."

"I will, Mag," he purred, as he one-handedly undid the top button of her shorts, slid down the zipper, and gently massaged the pale skin below her tan.

44

Maggie's heart began racing, and her blood roared through her veins. His whispered voice came to her as though from a distance. "I love you, Maggie. . . . I want to give you more pleasure than you've ever felt before in your life."

She eased out her words. "You are giving me pleasure, Peter! I've never felt so much love in my entire life!"

Later, they lay quietly in the grass for a long time, absorbing the pleasure of being physically a part of each other, before Peter finally spoke, "We'll have the rest of our lives to share these feelings. Nothing can change that." She recognized a certain determination in his voice.

"I know, and I'm happy that we will. There's nothing in this world I want more than being with you, Peter," she answered, while visions of their lives together flowed through her mind.

Gradually, Peter's penis withdrew from inside Maggie of its own volition.

"I don't ever want to be without you. I'll love you forever," he said to Maggie as he moved to one side and kissed her forehead, each eye, then her mouth.

Not wanting to end their feelings, but knowing that time was passing swiftly, she suggested, "Maybe we should get dressed and go to the waterfall."

Sitting up and pulling on her blouse, Maggie wanted Peter to know how she felt and said, "That was beautiful the way you made love to me, Peter. You won't tell anyone, will you? . . . Not even Jaako?"

Getting dressed, Peter tried to ease her mind. "Don't worry. I won't tell anyone." Then he changed the subject. "You sure zapped my energy. But, that's all right, it was worth it. It was too good for words to explain."

Maggie was still concerned. "Do you still respect me?"

He kissed her. "Of course I respect you. I'll always respect you, Maggie. You know that."

Her eyes lit up. "I know it, but I had to hear it from you."

They walked hand in hand to the waterfall. When they reached it, Maggie surveyed the area. To their right across the pool that formed at the base of the falls, a line of tag elders were dwarfed by a tall white pine tree. Foam gathered near the top of the falls where it swirled around a fallen maple tree. Her eyes came to rest on a pair of black ducks swimming in the pool below.

Pointing, she exclaimed, "Peter, look at those ducks! They look like they're really enjoying themselves!" Quickly she added, "I never would have thought it could be this beautiful here."

"It sure is. . . . Want to go skinny-dipping?" he invited, as they walked to the edge of the water.

"Do you think we should? It'll be cooling off soon."

Peter knelt down and felt the water. "It's really warm. We can get dressed if the air gets too cool later."

"Okay! I'm with you!"

Challenging Peter, Maggie shouted, "Beat you in!"

Popping off her blouse, dropping her shorts, and kicking off her tennis shoes, she quickly dove into the foamy pool. Peter followed close behind.

The thick, soft, white foam clung to their bodies as they surfaced. Feeling totally relaxed, Maggie enjoyed the tantalizing flow of warm water against the length of her naked body. A contented feeling enveloped her. Such freedom she'd never felt before. She turned and swam on her back and watching Peter clumsily thrashing behind her, she laughed to herself at how uncoordinated he was in the water. To her, swimming came naturally.

They circled the pool and neared the misty spray of the falling water. Calling out excitedly, she pointed. "There's a cave behind the falls!"

"I see it," Peter acknowledged. "Let's have a look around inside."

They swam to the left side edge of the falls and carefully climbed out over the slimy rocks on the shore. With Peter in the lead, they started along the narrow ledge leading in. As they entered, her foot slipped on the rocks underfoot, which were moss-covered and very slippery. Peter found handholds and assisted Maggie, who proceeded gingerly, as though she were walking on eggs.

Maggie thrilled to the sight of multicolored light, caused by the sun as it passed through the spray of water that was dancing like fireworks on the limestone walls of the cave. "It's beautiful but spooky in here! Do you suppose it could be haunted?" she questioned.

"Of course not," he encouraged. "Let's go in the cave a little ways."

"I'm not going! I like it here . . . but you can if you'd like. I'll be all right here."

Trying to be agreeable, he said, "Maybe some other time I'll explore it."

A light, misty spray of water filled the mouth of the cave. "It's cool in here. Let's go back into the sunshine," Maggie requested.

Peter put his arm around her and pulled her naked body against his. Face to face, he looked into her eyes and massaged her moist skin. The heat of his body against hers warmed her. When his hands cupped the round cheeks of her buttocks, she resisted. "Not here," she insisted, then directed his attention. "Look, Pete. There's a small rainbow behind you on the wall."

He looked over his shoulder, then back at her. "Pretty, but not as pretty as you are," he complimented her. Then, leaning forward, he asked, "Ever been kissed under a waterfall before?"

Unexpectedly losing his footing before she could respond, he dragged her down with him. Sliding, they tumbled into the churning foamy water.

Coughing, sputtering, and slightly scoured by the undertow, they emerged downstream. They then swam to the shallows near a sandbar that jutted out near the pool outlet and stood up in the knee-deep water.

"I'm really sorry, Maggie-Loves. I should have been more careful. . . . Did you hurt yourself?"

"Just a couple of scrapes. . . . It happened so quickly I was more surprised than anything. . . . Nothing to worry about, though."

Hand in hand, they walked onto the sandbar.

"Let me check to be sure you're not injured," he insisted.

Upon thoroughly examining her naked body, he found only a few reddened areas. When he had assured himself that she was all right, he sat down on the warm sand. Maggie sat beside him. Apologizing he said, "Sometimes I can't do anything right."

Her eyes twinkled. "Oh, for sure!" she exclaimed kiddingly. "But you can't help it. You're just like any other careless, clumsy klutz."

His smile disappeared.

Seeing his distressed look, her eyebrows wrinkled into a frown. "Don't take it seriously. I'm only kidding you."

Quickly, his face brightened. "Race you to shore," he called out as he jumped to his feet, ran into deeper water, and dove in.

Maggie was hot on his heels. She easily caught him and swam alongside. Reaching the shallows near shore, she playfully caught him square in the face with a shot of water from her cupped hand. Then, jumping to her feet, she ran for shore.

Springing to his feet in a flash, running after her, Peter quickly caught her. Pulling her down into the water, he grasped one foot and began tickling it.

Screaming, kicking, and squirming, she tried freeing herself.

"This will teach you not to mess with a cave man." He talked between his teeth. His face compressed in a grin, he struggled, trying to hold onto her. "When I'm through here, I'm dragging you back into that cave so you can hatch up a whole flock of cave kids that you can cook and clean for."

Struggling and yelling, she exclaimed, "You'll pay for this."

Maggie's foot caught Peter in the stomach as she kicked at him. "From now on, I'm crossing my legs any time you get any funny notions."

He let go of her ankle and jumped into the water, enclosing her with his arms. "Like now?" he asked, as he rolled over, trying to get on top of her.

Quickly she raised her knee for separation, their naked bodies wrestling for control. Exhausted, Maggie gave in and Peter floated above her. Using her hands on the bottom, she pushed her way to the sandy beach along the side of the pool. Separated only by a thin film of water, lightly their bodies touched and aroused her senses. Her desires rose, the feelings of wanting returned, but she was determined to tease him first. She felt his hand on the inside of her leg, moving slowly toward her crotch. He lowered his head, and she allowed their lips to touch. Then quickly she turned her head to the side. As she did this, she felt his hand stop as it covered her genital area.

"I want to make love to you, Maggie," he pleaded, his eyes filled with desire.

Her eyes gleaming, she retorted, "Not till your grandmother turns blue in her grave."

Without hesitation, Peter answered, "When I visited her grave this morning, I asked her, 'Grandma, are you blue yet? I know this chick that likes to screw when you're blue.' . . . There she was, blue as blue can be. In fact, she was even singing the blues."

Maggie pretended to struggle to break herself free. "I know who'll be singing the blues when he doesn't get what he wants anymore."

Peter's eyes sparkled. "Not any less either, I hope."

"It'll be so long before you get any, you'll think a piece of ass is something you eat with a fork," Maggie teased.

"Not me. Cave men never use forks." He tried to hold her down and kiss her. Once more she quickly turned her head to one side.

"Oh, yeah? Well, my cave is one that you'll never enter again."

"Why? Did it cave in?"

"You're crazy!" she rebuffed him, kiddingly.

"I know! . . . I'm crazy about you!" he answered, his eyes still gleaming.

Maggie relaxed, looked deep into Peter's blue eyes, and saw the fire of love that was consuming his being. She felt her own love burning in her breasts and responded by putting her arms around his neck, pulling him to her waiting lips. Their passion couldn't be contained. No water could quench the fire that consumed their bodies. Exploring ecstasy together, they made rampant love in the warm shallows of the pool.

Later, Peter trickled small handfuls of sand over Maggie's white breasts as she lay on her back on the white sandy shore.

"I can't believe I've made love with you twice now, Peter. You were so good, I didn't want you to stop." She paused and looked at him, then added, "I didn't know what I was missing, or I'd have been begging you to show me your love a long time before this."

Maggie lay naked, totally exhausted on the sandy bank, in the early evening sun. He knelt beside her and said, "Maggie, I don't know how to thank you enough for the love and understanding you've given me. You've stolen my heart and given it back to me filled with your love. You've done more to help me in such a short time than anyone else has done for me in my entire life."

Emphasizing her reasons for helping him, she responded, "It's because I love you. Do you know that love means GIVING OF YOURSELF WITH NO EXPECTATIONS! That's the way I feel about you." To her, it was the only way real love could survive, and she desperately wanted their love to last forever. She continued, "Too many people set themselves up for unhappiness in this life by putting expectations on everything, even love. They're so materialistic."

She slowly ran her hand over Peter's body, coming to rest on his shoulder. Leaning over, she massaged his neck muscles before continuing. "They're not willing to give of themselves in any way without expecting to gain something in return."

Peter realized more about Maggie than he was previously aware. "You're so logical. Where do you get your ideas from?"

"It's the way I've always believed that life should be. I want love that's plain and simple, but true. I don't want all of those implications and complications people place on love," she said in earnest.

Peter looked thoughtfully at Maggie. He said, "It's funny but I've never thought of the 'Big L' in that way. But, you're right, though. It could be better for everyone concerned if people didn't play stupid games with each other. Life could be much simpler."

Maggie added, "And happier."

Peter sat up. Reaching forward, he turned on the small radio he'd dropped in the sand, when they first arrived. Her senses still aroused, Maggie leaned toward Peter. "Let's kiss like the birdies kiss," she invited. Peter looked at her questioningly.

"You don't know how they kiss? . . . I'll show you." She puckered up her mouth and placed small kisses all over Peter's face. He caught on immediately and responded by taking hold of her head in his hands and kissing her the same way.

Jumping to his feet, Peter suggested, "Let's dance." Reaching down, he grasped Maggie's wrist to assist her.

Twisting her wrist free, she resisted. "I don't think we should. What if someone comes? I'd be so embarrassed."

"You let me make love to you here!"

"But we were in the water, and they couldn't see much even if they wanted to."

Peter persisted. "No one will come. . . . Besides, I know you're the kind of girl who would do just about anything with me. If I said, 'Let's walk down the main street and pick our noses,' you'd be right there with me."

She laughed. "You ARE crazy. Didn't your mother tell you not to pick your nose?"

He answered, "It's dirty business, but since no one else will do it for me, someone has to."

She laughed and allowed him to help her up. "I do like to dance. But, we've never had a chance to dance together."

Pausing, looking at him sheepishly, then smiling, she gleefully said, "Why not make this a day to remember? I don't even care now, if someone does see us! . . . BUT DON'T EXPECT ME TO PICK MY NOSE WITH YOU IN PUBLIC!"

They became engrossed in the music, and their emotions rode high. Wildly twisting, twirling, and singing the words of the songs to each other, they didn't notice the sun sinking lower on the horizon and the temperature dropping. After what seemed to Maggie to be magically endless moments, they sank to the cool soft sand. Feeling a slight chill, as the perspiration dried on her skin, Maggie suggested, as she reached for her clothing, "Let's get dressed. I don't want to get sick."

Peter stood up and helped Maggie to her feet. As she leaned over to put on her shorts, she noticed indentations in the sand. Chuckling, she said, "Look, Peter, we've left our prints in the sands of time."

Peter look down at the marks left by the cheeks of their buttocks. "We could make them permanent if I had some plaster. That way we'd have them last forever to remind us of this special day."

"I don't need that to remind me. Everything is written permanently indelible in my mind," she answered with a contented smile.

Peter took her hand and squeezed it. "I'll never forget the pleasure I've had being with you today, babe. It will live forever in my mind, too."

Regretting the day was ending, but looking forward to the many ahead that they would spend together, Maggie walked a little ahead of Peter, humming a song. He noticed the cheeks of her butt as they bounced slightly to and fro beneath her shorts, and how they kept perfect rhythm with her humming. He moved closer and flicked one cheek with the tips of his fingers. With a quick smile over her shoulder, she responded, "That's the closest thing you're going to get to a piece of tail for a while."

Peter grinned. "Just wanted to get your attention."

He changed the subject. "The trail to Natural Wall is up ahead. Want to take a look at it before we go back?"

"It's a bit cool, but if it's not too far, we can."

He caught up with her and held her hand. Before long, they entered a clearing. Peter pointed forward and remarked, "This must be it. I can see some huge rocks along the side of the cliff up ahead."

Walking a little farther, they could see why it was named Natural Wall. Huge rectangular rocks of about four feet high by eight feet long lined the side of the cliff. Appearing as though they were placed by human hands, they were set in perfect alignment, with spaces of one inch between them. These spaces were filled with soil, as though the mortar had deteriorated away. The size of the wall was larger than they'd expected, as it covered an area of about fifty feet high by five to six hundred feet long. Maggie stared in wonderment. "It's simply amazing. I've never seen anythng like that before."

Peter's astonishment was evident as he stood mouth agape. Becoming aware of it being open, he quickly closed it and said, "It doesn't seem possible they could be arranged like that by nature. They're too perfectly matched and plaed too uniformly to believe someone didn't put them there for some reason."

Maggie looked at Peter. "But, what kind of a reason could there be for putting them here? I'm sure no one would go through that much work, unless it served some purpose."

Peter replied as he turned to leave, "I'm going to try to find out if they're really here naturally. If they are, it could be the eighth wonder of the world." Then he quickly added, "Let's get back, now. We don't want you to get into trouble with your mother."

The next day, Peter met Maggie in her uncle's office. After talking briefly with his secretary, they seated themselves while they waited.

Maggie wanted to give Peter a poem she had written for him. She felt a little self-conscious about giving it to him, not knowing how he would react to receiving a love poem. Turning toward him she shyly handed him an envelope and announced timidly, "I wrote you a poem."

Reaching for the poem, his eyes beaming, a smile spreading across his face, he replied, "You did? No one's ever written a poem for me, before."

Opening the envelope, he read the poem.

Destined to Love

When alone, there's a longing deep within,
to know someone, with life to begin;
and share the feelings supressed for so long,
freeing them now, cannot be wrong.

Just knowing you truly care for me,
togetherness that is simply heavenly;
telling secret thoughts and desires,
blends our souls with shimmering fires.

I've learned of your love, so true and real,
and your flashing smile projects sweetness that I feel;
I know time does rob, so we cannot know,
how our destinies will flow.

So look not to the way it's been,
but cast your mind forward and then;
try to feel and see,
far beyond, what used to be.

It's known that fate can twist and turn,
our lives in space, until we learn;
what gives us true meaning and content,
before which, sometimes, our lives are spent.

As our hearts do now combine,
as ivy, our lives can entwine;
and now you feel free to say,
I've stolen your heart away.

Our love can now surely bind
us together, deep in our souls and mind;
Through what we've shared now I feel;
your love for me is true and real.

We know not how or why,
this special caring has grown for you and I;
maybe it's because it was destined to be,
THAT I LOVE YOU AND YOU LOVE ME!

Peter looked up after reading the poem and saw Maggie's love lighting her eyes as she watched him read. "I'll keep this with me forever. Whenever we can't be together, this will bind your feelings for me to my heart."

A pleased look spread across her face. "I'm glad you like it. I stayed up thinking about you late last night. I wanted to write you something to show you my real feelings for you."

Tears glistened at the corner of Peter's eyes. Leaning over, he kissed her softly on the lips before admitting to her, "It gave me the shivers when I read it. I don't know how you could write something with such meaning. I know I never could. Thank you, Maggie-Loves. I'll treasure it forever."

Maggie's uncle called his receptionist, Jean, into his office. She returned a few minutes later. "He wants you both to go in now."

Mike O'Neil was smiling when they entered. Extending his hand to Peter, he greeted them. "Hi, Peter, . . . Maggie. I have good news for you, both." Then, looking at Peter, he informed him, "They've dropped all the charges against you."

Maggie felt a surge of gratitude. She blurted out, "That's great!" Then, turning to Peter, she threw her arms around him and kissed him. "I told you Uncle Mike would help you!"

Peter's eyes sparkled as he returned her kiss. Then, turning to Mr. O'Neil, he grabbed his hand and pumped it up and down in his excitement. "Thank you!" he half-shouted.

Mike O'Neil explained, "I've been on the phone most of the morning with the DA. He knew he had a weak case, with only circumstantial evidence, but he didn't want to let you off. A few minutes ago, he called. One of the girls who was in the area of the gym informed the police that you and Maggie were only talking in the hallway and didn't have any cigarettes. She knew who it was who discarded the ones that caused the fire. They're looking for them now."

Peter's eyes sparkled with relief. "Thank you again, Mr. O'Neil! You're a life-saver, in more ways than one! I don't know how to thank you enough for what you've done for me! I could never survive if I had to go back to jail! That was the worst experience of my entire life. I kept thinking I'd die in there."

"I understand. Maggie explained to me about you having claustrophobia. You can thank her. It was her concern and belief that you were innocent that made me want to look into your situation."

Peter turned to Maggie as she said, "I knew you didn't do it, but those dumb cops wouldn't believe me."

He caught her in a bearhug, raised her up off her feet, and spun around, kissing her. "You're the best girl in the whole wide world. You know that I'll make it up to you for helping me. Thank you, Maggie-Loves."

Mike O'Neil was quiet momentarily, observing their reactions to the good news. Finally he stated, "I don't want to interrupt your excitement, but I have to leave now. You two kids enjoy yourselves this afternoon. I'll go over to the police station to make sure that all of the records are cleared so you don't have problems over this in the future."

Maggie felt very excited inside. Feeling almost as though she would burst with gratitude and happiness, she watched Peter as he shook hands once more with her uncle before leaving.

She heard him saying, "Thank you again, Mr. O'Neil." It pleased her to see the joy written on Peter's face. A flush of renewed love for him filled her being. Anticipatory visions of their future together filled her mind. Her thoughts quickly turned to the last hurdle they would have to overcome in order to be free to share their love and their lives together. Her mother. How to convince her that Peter was a good person . . . to convince her that she should allow her to be with him.

Maggie's mind returned to the reality of the present as she heard her uncle say, "You're very much welcome, Peter. Take good care of Maggie, will you?"

Peter's smile broadened. "Sure will! You can depend on that!"

With sparkling eyes, Maggie stretched upward to kiss her uncle's cheek, "I really do appreciate all you've done for Peter and for me, Uncle Mike."

Maggie spent that afternoon with Peter. Although they didn't do anything special, just being with him filled her heart with a joy she had only been able to know in her dreams until recently. Now it became an all-consuming fire that burned deep in her heart. Later that night Maggie's mind kept laying out plans of how she and Peter would be spending their lives together. Sleep wouldn't come to her. It was early morning before she slowly drifted off into a deep slumber.

At mid-morning Peter was at home alone when the telephone rang. It was Maggie and he could tell she was crying. "Peter, this is Maggie!"

Something tugged at his heart as he read the distress in her voice. He answered her, "Hi. Is something wrong? Your voice is trembling."

She blurted out, half-crying. "It's awful, Peter! My mother is taking me to Maine to live with my Aunt Hattie! She saw me with you yesterday when you walked me home! She wouldn't listen to me this morning when she accused me of lying to her about being with you before!" She

54

paused, then her voice turned into a sobbing wail as she continued, "Sissie saw us on the motorcycle the other day, too, and told her! She still thinks that you set the fire at school, too! I couldn't call you before this because she's been watching me!... Oh, my God, Peter, I don't know what I'm going to do up there without you!"

"We can go away together, Maggie!" His eyes blurred with tears. He forced his tongue to form the words. As frenzied thoughts roared through his mind, he half-yelled, "I'm coming right over to get you now! We'll get out of here!"

"Get off that phone!" Maggie's mother's voice was shrill and harsh.

"I'll always love you, Peter!" he heard Maggie say, before the phone clicked dead. With Maggie's troubled voice resounding in his brain, Peter bolted out the front door and like a scared gazelle, ran to his love, Maggie. But, he was too late to be able to talk with her. He sank to the sidewalk crying uncontrollably, losing track of time. Finally he dragged his empty, miserable body home.

Later, upon entering his house, Peter couldn't help feeling confused and cheated of happiness. The recent events in his life were too staggeringly real for him to deal with. They tossed in his head like a leftover salad with important ingredients missing. Maggie was vividly clear in his mind. He remembered the anguished look on her face the last time he saw her, when her mother, after screaming at him through the open car window, "Don't you come near her!" had whisked Maggie off to somewhere in Maine. Where, he had no way of knowing. Seeing the hurt on Maggie's face and tears in her eyes as they drove off, was more than he could bear. "WHY?" he questioned half out loud. It didn't seem fair to him to have to lose her, especially now when everything had seemed to be right between them.

Chapter 4

A HAUNTING EXPERIENCE

THE communication barrier between Peter and his family increased while his father's abuse worsened by the day, until a few weeks later he found that he could no longer stand remaining at home. And, his loss of Maggie sent him into depression.

Feeling there was nothing left for him there, now that Maggie wasn't around to share his life, he decided it would be best for him to leave without delay and make a new life for himself elsewhere. Having thought about it a long time, he decided upon taking only the few things he needed to survive on the road.

Walking in and finding no one at home, Peter went directly to his room. Spreading out the used sleeping bag Jaako had given him, he used it to hold what he would take. Having finished filling it, as he searched for remaining items of importance, his eyes fell upon a picture of himself and John, taken when they were much younger. Tears formed in his eyes as he remembered when it had been taken. It was long before John had turned on him. They had been in the park with their Uncle Joe, tossing a baseball around, when his Aunt Amy snapped it. *If only we could still be close*, he thought.

Swinging the bag over his shoulders, he felt regretful as he headed down the stairs. Thoughts of writing a note before leaving entered his head, but they were quickly dismissed. He reasoned they wouldn't care that he'd gone, so why bother writing one? Pausing momentarily on the street, he took a long last look at the house before heading south across town to the expressway.

One month later, after wandering across the Southeastern part of the country, he found himself in the Ozark Mountains. Depressing thoughts of life without Maggie had flooded his mind everywhere he'd gone. Nagging feelings of despair accompanied him, always tying his guts into knots. Reading and rereading her poem kept her image before him constantly.

His desperate longing to be with someone who cared about him became an obsession with him. He needed someone to share his life, now that Maggie could no longer be in it.

The money he'd earned at his last job was almost depleted when he walked into a store to buy a pack of cigarettes. As he approached the checkout counter, a girl who was waiting in line just ahead of him caught his eye. Her coal-black hair, deep tan, and slender build made her strikingly beautiful. Desires swelling in him, Peter tried to approach her, but either she didn't see him, or was ignoring him.

He attempted to wedge himself sideways ahead through the checkout aisle to get to her. In his haste he elbowed a short stubby man who was placing a bottle of orange juice onto the counter. Falling to the floor and breaking, it splashed everyone in the line. He offered to pay for it and attempted to apologize, but everyone looked at him with contempt.

Taking her groceries and heading for the exit, the girl he was trying to meet turned to face him. She gave him a "You dumb fool" look before turning and walking out the door.

Leaving the cigarettes on the counter, Peter rushed for the exit, trying to catch up with her. Upon reaching the parking lot, he saw her entering her car.

He yelled to her, "Wait! I'd like to talk to you!"

Starting her car, she turned to look at him with distaste written on her face. Then, squealing the tires, she roared out into the street.

"Shithead, you sure can be stupid," he muttered to himself, as he returned to the store to buy the cigarettes.

Later that day, Peter found work at a sawmill about four miles from the small, desolate mountain town of Loganville. The mill was located near a rapidly flowing river that coursed through a small wooded valley. The shade of a large pine tree, which stood in the woods a few hundred yards in back of the mill, became his home. Each day he hid his few belongings, then slept beneath the pine at night.

The pay was meager, but the work was something he liked and it was steady. A routine that involved moving and stacking the sawed lumber onto the drying piles kept his mind busy. At night thoughts of Maggie crept into his brain, bringing with them an inevitable feeling of despair and loneliness. The accompanying all-consuming emptiness attempted to devastate him, by quenching his will to live.

After working at the mill for a few weeks, Peter had become acquainted with some of the other workers. One of the men asked him to share expenses on a house where he was sharing rent with two girls. Peter accepted, as it meant a chance to move indoors. Within a few days, he would be moving in with them.

Dangling his sleeping bag from one hand, he approached the house. It stood on a hill and loomed through the dim evening light like a relic out of the past. A cedar rail fence with weather-beaten poles protruding from the ground in a scattered pattern protected an overgrown yard. Young elders filled most of the lawn, except for a narrow pathway that led to the front porch. The house itself had a foreboding air, with its weathered shudders that hung haphazardly from many of the windows.

Feeling second thoughts about living here, Peter wanted to turn and leave. Deciding against them, he walked up onto the porch and knocked on the door. An uneasy feeling crept over him. But, he reasoned that since Jake Strauts and two girls were living there, it couldn't be too bad. Besides, he thought, Jake hadn't mentioned anything unusual about the house, so he decided it must be all right.

A young, slim, petite girl answered his knock and let him in.

She introduced herself. "Hi. I'm Lynn White. . . . You must be Peter."

His eyes passed beyond her and into the house, before returning to meet hers. "Peter Dunn. Nice meeting you," he announced while extending his hand.

Shaking hands, she invited, "It's nice meeting you. . . . Come on in and sit down. We have fresh coffee on, if you'd like some. Jake and Linda should be back soon."

Peter smiled, shyly. "Sounds good to me, thanks. It's getting a bit damp out and looks like it might rain tonight. It'll be good to have a roof overhead." As they walked in, he added, "I like the outdoors, but it's been getting a bit nippy out lately."

"Jake told us you've been sleeping out under a tree. I don't see how anyone could do that."

"It wasn't too bad at first when the weather was warmer. We haven't had rain since I've been here, so it didn't bother me."

He looked around quickly before looking back at Lynn and saying, "Looks like I found a place just in time."

Peter walked into the living room and looked around. "This must have been quite a place in its day. That huge fireplace in the vestibule, with the hand-carved brick, is something else."

Lynn smiled and agreed, "It IS beautiful, isn't it?"

Walking toward a couch, he commented, "That stairway looked like it's made of solid oak."

"It is. . . . There's a lot of oak in the place. The archway between this room and the dining room," she said, pointing at the large opening, "has huge, solid oak, sliding doors. I'll show you around later on. Why don't you sit down and kick back?"

Noting his duffel bag, she suggested, "You can leave the bag in the entranceway for now." Turning to leave, she said, "I'll bring some coffee."

"Thanks, that'll be great," he responded.

Peter noted that she appeared to be about eighteen years old. Her light brown hair was tied up in a bun and her crystal blue eyes were in striking contrast to her tight-fitting yellow dress, which was cut short at the knees. Latent feelings of desire stirred within him. Briefly he watched as she walked toward the kitchen. *Not bad looking*, he thought.

He walked over and set the bag down before returning to seat himself in the living room.

Peter's attention turned to the grandfather clock that stood next to a fireplace, in the living room. It appeared to be made out of mahogany, with a carved eagle at the top. He noted that it wasn't showing the correct time. *Must not work*, he thought. He admired the fireplace, which had a cherry-wood mantel with a scene of two deer carved into it.

Small speckled white-and-tan tile surrounded the fire box opening. Looking around the room, Peter noticed the window drapes appeared to be original, as they hung limp in a tattered condition. The room appeared dim with eerie shadows cast onto the dark walls, caused by dirty patches on the chandelier light globes.

Lynn returned with the coffee. "This'll warm you up."

She poured out a cup for Peter, then asked, "Would you like a piece of cake to go with it? I think we have some left in the fridge."

"This'll be fine," he replied as he accepted it. "How long have you been living here?"

She smiled as she seated herself. "About two months. We haven't had time to do anything with it, yet. The place has a lot of potential if someone were to buy it and fix it over. But, we don't plan on living here long enough to do much, except clean up a bit. The owner said he would supply the paint and materials if we wanted to do the work." She sipped from her cup before continuing. "We were thinking about redoing this living room, the kitchen, the bath, and the few bedrooms we're using. A little paint hides a multitude of sins."

Peter offered, "I'd be glad to do my share—course I've never done anything like that, but I'm sure I could learn."

Lynn spoke. "We plan on doing a little at a time. It's kind of creepy the way it is. . . . When we first looked at it, I told the others that I wouldn't live here." She paused and looked at Peter. "The rent is only about one-fourth of what the other places we looked at were and there is so much more space here, so they convinced me." She shuddered. "But I'm still not comfortable here, yet."

Peter sipped his coffee and reasoned, "You sure won't get shack-wacked here in the winter months. I'll say that for it."

"Right. I don't like being here alone, though. They're taking an evening class tonight, so I told them I'd wait here for you. Otherwise I'd have gone with them." She paused and added, "I'm glad you came early."

"I appreciate your waiting for me," Peter said, then paused and looked at her saying, "I don't blame you. It's such a big house. I don't think I'd want to be here alone at night by myself, either."

While Lynn and Peter were sitting in the living room talking, Jake and Linda returned. As they entered Peter rose from his chair. Jake said, "Hi, Pete. I see you found the place. What do you think of it?"

Peter grinned and kiddingly said, "Great place for spooks."

Jake smiled. "That's what we thought when we first looked at it. It was a hard decision to make, but we decided that it can't be all that bad. Once we get it cleaned and painted a bit, it should be livable. Besides, we're not planning to stay too long." He paused as he walked toward a chair, then asked, "Have you been through it yet?"

Lynn answered for Peter. "No. We decided to wait until you got back."

"By the way, you haven't met Linda, have you?" Jake asked.

Linda interrupted Jake with, "No, we haven't met. I'm Linda Arnst and you're Peter Dunn, right?"

"Yes, pleased to meet you, Linda."

"Now that we know each other, what do you say we have a bite to eat? We can show you around later, if that's all right with everyone," Jake suggested and they all agreed.

The girls went to the kitchen to prepare the meal while Peter and Jake remained.

Peter settled himself back on the couch. "It was hard at first. I'm not used to heavy work. My muscles ached the first week. Now I'm getting used to it, but it's putting me in shape quickly. I needed something like that. . . . They're all great guys to work with."

Jake leaned forward and put his hands on his knees. "Yeah, I had the same problem. It takes a while to get used to, but once you get past the first few weeks, it's not too bad. I've been there about a year and a half. . . . By the way, where are you from?"

Peter relaxed and answered, "I'm from Boston. I've been traveling lately. I've hitchhiked down into Virginia, the Carolinas, Florida, Georgia, and a couple of other states before ending up here. I saw a lot of great country and met some good people, too."

Jake threw one leg over the other as he changed positions. "Sounds interesting," he replied.

"It was. The problem was there wasn't any full-time work available. I like it at the mill and will probably stay here as long as they keep me on." Peter paused, then asked, "Are you from around here?"

"No, I'm from Kentucky originally. My parents moved here about ten years ago. When they moved back three years ago, I stayed. I like it here. . . . I worked at the Superette before getting this job, but the mill work pays more and is better for me." He paused and looked toward the kitchen, then back at Peter. He continued, "Lynn's from New Jersey and Linda's from a town called Thornwood, a few miles from here."

Peter nodded his head knowingly. "I've heard of that place. I had thought of going there if I didn't find work here."

Soon the girls called them to the kitchen to eat. Peter glanced around and noted it was a small room with an old sink in one corner. Ivory cupboards lined one wall with a base cabinet underneath. An old table and four chairs provided the dining area. The walls had been papered, but they were so badly coated with soot from the wood cookstove that the original pattern was barely visible.

"Sure smells good," Peter offered.

Jake smiled and said, "The girls are good cooks. They like doing it, so I let them."

Linda gave him a quick look and commented, "You let us, eh?" She looked at Peter and added, "You should taste his cooking. He tried to make a beef roast once, and it turned out burned. We decided to cook from that point on. It's better and cheaper than letting him experiment."

Jake grinned. "A guy is entitled to one little mistake, isn't he?"

"Not when we're paying for it," Lynn retorted with a firm look on her face.

After they'd finished eating, Lynn showed Peter through the remaining part of the house that he hadn't seen. When they reached the room they'd intended for him, she said, "You will have the best room in the house. The view is beautiful. Course, it's the only good room left, unless you want the one where the ceiling has fallen. There was a leak over it, but Jake fixed it." She pointed to the only window in his room. "The sun shines through your window in the morning. It's a great waker-upper. Jake's, Linda's, and mine are on the side where we can see the sunset."

Peter watched her as she talked and felt he would like it here. "This'll be fine." He glanced at the layer of dust that had collected on everything.

"It shouldn't take much to clean it up. It'll be the best place I've had since I left home."

"I'm sure you'll like it. It even has a view of the cemetery," she reflected with a huge smile, as she watched Peter's face turn pale.

"Cemetery?"

"Yes, there's a small one." She pointed to the window. "You can see some of the stones in the daytime, but most of it's overgrown. I guess they must have buried people on their own land years ago."

Peter shivered inwardly, trying not to let his feelings of uncertainty show as he answered, "I suppose I'll have to get used to that idea."

Lynn tried to be reassuring. "It bothered us girls at first. Now we don't even think about it anymore. Jake thought nothing of it. He said, 'What you believe the dead do is all in your mind.' He said he wasn't going to let it worry him none."

"I guess I can hack it, too," Peter claimed, with renewed courage.

Peter's life started to settle down to the routines of the day, but he spent many hours rehashing the events that had sent him away from Boston. He still thought about Maggie often and missed being with her. He sat alone at night on his bed, reading her poem and thinking the same thoughts over and over again. His mind became filled with wondering what she might be doing at that moment. Or what they might have been able to do together.

Peter's travels had been very difficult, but they'd toughened him to the world. It had become more of a dog-eat-dog existence until he moved into this house that he was now sharing with the others.

But, he felt content here. It pleased him that there was no dissension here, as they all got along well together. It was to him more of a home than he'd experienced with his family.

As time went on, Peter and Lynn became very close, and he was able to talk with her about the parts of his life that had been so difficult for him.

One day, six months later, Lynn and Peter were alone in the house. He'd been upstairs and was entering the living room when he noticed the upholstered chair that was beside the fireplace had been moved. Not that it mattered to him where the chair was, but he noticed that it didn't look right beneath the large window. It occurred to him that this was the second time he'd seen it there and he'd moved it back the other time. He decided to leave it where it was now and ask Lynn if she knew why it had been moved. She was in the kitchen making lunch, when he entered.

"Do you know why the brown upholstered chair is over under the window?" he asked, as she turned to face him. Then, he added, "I think it looked much better where it was."

"No, I saw it there earlier and wondered about it myself. I agree it looks out of place by the window. I thought about asking you to move it back beside the fireplace. I'm not sure why Linda and Jake put it there." She turned back and spoke as though she were talking to the sandwiches she was making. "They were up late last night. . . . There must have been some reason they did it. Maybe we should ask them when they come home."

Later that evening, as they all sat around talking, Jake casually asked Peter, "Who's been changing the room around? That chair by the window looks out of place there."

"We noticed it today and thought you and Linda had decided to put it there," Lynn interjected.

Jake scratched his head. "That's the third time I've seen it over there. I've put it back a couple of times in the past couple of months. I had meant to ask about it then, but I'd forget to." He looked at Linda whose face reflected her puzzlement. She shook her head, indicating she knew nothing about it. He asked, "If we didn't put it there, then who did? Why would anyone want it there, anyway? Something strange is going on around here."

Linda was concerned and bewildered. "That's not all that's happened. Someone's been moving things around in my room. I didn't say anything before, 'cause I didn't want to cause any trouble. But, the things on my dresser have been moved several times."

Lynn became defensive. "I sure didn't do it."

"I didn't mean that you did. I know you wouldn't. I know I didn't do it, and I know that you guys wouldn't. So who did?" she asked, in disbelief that it could happen by itself.

"Sure beats me," Lynn answered. Then she turned to Jake. "Maybe some of your friends at the mill have been playing tricks on us. They've been teasing you both that we live in a haunted house, haven't they?" Lynn reasoned.

Peter agreed. "Sure, that must be it. They think they can have a good laugh at our expense."

Then he offered what seemed to him to be a solution. "I suggest we lock the house up tight whenever we leave. That way we'll take the temptation away from them."

Linda spoke up. "Good idea. Just don't mention anything to them. We don't want them to know we're aware of anything being wrong."

Lynn, who had been lying on the couch, suddenly sat bolt upright and cried out, "What was that noise in the kitchen?"

"Sounded to me like Spike lapping his water. All this talk about strange things has got you nervous," Jake answered, as he got up. "I'll go and check on it to ease your minds. . . . Here, Spike," he called, as he walked toward the kitchen door.

Emerging through the open doorway walked Spike, their Irish Setter, wagging his tail.

"You scared poor Lynn," Jake said to the dog, while patting its head.

Lynn looked at Jake. "I'm not sleeping alone tonight. You and Linda are together. All this talk has given me the jitters." She looked over at Peter and implored him, "Will you stay with me, Peter?"

"No funny stuff, either," Jake cautioned kiddingly.

Rubbing his hands together, Peter looked at Jake and said, "Sure will enjoy this." Then he comforted Lynn with, "I was just kidding, Jake. I know how you feel. It's probably just the guys at the mill. . . . There has to be a logical explanation of what's been happening."

Smiling at Lynn, he suggested, "It's getting late and we've got to get up early. Why don't we go up now?"

Jake continued his teasing. "Can't wait to molest her, eh, Pete?"

Lynn gave Jake a quick glance. She smiled and said, "It'd be all right by me." Then, turning to look at Peter, she continued, "I'll feel much better with you being with me. . . . I'm sure I'll be all right tomorrow. . . . You're right. It's late. . . . Maybe we should all get to bed. Things look better by the light of day."

Rising from her chair and holding out her hand to Jake, Linda concurred. "I agree."

The following morning, Linda sat in the living room reading a magazine. Looking up, she noticed a flower vase on the mantel begin to slide sideways, ever so slightly. *My mind is playing tricks on me. What happened last night is getting to me.* She consoled herself, *Don't let this thing get to you.* Looking back at her magazine, she began reading once more. In an effort to double-check her sanity, she couldn't resist glancing up at the vase from time to time.

Lynn entered the room after finishing with her bedroom.

Linda waited until she'd seated herself on a chair before commenting, "I could see that you were beside yourself last night. . . . How'd you sleep?"

"It took me a while to settle down before I could get to sleep."

Linda teased, "That's understandable, with a guy like Peter beside you!"

Lynn took it the way it was meant, but she acted as though she was upset with Linda. Her eyes narrowed slightly as she spoke. "Now don't get any ideas. He was a perfect gentleman. We sat and talked, that's all. Nothing happened."

"I was just kidding," Linda returned. Then she questioned herself, *Should I mention to Lynn about the vase moving?*

Seeing a perplexed look on Linda's face, Lynn answered, "I know you're kidding, but you looked so strangely at me for a minute, I wasn't sure."

"That had nothing to do with you. I was just wondering if I should tell you about something that happened, before you came down."

Lynn immediately questioned, "Like what happened?"

"It was probably all in my mind because of what we were talking about last night, but I thought I saw that vase on the fireplace move."

"What!" Lynn exclaimed somewhat startled.

Immediately realizing it was a mistake to have said anything, Linda said, "Like I said. It was probably all in my mind. It appeared to move slightly just as I looked up from reading. I shouldn't have mentioned it." Apologetically, she added, "Please, don't let it upset you."

Lynn felt determined. "Okay, but if anything else happens around here, I'm moving out. I don't want to live in a haunted house!"

Later that night, while the girls were finishing cleaning up after their meal, Peter and Jake sat talking in the living room.

Jake spoke. "I know Lynn was emotional last night, thinking there may be ghosts in the house. Though, it's still got me wondering, too. I really don't think the guys at the mill would do that sort of thing, especially since it's happened before, quite a while ago."

Peter could see by Jake's eyes that he was concerned. Peter said, "I had to do a lot of talking to get Lynn calmed down last night. Even if we'd have wanted to screw around, we couldn't have—she was too upset to even think straight.

"It seems almost as if that chair has a mind of its own and wants to be under that window," Peter commented, half-kidding and half-serious.

"We shouldn't be talking about this when the girls come in. It would just upset them all over again," Jake cautioned, as he got up to go to the bathroom.

"Right," Peter agreed, while reaching for the newspaper.

Jake returned a few minutes later, and anxiety was written on his face. "Damnedest thing I've ever seen! When I flushed the toilet, the water was all black and greasy-looking. Like it was mixed with dirt and oil!" Then, to prove his point, he challenged Peter. "Go and take a look! See what you think. Don't say anything to the girls about it, though. We don't want to spook them anymore than they already are."

Peter returned, shaking his head. "Sure is shitty-looking stuff. I don't know what to make of it, either."

Jake remarked, "They should be through in the kitchen any minute now. Let's not talk about this ghost business anymore tonight. We'll have to call a plumber tomorrow and have him check it out—let's forget about it now." Then, heading for the mysterious chair, he seated himself, saying, "I don't really believe in ghosts. Even if I did, from what I've heard, they don't ever hurt anyone."

Peter nodded his head in agreement. "Guess you're right," he said, "There isn't anything to be afraid of."

Jake had hardly seated himself, when he was suddenly hurtled across the room by some unseen force. Sliding on the varnished floor, he crashed into a heap against the wall.

Stunned by the suddenness of the attack, Peter leaped to his feet, as if catapulted. "What the fuck?" he blurted out in disbelief. Then he ran over to help Jake and shouted, "Lynn, Linda, get in here!"

Having heard the noise, they were already racing for the living room when they heard Peter shouting. Fear imprinted across their faces, they stopped short upon reaching the room. Jake, holding his shoulder, was staggering around dazed, with Peter assisting him. The chair stood suspended in mid-air, held by some invisible force.

Peter shouted, "Help me with Jake! We're getting the fuck out of here! This place is going crazy!"

Linda ran to help Peter while Lynn charged for the front door.

Materializing from a misty blue smoke, a head formed above the suspended chair. Its long black hair matted in tangles was visible above hollow, glowing green eyes. A full black disheveled beard rested on the back of the chair.

Seeing this apparition, standing seven feet tall, sent fright through Jake's disabled body. A surge of energy rushed through him, enabling him to move with a sudden urgency.

A growl of ear-shattering ferocity pierced the air, as blue-yellow flames shot from the creature's mouth, narrowly missing Peter.

Reaching the open doorway at the same moment, Jake and Linda collided, landing in a pile on the front porch. Running at full tilt, Peter suddenly had to hurdle them to avoid injury. He came to an abrupt halt and returned to help them up. Together, they rushed from the house in a mad dash as a second bolt of flames struck the front door exploding, shattering it into splinters. Burning, the flames spewed forward in all directions.

Once they'd reached a safe distance from the house, they stopped to search for Lynn.

Panic in her voice, Linda shouted in a hysterical rasp, "Lynn, where are you? Can you hear us?"

The night was dark, making it difficult to see. "I'm over here!" they heard Lynn shout, and it came to them from down the road.

Rushing toward her, they heard her shout once more, "I've twisted my ankle! I couldn't go any farther!"

Within minutes they reached her and helped her up from the mound of dirt where she was seated.

Peter turned and looked back at the house. Momentarily, he stood shocked, in bewilderment and disbelief. The sky behind them brightened as the fire spread and engulfed the porch.

Peter turned to Jake, who still looked dazed and asked, "How you doing, Jake?"

"My right shoulder is paining me something awful, but I'll be okay. Let's get out of here before that ghoulish devil attacks us, again."

For them, making good time was difficult. Lynn hobbled along with Peter and Jakes' help. Linda set the pace and said breathlessly, "I think they have a telephone at the Marrits! If we can make it that far before that thing decides to attack us again, we should be safe!"

Lynn's voice was high-pitched and half-hysterical. "They won't believe us, though! I'm sure, they'll think we set the place on fire!"

Between short breaths, Linda exclaimed, "My God! . . . They'll have to believe us! . . . Who would think . . . we'd do this . . . to ourselves!"

Jake's pain was becoming excruciating. "I think that fuckin' bastard broke my shoulder. . . . It's killing me!"

Lynn's breath came in short spurts. "I just knew . . . something terrible . . . was going to happen . . . when Linda told me about the vase . . . moving this morning." She paused to breathe deeply before continuing. "I could feel . . . evil in the air, all day . . . can we rest a second? . . . I'm all in," Lynn pleaded in despair, between breaths.

Half-questioning his own reasoning, Peter stated, "I think we're far enough away from that damned house! If it was coming after us, it would have been here by now! I guess it'll be all right here." He paused and looked at Jake. Then he continued, "I think the Marrits' house is just a little farther."

Easing Lynn to the ground and trying to get her to relax, Peter said to her in a controlled voice, "Let me check your ankle for you." He pulled up her jean pants leg and felt her ankle. "Seems a bit swollen, but I don't feel any bones out of place. It probably is just a bad sprain." He turned to Jake and asked, "How's your shoulder doing?"

"I'm sure it's broken. The pain's going down into my arm and chest, but I can stand it . . . at least we didn't die." Changing the subject, Jake commented, "That thing was ugly beyond belief." Then his voice filled with anger. He asked. "Did anyone else see it?"

Feeling somewhat calmer, Linda answered, "It was horrible. The eyes were like sunken glowing embers. I think they are burned in my mind forever."

"I ran like hell as soon as I saw the chair hanging in the air," Lynn revealed. Attempting to get back onto her feet, she assured them, "I can make it now. Let's get going."

"Right! Here, put your arm around my shoulder," Peter instructed, as he assisted her to her feet. "I think that we can take it a bit slower, now. It'll be safer in the dark if we don't rush like we were."

Turning to watch the house become engulfed in flames, his voice quavering with emotions, Jake shouted, "Look at that sucker burn."

Linda turned momentarily to look. Pumping her arm into the air, she shouted, "Burn, you bastard, burn! I hope you go straight to hell!"

"Come on," Peter urged them. "We've got to get you and Lynn to a doctor as quickly as possible."

Abner Marrit and his wife, Janet, were about to get into their car to drive to the fire when they heard voices up the road.

"Who's there?" Abner shouted.

Peter yelled forward, "Can you drive us into town? We've got two people here who need a doctor."

Linda shouted to them, "The Krat house is on fire and we barely escaped being burned up with it."

Mr. Marrit rushed to get his car started while his wife ran up the road toward them. "What happened?" she asked when she reached them.

Peter noticed how Lynn's eyes opened wide as she exclaimed, "You'll never believe us. It's too crazy. No one will believe it."

Mrs. Marrit took her arm to help her and excitedly requested, "Please tell me what happened. I'd like to know."

Before anyone had time to explain, they had reached Mr. Marrit, who had just finished backing the car out onto the road. His wife opened the door to the back seat. "You two get in back. It'll be more comfortable there."

Lynn joined them in the back, while Peter climbed into the front with the Marrits.

During the drive into town, they explained to the Marrits what had happened.

Abner Marrit drawled as he chewed on his empty pipe. "Sounds like old Krat came back. He was a huge lumberjack, taller than a smokestack and ornerier than a pig-headed mule." He sniffed. "He used to strangle his chickens by taking them by the head and swinging them over his head until their necks twisted off." He glanced at Peter to check his reaction before continuing. "Then he'd let out a hoarse laugh. He always had a wild look in his eyes. . . . Never was right since his wife ran off and left him. He was the terror of the whole area, while he lived. . . . No one would cross him. Fell down his well, they say." He glanced at Peter, then back at the road. "No one went on his property, even to check out how he died. . . . His nephew inherited it, but he wouldn't go there, either. . . . Been vacant a long time before you folks moved in."

A few days later, with no place to live and all of his possessions destroyed, Peter decided it was time he moved on. After collecting his earnings, he said good-bye to his friends and set out on foot for the expressway heading out of town.

Somewhat questioning his reason for leaving this life that had brought a semblance of contentment for him, Peter found the decision difficult to make, but he knew it would never be the same again if he remained. Blinking back tears of regret, he walked halfheartedly down the dusty road, his thoughts being warmed by the hot fall sun.

At the roadside park, on the expressway near the edge of town, he attempted to hitch a ride with no success. By evening a chill was in the air as he settled down to spend the night. Curling up in his new sleeping bag, he let his thoughts drift back to Maggie and the time they'd made love. He wished desperately that he had some way of contacting her, but this only left him feeling empty inside. He read and reread her poem by the dim light from the park lighting. After he had tossed and turned restlessly, his tired eyes allowed him the peace of a deep sleep.

In his dream he found himself searching for Maggie everywhere, but he couldn't find her. Then, suddenly finding himself in an elevator with other people, Peter recognized a small blond girl who appeared to be in her early twenties. He'd seen her before, but he couldn't remember when or when. As the elevator stopped at each floor in its ascent, people got off, but none got on.

Finally he and the blond girl were the only two left in the car as it approached the thirteenth floor. When the elevator stopped, the door opened and the girl stepped out, but an unseen force held Peter in. The doors closed and the elevator car rose with accelerado. The walls disappeared and the floor became suspended by a rope at each corner. Suddenly, the car came alive. It twisted, rocked, and began sudden up and down movements, attempting to dislodge him into the black murky void that surrounded him. He retched while he lay on the floor, clutching the raw edge, trying to sustain himself. A sense of finality grasped him as it neared the top.

Suddenly, he awoke, sweatfully cold. He recalled the dream. It was the same as others Peter'd had. Each time the elevator had not reached the top and upon remembering it, he'd wonder what might happen when it did. A bit shaken, he arose and prepared for the day.

The sun had come upon the day from across the park. The sky was speckled with clouds and the sun's rays, showing through slight openings in the trees, were melting the overnight frost. The beauty of the spray of sun against the trees gave the impression of a cluster of fireworks. Shaking inside, Peter paid no heed to this beauty surrounding him as he rolled up his bag and headed for the expressway to catch a ride.

Having walked along the exit road from the park to the highway, Peter began thumbing a ride. No one stopped for him; no one cared about his needs. By noon, his attempts fruitless, he sat by the roadside and ate the few crackers and cheese he'd taken with him.

Glancing up occasionally while eating, he'd check the oncoming traffic, which was light in this area, even at mid-day. His thoughts carried him back to Maggie, and he dwelled upon his loss.

Finally, in the late afternoon, a pickup with a camper approached. He jumped up and held out his thumb. It rolled to a stop down the road from him. Hurrying, he grabbed his belongings and running to it, he swung open the cab door. A man in his fifties leaned on the steering wheel, peering at him.

"Hi. Bill's my name. Where you heading?" he inquired while extending out a bearlike hand.

"Peter Dunn. . . . Out of town. I'm not particular," Peter responded, as he submitted his hand. Dwarfed by size, he felt his hand being clenched viselike.

"Sounds all right to me; climb in. I'm heading up north, then west toward Seattle, but I'm not in any particular hurry to get there." He paused while Peter pulled himself up into the seat and slammed the door shut with a bang. As Bill shifted the truck into gear and they started moving, he began talking, "It's been some time since I've been to Seattle. You're welcome to tag along as far as you like," he offered. "It'll be good to have company along the way. It's beautiful country up north—ever been up that way?"

"No, never," Peter admitted and added, "I'm from Boston and decided I'd like to see what the rest of the country is like."

He looked over at Bill, whose shoulders filled his black-and-red checkered flannel shirt to the bursting point. Bare skin erupted, through a ruptured seam at the sleeve-top. His paunchy stomach pressed against the steering wheel and flowed down onto his thighs.

Noticing Peter examining him, he drawled, "It's all bought and paid for. . . . I've gotten somewhat out of shape since I sold my stores a couple of years ago. . . . Once, though, I prided myself on my physical condition. But, since my wife, Emily, died, I've been on the bum." He glanced down

70

at his stomach. "I guess in more ways than one."

"I'm sorry to hear that you lost your wife," Peter remarked in earnest. "I really don't have anyone, either. Oh, I've actually got a family of sorts back there, but I'd have been better off if I'd have been born an orphan. Maybe then I'd have been adopted into a good one." Peter's regret hung heavy in his revelation to this stranger.

"Run away from home, did you?"

"I just left. There wasn't anything for me back there anymore."

They had covered many miles before Bill broke the silence by announcing, "I have to stop for gas. How's a cup of coffee sound to you?"

Peter moved from his slumped position and stretched. "I could go for that."

Later, back on the road, Peter, becoming drowsy from the drone of the pickup, dropped off to sleep. Some time later he awoke, opened one eye, and saw Bill slumping forward toward the steering wheel. Becoming concerned, he blurted out, "Are you all right, Bill?"

He'd known him a short time and though his first impression was questionable, he was beginning to like him as a friend.

Immediately Bill's head perked up. "Sure, I'm all right. This helps me to relax. Earlier you had said that you left home. Something to do with your family?"

"I wasn't getting along with them."

"Care to talk about it?"

Believing this stranger to be honestly interested. Peter explained the circumstances that led to his being on the road.

"That's some story. This ghost scared the pants off of you, did it?"

Peter found Bill easy to talk to, so he ventured, "I guess you could say that. I'm lucky that I didn't shit them full."

Bill laughed and responded, "You've got that right. . . . You know, I was reading in the paper yesterday about these things they call poltergeists or poltragists, something like that. Anyway, these people over in Bay City, Michigan, struck oil. . . . Not the way you're thinking, though. This here oil was coming out of their faucet in the kitchen and toilet. Sort of like what happened at that place of yours. Anyway, in the rest of the house, it was just plain water. The water company checked it out and couldn't find anything wrong. They called it the work of one of those things."

The weather was starting to change. A strong wind beat against the side of the camper. "Looks like we're in for a storm," Peter commented.

"I've driven in a lot of rough weather. This doesn't bother me none," Bill replied.

There was silence for a few minutes, which was broken by a ripping sound. Looking toward it, Peter could see Bill's red hairy calloused elbow pointing at him through a large hole. "This old thing is ripe all over, but that's when they're the most comfortable," he declared, looking at Peter and smiling.

Peter's mouth formed a slight smile, and he agreed, "That's when I like mine the best, too."

Bill, glancing at Peter then back at the road, said, "That experience you had with that banshee, as you called it, reminds me of what happened to me and my wife in upper New York."

Suddenly, without warning, he swerved to miss a pothole, tossing Peter against the door.

Bill apologized. "Real sorry about that."

Rubbing his elbow, Peter recovered and straightened himself up. He noticed Bill's concerned look. "No problem," he said and added, "You were saying?"

"Oh, yeah. That was a strange thing there, too. We'd bought a nice rustic home on the edge of town and had only lived in it for a couple of months when, late one night, what sounded like someone banging things together woke us up. It quieted down, so we thought it was the steam pipes. You know how they crack and bang sometimes. Well, we just went back to sleep. Anyway, a few days later, one morning when we got up, the kitchen was all in a mess. . . . Silverware and broken dishes were spread around, all over the place. Emily's favorite flower plant was turned upside down in the sink, and there was mud on the kitchen carpet," Bill explained, while blinking to keep his strained eyes on the road.

What had begun as rain was quickly turning to sleet. Driving was becoming more laborious, but Bill refused to give in to the difficult task. Reaching behind the seat, he pulled forth a pint of brandy. Taking a snort, he handed it to Peter. "Here, have a drink, it'll put lead in your pencil."

Peter waved his hand. "Thanks, but I'll pass." He became concerned. "Maybe we should pull over. . . . You've been driving a long time now. You must be getting tired," he ventured, knowing that it was not his place to decide when they stopped.

"I'm all right. I'm used to this kind of driving."

Ice had been forming on the wipers for some time, now. Peter noticed how the wiper on Bill's side waved to and fro, leaving only small areas for him to see through while Peter's cleared the entire windshield. Peter commented, "Maybe you should stop and clean your wiper."

Bill responded, "Modern technology they call it. They haven't changed the style of these wipers since they were invented. The only thing they've changed was to move them from the top of the windshield to the bottom. You pay twenty thousand for a vehicle and they put fifty-cent wipers on it!" He kept right on driving.

After a few minutes, Bill spoke again, "Now where was I? Oh, now I remember. One of the dish towels was full of dirt from the plant and had been wiped across the refrigerator. Nothing seemed to be missing, though. When we moved there, everyone had told us that it was a peaceful community. We never locked our doors, so we figured kids had done it. We reported it to the police, and they agreed and called it vandalism. From then on you can be sure we locked them. Even after that we'd occasionally hear noises at night, but when we checked, we didn't find anything unusual."

Bill shifted in his seat, then continued, "It was strange, though, because each time it happened, I felt a presence of some kind. Emily said she'd felt it, too, but she didn't let it bother her." He paused and shifted his position again, glanced at Peter, then back at the road.

"We'd been at a party one night at the neighbors. We were both kind of loaded and had just gotten to bed when all hell broke loose. It sounded like it came from the living room. We got down there quicker than you can split a cunthair. But, we couldn't find anything out of place. That night, we'd forgotten to lock the door, so after locking up, we went back to bed. Funny thing was, though, we could smell a slight odor of flowers. Then, at about four-thirty or so, I woke up again and caught a glimpse of something moving near the dresser. It was only there for a second."

Bill coughed and rubbed his nose and glanced at Peter before continuing. "I was about to go back to sleep, thinking I'd imagined it, when I saw the closet door opening. Then, a few seconds later, I heard a swishing sound near the bedroom door."

Bill stopped abruptly and hit the brakes. Heading straight for them was a semi passing a car. Turning the camper sharply toward the side of the road, Bill avoided a collision. Spraying the camper with mud and slush, the truck sped on past, swaying the camper in its backdraft.

Bill blurted out, "Those DAMNED GASOLINE COWBOYS! They think they own the whole damned road."

Reaching behind the seat, he produced the brandy and took a healthy swallow, then handed it to Peter. Feeling very nervous, Peter chugged one down, coughed and handed the bottle back to Bill.

Peter shook his head before commenting, "That stupid guy could have gotten us all killed. They're always in a hurry. . . . When they get where they're going, they have nothing to do but sit at a bar and hustle the local chicks. . . . Why is it they always drive at night?" he inquired, as he tried to calm his frazzled nerves.

Bill glanced over at him and frowned slightly. "Can't answer that. Except, I suppose, there's no way stations open, less traffic, and they can make better time."

Bill continued to drive even though the weather and road conditions were getting progressively worse. "Let's see now, I was saying, when that wheeled devil came at us, I had heard this sound near the bedroom door. I turned and saw a partial outline of someone. It was a misty, silverish shadow with the lower part trailing off into a thin line. You know, the way a genie comes out of a bottle. That's the way it looked before it vanished. I was still real tired and half-drunk, but that sobered me up."

Bill's voice portrayed his tension. "I can still feel the chills running up my spine when I think about it."

He paused while directing his concentration on the road. The camper swayed threateningly as wet snow driven by high winds slashed at its side.

Peter had become intent on what Bill was telling him and wasn't paying attention to the road conditions. Seeing Bill's intensity, he suggested, "Don't you think it would be better to get a rest? The weather will probably be better tomorrow."

Bill slouched over the wheel in an effort to see. He answered, "Could be worse. It could turn into a blizzard. Early fall like this, the weather is really unpredictable. Besides, I still feel alert." Then Bill continued his story.

"My sudden movements in bed woke Emily up. While I was telling her what I'd seen, we started hearing a commotion going on downstairs. We lay there listening for a few moments, too scared to move. We heard people talking down there and they were arguing about something." Bill became silent while he rubbed his strained eyes, then he continued, "Emily whispered something to me about my not wanting a telephone in our bedroom. . . . Finally, I decided to go down and see what was going on. . . . By the time I was halfway down the stairs, they were shouting down there."

Suddenly, Bill, no longer talking, his face ashen white, his hands gripping the steering wheel in a death grip and his knuckles in reddened tenseness, swerved the camper sharply to the left. It skidded along the left shoulder of the road. Finding traction, it careened to the right, with Bill trying frantically to steady it on the road. Zig-zagging from side to side, it slid into the soft shoulder on the right side of the road and halted abruptly in the ditch.

He tried to back it out, but the shoulder was soupy with mud and snow. It would not budge, but was held fast in place. Realizing he would dig it in deeper if he continued, Bill decided that it would be better to sleep in the camper and try to get help in the morning.

Leaving the motor running, he explained to Peter, "Thought I saw something on the road back there. . . . It was shaped like a man bent over looking at the ground—it just disappeared before I would have hit it. I guess this talking about ghosts has got me jumpy. My mind must be playing tricks on me." He wiped his hand across the stubble on his chin and looking at Peter, he said, "I'd better finish telling you in the morning."

Bill reached for the bottle of brandy, took three long swallows, and handed it to Peter, "Here, finish this off. It'll be good for you—spruce you up a bit." Then peering at Peter in the darkened cab, he said, "Looks more like you were the one who saw the ghost."

Peter finished the contents, tossed the bottle into the back of the seat, and stretched out his legs. "Thanks, I really needed that. I'm not much of a drinker, but at a time like this. . . . Who cares?"

Bill kept the heat on while they talked. "We'll stay up front and settle our nerves." Then, admitting his error, he commented, "I should have listened to you when you suggested stopping. But being a bull-headed Frenchman, my thinking isn't always the best. I have to admit sometimes I do push myself too far. Then, when something like this happens, I pay the price."

Peter looked at Bill and said, "I had second thoughts about saying anything. It's your vehicle and it's not my place to tell you what to do."

"Don't waste your time worrying about it. If you think I'm wrong, just say so. I may not listen, but that doesn't stop you from having the right to say what's on your mind."

Peter felt he was beginning to like this man more right along. Still shaking beyond his control, he admitted, "With this talking about ghosts, I—I—I'm afraid to go out of the cab. I shouldn't admit it, but I am."

"We can stay in here for a while. I couldn't get to sleep now myself, anyway, until I settle down." Bill paused, and after slumping forward onto the steering wheel, he commented, "Wish I had thought ahead and bought more brandy." Then, looking intensely through the dark toward Peter, he went on. "I'm going to tell you something that happened to me years ago. It was when I was in my twenties. I owned a small movie theater. After the last showing, I had to check it, turn out the lights, and lock up. It had a stage in the center, in front of the screen. I don't remember why I did it, but there were steps leading from the aisle up to the stage. I know the idea was crazy, but I decided that I would turn off all the lights and walk down those steps in the dark."

He paused and wiped his dripping nose on his sleeve. Then he continued, "Well, the controls were near the side of the stage. I turned them off, and the place was pitch dark. I felt my way along the floor with my feet until I found the top step. I had counted them, so I knew there were exactly eight steps that I had to go down."

He glanced up the road, then back at Peter who was absorbed in what Bill was telling him. He continued, "Then, I started to tell myself there was no bottom step, just a deep black endless pit. Each step I'd take down, I'd repeat this over and over to myself, attempting to convince myself. I did this all the way down, until I reached the seventh step. By then I had, beyond a doubt, convinced myself the last one didn't exist. That I'd just fall into an abyss of some sort. Finally, I really tried to take that last step, but couldn't."

Bill felt uncomfortable and shifted his position. First looking into the night at his side of the road, he then turned toward Peter. Feeling a bit nervous and not wanting to reveal it in his voice, he tried to contain himself. He paused a few moments, then continued, "You know? I had to feel my way back across the stage to the light switch boxes. They were of the open type, so I knew I had to be damned careful not to electrocute myself. Finally, I reached them and cranked them on. Since then, I've thought many times about how stupid I was and could have killed myself with those power switches."

Peter remained silent as Bill paused, breathed deeply, and added, "You're probably wondering why I'm telling you this and what it has to do with us now. Well, it taught me a valuable lesson. . . . There is nothing to fear in this life, except fear itself. Fear is a normal reaction to things we can't see or don't understand. Believing this has gotten me through many situations, when otherwise I might have recoiled back in fear. Instead I'd plunge right on. . . . Now don't get me wrong. I'm not saying a person should be foolhardy. When there's real danger, you need caution, not fear. Fear clouds your mind, so you can't think clearly. Fear is all in your head."

Peter knew Bill was impressing this upon him in order to teach him what he himself believed. Thinking about this, he nodded his head. "It makes sense to me. I would never have thought of it in that way. I feel better already."

They had been on the road all day and part of the night. Peter was very tired when he drifted off to sleep in the camper.

Sometime during the night, Peter was awakened by an insistent rapping noise. At first, he thought he was dreaming. Shaking the sleep out of his head, he tried to collect his thoughts. The rapping continued and kept getting louder.

Finally, he realized the pounding was in the back of the camper. Stumbling through the unfamiliar truck, he reached the door. Unlocking and opening it slightly, he peered out. Blinded by a bright light, he quickly pulled it closed and was attempting to lock it when he heard, "Police. Is everything all right?"

As he reopened it, the officer spoke, "We saw that your vehicle was in trouble. Is anyone injured?"

Seeing the patch on his shoulder, Peter was about to speak when Bill called out, "What's going on?"

Peter informed him, "The police are here."

"Can we be of any assistance? Is anyone injured? . . . We'll call a wrecker, if you'd like us to."

Bill yelled back, "No one was injured. But a wrecker'll be fine. Have them here around eight. We're all right for the night. . . . Thanks for stopping."

"No trouble at all. We'll have them here at eight. Good night."

What a day, Peter thought, as he tried to regain his sleep.

Bill stirred, then woke up. *Is that the wrecker already?* he wondered, as he groped for the light switch. Turning on the light, he checked his watch. "Only six-thirty," he mumbled to himself. "The dumb cops sent them here too early!"

Pulling on his pants, he went to the door bare-chested. Jumping to the ground, he felt the chill of the crisp morning breeze strike him. As he walked around the corner of the camper, a man in a heavy jacket spoke. "Morning. Thought you could use some help getting out."

Bill began to shiver. "Thanks, but we have a wrecker coming around eight."

"Better get something on. You could catch a bad cold that way," the man said. Then, pointing up front, he added, "I've already got a chain hooked onto the front. It won't take but two licks to pull you out. Could save you the cost of the wrecker. But, it's up to you."

Bill wrapped his arms around his body for warmth and silently cussed his stupidity of neglecting to get fully dressed. "Thanks, maybe you're right. I'll be right back."

After putting on a jacket and boots, Bill headed toward the cab of his camper. He was surprised to see a semi backed up to the bumper of his vehicle. He looked in wonder at the load it was carrying. Protruding through the slats of the trailer were the legs of live pigs. To his amazement, they were piled into it to a height of five to six feet. *Inhumane,* he thought to himself, as he pulled himself into the cab and started the engine. Once he was back on the road, he went over to thank the driver. "How's twenty for your trouble?"

"Wouldn't think of accepting it. Glad to be of service. Maybe someone will do the same for me, someday." He paused, then continued, "I'll call the wrecker on the CB, so they won't make a wasted trip."

Bill couldn't help commenting, "Sure is a hell of a pile of hogs you got there. Any of them make it alive?"

The young driver produced a grin. "They'll be all right. It's only a short haul. . . . Take care driving. The roads have melted some, but they're still slippery in spots."

"Thanks. I'll be more careful. Thanks again for the help."

Peter could feel the thump of the camper on the joints of the road, as he awoke. *Must have slept pretty sound. I didn't even hear the wrecker,* he thought.

He opened the connecting window to the cab. Bill, hearing the squeak of the window sliding, looked back. "You slept through all the fun. Some help you are," he kidded Peter.

"What time is it?"

"About eight-thirty," Bill answered, while pausing to look back at the road. "You know how I was bitching at those semi truck drivers? Well, damned if one of them didn't stop and pull us out early this morning. I thought it was a wrecker at first, but it was only six-thirty when he showed up." Then, handing a thermos through the opening back to Peter, he offered, "Here, have some coffee. It'll warm your innards."

"Thanks, it'll sure hit the spot."

"I'll be stopping up ahead, and you can climb in front then." He glanced back. "How'd you sleep?"

"Not bad after the interruption."

Later, when Peter was in the cab and they had started back on the road, he asked Bill. "What about that story you were telling me last night. Does it have an ending?"

Bill poured himself a cup of coffee from one of the refilled thermoses and took a drink. After wiping the drip from his mouth onto his sleeve, he continued his story. "We went down the stairs to the vestibule and stopped there. We stood back far enough so that we could see through the archway into the living room." Bill paused.

The sun had cleared the road of ice and snow. Thus relieved of the need for continual direct attention, Bill would glance at Peter frequently while talking. This time he sniffed deeply, wiped his nose with his sleeve, and continued. "They were arguing about something, and there was a baby crying. I tell you we were mighty scared. I was shaking like a leaf

78

in a high wind. We couldn't imagine what could be happening. We peeped around the corner of the doorway into the living room. What we saw was a real shocker."

Bill sipped some coffee, then continued. "The whole damn room was different from ours. It was like it had just appeared from out of the past. The furniture we had was gone. In place of it was old-style furniture in new condition. It dumbfounded me completely. It made no sense to us, how it could have been changed. Even the wallpaper was different. There was a pull-down kerosene lamp hanging in the center of the ceiling. The carpeting we had was gone. In place of it was a varnished floor with a homemade circular rug in the center of the room. There was a fireplace, too. . . . We never had one!"

He sipped coffee once more, set the cup on his knee, checked the road, and turned to Peter, who sat motionless, intrigued by the story.

"A bearded man of about thirty-five was standing there shouting at a woman, who was trying to quiet the baby. It was young, possibly a year or so old. The guy kept slapping his hand with his fist, sometimes shaking it at her. I heard him tell her, 'Martha, I can't take your nagging anymore. You've got to stop your spending money foolishly! People we don't even know coming over, eating and drinking . . . spilling wine all over the furniture!'

"She was yelling back at him, 'You never want to do what I like doing! You never take me anywhere!'

"He yelled back, 'And I'm never going to, either.'

"She yelled at him again, 'You no-good weasel! I wish I never knew you! My mother told me that you were no good! I should have listened to her!'

"He yelled back at her, 'Didn't I take you to New York City last year for your birthday? But, oh, no! That's not good enough for you! That city has half a million people! . . . I should have left you there! Maybe I could have found someone there better than you!' "

Bill took another drink and continued. "Well, they carried on like that for about five minutes, while Emily and I, stood in shock. I just knew something terrible was going to happen."

Bill paused, checked the road ahead, then looked at Peter. "All of a sudden, he ran at her, threw the baby aside, and started choking her. When I saw that happen, I lunged right for him. But, there was nothing there. I went right through them. Just like shit through a sieve. . . . I slammed into the wall, and it knocked me on my ass."

He paused, cleared his throat, and continued, "I got up dazed. I was bewildered. I had tried to help her, but there was nothing that I could do. We were in different dimensions. I tell you, it was horrible to just watch her getting strangled, and I couldn't do a thing about it. Emily was screaming, the baby was screeching."

Bill wiped his dripping nose on his sleeve and continued. "Well, he done her in right before our eyes. When he finished, he dropped her, looked at her for a second, then ran right through the closed door, holding his face in his hands, sobbing. Suddenly, it got very cold. We were both shivering. The woman just lay there, with the baby still screaming. Emily, forgetting what happened to me, went over and tried to pick it up, but her hands went right through it, too.

"In an instant, it all disappeared and our room was back to normal. There was only dead silence left. We were still shivering. I held my knees, but they wouldn't stop shaking. Emily insisted we leave that night, so we took some things and got a motel. The next day I got the rest of our things, and we never went back. It took Emily many months to get back to normal. Even though we sold the place, for years after that, she'd wake up at night having nightmares. It's still crystal clear in my mind."

He paused, shaking his head. Peter, wide-eyed, just stared at him. He was glad Bill had finished his story during the day.

After lighting his pipe, Bill looked at Peter, glanced back at the road, and said, "That was the most terrifying experience I've ever had. You know, I even broke a tooth in my upper plate in the excitement. . . . When I saw the ghost house in Disney World, many years later, it brought it all back. It's like, you can watch it all happen, but it isn't really there."

Squirming in his seat, Bill shifted until he felt comfortable, then he reaffirmed his disbelief. "I still find it hard to accept we witnessed a murder, but we couldn't do anything about it."

Peter's face was drawn tight. He shivered slightly, involuntarily, and said, "It gives me the chills just thinking about it. I never would have believed that these kinds of things happen, but my experience made a believer out of me. It brings back memories I'd just as soon forget."

Chapter 5

A TRUE FRIEND

DRIVING along leisurely through Missouri, time passed quickly for Peter and Bill, giving them a chance to get to know each other. Before long Bill turned the camper into a truck stop for gas and a bite to eat. After placing their order, Peter couldn't help noticing that Bill was giving the eye to a girl who sat at the end of the counter.

She hadn't noticed him, but everyone else appeared to have. Being unsucessful in his attempt, Bill stood up and walked toward her. As he was about to make a play for her, she looked his way, right on past him, at a young man behind him. Noticing her looking on past him and avoiding a situation, Bill changed direction and headed for the cigarette machine.

To Peter, he appeared awkward in his attempt at capturing her in his net by engaging her in conversation, before moving in for the kill. He wondered if older people like Bill were all in such a hurry because they feared getting too old, too soon, to continue being successful with the opposite sex. Peter smiled slightly and couldn't help but laugh to himself, seeing how quickly the events had changed. He further wondered what would have happened, if Bill had made it to her before the other man appeared.

Peter was fast learning that Bill was basically a gentle man. He felt comfortable with the idea that Bill would not hurt anyone purposely, but could turn tiger if threatened.

The next few weeks were spent at a lazy pace, meandering aimlessly. Bill never once asked Peter where he wanted to stop to get off. When Peter's money finally ran out, he confessed it to Bill, who just let it slide. His only comment was, "Stick with me. We've got a lot of enjoying to do. Someday when you have a chance to help someone, do it in my name. Somehow I'll know."

Bill liked to talk, and Peter was frequently lulled by his monotone drawl. On one of these occasions, Bill was talking about God. "I look at it this way. He must know what He's doing. Nothing has changed in the last million years. Everything has its place and order and is dependent on everything else. Until someone proves otherwise, I believe He's supreme."

Peter hadn't given much thought to God, but he found Bill interesting to listen to. Bill continued, "I know that it all makes a lot of sense. If you think about it—the Golden Rule, the Ten Commandments, the Constitution of the United States, and the Bill of Rights all say the same thing. Do what you want to do, as long as you don't hurt someone else while doing it. It's like this: you can stand on a corner and swing your fists as long as you like, just as long as you don't connect them with anyone."

Pausing to catch the drip from his nose with his sleeve, Bill continued, "I figure live and let live. Enjoy each moment for what it's worth. You may never have another chance."

Bill was silent for a while before starting on another subject. "Worry and guilt are useless burdens on your mind. Worry deals with a nebulous future and guilt with the past. You can only do something about them in the present, and that's what I aim to do. I create my future each moment of every day."

Peter interrupted him. "I'm not sure I'm following you."

"The best advice I can give is to develop a zest for a meaningful life. Be totally involved, but don't take it too seriously. It can get serious enough by itself. That's not meaning to say you shouldn't make plans and take action on them, but when you do make them, accept the fact that they may have to be adjusted as changes occur. Change is the most constant thing in your life. It's good too, otherwise we'd always be bored. When you anticipate it happening, you don't go down for the count when it does occur."

Then Bill turning reached to the back of Peter's seat and brought forth a new bottle of brandy, took a couple of drinks, then handed it to Peter. By now, Peter was accepting of the routine and drank down his share before it was replaced behind the seat in anticipation of future considerations.

Bill hunched himself forward and continued, "I like challenges in my life. That's what strengthens a person. Overcoming them can be fun. It gives you a different perspective on life when you realize there is no such thing as failure. That's just someone else's opinion of how you should accomplish something. You know, schools put so much emphasis on not failing that people lose the value of it. It's really just one of the steps to succeeding. We all have to go through failures of one sort or another in our lives."

Peter listened in awe to this big man whose rambling conversation made sense to him. When Bill stopped momentarily, Peter glanced toward him. He watched silently as Bill reached down, scratched his oversized leg, then continued. "Life has a leveling effect. When you're with people who are depressing, or tear others down, it rubs off. Best to avoid those kinds of people as much as possible. You don't need that in your life."

Peter interrupted him. "Your talking about depression reminded of what I read once about negative feelings creating negative chemicals in your body."

"That's right, kid. The negative chemicals create negative feelings and you're on a whirlwind down. . . . As I was about to say, there are also people who are takers. They take your life blood and leave you nothingness and frustration in return. Best to avoid their kind, too. There are enough good and pleasant people in this world to be with. I never let the bad kind get ahold of me. . . . Enough preaching for one day. The next turn-off, we'll bed down for the night."

They stopped in Oklahoma City. Bill's maiden sister, Gwin LaBark, lived there, and he wanted to spend time with her and planned on staying two or three weeks before moving on.

Bill liked to play golf, but he hadn't had much chance during the past several weeks, so he planned to spend a considerable amount of time on the links here. This left Peter time to get to know the city.

"Use the camper anytime you need wheels," Bill had told Peter and on the first day, he borrowed it and drove through the streets, trying to determine places that might promise a glimpse of interest. Bill had given him twenty dollars for the day, promising him more if he needed it. He disliked accepting Bill's generosity, as it made him feel like a taker, one of those people he had advised Peter to avoid. Because he liked Bill and considered him to be a true friend in every sense of the word, Peter wanted to be with him as much as possible.

Peter knew that Bill had done more for him in the very short time they were together than anyone in his entire life, had. It was because of this that he made a promise to himself that he would repay him someday, when he was able. Every offering he considered a loan and recorded it in a small book, which he kept in the camper.

More than a year had now passed since Peter had last seen Maggie, but her memory lingered in his thoughts. When they had been together, he'd made a considerable amount of plans in his mind, which included her. Now, with them shattered, he continued to long for a relationship with a girl.

Bill and Peter had been moving from place to place, never stopping long enough to allow him to get to know anyone. This was his first chance, and he was determined to make the most of it. He knew that it couldn't be a lasting relationship because of the limited amount of time they would be staying. Even so, he set out to check the places where there might be an opportunity to meet girls.

Driving along East Main Street, Peter noticed an interesting-looking place. The exterior was white stucco with a beach and palm trees painted across the front. The sign read simply, "Nick's Bar."

He entered a long, dim barroom. At the far end was a lighted pool table with several people playing. As his eyes became accustomed to the dark, he could see the thatched huts along one wall that provided individual booths.

"What can I get you to drink?" the pretty brunette behind the bar inquired.

"Whatever you have on draft."

"We have Mick, Coors, and Bud."

"Coors sounds good to me."

Picking up the beer glass, Peter asked, "Is there any place around here that has dancing at night?"

"Sure, lots of them. It depends upon what kind of dancing you're looking for."

This remark surprised him. "How many kinds are there?"

"Well, there's the kind where you go to dance and the kind where you go to watch go-gos dance."

"I was thinking about the kind where you go to dance, but if you know of a go-go place, I'll check that out, too."

"There's a place a couple of blocks from here called Dreggs Diggins. They have live music on Wednesdays and the weekends. Kids your age hang out there."

Peter looked at her questioningly. "My age? Looks to me they'd be about your age, too."

She held up her finger. "See that? It means that I'm married to a pack of kids. Six in all. Actually, I'm thirty-three, and I've been married more than half as long as you are old. But thanks for the compliment."

"Sure could have fooled me. You look to be about twenty."

She laughed. "I guess you could say I'm well preserved." She added, "If you're interested in go-go dancers, there's a place called Fletcher's over on Broadway. They have female dancers every night but Sunday."

"Maybe I'll check that out, too."

Peter drank and watched the pool players. He had an urge to play a game with her. "Say, do they allow you to play pool?"

"During the day when it's slow like this, it's okay. If you want to challenge the table, put your quarter up."

Then, reaching into a glass, she withdrew a quarter and handed it to Peter. "Here's mine. Put it up for me. . . . You'll have to win first to get the table, though. Are you any good?"

"Can't brag about it. I haven't played much pool in a year or so."

Peter spent the rest of the day in the bar playing pool and talking with the bartender. That night he went to Dreggs Diggins, but he didn't enjoy himself. He felt alone in a crowd. Not knowing anyone, he talked superfluously and danced occasionally. When he'd finished the dance, the girl would thank him and walk away. If he asked them a second time, they'd make an excuse not to, or would ignore him. He knew that he never was a good dancer, but it had gotten him by before. The kids here were different from those he'd grown up with. His Boston accent was still quite pronounced, and he wondered if that had anything to do with their unfriendliness.

Late that evening when Peter returned to Bill's sister's home, he was still up. "How was the dance?" Bill greeted Peter from the couch, as he entered the living room.

Feeling somewhat depressed, Peter looked at the floor as he answered, "Nothing special. I guess it takes a while to get to know anyone."

"Don't let it get to you, kid. There are a lot of girls out there. When they get to know you, you'll have to fight them off," Bill answered as he set down his magazine, stood up, stretched, and asked, "How does a cup of coffee and a piece of homemade apple pie for a midnight snack sound? Gwin made it this afternoon. I was just going to have some myself."

"Thanks for the vote of confidence." Peter walked with him to the kitchen. "Yeah, that'll be good. How was your day?" he questioned as they entered the kitchen.

"I totally enjoyed it. Gwin's neighbor, Sam Engles, and I played eighteen holes. It was such a beautiful day; a lot of birds on the course kept it bright and cheery. We sat around the clubhouse and had a few drinks—actually, quite a few. When I got home, I took a long nap. That exercise got to me. Not that I don't need it. It got me thinking that I'd better do something about this paunch. I've been getting fat and lazy, with all this bumming. . . . I've decided to go on a diet of sorts." Then, pausing to pat his stomach, Bill continued, "Course, it'll have to start after this pie."

The following day Peter slept in late. It was noon by the time he took the camper and stopped to eat. Addressing his urge when the waitress approached, he ordered, "I'd like bacon and eggs, with coffee."

The dark-haired waitress was pleasant but firm. "Our breakfast menu ends at eleven-thirty. Would you like to order something else?"

"I know that it's late, but I had this feeling for eggs and bacon."

"I'll check with the owner to see if we can make them for you. Be right back." She hurried off.

Peter watched her as she moved from his table to the kitchen. She was slender and had a wiggle to her walk. *Very sexy*, he thought.

Returning with his coffee and smiling, she said to him, "I talked him into it. They'll be ready shortly. Do you use cream or sugar?"

He returned her smile. "This'll be fine. Thanks for getting me the order. I just had the urge—you know how it is."

Wanting to talk to her, Peter commented, "Looks like you're not too busy today."

"Some days are like that. Guess this is one of them. . . . Your accent is different. From out East somewhere, I'd say."

"Yeah, I'm from Boston. . . . On my way to Seattle. We'll be here a couple of weeks or so."

She looked toward the kitchen. "I'll check on your order."

Returning with his food, she asked him, "Ever been in here before? You look like someone who I've seen around a few times."

"Never before today. . . . You look like you've got some Indian in you. Mind if I guess your nationality?"

She looked at him inquisitively. "Be my guest," she answered with a blush and a twinkle in her eyes.

Looking at her over his cup of coffee, Peter speculated. "I'd say you're English, German, and Cherokee."

"That's real close. Actually, I'm German and Irish on my mother's side. My father is a full-blooded Comanche. How did you know that I had Indian in me?"

"Your high cheekbones and black hair immediately made me think you were. That's why I asked."

This caught her interest. "What nationality are you? Let me guess. French and German."

"My father is German. I don't know what my mother is. She was adopted and she doesn't know what she is."

Looking toward a table that had begun filling with customers, she smiled and said to Peter, "Nice talking to you. I have to get back to work. Enjoy your meal."

86

Leaving the restaurant, Peter decided to stop at the go-go club to see the girls.

"Fletcher's Naked Beauties" was plastered above the bar front in bold, red, flashing neon. He'd been to a few go-go joints and to him, they were all pretty much the same. *Stand them on their head and the girls all look alike,* he mused as he entered. The stage, a small area with large mirrors behind it, was empty. At the far end of the barroom, Peter noted a couple of guys were playing pool with two girls who were naked from the waist up. He sat up to the bar and ordered a brandy and Coke.

"Three dollars," the bartender requested matter of factly, his face reflecting an absence of thought.

After paying for the drink, Peter picked it up and wandered toward the pool table. He set up a quarter and settled back in a chair watching.

Shortly, a black-haired girl with tits the shape of lemons looked in Peter's direction and called, "Your quarter's up. It's boys against girls. We only play as a team. Pick your partner."

Having only two people to choose from, he made a quick decision. "Red, you think we can beat them?"

"They skunked us three in a row, but I'm game to try. Are you any good?"

"I've played a while back. Not much lately, though," Peter answered, as he racked the balls.

The blond with a superb shape walked toward him. "Hi, handsome. You ready to get your ass whipped?" she challenged.

His face deadpan, Peter retorted. "When I make these balls talk my language, you'll know whose ass is going to get whipped."

Glancing downward at Peter, the black-haired minx cut in. "You know which balls you can make talk my language, honey."

The blond seemed perturbed and stated. "Enough bullshit. We'll cut your ass to ribbons."

"Eight ball or straight in?" Peter asked.

"Straight up," the blond returned, as she one-handedly broke the rack of balls.

"Looks like an open table," Red surmised, as he took his shot.

The blond chided Peter. "Shitty accent you've got there. Where you from? Lower Slumbovia?"

Peter was never one to be outdone. His face still deadpan, in a flippant way, he shot back, "Are you trying to be wise or other-wise? . . . Keep it up and you'll be lengthwise."

"Oh. We've got ourselves a live one by the tail," the blond quipped.

Peter didn't respond as he studied the table. The blond was clearly irritated. "Shoot already. What's your problem?" she demanded.

His face in a half smile, glancing at her bulging bare breasts, he

87

answered, "Keep your shirt on."

"Oh. You're a wise ass too, eh? Well everyone likes a little ass, but no one likes a wise ass," she spit out, hotly.

"She's trying to be witty," Peter fired back calmly and finished with, "I think you're only half that way." Then, to aggravate her, he purposely delayed the game by looking down his stick to check its straightness.

The brunette, clearly pissed off by the delay, spit out, "Get with the program! Either we play the fuckin' game or I go up and dance!"

"All right, already! We'll play. But tell your friend to cut the shit," Peter said, as he took his shot.

While they were playing, a third go-go dancer that Peter hadn't seen before took the stage and began dancing. A few more patrons had come in and were seated at the bar watching her. As the pool game progressed, tempers cooled. It lasted a long time, and before long, the four of them were joking and kidding as they played. With the game finished, Peter wanted to get to know the blond and offered, "Can I buy you a drink as a peace offering?"

"Earlier, I'd have refused. But, what the hell? You're really not that bad a guy. Sure, you can buy me one. By the way, my name is Marie Louise." She smiled and offered her hand. "We sure got off to a hell of a start, didn't we? I thought I was sure enough, literally, going to have to whip your ass."

"Mine's Peter. It was my fault," he confessed. "I started out kidding, but I never know when to quit."

"We both should have known better."

Marie Louise called her order to the bartender, who was at the far end. "Mike, I'll have a scotch with a beer for a chaser on my friend here."

"Give me a Coors," Peter requested.

Serving the drinks, the bartender informed him, "That'll be ten dollars."

Handing him the money, Peter's look was obvious to Marie, having experienced seeing it many times before on the customers. "My drinks are double price. I get a commission."

"Guess I should have known. When you have entertainment, it doesn't come cheap."

"But I'm worth it." She smiled, then downed the scotch and sipped the beer.

"I'll let you know," said Peter, kidding. Then, realizing it could be taken seriously, he quickly added, "Just kidding. You probably are very good."

In an effort to make it last, Peter sipped his beer slowly while they talked.

Soon it was Marie Louise's turn on stage. Sensuously she moved; muscles rippling in rhythm with the music absorbed Peter's every thought.

Whirling, twirling, and changing expression, she gave the clear appearance of being high on something other than the music. Her queen-sized tits bounced in wild frenzy to the beat, as Marie Louise whipped the crowd into wild hysteria.

"How can such a vixen be blessed with so much beauty?" Peter wondered.

With her dancing finished, she returned to the bar stool beside Peter. He offered, "I'd like to buy you another drink, but I've got to admit I really didn't bring enough money with me. I'm sorry, too, because I'd like to get to know you. I think you're cute."

"Thanks," she answered, then smiling, she continued, "I was thinking the same thing. I'd like to talk with you. . . . Tell you what. . . . How about me buying you a drink instead? It goes against what I usually do, but there's something besides your accent that I like about you. Aside from the fussing we did at first, you seem to be a really sincere person. I don't see many of your kind in these places."

"Thanks, but I could leave and come back later on with more money. I didn't expect it to be so expensive here."

"Forget it. I said I was going to buy you one, and I am. What would you like?"

Peter looked at the bartender and ordered, "I'll have another Coors." Then he turned back to Marie Louise. "I'll make it up to you. You know, you're the first girl who ever bought me a drink."

"Don't worry about it," she insisted, then she started twisting her head from side to side. "I've got a bit of a headache."

Peter was quick with a suggestion. "If you want to get rid of it, there are pressure points on the back of your neck. When they're squeezed for ten seconds, your headache vanishes." Trying to be helpful, he asked, "Want me to try it?"

"Okay. Not that I believe you, but what have I got to lose?"

He applied pressure to her neck and when he released it, she exclaimed, "You must be a magician! I've never had anything work that fast before. Thanks, I really appreciate it."

He explained, "I learned that from a good friend of mine. He knows just about everything. Maybe one of these nights, I can talk him into coming here. I'm sure you'd like him. He really IS something else!"

Sitting together, they talked while Marie Louise screened her records for her next set. The girl dancing on the stage finished her set and walked over to talk with her. "Who's your friend?" she inquired.

With a wave of her hand, Marie Louise introduced them. "This is Peter, and this is my friend Sunshine. We dance at a lot of places together."

"Nice meeting you, Sunshine. Been dancing long?" he asked, attempting conversation.

"Bet you could come up with something more original," she answered. "Everyone asks me that. It tires me having to answer the same question a thousand times."

Peter felt a bit embarrassed and tried to apologize. "Sorry, I didn't know."

Speaking to Marie Louise, Sunshine began with a grin on her face. "You see that old geezer over there? He's in his eighties and still up to coming in here! Anyway, he was telling me about how he took his little poodle to the pet shop today for a clipping and it died. He said the woman didn't seem too concerned when she told him it was dead. He said it was his only friend, and I could see he was feeling lonely. He told me he's here to try to forget about it, and I got to feeling sorry for him. Then, with a twinkle in his eyes, he said that he got a hard-on while he was watching me dance. He said it was the first one he'd had in a year. I couldn't help but laugh."

Giggling loudly, she finished telling Marie Louise, "He was laughing, too, when he asked me if I was a trollop and would I go home with him, but I know he was serious. I guess they're never too old, eh?"

"That's great. The best I've heard in a long time. . . . I noticed him, too, just sitting and grinning when I was up there. I could see a fascinating sparkle in his eyes. I wonder where he gets all his energy from?" Marie Louise mused, while laughing along with Sunshine. Then she added, "I think he's real cute."

The bar was full of customers when Marie Louise walked out onto the stage for her second set. Sunshine was left sitting with Peter.

Sprouting an impish grin, she inquired of him, "I hope you're not one of those CPA's or PhD's."

"I'm not old enough to have a degree," he stated matter of factly, wondering if he appeared to be old enough to have graduated from college.

"You don't need a degree to be a Certified Public Asshole, or a Prick Head," she said. Then, she burst out laughing at the surprised look it produced.

"You got me there." Peter admitted to being sucked in. "All right. If you're so smart, how do you get rid of crabs?" Peter inquired.

"I hadn't thought about it before. I really don't know. How do you?"

Looking smug, Peter answered, "Find a cocksucker who likes seafood."

90

"Real cute. Sounds like something I should have expected from you. . . . I've got to get ready. I'm up next," Sunshine announced, as she arose from the bar stool. "See you later."

"I'll be waiting," Peter offered an encouragement, hoping she would return.

Later, Sunshine emerged from the changing room. Peter watched her as she walked toward him, sat down, and began talking with a customer next to Peter. Through the corner of his eye, Peter watched her as she flaunted her curvaceous body, which was clad only in a G-string. He took note of the fact that she was a beautiful, hypnotic girl and appeared to be about Marie Louise's age.

Doused with a strong pleasing scent designed to attract, Sunshine was keenly aware of each head that turned her way. Even as she talked with the man next to her, she checked out Peter in a subtle way. Wanting to get to know her, he turned toward her and complimented her when she looked his way.

"I noticed that you're a very good dancer. You have the music in you."

She smiled and replied, "Thanks. I practice a lot."

"Looks like you enjoy it a lot, too."

She leaned toward Peter to answer. "I do get into my music. Marie Louise and I started doing dance routines together when we were in high school. We're both from Fargo, North Dakota."

"I figured you must dance together quite a bit. Your movements are similar in many ways."

"We started dancing professionally at the same time, too. We've even made our own outfits. We worked together on them and being the same measurements, we change off. It doubles our wardrobe. If you buy them, they can run into mega bucks. That pink bikini she's wearing up there now was one of the easiest to make." She indicated the stage with a handsweep.

Peter followed her hand and found Marie Louise on stage flirting with a young Marine sergeant. His attention drawn to the stage, Peter's ears caught what the Marine was telling her. "Sit on my face, baby, and I'll guess your weight," he shouted at her.

Although he'd known Marie Louise for only a couple of hours, a tinge of jealousy spurted through him. Reflecting on how quickly he was aroused, he suddenly realized hidden feelings he felt for her.

Sunshine looked at Peter and appearing concerned, she asked, "Is something wrong? Your face tensed up like something was bothering you."

"Nothing really," he replied. "That is a classy outfit with the matching pink lacy top. How'd you get the rhinestones attached?"

"With much difficulty," she answered, then added, "Sorry if I was butting in on your private thoughts."

"No problem. I was just thinking about how you remind me of someone I once knew."

"I'd like to talk with you again, but now I've got to get my records ready for my next set."

"I'd like that, too."

"Talk at you later then." She stood up and headed for the back room.

Peter responded with a wink. "Sounds good to me. I'll be waiting."

Chapter 6

THE APARTMENT

MARIE LOUISE walked toward Peter after leaving the changing room. He thought about how pretty she looked, wearing a stunning gold, lace-sequined bathing suit for her next set. She looked his way, then she half-smiled as she walked over and sat next to him.

Peter's curiosity got the better of him, and he couldn't help asking, "How'd you get into dancing, if you don't mind my asking?"

"I get asked that a lot. I don't usually tell anyone, but I don't mind telling you, 'cause I like you," she said, as she coyly looked away.

Peter looked at the floor and said, "I've been thinking the same thing about liking you." He looked at her. "I shouldn't tell you this, but I felt a little jealous when you were talking to that Marine."

"I think that's cute. . . . Anyway, getting back to your question, Diane Stone—that's Sunshine's real name—she and I got loaded one night at a party. We ended up at a bar. The guys dared us to strip down altogether and dance on the bar. I wouldn't do it at first. When she did and I saw the attention she was getting, I guess I figured I wanted some, too. It turned out that one of the people in there was an agent, and someone gave him my address. The next day he dropped by and wanted to sign me. We talked and smoked some weed he had. He said I'd have to audition at a go-go club. I asked how much it paid and was surprised that it was three to four hundred a week for about three to four hours a night." She paused, then chuckled impishly, saying, "I got to thinking, 'What the fuck. If they've seen it before, then it's nothing new. If they haven't, they won't know what it is.' "

Peter laughed. "Guess that's one way of looking at it. Never heard that expression before."

She continued, "The club owner signed me right off. It sure beats the minimum wage I was getting at the dry-cleaning shop." Waving her

93

hand toward the stage, she added, "Diane waited about six months before she started."

"You appear to flow with the music. Have you had lessons?"

"I've thought about taking some, but most people tell me I don't need them for this kind of dancing. Most of the guys who come to these places just want to see your snatch. They don't give a fuck how you dance, but the owners do. They don't want pigs on their stage."

"Can't say I blame them. You are a real asset. I'd say you're a good drawing card for them."

She became seductive, her cheeks dimpled, enhancing her smile. "Thanks for the vote of confidence. . . . We'll be through for our supper break after this set. We're going back to our apartment to eat so we can get some rest, too. Would you want to come with us?"

Peter quickly thought it over. "Tell you what. Give me your address, and I'll stop in. First I have to go and let my friend know that I won't be eating at his sister's with them. . . . He's a great guy. . . . Maybe I can talk him into coming here tonight with me. I know that you and Diane would like him."

"Sure. I'd like to meet him. Why don't you bring him to the apartment with you? We'll rest first, then eat at about six-thirty. We don't have to be back until eight-thirty. I know it'll be all right with Diane."

Peter convinced Bill that he had two hot chicks lined up. Not being one to miss out on possible action, Bill's excitement was obvious to Peter as they approached the apartment building.

Peter chided him. "I don't believe you. You're like a mad dog after raw meat."

Bill returned the carp in a teasing tone of voice. "Speak for yourself. I've never seen you cream your jeans before tonight. Bet you thought I didn't see that wet spot when you came in. Good thing Gwin was out visiting. She would have razzed you to no end if she saw it."

"You're not living, you're dreaming," Peter kidded him back.

Peter noticed how dreary the outside of the building looked. The front had a wide set of steps made of sandstone blocks, some of which were missing. The many-layered paint curled from the door frame in spots, leaving bare wood showing beneath. The door handle was loose and seemed to want to remain in his hand as he opened the door. Once inside, the dimly lit walls of the stairwell revealed poor workmanship. Mismatched paneling was overlapped in some areas and open in others where the paint underneath showed through. Adding to the feeling of desolation was a dirty yellow ceiling.

As they climbed the stairs, which had been gouged by hobnailed boots, the creaking echoed mournfully.

"What's their number?" Bill asked, as he led the way.

"They said it was number six."

Bill reached the top of the stairs and turned left. "This is it. You'd better do the knocking."

Marie Louise answered the door and invited, "Hi. Come on in."

Peter introduced them. "This is my friend, Bill LaBark, and this is Marie Louise."

"Diane is doing her hair. She'll be out in a minute," Marie was saying when Diane walked into the room with her hair tossed up on top of her head.

"Hi. You must be Bill. I feel like I know you. Peter's told us a lot about you."

Bill looked at Peter as they walked into the living room. "All good, I hope?"

Peter just grinned. "All good," Marie confirmed.

Once they were seated in the living room on the couch, Bill spoke. "Peter told me that you two girls were good-looking. I'll have to agree wholeheartedly with him."

"Thanks, Bill. Peter told us you were very observant. He also told us you were full of bullshit," Diane said while winking at Peter. Then she continued, "I'm not sure we can believe you."

Bill's eyes twinkled. He enjoyed teasing. "You can't believe him. If brains were dynamite, he wouldn't have enough to blow his nose. But you can believe me. You're both good-lookers."

Feeling compelled to defend himself, Peter responded, "Can't be nice in front of the ladies, can you? Do I have to teach you everything?"

Bill grinned. "I was only trying to be honest with them. No need to get uppity about it."

Feeling it was a good time to change the subject, Marie Louise suggested, "We'll have to get back soon, so maybe we should eat now. Diane and I will get the table set. I hope you don't mind leftovers from last night. We don't fuss much when we're here."

"Go right ahead. We don't mind what it is. Any grubbage you've got is all right by me," Bill responded.

Peter agreed, "Sounds good to me, too."

Peter looked around and wondered why the bar would rent this bad a place for the dancers. The room reflected the same shoddy lack of repairs as the stairwell. Plaster had fallen from the ceiling near the light fixture, where a kerosene lamp appeared to have hung in times past. The walls and ceiling were sorely in need of paint. The furniture was placed haphazardly and had surrendered its value years before.

"Real cruddy place they have to live in," Bill observed when the girls had left.

Peter, crossing his leg onto his knee, leaned back and relaxed. "I was thinking the same thing myself."

Bill followed with, "I'd offer to put them up at Gwin's, but I know she'd never let them in her place."

In a hushed voice, Peter admitted his lack of contact with this type of girls. "I've never gotten to know any dancers before. These two seem like ordinary people. I've heard most of them are bad news, though."

Bill agreed. "They are different from what I'd expected them to be like."

The tantalizing aroma of freshly brewing coffee, mingled with an appetizing smell of food, flooded Bill's nostrils and set his gastric juices in motion. "Whatever they're making is tuning my innards for some mighty good eating." He verified his remark with a quick rub of his stomach. "It's been a while since I've eaten. Right now I could eat a horse and chase after the rider."

Peter was in agreement. "I was thinking the same thing. I had breakfast at noon and nothing since."

Bill queried as if serious, "Sounds a bit mixed up to me. When are you going to get your times of day straight?"

Peter stretched his arms out onto the sides of the overstuffed chair that was sorely in need of repairs, and uncrossed his legs. "Any law against being different?"

"You've got a right to be any way you want. Confusion and mental derangement can be an asset if you have state-certified release papers to prove it. Then people accept you for what you are and don't question anything you do."

Bill had a way of turning situations around and using them as the basis for teasing. When he saw that it got a rise out of Peter, he would continue unmercifully. This drove Peter up the wall at times until he adjusted to the onslaughts. At first, he'd taken him seriously and would attempt to defend his position. Gradually, he learned to accept this in a good-natured way.

Peter became quick with his own comebacks. "People like you have their brains just like cement. All mixed up and permanently set," he responded. Bill laughed.

Marie Louise appeared in the kitchen doorway. "We're ready, if you don't mind our meager offerings."

"I'd say it must be very good, judging by the way my stomach is reacting to the inviting smell emanating from yon kitchen," Bill commented as he rose from the couch.

Marie Louise's face scrunched into a smile. "Thanks, but I'm still not sure I can believe you."

Peter winked at her. "You can believe him this time. I have to agree, it smells real scrumptious to me, too."

They followed Marie Louise into the kitchen. Diane said apologetically, "We're just simple folk. We don't put much stock in appearances."

Marie explained, as she set out the food. "Yeah. The mismatched dishes and silverware are compliments of the house, but they serve their purpose."

"We don't eat the place settings. The important thing is what's on them," Bill remarked while settling himself at the table.

Steaming hot-cross buns, multi-colored homemade soup filled to occlusion with garden-fresh vegetables and large chunks of beef, served up in the cooking pan, occupied the center of the table.

Placed neatly beside each place setting was an etched crystal wine glass filled with red wine.

Diane pointed to the glasses. "The only thing I have of my mother's is this set of glasses. There are eight of them. I keep four at home and take these with me. I know they look out of place here, but when I use them, I feel close to her."

Marie Louise explained, "Her mother died a few years ago, and her father got remarried. She doesn't get along with him, so she moved in with me."

Bill's face turned sympathetic, reflecting his feelings upon learning of her loss. "Sorry to hear that. We'll be extra careful with them."

"Enough talk. Let's eat," Diane advised.

After dropping Marie Louise and Diane off at the club, Bill and Peter went back to his sister's. "What you two been up to, coming back so late?" she asked with an all-knowing smile.

Bill looked at her, paused, turned to Peter, winked and answered, "Peter's trying to convert me."

Gwin's eyes squinted disbelievingly. "Convert you? You'll never get religion."

"Not that kind of conversion."

"Come clean. I know you're putting me on again. You can never tell me anything straight."

Bill winked at Peter. "He's trying to get me interested in girls. He wants to make a heathen out of me."

"I knew it must be something foolish. You always did drool at every skirt that passed. I'd believe it's the other way around. You're trying to get him in the sack with some harlot."

Trying to conceal his smile, Bill replied, "Be nice, Gwin. I'm not at all that bad. I'd never have him do what I wouldn't do myself."

"That's just what I'm saying. You'd be right there with him and loving every minute of it."

"So you think you know me, do ya? I'll have you know that I've led a good clean life."

Gwin was ready for him. "That's what I mean. There are three kinds of good: Good, no good, and good for nothing. I won't say which kind you've led, but it's not the first one."

"All right. You think you've got me tagged, eh? Tell her, Peter. Who's been leading who astray tonight?"

Using every effort Peter tried to appear serious. "You can't fool her, Bill. She knows you too good." He watched Bill's reaction through the corner of his eye.

"Siding with my kin, are you?"

Not able to keep from laughing, Peter explained where they'd been.

"I guess I'm entitled to be wrong at least once in my life," Gwin admitted.

"I won't comment on that," Bill blurted out, unloading a horse laugh.

She looked at him sternly. "You think that's funny, do you? If it weren't for my guidance, you wouldn't have amounted to anything. Not that you did anyway."

"All kidding aside, we'll be out late tonight. The girls want us to go to their place after they're through working. In fact, we may not be home at all tonight," Bill advised her.

"I can't say that I blame you. You've got to do your living while your blood is still circulating." She smiled cajolingly.

Bill and Peter arrived at Fletcher's at eleven-thirty. The room was still quite empty. Diane and Marie Louise were on their break while the third dancer was on stage. Marie Louise had been sitting by herself and came over to their table. Diane was talking with a young man in his mid-twenties and waved when she saw them. Seating herself, Marie Louise, a slight smile on her face, said, "I'm glad you both decided to come back. It was getting late, and we thought you might not show up tonight."

"You couldn't keep us away," Peter volunteered.

"You've got that right. Show me a beautiful lady that's interesting, too and I'll be there. . . . Can I buy you a drink?" Bill offered.

"Thanks. I'll have a brandy and Coke."

"What about you, kid?"

"Coors'll be fine," Peter answered.

Bill went to the bar to get the drinks.

While leaning into her cupped hands and looking at Peter, Marie Louise said, "This place has been dead tonight. There's probably other things going on in town. It gets that way sometimes. It's hard to get all fired up when there's not many people to dance for."

Bill returned with their drinks, and within minutes Diane joined them.

While they were talking, the entrance door suddenly burst open and a troop of young men marched in with their right arms extended, forearms raised, chanting extremely loud, "Ho-ho-ho-ho-ho," as they entered the barroom. Numbering about twenty-five to thirty, they gathered around a table where a few others were seated. Some took seats, others stood milling around. Shortly, a few started yelling at the dancer on stage, "We want to see some beaver!" "Get naked!"

"Come on, Art," one of them hollered at one of their own. "Get up on the stage and show her how to dance!"

But Art, in the meantime, was precariously perched with one foot on a chair and the other on a table, looking for encouragement from his buddies, to dance on the table. The bartender was hustling to fill orders for drinks and paying no attention to the crowd that was getting vociferous.

Suddenly Art plunged headlong to the floor, sending his beer bottle flying from his hand high into the air, splattering the mirrored back wall. He lay piled in a drunken heap on the floor. The clamor of the crowd drowned the music, which was raised to a high pitch. Some of them were dancing between the tables, kicking their heels high into the air.

One shriveled, skinny runt, just old enough to gain entry, wriggled in front of the stage. Suddenly he pulled off his T shirt, shed his pants, undershorts and boots. Then he leaped to the stage, frightening the dancer off. He wriggled, twirled, cart-wheeled, and did bumps and grinds 'til he was wrestled from the stage by the manager, who threatened to call the police. By now the boisterous mob was yelling, swearing, and pushing each other, dumping over tables.

Marie Louise, having had previous experience with these kinds of situations, held an empty beer bottle at the ready. Bill and Peter, not having been affected, restrained bristled muscles ready for their defense.

Finally, the manager succeeded in quieting the crowd to a mild uproar. He told Marie Louise to get onto the stage and dance. She raised the bottle to her lips, pretending to be drinking from it as she ascended the stairs to the stage. Setting it within easy reach for protection, she cautiously started dancing.

Seeing her on the stage, the crowd became rowdy once more. "Show us your pussy, honey," someone yelled. A few started throwing coins onto the stage and almost immediately, she was being showered with them.

Grabbing the bottle, Marie Louise headed for the change-room. Seeing her leave, Diane also made a dash to it for safety.

A loggerhead developed and gathered steam. Out of nowhere a glass of beer appeared, sailing through the air and smashing onto the stage.

Someone yelled, "He's calling the cops," and the entire buffalolike herd pushed toward the door in mass confusion. Just as suddenly as it started, the riot ended and the bar returned to normal. The ear-piercing music took over once more, the entire episode having lasted less than fifteen minutes.

Marie Louise and Diane returned to Bill and Peter's table. Marie Louise spoke. "The manager told us that he'd allowed them to remain as long as he had because he knows most of them. They were at a bachelor party down the street." She paused, shaking her head. "I don't trust that kind of scene. I was leery of dancing and decided to split when it got bad. Throwing coins at a dancer is an insult," she complained haughtily.

Diane interjected, "They did agree to pay for the damages, so I guess nothing serious resulted, but someone could have gotten hurt."

Bill and Peter remained at the club until closing time, then they drove the girls home. Once inside their apartment, Diane brought out a twelve-pack of beer. "This place is shit. I don't like to entertain here, but it's the only place we have. Our contract requires us to live here."

"What about the other girl? Does she stay here, too?" Peter inquired.

"It's in her contract, too, but she lives with a local guy. She only leaves enough of her things at her apartment so the owner of the club doesn't know she's not there. He doesn't want us living with anyone. That's why he requires us to live here," Diane said with disgust as she opened their beers.

Marie Louise picked up the conversation. "He's a real asshole. One of the girls told me once that he set her up with a date for one hundred dollars. The guy required her to spend the night for it. . . . When she collected her pay, she was short the hundred. The manager told her that he docked her for it because she slept out that night. She found out later that the guy was a friend of his and he'd done that same thing to other girls."

She sipped her beer and continued. "They say he has the city council in his pocket, too. You can't fight him legally. She swore she was going to burn his place down. It wouldn't surprise me if she does it someday. She was royally pissed about it."

Bill, shaking his head in a slow motion, said, "I can't imagine anyone being that hard up for money."

Seating herself beside Bill, Diane took a drink then spoke, "There are a lot of these places owned by jerk-offs like him.. 'Course, there are a lot of good ones, too, where they treat you like a lady and demand that everyone else does, too. I hate the sleaze places where they let them grab your ass and don't do anything about it."

She leaned back to get more comfortable, then continued. "Once in Nebraska, I was bending over on stage and this young asshole grabbed my crotch. I took my drink and threw it in his face, then I jumped off the stage. The owner didn't see it and asked what happened. When I told him what he'd done to me, all he said was, 'Maybe he thought you were sleeping and wanted to wake you up.' I was so pissed-off I saw red. I threw one of the drinks from the bar in his face, got my things, and boogied. He owed me a week's pay, too. I didn't get it and never went back to try to collect."

Peter felt sympathetic. "It's hard to believe that anyone can be that dirty."

Diane looked at him. "You've got that right. If they were all like that, I'd have quit dancing years ago. Most of them know they have to depend on us to make big profits for them, so they treat us right."

Bill looked first at Diane, then at Marie Louise. "It must be interesting, though. You get to meet a lot of people."

Diane was about to answer, but she was interrupted by a knock on the door.

Bill went to the answered it. A large, red-bearded man stood in the entranceway. Close behind him were two others. Drunkenly the bearded one stated, "We're here for the party."

"There's no party here," Bill explained in a gruff voice that was permeated with his annoyance.

"We were told there was going to be a party here, and we want in on it," the man insisted.

Bill blocked the doorway from entry. "There's no party here, so try someplace else." Bill was peeved and showed it in his strong eye contact.

The brute became demanding. "Isn't this where the girls from the strip joint live? Let me in, so I can see for myself."

"We told you there's no party here!" Peter joined Bill. "You're drunk. You'd better go on home."

"Who the fuck's drunk, you cocksucker?" the man yelled and reaching past Bill, he grabbed Peter's shirt.

"Come on, Red. Let's get out of here!" one of the others said, trying to convince their companion to leave.

Bill, upon seeing the attack on Peter, swiftly chopped the edge of his left hand into the man's neck and shoulder joint. Then, he quickly followed up with his right into the man's rib cage, causing him to stagger backward into the hallway. Stumbling, he lost his balance and tumbled headlong over the railing and into the stairwell. Sliding, yelling, and kicking, he went careening down the stairs to the bottom. His buddies ran after him. He lay in a disheveled lump, refusing assistance from them.

Peter rushed to the top of the stairs and peered over in time to see the red-bearded man drag himself to his feet.

"I'll cut your fuckin' throats for this, you sons-of-bitches," the red-bearded man yelled up at them as he wobbled out the entrance door. Before Bill closed their door, they could hear him yelling and swearing at his friends for not helping him as they left.

Walking back into the apartment, Peter straightened his shirt as Bill closed the door. Looking at Diane, Bill asked, "Do you get this kind of action often?"

Shaking from the excitement, Diane answered, "Most everyone knows where we live. They don't usually bother us though, because they know it's owned by the manager of Fletcher's and we're under his protection by the police."

Feeling afraid, Marie Louise implored, "Would the two of you stay with us tonight? They may come back later when they think we're asleep." She shuddered. "He had mean-looking eyes. I don't trust him not to try to get even."

Bill reassured her. "Sure thing, honey. I don't trust them either. If they do come, we'll give them more than they've bargained for."

Peter elaborated. "Bill could handle all three of them at one time. His fists are like loaded dynamite ready to explode."

Bill's eyes lit up, and he slapped one fist into the palm of his hand. "You can say that again. The dynamism in these mitts will stop them dead in their tracks. Just let them try anything."

Shortly, there was another knock on the door. Bill jumped to his feet, prepared for the worst possibilities. He walked over and in one quick sweep, he swung open the door. In the doorway stood a small old man, wrinkled with age. He blinked, then trying to peer around Bill, he addressed the girls. "I heard a ruckus in the hall and thought you girls needed some help."

"It's all under control," Bill assured him, then added, "Thanks for your concern."

Marie walked over to him. Smiling, she said, "Mr. Dudley. That was sweet of you to want to help us. We appreciate your thoughtfulness. Thank you." Then she invited, "Would you like to come in and have a drink with us?"

"Thanks, but the Mrs. would be scared back there by herself. Maybe some other time."

Diane called over, "Ask her to come over, too."

"She's been feeling poorly again. Arthritis has been acting up in her knees, so she doesn't get out much. . . . If you need help at any time, just holler and I'll come a-running," he offerd and as he turned to leave, he cautioned, "Be careful now, you hear?"

Walking out into the hallway with him, Marie Louise said, "We will. Thanks again for coming to help us."

Closing the door, Bill looked from one of the girls to the other, then asked, "Do you girls party much? Could they have thought there was one going on here?"

"We had a small one the first night we were here. Only a few guys, though. They brought some grass and speed. I'll bet those guys must have heard about that one and thought it was tonight," Diane reasoned.

Seating himself, Bill agreed. "That could be it." Then he commented, "I'll bet you girls run into some real butt holes on the road."

Diane lifted her legs up onto Bill's lap. She answered him, "We try to stay away from them. But sometimes you end up with one when you don't expect them to be that way. I ran into one once who was willing to pay me one hundred and fifty dollars to beat him and call him down to the lowest. I sat on his stomach and slapped his face, bit his nipples, and spit in his face. He loved it and kept asking for more, so I leaned back behind me and pinched his balls. All the while, I kept telling him he was a fat ass and should be ashamed of himself and things like that. He got up and jacked off while I punched and kicked him. The only halfway normal thing he wanted to do was eat my pussy, so I let him. I figured for a hundred and fifty I would, but I don't usually let anyone."

She looked at Bill and admitting to being a *fille de joie*, she said, "Most of them just want straight sex. They get on, hump a little, and I make fifty easy bucks."

Bill and Peter sat listening without comment.

Marie Louise lit a cigarette, then spoke, "Once, I had a guy want me to beat him, too. I'd never done that, but he offered me a hundred and fifty to do it. He had a whip and ropes, and I tied him to the bed. Each time that I beat him only increased his wish for more. When I stopped, he was bleeding and had welts all over, but he didn't want me to stop. When I said I wouldn't do it anymore, he offered fifty more dollars, but I just couldn't. I was getting sick and wishing I'd never gotten into doing it. I untied him and went back to my room and threw up. I'll never do anything like that again."

She paused and puffed on the cigarette before continuing, "Once, a couple stopped me on the street. The guy offered me two hundred to make love to his wife. I thought, *What a sickie. I'm not a dyke.* I'd never do that kind of thing." Slowly she shook her head in disgust.

Diane admitted to her desires. "You know, every man is different once you get them into bed. You never really know what they are like until then. Sometimes, I find myself looking at a man and wondering what he's like in bed."

Marie Louise spoke up. "Once, a guy gave me a fifty just to spit in his face. I'd been speeding a lot and had cotton-mouth. I told him I couldn't do it, so he bought me a bottle of soda so I could, and I did. I don't like to hurt anyone, but these kooks pay good money. I figure, if I don't get it, someone else will. They get hurt anyway, so why shouldn't I make the money?" She paused and blew a smoke ring before continuing. "Competition is really keen for the better paying guys and generally, you are less likely to be hurt by them than by the creeps who want everything for nothing." She paused, blew another smoke ring, then continued. "Once, one really ugly fucker wanted me to shit and feed it to him for a hundred bucks. I draw the line on some things. Many of the girls would have done it. Some want a golden shower and pay up to fifty bucks for it."

Rolling his beer bottle in his hand, Peter asked naively, "What's a golden shower?"

Marie Louise answered with a grin. "That's when you squat over them and piss in their face."

Seeing Peter and Bill's interest in their way of life, Diane took over the conversation. "A couple of weeks ago, I had suspected this guy might be weird, so I had a girlfriend come with me. The guy kept pumping in me and couldn't come. I told him that I didn't know about guys, but girls get sore and he had to quit and get off. I couldn't believe it. He was still hard. I think he enjoyed hurting me. He got mad and called me a bitch."

Peter voiced his curiosity. "Do you get paid when they don't come?"

Looking at him, Diane continued. "Sure. I made him pay me up front. He paid a hundred and forty, and I didn't feel a bit sorry for him, either." She paused. "He really hurt me bad. . . . Sometimes, these guys have a problem. Like the one who used to pay me and would come before he even got it in. It was always the same whenever I'd see him. I finally told him to come back when he grew up."

Marie Louise spoke up. "There was this crud who never took a bath, and when he finished screwing me, I stunk just as bad as him. I finally quit him. I couldn't take it no more." She paused. Lying on the floor, she rolled onto her side, took a drink, set the beer bottle on the floor, and continued. "Once, I lived with a guy and he wanted to be in bed all the time. I'd get so sore that I'd get drunk or high so it wouldn't hurt so much."

Bill queried, "Did you tell him about it hurting you?"

Marie Louise put out her cigarette, before continuing. "No, because I was nuts about him and didn't want to lose him. I know I should have told him. . . . Finally I just left one night while he was asleep. I didn't have many things there. I packed all of it outside, got a taxi, and never went back. All this was in my earlier days. Now I get better class customers. I tell them. 'I have class and finesse. If you want me to respond, treat me with kindness and respect.' You've heard the saying: 'You can get more with honey than with vinegar.' They treat me good and pay better, too."

Bill was curious and asked Diane, "Have you ever had a pimp?"

She frowned. "No! Those fuckers will kill you! I had a close friend who lived with her pimp. He put her on the streets every night and would give her two or three dollars a day from what she earned. He kept her on drugs and would beat her if she refused.

"One day, she got away from him, and his brother told me he had a contract out on her. I never saw her to warn her. They found her out in a cornfield strangled to death. He had two other girls, and they were scared shitless of him. . . . Let me tell you, I would be, too. He'd drive around checking on them.

"Well, one night, he picked up a chick from Montana who was only thirteen. She was lonely and scared, so he treated her good for a couple of weeks, then put her out with the others and threatened to kill her if she didn't go. He went out of town one day and thought she was too scared to do anything. Well, she called her mother, who called the police. They put his ass in jail. The police gave the other girls protection, too, and they testified against him. He's still in jail, but he will be out on probation soon. I know he'll try to have them killed. He's got the money to do it. He made thousands on them and drug dealing."

Bill corrected her. "He'll be out on parole, not probation."

"Probation, parole, whatever. They should starve him to death instead of letting him out, the fucking bastard. Or better yet, hang him by his dick 'til he dies!"

Peter kidded her. "I take it you don't like pimps."

"I know a lot of girls who live in fear of their pimps. Some treat their girls okay, but they're few and far between. The pimps get rich and the girls get VD, jailed, or even killed. They get a record, and the pimp gets off scot-free. Me, I choose my customers. I check for VD by watching for a yellow discharge and usually require them to use a rubber. I've lost a lot of money by those who won't use one, but I don't care. I had gonorrhea in my throat once, and I couldn't handle that again!"

"I never realized there were so many weird people," Peter said, after listening to the girls.

"The world's full of 'em. I could tell you a whole lot more, but it's getting late. We should be getting to bed," Diane remarked as she glanced at her watch. "It's going on five. Time sure flies when you're enjoying yourself."

Marie Louise felt anxious. "You will stay the night, or what's left of it, won't you?"

Pretending to have ulterior motives, Bill asked her, "How do you know that we're any different from the ones you've been telling us about?"

"I can read people pretty good, and you're both good people."

Figuring he'd better know up front what he was getting into, Bill asked, "How much are you going to charge us?"

Marie Louise bantered, "We usually charge old farts like you five hundred dollars, but you have a kind face," and Diane finished with, "Yeah, a funny kind," and she emitted a rolling laugh that ended in an ear-to-ear grin.

"Seriously, we'd feel a lot safer if both of you are here. . . . No charge for the services." Marie Louise smiled as she got up. "I say we hit the sack and catch some Z's." Bill nodded his agreement. "Sounds like a pregnant idea to me," Diane agreed as she got up. Taking Bill by his arm, she helped him to his feet. "Come on, big daddy, you're sleeping with me."

"You won't catch me complaining." Bill winked at Peter. "Consider this a learning experience. It's better than learning the hard way."

Diane glanced down, then back at Bill and kidded, "If you're not hard tonight, you'll learn what it's like not to sleep with me."

Peter found Marie's bedroom was no better than the rest of the apartment. Her mismatched bed and dresser were old and cigarette-scarred. The walls were devoid of character, painted in an off-green shade, which showed through swirled streak marks where someone had attempted to wash them. Peter tried to get comfortable in the lumpy bed that intruded on his spine, as he lay in anticipation, not quite knowing what to expect. Marie returned from the bathroom dressed in a soft, see-through, flowing pink negligee.

Spreading the gown out to both sides with her hands, she asked, "How do you like me now?"

"Right here beside me, you beautiful angel."

"I don't want a quickie. I like to get real meaning from it when I'm with someone I like. I get too many of those 'Wham Bam, Thank You, Mam' kind and not enough where I can enjoy myelf."

Peter looked at Marie as she glided toward him. "There's something about you that makes me think you're still a little girl who hasn't had a chance to be young."

"You could be right. I never got a chance to do the things other girls did. I skipped school and got in with a lot of older kids. My father died around then, and my mother remarried. Unfortunately, her husband and I couldn't stand each other." She paused and kicking, she flipped her slippers off, sending them flying. "My mother couldn't do anything with me. I finally left . . . but enough of that," she finished, as she sat on the bed beside him. "Right now, I want to get on the outside of you."

Peter reached out and pulled her down onto his chest. She lay sprawled sideways on the bed as she turned to face him. Looking into his eyes, she leaned forward and kissed his lips, withdrew, looked at him again, and then began a long kiss, locking their lips in a sucking embrace. Then, getting up from the bed, she removed her gown. "I can already see that you're different from the others, and I like it."

Peter threw off the sheet he'd covered himself with and waited. In one leap, Marie Louise sprang to his side, then reached down between his legs. "I like these," she murmured.

He rolled over onto his side and put his arm underneath her shoulders. Then, he pulled her close to him and kissed her. Shivering with emotions that were swelling within him, Peter had trouble restraining his desires to enter her and fulfill the immediacy of his urge. "You're driving me wild," he panted.

"I want to make you feel good," she whispered in his ear as she slowly and with skill, used her hands to bring him to heights he'd never before thought possible. Their kisses became torments of fire in him, with her darting tongue lashing desperately into every crevice of his mouth and entwining with his. In his passion his hand began caressing her body. Gently, he moved it through Marie's tassled mound of dark, black, pubic hair.

"Oh, Peter, you're making me so horny I can hardly wait for you to make it with me."

"Your fire is burning me up," he whispered, resisting a quick entry into her waiting body. With their passions rising, Peter lowered his mouth to her bulging, tanned breasts, kissing and sucking them. Then, he began biting her nipples ever so gently. First one, then the other. He caressed her genitals with his hands, then began kissing down the entire length of her body.

Unable to restrain herself, Marie cried out, "I WANT TO FEEL YOU INSIDE OF ME!"

Peter could see that her eyes were burning with desire as she instructed, "Lay behind me. I want to do it that way first!"

Quickly, Peter changed position and snuggled up tight behind her. Marie Louise was ready and with her hand, she took hold of him and guided him into her vagina.

"Not too fast, Peter. I want to absorb as much of you as I can," she whispered. "You've made me so horny, I'm going out of my mind needing you."

She involuntarily jerked in spasm as he pushed in to full entry. Her emotions burned hotter as he reached around and cupped her right breast.

Marie Louise reached back and pulled him tight against her. A short while later, she leaned over her shoulder and looked back into Peter's glazed eyes. He leaned forward and passionately kissed her. Finishing the kiss, she whispered, "Come on top of me now. I want to look at you while we're making love."

"Yes, babe, I want it to feel good for you," he panted. Their rapture intensified as they changed positions. Marie Louise moaned deeply as her emotions took control.

Peter drove harder with more desperation to culminate his urgency. Feeling his sudden release within her triggered Marie Louise's own eruptions. Within moments, Peter felt Marie's entire body quiver beneath him. Unlocking her legs from around Peter's body, she pulled them down and beneath his, and they stiffened in involuntary spasmic jerks.

"YOU'RE WONDERFUL! . . . IT WAS UTTERLY BEAUTIFUL," Marie Louise shouted, as if to someone other than Peter, perhaps to herself.

Sweating and panting, Peter whispered to her, "That was really terrific for me, but you tire me out." He grinned and added, "It was worth it, though."

He leaned down and kissed her repeatedly, while they absorbed as much of each other as possible.

Catching her breath, Marie Louise said, "You really are good at making whoopie." Her eyes gleamed as she added, "We're good together. That was some really good loving . . . the best I've had in a very long time. . . . Most of the guys want to get in and out quickly. Once they come, they're like dead fish."

Peter glanced down along her nakedness and admired her beautiful body. A golden tan covered her entirely, except for the white area on her succulent breasts that had been covered by a bikini bra and the patch of white surrounding her black pubic hair that was created by a G-string.

Marie Louise rolled onto her side and looked at Peter, saying, "We were great together. I wish we could always be together like this." She looked away, then back at Peter. "I've held my feelings in for so long now that I didn't think I could ever feel anything that resembled love. You opened the door for me to feel that way, again. Thank you for giving these feelings back to me."

Lying beside Marie Louise, Peter slid his arm beneath her shoulders and pulling her close to him, he kissed her. Then, pushing himself back slightly so that he could look into her eyes, he whispered, "I thank you for letting me make love to you. It's been a long time since I've been with a girl in this way. But, it was well worth waiting for."

Marie Louise looked deep into Peter's eyes and answered, "You don't have to thank me. It was special for me, too. . . . I really like you a lot. Maybe that's why it was so good with you." She stroked his hair softly for a few minutes without speaking. Finally she said, "I'm thinking about not hooking anymore. After being with you, I know there's more to sex . . . and that's feelings. All that fucking without meaning will eventually kill my feelings altogether, and I don't want that to happen."

Peter brushed her sweat-filled hair to one side. "I've often wondered what makes you girls screw so many guys. I didn't think it could be that you actually couldn't get enough, or that you enjoyed it that much. And, I didn't think you could have good feelings with all of them, when you don't really know the guys. The girls I've known don't like to have sex with a guy unless they have feelings for them. Most of them want to be in love first."

She rolled onto her back and looked at Peter. "It's strictly the money I've been doing it for. Sometimes, though, I like them, so I figure that's a plus. But, it doesn't give me the real feelings of love that I need. I get lonesome a lot, want to be married and have kids, someday. I know that it wouldn't be a good life for them to have a hooker for a mother. That's why I've been saving my money to go back to school and be able to support myself without hooking, unless I get married and have kids first."

Peter's eyes brightened. "I think your going to school would be great for you. I know you'll feel better if you can get away from prostitution."

Marie Louise's eyes relaxed. "I know that it's best to stop now before it's too late and I can't get my real feelings back."

Peter kissed her shoulder. "It may not be easy for you to manage without the money, but it isn't everything. I know you'll feel better about yourself, and that's more important."

They continued after-love-making with touching, kissing, and talking for a long while before falling asleep.

After awakening the following morning, Peter stumbled to the kitchen to get a drink of water. He found Bill sipping from a cup of coffee. Looking up at Peter, he said, "Judging by the way you look, that gal must have taken all the piss and vinegar out of you last night. I thought she might have even killed you with love-making. I'd say from the sounds coming from her room, you got your money's worth."

Peter rubbed his bloodshot eyes. "What time is it?"

"A quarter past ten."

He picked up a glass and ran the water. "She was something else all right." He took a drink and said, "We talked a lot afterward. She told me I was so good that she's giving up hooking for me."

Bill felt a tinge of jealousy. "So you're planning on moving in with her, are ya?"

"Not really. I'm just kidding. She's not doing it for me, but for herself. I think she wants to straighten out her life and get back to a normal one. I just encouraged her to do it, that's all." Peter sat down at the table with Bill. "Don't tell me that you and Diane didn't hit it off?"

"We did all right. She sure is a looker and no slouch in screwing, either. She was tired, so we got to sleep right afterward."

Bill got up and poured Peter a cup of coffee. "Here, drink this and you'll feel better. It'll grow hair on your chest."

Peter sat quietly and drank his coffee. After a few minutes of silence, Bill could see that something was bothering him. In a fatherly tone of voice, he remarked, "You look like things aren't setting right with you. Did anything serious happen between you and Marie last night you'd like to talk about?"

"It's not Marie," he answered, feeling depressed. Then he became silent.

"If it's not her, what is it? You look like the living dead sitting there hanging your head like it was in a noose."

Beads of perspiration broke out on Peter's face. "I had that dream about the elevator again last night. . . . I have the feeling that whatever it represents is getting closer to happening. You know the problem I have with the feelings of enclosure I get. They haven't been too bad since we've been traveling, but when I have that dream, they get intense. Maybe it's because I have no control over what's happening to me in it."

"It's been a while since you've had it. Is it still the same dream?"

Peter's head drooped. "It always starts out different and ends the same. Each time it becomes more real and vivid. I'm afraid that it has some hidden meaning. . . . This time I recognized the blond girl. . . . It's Marie! You and Diane were in it, too!"

"Tell me what you can remember about it."

"It was just before I woke up, so I remember more of it this time. When it started, I was running around naked in the woods. There were rabbits and deer around me, and they were all wearing designer clothes."

Bill let out a soft chuckle. "That is a strange dream all right, even a little funny. Sounds like reverse roles, but that doesn't mean anything to me."

Bill's skin was drawn tight over his cheekbones as he contemplated, trying to interpret Peter's dream as he listened intensely.

"It gets much stranger than that. While I'm in the woods, a naked girl rides by, on a large deer, clothed in a buckskin jacket and matching pants! It was Marie and she yelled at me, 'Peter, you'd better hide quickly! He's hunting for you! Don't let him catch you!' She disappeared and I had a feeling something terrible was after me! I was scared and started running, but I could barely move my legs."

Beads of sweat ran down Peter's face. He wiped it off with his hand. Taking a drink of coffee, he continued. "Finally, I got to the edge of the woods and was immediately drawn with terrific speed toward a building. I went right through the wall and straight into an elevator. It was full of people who were dressed in white. I tried to get out, but the doors were closed. As we started going up, I noticed one of them had a can in his hands. It was shaped like the ten-pound canned hams in the store. The cover was open, and the can was empty. No one got on, but each time it stopped at a floor, people got off. Then, as it started moving again, its speed increased more rapidly. When there were only a few people left, I recognized them as you, Marie, and Diane. We were on the thirteenth floor when the elevator stopped, and the three of you got out. All of you acted like I wasn't there. I tried to get off, too, but something I couldn't see held me in. As soon as the door closed behind you, the elevator went wild, just as it did in the other dreams."

Peter paused and rubbed his hands together. Then he continued, "I fell to the floor. When I tried to hang onto the edges as it skyrocketed upward, my hand bumped against something on the floor. It was the empty can lying there with the cover open. On the top of the cover was a picture of the contents." Color drained from Peter's face.

Bill waited patiently for Peter to continue, and finally he had to ask, "What was on it?"

Peter looked at Bill and let the words fall out, "It was my face on the cover! . . . When I saw that, suddenly I woke up in a cold sweat! It was so real that it scared the living hell out of me!"

Bill could see the effect the dream had on Peter. Unable to determine the meaning of his dream, Bill admitted, "It would scare me, too. . . . It doesn't seem to make much sense to me. You say the three of us were on the elevator with you?"

"Yes. All three of you were there this time! . . . When all of you ignored me, I felt a terrible gnawing feeling of loneliness consuming my whole body."

"It's beyond my understanding why we'd ignore you . . . even in a dream. I feel as though I should apologize to you. . . . But then, it was only a dream."

The fear created by the dream still in him, Peter's eyes appeared gloomy. Looking at his cup of coffee, he sighed a big sigh of relief and looking at Bill, he said, "Thank God it's over! I don't ever want to have it again!"

Bill tried to be understanding and agreed, "It's not anything anyone would want to have recur. . . . I remember your mentioning the blond girl before. Now, your knowing it's Marie would definitely make it appear more real to you. . . . Are you sure Diane and I weren't there before, too?"

"Diane could have been. I didn't know her then. I remember the blond girl because I had a feeling about her that I didn't understand. Even though I've had the dream several times since knowing you, I don't remember seeing you there, but you may have been. Last night you definitely were there!"

Peter looked at the table, then back up at Bill. "You looked right through me like I didn't exist. All three of you had such long and sad looks on your faces that I felt I was at someone's funeral. With the way it ended, it could have been mine! . . . I had the feeling that if we reached the top, they were going to chop me up, cook me, and put me in cans, just like a canned ham!"

Bill shook his head. "It beats me, as to what it could mean. Probably nothing, though. . . . I've read that recurring dreams have to do with the way a person feels about something. You've told me about how you get claustrophobia in elevators. That may be why you have these dreams. Some inner fear is working on your subconscious, and it comes out as a dream."

"That could be it. But this one was TOO REAL! It scared me shit-less!"

Bill wanted to set Peter's fears to rest. Trying to be helpful, he said, "They say that when you're almost asleep, in what they call the twilight zone—half-awake and half-asleep—you can control your dreams. What you have to do is, before you actually fall asleep, tell yourself in a positive and firm way what you want to dream. . . . In your case, what you don't want to dream. Then reinforce it during the day by repeating it over and over whenever you think about it. Try to visualize something good happening and erase the bad."

Peter relaxed and felt somewhat better. Spreading his legs forward from their tense position, he took a drink of coffee. Setting his cup down, his eyes moved toward Bill, as he was saying, "I'll have to try that. I sure don't ever want to have it again!"

Leaving and not wanting to awaken the girls, Peter wrote a note, telling them he and Bill would see them that evening at the go-go club. Then, they went directly to Bill's sister's home for lunch. Because the camper had developed a miss in the motor, Bill parked it on her front lawn. While he was working on it, Peter tried to be helpful by handing

112

him the tools. He had no experience with motors, but he was keenly interested in learning and found Bill a willing teacher.

Sam Engles called to Bill from his yard. "What are you doing, Bill? . . . Trying to overhaul that thing out here in the yard?"

Bill looked up and smiling recognition, he answered, "It has a bit of a miss in the engine and sounds like a tractor. But I think I've found the problem."

Holding a part up to the light, Bill explained. "I've had a leak in the valve cover gasket for a while now, but I haven't gotten around to fixing it. There's a small crack in the distributor cap, and oil must have leaked in through it and gotten all over the rotor."

Sam came over to observe. Bill worked on the cap with a rag, while holding them on the top of the fender. "I'll have to wipe it clean for now and get a new one later."

Running out of the house screaming, Gwin yelled out, "Bill! Get in the house right away! I need you! Hurry!" Then she ran back in.

He was leaning over the truck fender looking into the motor at the time. Upon hearing her, he quickly stood up to see what she wanted. Forgetting about the hood in the excitement, he cracked the top of his head into it with a sickening thud. Holding the top of his bleeding head with his hand, he looked at the house, muttering, "Damn women! Everything's a crisis to them."

He called to her, "What's so important this time?"

Holding his head with his hand, he walked slowly around the side of the camper to see what she wanted, but she had disappeared back into the house. Figuring it wasn't too urgent, he took his time walking, while he applied pressure to stop the bleeding. By the time he reached the front door, Gwin was there again. "Hurry up, before he destroys my entire house!"

Puzzled, Bill rushed into the house, asking, "Before who destroys your house?"

Once inside, he saw the drapes torn from one window. A floor lamp was toppled over, and her squirrel monkey was flying through the air with Gwin in hot pursuit. Bill joined in the chase, which led from the living room, to the dining-room chandelier, to the drapes, and on into the kitchen.

Peter joined them in the chase as it darted to every conceivable place it could get a handhold. Just when Peter had cornered it on top of the refrigerator, it made a mighty leap and landed onto the handle of a pan that was setting on the stove. Landing with ease, it suddenly flipped to the floor, spilling the contents onto itself. Sitting stunned, covered in a dowdy mess of hot pea soup, the monkey shook frantically to free itself of the burning liquid.

113

Quickly, Bill grasped the impish creature by the hind legs and swung it upside down. Dangling it in this way, he headed for the sink. Recovering from its initial shock, the monkey tried to turn itself upright. Baring its teeth, it snapped at Bill's hand. This only maddened him, and he cuffed it with his open palm. Reaching the sink, Bill yelled to Gwin, "Hold its damned head still!"

She had the water running, grabbed it behind the head, and thrust it under the spout.

What followed was a test of the monkey's prowess and Bill's endurance as the water sprayed everyone close by. Attempting to scrub the creature clean, Gwin struggled as it twisted and turned in its attempt to break free. Its head broke free of Gwin, and Bill quickly grabbed it.

"Move that goddamn scrub brush, woman. I can't hold this bastard too much longer!" Bill yelled.

Finally they were successful in cleaning it, and Bill thrust it into Peter's waiting towel. "It's your turn," he said while stepping back to watch.

Bill caught the humor of the situation while watching Peter wrestling with the monkey. Suddenly, he began to laugh.

Managing to keep the monkey within the confines of the towel long enough, Peter finished drying it. When he felt he'd succeeded, he wrapped it into the towel. With only its head left poking out, it appeared as two eyes in a soggy mess of tangled hair.

As Peter carried it to its cage, he laughed and commented, "The little sucker looks like a drowned rat."

Gwin held the cage door open for Peter, and he tossed the soggy monkey from the towel into its cage.

Looking at Bill and Peter, Gwin expressed her appreciation and tried to explain, "Thanks. . . . He's never done that before. . . . I really didn't expect him to leap out when I was cleaning his cage."

Grinning, Bill teased, "Maybe he thought you were a monkey in heat?"

A stern look crossed her face as she responded, "I might have expected you to say something like that. . . . Look at the mess he's made. And, I had that soup for your lunch. . . . It'll take me forever to clean up after him, so you'll have to make your own, now." Shaking her head, she surveyed the damages.

Bill smiled and stated, "We'll eat out." Then he asked, "Can we help you with some of the straightening up?"

"Thanks, but I have time today. Now, if this had happened yesterday when I had to go out, I'd have taken you up on it."

Sam looked at the mess Bill's clothes were in. "He sure did a number on you." Then Sam smiled and continued, "I don't know why she keeps that thing around. It's the horniest beast I've ever seen. Sometimes, it'll sit on its stick in the cage and suck its prick. I've been embarrassed for Gwin when she has company with small kids." He shook his head, displaying noticeable disgust.

Bill agreed. "Yeah, it's a real menace." Then his face broadened into a grin. "That's not all it does. Twice I've seen it stand up holding onto the bars of the cage and wait until some pretty young girl would go over to admire it. When they got real close to the cage, it would piss all over them! . . . They'd jump back in disgust and say something like, 'SHIT! LOOK WHAT HE DID TO ME!' and Gwin would have to apologize." Then he finished, "But, usually she would see them going over to look at it and warn them ahead of time." Then, looking down at himself, he continued, "I'll have to go in and change, before leaving."

When Bill had finished working on the camper's motor, they climbed in and he headed for Fletcher's bar. As they drove through the city, Peter remembered the incident and commented, "I'll bet that monkey doesn't try that again. He must have thought we were trying to kill him."

Bill checked the traffic and looked toward Peter. "It wasn't funny when we were chasing him, but now that I think of it, that was quite a riot. . . . He pissed all over me while I was holding him. I had him by the head, and I felt like twisting it off for him, right then and there."

Pointing up the road, Bill diverted Peter's attention. "That Red Rooster restaurant looks like a good place to eat. . . . What say you? . . . Want to stop there and get on the outside of some food?"

Peter agreed. "I'm with you on that. I could use some vittles about now."

Seeing that the restaurant was filled with people, Peter and Bill seated themselves at the counter. One of the waitresses glanced in their direction, and Bill winked at her. She quickly looked away. He commented to Peter, "She's cute. That queue of amber hair would be easy to latch onto when you wanted her to do something for you. If you had papers on her, that is."

"Where do you dig up some of those words you use?"

"It's called education. I had a lot of time on my hands when I was in the Navy, so I read the dictionary to pass it."

"Sounds boring to me," Peter answered, paused, and continued, "So I take it that a queue means long hair."

"It refers to the braid." Suddenly Bill's eyes turned away from Peter, and he looked down into his lap to see what had dropped there.

Smiling sheepishly, a dark-haired waitress tried to explain. "Sorry about that. You're sitting in a bad spot. Those kids' place mats get bumped off the counter pretty regularly."

"It could have been worse. . . . Mustard stains!" Bill kidded her, then added, "But, since you're so cute, I can't fault you for being so clumsy."

She cocked her head to one side and responded, "So you're one of those kind, eh?"

"Which kind?"

"The kind that gives a girl a compliment and slur in the same breath."

"All right. You've got me there. We'll just say you're cute. How's that set with you?"

"I'll accept that."

She took the place mat from Bill and placed it back onto the pile. "Since I'm here, I'll take your orders if you're ready."

Peter ordered, "Make mine a hamburger deluxe, a large fries, and coffee."

"I'll have the same. . . . Do you come with the order?" Bill couldn't resist asking.

She winked at Peter. "I come sometimes. . . . But I'm not cheap."

Leaning on the counter, chin in hand, looking up at her wide eyed, Bill commented, "Nothing worthwhile in this life is cheap. Skip the hamburger. I'll just have you between the buns, instead."

"You don't know what you could be getting yourself into, talking like that."

Keeping his voice low and looking up at her in a kiddish way, Bill tried to see how far he could go with her. "That IS what I'd like to get into. I'll know it when I feel it. . . . You still have a chance to back out."

Her smile deepened. "Sure. . . . And you'll be right there behind me if I do, won't you?"

Bill lifted his head from his hands and looked squarely into her eyes. "Can't fault a guy for being honest."

"I'd better get your order before I get myself into trouble." She smiled and went to the kitchen.

Peter chided Bill, "You've always got to give the girls a hard time, don't you? You're a real meat hound."

Bill laughed as he answered, "When you get to be my age, you don't pass up a chance to have fun. You never know if you'll ever have another."

Later that evening Peter and Bill went to see the girls at the go-go club. Marie Louise was just finishing her set on stage as they walked in, and she came over and joined them. Dressed in lavender-embroidered panties and a matching halter, which set off her deep tan, she looked stunning to Peter.

"I like lavender, no matter what color it is," he said to her with a coyish smile.

116

She looked at him seriously. "Thanks. . . . When I woke up, I was surprised that you both had left!"

"We left you a note," Peter explained. "Bill had to work on the camper, and we didn't want to wake you girls. We figured that you needed your beauty sleep, since you have to work late tonight."

A look of surprise crossed her face and she asked, "What note? We didn't find one! I thought you might leave one, so I looked, but there wasn't any!"

"I wrote it and left it on the kitchen table. Bill was there with me." Peter was surprised and his face showed it. He turned to Bill.

"Tell her, Bill. You saw me put it there."

"I was there. He wrote it and left it on the table, like he said. Maybe the window was open and it blew on the floor?"

"I'm not sure if the window was open. I suppose that could have happened, but I didn't see it on the floor, either."

"That's strange. I'm sure I left it there," Peter asserted.

Still wondering what could have happened to the note, Bill changed the subject. "So what did you girls do today?"

Marie Louise replied, "Not much, really. We lazed around for a while, then went to the YWCA for a swim and took a sauna. Then I took a tan."

Bill's face was absent of expression as he commented, "My father taught me how to swim when I was about five. He took me out to the middle of the lake and threw me in."

"That's one quick way to learn!" Marie Louise said with noticeable concern in her voice. "Weren't you a little young to learn that way?"

"Right, I learned quick all right." Then ignoring her second question, he continued with a deadpan look. "The hardest part was untying the gunny sack and getting out of it."

She burst out laughing. Then, she chuckled as she responded. "I should have expected that you'd be putting me on. I'll know better than to believe you next time." Then, glancing at her watch, she said, "I've got to go to the change room before I go on. See you both later."

"Right, catch you later," Peter acknowledged.

The bartender delivered the drinks to their table, and Bill paid for them. Casually Bill said to Peter, "I've been thinking about moving on when the girls are through working here. Diane said they have their next job in Spokane. . . . Since we're going to Seattle anyway, we could drive them over and save them travel expense. It won't be far out of our way."

"That's fine with me. It'll give us more time with them."

Bill's eyes searched the dimly lit room. "I haven't seen Diane around, yet." Then he added, "She's probably in the change room."

"I would think she must be here somewhere or Marie would have said something."

Bill and Peter had been sitting talking for about ten minutes when Diane appeared. Bill watched her slow, sexy walk as she came over to their table. He waited until she was seated before he spoke. "Hi, Diane. My, but aren't you the pretty one tonight?"

She crossed her bare legs and leaned one elbow on the table. Then, looking into his eyes, she smiled and answered, "Thanks, but I don't feel so great. I'm still tired from last night's go 'round."

Bill spoke again. "Sorry to hear that. Maybe this will cheer you up. We've been thinking about leaving when you and Marie are through working here. We can drive you to Spokane and stay there for a few days. Since we don't have a timetable, it doesn't matter when we get to Seattle and it would help you girls out."

Her eyes lit up. "That's great. I don't like riding the bus. It's a boring waste of time."

"Then it's settled, if it's okay with Marie," Bill said. Then he inquired, "What would you like to drink?"

Diane dug in her purse. Finding what she wanted, then looking up at Bill, she answered, "Thanks. I'll have a tequila sunrise. I haven't had one of those in a long time."

"That drink sounds romantic," Peter commented.

"It's a good drink when you want a picker-upper." She flashed her eyes at Bill and asked, "So, how was your day?"

He responded, "I had the camper parked in the lot at the Main Street Mall and when I came back from the hardware store, there was a couple in the front seat making out."

Shock was plain on his face. "My God. In the daylight . . . in a public place, yet? I could never do that. . . . What did you do when you found them?"

"They sort of ignored me, so naturally, I called the police. What pisses me off though, is that when they finally came, they gave ME a ticket."

Peter held back his smile as he watched the expression on Diane's face change as she asked, "What the fuck for?"

"For disturbing the piece!" Bill answered her matter of factly.

She couldn't help but laugh at the way he presented it to her, but she blurted out, "You bastard! I really believed you, too."

Peter grinned. "Now, don't say I didn't warn you about him. . . . You'll know better than to believe him, once you get to know him."

"Now, tell me what you really did today," she inquired.

118

Feeling Diane might not believe him, Bill instructed Peter, "You'd better tell her about the monkey."

Not being sure she wasn't going to be set up again and frowning, she asked, "What monkey?"

Peter explained what had happened.

Later that evening, Bill and Peter were having supper at the girls' apartment when Peter said, "This food is a whole lot better than what we've been having, on the road."

Bill pretended indignation. "So, what do you call the stuff we've been eating all this time? If we had to depend on you to cook, we'd have starved to death."

Peter responded, "I didn't claim that I could cook, EITHER."

Bill answered, "You've got a lot of lip for a kid who couldn't even tie his shoes when I found you on the side of the road, looking like a stray alley cat. If it had been a pig that I found, at least now I'd have pork."

As he was about to take a bite, Peter said, "We'll let you know if it needs pork in it, when we've finished eating."

Turning to Bill, Marie Louise changed the subject. "That was really considerate of you to offer to drive us to Spokane when we're finished working here."

Bill washed his food down with his milk, then he answered, "It's no problem for us. I was thinking of a way Peter and I could be able to spend some time with you girls, and it came to me that we're going that way anyway, so why not? It doesn't matter to us when we leave, and it will help you both out."

Excitedly she spoke. "We accept!" Then she paused, looked at Diane and Peter, then back at Bill, "We can have a good time along the way. It could be a fun trip."

Bill was pleased. "Then it's final. We leave right after you finish work, if that's all right. You three can sleep in the camper while I drive."

"It would be better to leave the next day. We'll be too tired to get packed up to leave right away," Marie Louise suggested. Then she asked, "Besides, you're not in any hurry, are you?"

Bill raised his fork and dangling a chunk of meat, he answered, "No. We've got as much time as we need. I hadn't even thought about that aspect of it."

Diane flashed her eyes and smiled at Bill. "I hope that you're planning on staying with us again tonight."

"Wouldn't think of having it any other way." Then Bill pretended to be serious. "Remember, you chicks need protection."

Winking impishly at Marie Louie, Diane asked, "From who?" She paused, then added, "If we want a good night's sleep, I'd say we need to be protected from you two."

"Are you telling us that you didn't enjoy getting so excited you couldn't sleep last night?" Peter asked.

Marie Louise chuckled. "No. I have to admit it was great. I know I enjoyed it."

When they'd finished eating, they sat in the living room talking for a short time before going to bed. When Peter and Marie Louise did finally get to her room, it was quite late. She was sitting at the mirror and Peter stood behind her, completely naked.

"Do you like to watch a girl remove her makeup?" she asked.

Peter flushed light red. "I'm just looking at you. I can't seem to get enough of you. . . . To me, this is like a dream."

"You're crazy," she answered.

"Yeah, I'd say I'm crazy about you."

"You make me nervous standing there watching me. Go and lie on the bed while I do this. I'll be there in a minute."

Peter walked over, sat on the bed, and complimented her. "You sure turn those guys on when you're on the stage."

Holding an eyelash brush in her teeth, she tried to speak. "I's yust laake." She removed the brush. "It's just like acting. You give them what they want."

She twisted her head around to look at him. "The problem is that when you get off the stage they expect you to be all hot and bothered over them."

"That could be a problem. I suppose they take you seriously and when they see you're not, they get pissed off and give you a hard time."

"You've got that right. But I'm used to it now. Besides, they're not all that way. It's just a few assholes who think because they gave you a buck in your G-string, they've bought you for the night."

Finishing at the mirror, Marie Louise strutted over toward Peter and taking her clothes off piece by piece, she threw them into the air.

Completely naked, projecting a captivating smile, she inquired seductively, "Would you do anything that I asked you?"

"Sure, hon, your wish is my command."

Her face changed to an impish smile and she asked secretively, "It may seem silly and childish. Would you still do it for me?"

Watching Marie Louise dancing about the room in her naked, tanned beauty was making Peter very emotional. Her deep brown eyes, in contrast to her white-blond hair, flashed untold messages. As she did a mixture of strutting and prancing around, she gently moved her hands over her bulging breasts, down onto her curvaceous hips, down the length of the cheeks of her butt, and then into her crotch area. Here she placed two fingers over her lips, revealing her dark black pubic hair on each side of them.

Peter remembered the pleasure she had given him the night before and knew that he would do anything she asked. He felt that if it was important to her and he refused, the spell she was weaving might be broken. He answered her, "Whatever it is, I wouldn't hesitate. Just say the word and you can consider it as good as done."

Having changed her expression to that of a very shy girl, she explained, "Like I said, it's silly." She hesitated. "When I was young, my father used to put me on his shoulders and dance around with me up there and my long legs dangling around. I've never forgotten how good it felt to have his strong body beneath me. You have such a beautifully muscled body that I was thinking you could do it without dropping me. . . . But, you don't have to if you don't want to."

Peter rose to his feet, walked over to her, and picked her up in his arms. Then, carrying her over to the bed, he stood her on it.

Seeing her naked body, he was persuaded to agree. "The pleasure will be all mine. Turn around and spread your legs," he instructed her.

She complied with his request. Unable to resist, he leaned forward and kissed the golden cheeks of her buttocks. He pressed hard and kissed intensely, first one, then the other. She chuckled while looking over her shoulder at him. "Don't put hickies on them. They're my work ass-etts."

Peter smiled, admitting to himself the thought had occurred, but he replied, "I wouldn't think of spoiling their beauty."

He tried to insert his head through her legs, but it wouldn't fit, so he suggested, "Spread your legs a little bit more, so I can get my head between them."

After he'd inserted his head in through her legs, she settled back onto his shoulders.

Peter could feel her juice-filled mound of pubic hair pressing tight against the back of his neck and felt a surge of excitement flowing through his body. Picking her up and with bulging muscles, he pranced and bucked about the room, with Marie Louise balancing herself above him. She swung her arms high in the air and pretended to be a cowgirl. Whooping, hollering, and yelling, she made it plain to Peter that she was completely enjoying herself.

He felt a wetness oozing onto his back. Soon the trickling love-juices became a flood and ran down his back and into the crack of his butt. This increased his excitement.

Suddenly, without a warning, she exclaimed, "Oh, Peter! I'm terribly sorry!"

Peter felt the eruption of her waterfall of pee spread over him. It ran like a broken reservoir down his chest and back. The sudden feeling of the warm piss shocked him momentarily. Regaining his composure, he laughed.

He exclaimed, "I've heard the saying, 'Being pissed-off is better than being pissed-on.' Now I can say that I've experienced being both, and I'm here to tell the world that being pissed-on by a beautiful girl isn't as bad as it sounds!"

They laughed together, presenting a strange sight. Two naked bodies bouncing around the room. Peter, dripping wet with pee, balancing Marie Louise on his neck, and now stepping out with exaggerated strides and holding her legs tight, he pretended to attempt to unseat her.

With unexpected suddenness, a shrill scream pierced the air.

Marie Louise sat rigidly upright on Peter's neck, as he stopped to listen. "What the fuck's going on in Diane's room?" she blurted out.

The scream was immediately followed by the noise of a scuffle.

A cold chill shot up Peter's spine, and the room became bitterly cold. Quickly he toppled Marie Louise onto the bed and ran to Diane's bedroom. She ran closely behind him.

More screeching from Diane pierced the air as Peter reached the door to her room. He threw it open and was shocked by what he saw.

Spread along the bed, Bill lay limp. His head was pinned down by a pillow held tight over his face. Racing around the room ran Diane, screeching at the top of her lungs. A large rag doll, clutching at her hair, swung with her every leap.

The pillow, held by an unseen force, immediately caught Peter's attention, and he rushed to Bill's assistance, attempting to wrest it loose.

The rest of the room immediately became alive! Struggling with the rag doll she had kept on her bed, Diane's grasping hands tried to dislodge it from her back. It clawed and gnashed its sharp teeth as she fought with it. Marie Louise quickly rushed to her rescue, and in one quick jerk she managed to pull it loose. Ripping its head off with instantaneous superhuman strength, Marie Louise threw the head across the room. Then, seeing that the body had remained alive, she yanked it into parts and throwing them piece by piece, she spread it out in every direction of the room. Dumbfounded, she watched each part move with a life of its own.

Tearing the pillow to shreds to remove it, Peter pulled the remaining piece from Bill's face and began blowing into his mouth, silently praying for his survival.

A throw rug rose up from the floor and wrapped itself around Peter's head. Marie rushed to him. Yielding to their combined strength,

122

the rug released its grip on him. Jumping from the bed, Peter threw it at the window, hoping to get rid of it. Before reaching the window, it swiftly changed into a thunderbolt. Then, with a bright blue flash and sickening force, it struck Peter in the shoulder, where it exploded in a volcanic eruption of burning flesh that spewed about the room. The smell of burning flesh and sulfuric-ozone smoke flooded the air.

Bill, dazed and in disbelief of what his recovering eyes saw, shook his head to clear it. He was about to rush to Peter's assistance when a large spider, a foot in diameter, with long orange-black hair and sharp spines, dropped from the ceiling onto the bed near his feet. He gave one kick at it before he felt the creature clenching its teeth into his ankle. Successful in shaking it loose, he kicked it across the room. Hitting the wall, it slid to the floor and lay stunned in a hairy mound with black-green blood oozing from its eyes and nose.

Diane ran toward the bedroom door, screaming hysterically, but the door slammed shut by itself as if it had a mind of its own. She struggled with it, but it was held tight, as if it were bolted closed.

A Gideon Bible bolted from the dresser drawer, and using its covers as wings, it flew at Bill. Dodging it, he leaped from the bed in a surge of fear-initiated strength. "Get out of the way!" Bill yelled at Diane, as he rushed headlong toward the door. Diane leaped aside as he struck it a crushing blow with his shoulder, that shattered it. The force carried him forward, and he slid into the couch in the living room, striking his head.

Diane burst out the door, chased by the attacking, flying Bible, which dove into the back of her head. Dashing down the stairs, she was followed closely by the book, with its loose pages tearing off and flying from it, while the covers, flapping determinedly, carried it in hot pursuit of her.

Back in the apartment, Marie Louise, supporting Peter with his good arm over her shoulder, helped his staggering body from the bedroom. Bill, who had jumped from the bed, rushed to assist her. As they reached the door, the remaining things in the living room simultaneously came alive in an effort to attack them. Beating off the attack, they rushed to the stairs and started down.

By now, other tenants, having heard the commotion, were in the hallway. A large-framed man yelled at Marie Louise, "Get yourself out. I'll help him." He swung Peter's body up into his arms and followed Marie Louise and Bill, who stumbled down the stairs, naked and covered in Peter's hot blood. A straight-back chair flew out of the apartment and crashed into pieces against the passageway wall.

"Everyone get out of the building!" Bill yelled over his shoulder.

"Use the fire escape! . . . The place is alive!"

The man shouted to Bill, "Get the door!"

Bill caught the door after Marie Louise had exited through it and held it open for the man who was carrying Peter. Looking up the stairwell, past the onrushing tenants, Bill saw a half-man half-beast, just standing there looking down at them. Its tangled hair surrounded ghoulish green, fiery eyes.

Suddenly, upon raising its arm, it shot a blue-red firebolt down the stairwell. Striking the entrance-door casement, it burst the wood into a fiery mass of splinters, some of which struck Bill, Peter, and the man carrying him. With one quick leap, Bill was on the porch and the man carrying Peter was swiftly running behind him. A second bolt struck the door as it slammed closed, splintering it and setting it ablaze. Screaming people rushed through the burning door out into the flickering firelit streets.

Upon reaching the camper, Bill found Diane sitting on the front seat shaking. "Can you drive?" he yelled to her excitedly.

"Sure! . . . The keys are in it!" she yelled to him as he rushed on by, heading for the back. Instinctively, she started the motor.

"I'll get in the back with Peter! I have a first-aid kit there! Maybe I can stop the bleeding!" Bill panted breathlessly.

Marie Louise stood holding the camper door open. "Help us to get him in!" Bill requested.

She climbed in and opened the bedding up, making a place for Peter to lie. Still very weak from being suffocated and dazed from the blow to his head, Bill climbed in and reached out to assist the man with Peter.

"There are some of Peter's clothes just inside the door on the right!" Bill instructed Marie Louise, once he'd put Peter on the bed. "Take them and you two get dressed! I'll see what I can do for Peter! . . . Do you know where the hospital is?" he shouted, silently hoping that Diane did.

"Sure, I've been there before!"she acknowledged while hastily grabbing whatever she could of Peter's clothing for herself and Diane.

"Better get moving fast!" the man who'd assisted them yelled to Marie Louise as she rushed on past him, heading for the cab.

Bill glanced at Peter's unconscious body on the bed as he turned on the light and pulled the door closed. Then, while he hastily dressed, he yelled to Diane through the connecting window, "Don't spare the horses! . . . Get this fuckin' thing moving, NOW!"

The camper careened and sped through the streets under Diane's expert guidance, on its way to the hospital. Reaching the emergency entrance, she pulled to a screeching halt and jumped out. "I'll tell them to get their asses out here!" she shouted as she ran toward the door.

Marie Louise rushed around to the back of the camper to help Bill. Peter lay motionless beneath a blanket on the bed. Excitedly, she shouted, questioning Bill, "How is he? . . . They'll be here soon! Diane went in to get help!" Her blood surged through her body in torrents as she looked at Peter.

Bill, his head throbbing mercilessly, looked into Marie Louise's wide eyes and said, "I don't want to move him until they come with a stretcher! . . . I did manage to stop most of the bleeding, though. . . . But, he's lost a lot of blood!"

Bill's body tensed and his eyes filled with tears as thoughts of fear for his friend Peter's life filled his mind. "Whatever it was, it did a lot of damage to his shoulder! . . . He hasn't moved at all! . . . I've been praying that he lives!"

After waiting a few minutes, Bill looked toward the emergency door and in disgust, he angrily cried out, "WHERE THE FUCK ARE THEY?" Then, looking at Marie, he blurted out, "He's been like a son to me, I don't want to see him die." A flood of tears cascaded down his face, soaking into his shirt. Trying to control his voice as he fought back the tears, he continued, "I know that you like him a lot, too. I've seen it in your eyes when you'd look at him."

Seeing this bearlike man crying, touched Marie Louise's heart. This and her feelings for Peter caused her eyes to swell with tears. She admitted, "Yes, I do!"

Through the corner of her eye, Marie Louise caught a movement. Turning in that direction, then pointing, she cried out, "Here they come!

Bill yelled to the attendants, "Get that stretcher over here on the double!" and they broke into a run.

Peter opened his eyes and found himself in an elevator. He noticed Marie Louise standing nearby, looking down at him, and she was sobbing. He tried to tell her that he was all right. But, although his mouth formed the words, none came out. Suddenly, he felt himself begin slowly to rise higher.

I'm dreaming about the elevator again, was his first thought. But somehow this time it appeared more real than before. TOO REAL TO BE A DREAM.

He glanced down. *Who's that on the stretcher?* he wondered. *IT LOOKS LIKE MY BODY! . . . IT LOOKS SO STILL! . . . I MUST BE DEAD!* The realization that he'd died hit him! He cried out, "NOT NOW, WHEN I'M JUST STARTING TO ENJOY LIVING!" but no words came.

A certain calming effect swept through his body, bringing with it a resolve of the acceptance of his plight.

Suspended on the ceiling, Peter looked down at Bill, Diane, and Marie Louise. He saw their sadness written on their faces as they stood observing his lifeless body lying on the stretcher. Amazingly to him, he found reading their shadowy thoughts came nearly as easy as breathing had been for him, when he was alive. He was struck with the sudden realization of how much they really cared about him. He tried once more to speak, but still no words came.

Swiftly the elevator rose up the shaft. Peter tried evaluating the situation. The familiarity of the scene leaped into his brain. "The dream! This is the way it was the last time!" There was the doctor, a registered nurse, and two attendants, along with his friends, just like in the dream. He noticed that the doctor was putting something on his body's shoulder wound. He heard him speak.

"I don't think we can do much for him. He's lost so much blood. These units he's getting now will help, but his life's in God's hands. His shoulder is shattered so badly, we may have to amputate the entire arm. . . . We'll be going directly into surgery with him."

Peter heard Bill plead on his behalf. "Please do whatever you can to save him! . . . And try to save his arm, too, if it's at all possible!"

He heard the doctor try to reassure Bill. "You can be assured that we'll do everything humanly possible for him."

Then he heard the nurse ask, "Does he have any family? . . . You'd better contact them if he does."

Peter adjusted to his new existence. The one thing that concerned him the most was his inability to communicate with his friends. He listened to Bill who held his hand on the lump on his head as he answered, "He has, but I wouldn't know how to get in touch with them. He never spoke to me about them much, except to say that he was from Boston."

Seeing Marie Louise and Diane openly crying bothered Peter. He wanted to tell them that he'd survived, even if it was only in spirit.

Without warning, the elevator stopped and the doors opened. It was then that Peter noticed a thin silver cord. Leading down from his floating form, it was attached to his body at the back of the head. The attendants wheeled the stretcher out of the elevator, and he tried to follow. But somehow he was stuck to the ceiling of the elevator and couldn't move. A dark gray form appeared near the cord's attachment to his body. He exerted every effort to leave, too, and to fight off the form, but, as his friends walked out behind the stretcher and the doors closed, he found he was locked in by himself.

Suddenly, he felt the elevator surge upward and increasing speed, it went out of control. His energy form sucked toward the floor, it slammed down hard. The cord tightened against the strain of the ascent. He realized in desperation. *There IS something trying to finish me off in this elevator! IT's JUST LIKE IN THE DREAM, but THIS TIME IT'S FOR REAL!*

Peter quickly realized his body's survival depended upon his getting out of the elevator and fighting off whatever it was that was trying to break his life cord. Now, he believed that if the cord broke, he WOULD SURELY DIE! His mind ran in circles. *I'm trapped here! I've got to get free of this and back into my body! But, how?*

Lying flat and clinging to the elevator floor, Peter prayed desperately as the elevator's speed increased upward. Suddenly, his life's cord jerked and sent a jolt shooting through his body, ripping at his soul. Immediately, he felt himself traveling at an ultra-high speed, being drawn through the elevator floor. Passing through the hospital walls, his spirit rocketed with lightning speed. His mind whirled in confusion.

In the operating room, the doctor shouted at his assistant, "He's going into cardiac arrest!"

Quickly applying the electrodes, she turned and threw the switch. Peter's body jumped involuntarily. "Give him another shot!" the doctor directed. The switch was thrown once more. Peter's body jumped, again. The room went silent momentarily, then the doctor exclaimed, "We've stopped his heart from fibrillating!"

After checking Peter's vital signs, he wiped his forehead and said, "I think we can start the operation now."

Bill had the lump on his head checked and with their finding it to be a minor injury, he was released. With the girls, he waited in the lounge for Peter to be brought out of the operating room.

Chapter 7

CHANGES

W HILE staring at the floor, Bill saw the doctor enter the waiting room and he looked up at him.

The doctor looked around the room and questioningly, he stated, "You must be Peter Dunn's friends. I'm Doctor Martin."

Bill stood up and walked over to him. He extended his hand and said, "Yes, we are. How is he?"

The doctor shook hands with him and replied, "He'll be in the ICU until we can stabilize his condition. Fortunately, he's young and has a strong heart, and these are two points in his favor. We did decide not to amputate his arm at this point. It was a difficult decision, but the surgeon wants to wait to see if it'll heal. But, he is in critical condition, however." He looked at the girls saying, "Whatever you can do to locate his family will help. He may need them with him if he recovers."

Upon hearing that Peter had not died, Bill felt relieved. He explained, "He wasn't close to them and didn't talk about them very often. When he did, it left him feeling very remorseful." Then Bill tried explaining further. "A nurse told us that the girls' apartment was destroyed by the fire. Whatever identification or addresses he might have had were destroyed with it, so we may not have much luck in locating them. But, I'll try, if it'll help him."

Marie Louise, feeling anxious about Peter, asked, "Will we be able to see him in the ICU?"

"The hospital has a policy that only immediate family can be allowed in the unit."

Bill interjected, "We are the only family that he has now. . . . And, we'd like to see him!"

"Right now, he's unconscious and may not come out of it for days, if at all. He went into cardiac arrest in the OR. . . . We stopped the fibrillation of his heart, but we don't know what damage, if any, might have occurred."

Bill looked at him and asked, "What are his chances of being normal?"

"I'd advise you to prepare yourselves for the worst. Even if he does survive, he could be comatose. It appeared to me that whatever happened to him, had a terrific force to it. He was in shock when he arrived. Adding that to the excessive loss of blood, it's hard to make a prediction. We'll just have to wait and see how he does. The next twenty-four hours will be critical. If he survives that, he may have a chance to recover."

Pain tore at Marie Louise's heart, and she wept uncontrollably. Bill fought back his tears as he asked the doctor, "What are you telling us? . . . That he might not survive and, even if does, he may not know us?"

"If he does survive, he may remain in a coma. We've seen these cases vary so much that I wouldn't want to venture an opinion. We'll have to wait and hope for the best."

Tears filled Bill's eyes. "Can you talk with someone about allowing us to visit him in the ICU? . . . Since he doesn't have anyone else, we'd like to be there if he does regain consciousness."

"I'll do what I can. They may make an exception under the circumstances. . . . I'll be looking in on him throughout the night." He paused, then he finished speaking. "The nurses will let you know how he's doing. I'll tell them that it's all right to inform you of his condition. In the meantime, I'll see what I can do about allowing you to see him."

Choking back the tears through her handkerchief, Marie Louise said, "Thank you for all that you've done for him, Doctor Martin."

Bill extended his hand. "Yes, Doctor, thank you. We do appreciate what you've done for him. And, we'll appreciate whatever you can do to get us permission to see him. I know he will want to see us if he does come out of it."

Turning to leave, Dr. Martin said, "I'll be happy to talk with you at any time you may have questions on his condition. He'll need all of your prayers."

Looking over from where she was seated, Diane spoke. "Thank you, Doctor." Then, as he left, she turned to Bill and with sadness in her eyes, she said, "I don't believe this has happened to us tonight! . . . Where is God when He allows these kinds of things to happen?"

Bill fought to control his emotions as feelings of despair loomed over him. He tried to answer, "None of us can answer that question. . . . But, it does make you wonder why they happen. They say it is supposed to strengthen a person when adversity comes their way. I know, a couple of hours ago, things were so much different and it's hard to accept this kind of thing happening. . . . I often wonder about life and why it has to be so damned upredictable and complicated."

Marie confessed, "I know that we shouldn't question God's intentions, but Peter was a good person. I don't want him to die." Choking back the tears, she continued, "It always seems that his whole world is mixed up. If that was me in there, it would be understandable. I've been living in sin for a long time now. I deserve to be the one there instead of Peter." Then, she wept outwardly.

After a few moments, she said, "I told Peter the other night that I was quitting hooking. NOW I KNOW THAT I'LL NEVER DO ANOTHER TRICK AGAIN FOR THE REST OF MY LIFE!"

Bill walked over and sat in the chair next to Diane. Marie Louise sat across the room from them. Bill spoke. "Peter told me you'd told him that. Maybe this is God's way of bringing you back into the fold. . . . I've never been a religious person, myself, but I do believe that there is a purpose for everything that happens. . . . You shouldn't be too hard on yourself. I know that you're a good person. It's just too bad all this had to happen, especially since you and Peter were just getting to know each other."

Through blurred eyes, Bill saw a nurse approaching. He stood up to meet her. Marie Louise also stood and walked over to her.

"Would you folks like some coffee and rolls? We have them in the nurses' lounge. . . . If you'd like, I could bring you some."

Bill answered, "Thanks. A cup of coffee would be all that I'd want. Maybe the girls would like a roll with theirs."

Marie Louise spoke. "Thanks, but I couldn't eat anything right now."

Diane said, "I'd just like a cup of coffee, too."

"Can you tell us how Peter Dunn is doing?" Bill asked.

The nurse answered, "There hasn't been any change in him." Then she asked, "Whatever happened to him that burned him so badly? I've never seen burns like that before . . . and he smelled foul, too . . . something like a mixture of burned flesh and sulfur. It was so strong that I was nauseated by it."

Feeling that she wouldn't believe the truth, Bill answered, "I noticed the odor myself, but I wasn't sure what it was. We don't understand ourselves. It happened so fast that I really didn't see what happened."

The nurse remarked, "He's lucky there were no broken bones, but he did lose a lot of flesh from his shoulder. I understand they'll have to perform skin grafts on him." She turned to leave. "I'll be back with the coffee in a few minutes. . . . Are you sure you don't want something?" she asked Marie Louise. "You may feel better if you do."

"No, thanks. My stomach couldn't take anything right now," she answered. Then, turning to Bill, she said, "Let's sit down. I feel weak."

"Good idea. I don't feel too good myself."

Looking at Marie Louise and shaking her head, Diane said, "I can't get what happened tonight out of my mind. I keep remembering those giant spiders and how everything was trying to kill us."

Bill felt compassion for the girls fill his mind, knowing the strain they were under was tremendous. He responded, "You'll have to try to forget about what happened."

He looked from one of them to the other, then he asked, "Would either of you want a sedative? I may be able to get some from the doctor who's on call."

"I'll be all right," Diane answered.

Her complexion pale, Marie Louise said, "I couldn't take anything right now, or I'd up-chuck it. My stomach is turnng in circles." She leaned back and closed her tear-filled eyes. She added, as if to herself, "I just can't get Peter out of my mind."

Shortly, the nurse returned with their coffee. Trying to be helpful, she offered, "I know this has been a long night for all of you, and you may want to get some sleep. If you give us a telephone number where we can reach you, we'll let you know if there is any change in his condition."

"I'll be all right. I'd like to stay here for a while at least," Bill answered. Then, looking at the girls, he suggested, "If you girls want to get some sleep, you can use the camper."

While covering her face with her hand, Marie Louise said, "I couldn't sleep. My whole body feels like it's been in a washer and gone through the spin cycle. I'll stay here with you, Bill." She removed her hand and looking at Diane, she suggested, "Diane, why don't you go when you're finished with your coffee? If we hear anything, we'll get you."

"I'll stay here, too. Even if I wasn't upset, I'd be afraid to be out there by myself. I don't trust whatever it was that was trying to kill us in the apartment."

Momentarily, the nurse looked at her quizzically. Then, turning to leave, she looked at Bill and said, "Whatever you decide will be all right. But, if you get too tired and decide to leave, just leave a number at the desk where we can reach you. . . . Doctor Martin said he will let us know if we can allow you to be in the ICU. If he gets permission, we can only allow one person in there at a time." Then she left.

Diane was not flashing her eyes now. Her face reflected the urgency of her doubts and insecurity, and she wanted Bill to reassure her. "This is the worst thing that's happened to me in my entire life. It's made me think about how short life could be. . . . I've always felt that I was immor-

131

tal and would live forever. Now, the reality of how quick things can change has me scared. I don't want to die! I have too many plans for the future to lose them now. . . . Bill, do you think that devil thing will try to get at us again? . . . Maybe even in here?"

Realizing that talking about it might be best to help ease their minds, Bill answered, "I think that we are out of danger. If it had wanted to follow us, it would have done so by now. . . . I've been in a quandary about the whole thing, myself. I wish that I knew what the intent of the attack was. It just doesn't make any sense. . . I believe that it must have had something to do with that building. . . . The state of disrepair gave me a gloomy and dismal feeling when I first entered it. . . . The two of you have lived there many times before. . . . Can you remember anything unusual ever happening there?"

After giving it some thought, Diane said, "The place always gave me the willies, but there was never anything out of the ordinary I'm aware of."

"I can't think of anything, either."

Bill, still shaking inside, spoke. "It sure beats me . . . but there's no use in worrying about it. We have no control over what happens in this life. . . . Right about now, I sure could use a shot of brandy."

Diane's eyes brightened slightly as she agreed. "I could use a double shot. . . . But, the way I feel, that might not even be enough."

Later that night, Marie Louise sat in the lounge by herself. Bill and Diane had left the hospital and were asleep in the camper. They had agreed that one of them should remain in the lounge in case of a change in Peter. She felt tired and had started to doze when a tall, slender registered nurse with long black hair approached her.

Seeing movement, she knew that Marie Louise wasn't asleep and asked, "Are you Marie Dartz?"

"Yes."

"My name is Lori. We have permission for you to go in to see your friend Peter. He's in Room 652. Before going in, you'll have to check in with the nurse who has charge of the unit. You'll also have to let her know when you leave."

"Thank you. . . . How is he?"

"He hasn't moved since he's been here, but his vital signs appear to still be good, considering what he's been through. The nurse in the unit can give you more information."

"What time is it?"

Smiling, the nurse replied, "It's quarter-past eight. If you'd like some breakfast before going in to see him, the cafeteria is on the first floor."

After yawning and wiping over her eyes with her hand, Marie Louise answered, "Thanks. I'll get some later on. Right now, I want to see Peter. How long can I stay with him?"

"They'll only allow you to stay in the ICU for half-hour periods."

Marie Louise checked with the charge nurse in the Intensive Care Unit, then went to Peter's bed. He lay motionless, eyes closed. An IV tube intruded into the vein on his wrist, and an oxygen cannula was inserted into his nostrils. The corner of his multi-bandaged shoulder was exposed above the sheet and bore evidence of the excessive swelling that it had sustained.

She took Peter's hand in hers and whispered to him, "Peter, I realize that we've hardly had a chance to get to know each other in the last few days, but there are qualities in you that I admire. I know that we got off to a bad start, too. That was my fault. I was becoming hardened by the way I was leading my life, and I didn't like what it was doing to me. I had a chip on my shoulder because I figured that every guy who went to those places was only after one thing, so I tried to put them in their place before they would get any ideas."

Marie Louise paused and gently ran her fingers across the top of his hand. "I know that I never should have started working as a dancer. I thought I could be different from the other girls and not do the kind of things they were doing, but it was too easy to slip into being like them. The money became too important to me. . . . It was more than I could make any other way, but I hated myself for allowing it to happen to me. At first, each time that I did it, I would promise myself it would be the last, but it never was. . . . When I met you and got to know you, and I saw the special person that you are, I wanted to be that kind of person, too. . . . Not only for myself, but so that you would respect me more."

Feeling an emptiness begin gnawing at her insides, Marie Louise sat silent for a few minutes. Then, she continued, "I've always had a dream of getting married to someone like you, but I've never before been attracted to anyone enough to really have the incentive to make the decision to quit, stick. Since I met you, I've been feeling you were that someone who could make the difference. I believed that if I quit this work and we got to know each other better, maybe we could share a part of our lives together."

She rubbed his hand as she spoke. "You created a new hope in me that at last I'd found the life I've been searching for. . . . You were the prince who came into my life, and I felt you would help me to be a good person, just as you are. Peter, I don't want to lose you now, just when I can see a ray of hope in my life. Please, don't die. Don't give up. I know you can't hear me, but I've read that even an unconscious person can hear and remember. I desperately hope that you can and you'll use all of your ability to get better."

She paused, breathed deeply, then continued. "I need you to be my friend . . . my buddy. Maybe someday it can be more. . . . If you care anything for me, Peter, please get yourself better."

Marie Louise choked back a flood of tears, as she confessed her innermost feelings to him. She watched his face intensely as she whispered to him, searching for some sign that he'd heard her. A twitch of a muscle, anything that might indicate he could hear what she was saying, but there was none. She sat in silence next to Peter's bed, for a long time, a kaleidoscope of memories passing through her mind.

An R.N. came over to Marie Louise and with a smile, she quietly said, "I'll have to ask you to step out for a few minutes. You can wait in the lounge, and we'll send for you when we've finished."

"Yes, I'll wait. Thank you for all that you're doing for him," she said before she returned to the lounge.

When she walked into the lounge, Diane and Bill were there.

Anxiously, Bill asked, "How is Peter?"

Marie Louise responded in a low, tired voice that projected her feelings of despair. "They let me in to see him. They're doing something with him now. . . . He looks so white just lying there and not moving. I tried to talk to him, hoping that he would show me some sign that he heard me, but there wasn't any." Then she asked, "How long have you been here?"

Diane answered, "We just got here a few mintues ago."

Marie Louise felt a sense of responsibility and guilt for having invited Peter to her apartment. She looked at Bill and stated, "They will only let one of us in at a time and then only for one half-hour. I've heard of people who became complete vegetables from brain damage caused by cardiac arrest. . . . I hope he comes out of this all right. . . . I feel like it's my fault he got into this."

Diane felt concern for her friend. "You had no way of knowing this would happen, Marie. . . . You look very tired. Maybe you should get some rest. . . . We could wait here until they finish. Bill, you can go in to see him, then."

Marie Louise glanced at the windows. Bright sunlight greeted her eyes. "I am tired, but I'm a little hungry, too. Have you had anything to eat? . . . The nurse told me that they have a cafeteria on the first floor."

Bill answered, "No, but I'm not hungry. Why don't you and Diane go down and get something? I'll wait here, so I can see Peter."

Admitting to herself the strain of not having a chance to rest was affecting her, Marie Louise answered, "All right. . . . Afterward, I think I'll take a quick nap in the camper, then I'll come back."

Bill handed her the keys and they left.

Picking up a sports magazine to read, Bill walked to a chair and settled down, resigning himself to the wait. His mind alternated between the magazine and the bleak thoughts of what his life would become if Peter died or was a bed patient for the rest of his life. Either way, he knew that Peter had made a very deep impression on his life, a part of which could become a void if he didn't completely recover. He waited for what to him seemed like an eternity before he heard someone approach the lounge door. It was Diane. She looked at him in surprise.

"I thought you'd be in with Peter when I got back."

"They haven't said it was all right, yet. I went over and asked the nurse once, but she said they were still working in there and would let me know when I can go in," said Bill.

"Where's Marie?"

"She's in the camper. . . . She was so tired she almost fell asleep while we were eating. I had to shake her, or she might have." Then, changing the subject, Diane said, "I think she's fallen pretty hard for Peter. She hasn't said much to me about it, but she's secretive in some ways. I can tell by the way she's been acting since she met him. I know this is very hard on her."

"I figured she was. I know Peter likes her, too. Her name kept coming up when he talked. I think he had her on his mind a lot. . . . I keep thinking about how quicky everything changed from having fun to this tragedy. It's like some kind of curse was placed on him."

Bill paused and looked at the floor. "First, the incident in the Ozarks and now this. I know it's absurd to think they are related, but it keeps coming to my mind how similar they are." Bill's face showed the tenaciousness of his determination to cut through the uncertainty of the mystery.

Diane had tried to forget about what happened, but unconsciously she dwelled on it. "I don't want to think about it any more than I have to, but I've been running it through my mind, too. I've been fighting not to because it only makes me sick when I do."

Bill turned to her. "I guess it's better for all of us to try to forget about it. . . . I wonder what's taking them so long in there? It's been almost an hour now since you and Marie went to eat. I hope there aren't any complications occurring."

"Relax, Bill. It shouldn't be long now. I know you're worried about Peter, but wringing your hands like that won't help anything."

"I've been trying to relax, but I'm a bundle of nerves inside. You are right, though. It really doesn't help to be upset."

Diane walked over and looked out the window as she said, "I've been saying some prayers for him. I haven't prayed in many years because I knew I didn't deserve to have them answered. Now I'm saying them for Peter . . . maybe He'll understand and answer them."

"I have, too. It seems the only time I pray any more is when things go beyond my ability to do anything, and I know that's not right. . . . I used to be really close to God, but I'm ashamed to say, I've drifted away from Him, too."

A young, auburn-haired nursing assistant appeared at the doorway. She glanced around the room, her eyes coming to rest on Bill. In an uncompassionate tone, she asked, "Are you waiting to see Peter Dunn?"

Bill answered, "Yes, we are."

Matter of factly, she said, "One of you can go in to see him now. You'll have to check in with the R.N. in the unit."

"What room is he in?" Bill asked.

"Room 652."

"Thank you,"Bill answered and, then, turning, he said to Diane who had returned to the chair beside him, "I won't stay too long, then you can go in."

"Go ahead. Don't worry about how long you're there, I'll be all right here."

Bill's heart sank into his feet when he saw Peter lying motionless on the bed with the IV in his arm and the monitoring equipment attached to him. He wanted to speak to him, but a useless feeling prevailed over him. He sat sphinxlike, just looking at him. Finally, after remembering what Marie Louise had said, he spoke, "Peter, . . . You've been like a son to me. . . . We've made a lot of plans of what we would do together. . . . We still can."

Peter showed no sign of recognition.

The silence was broken only by the steady beep of the monitoring equipment. He consciously avoided thinking about the attack, but the thoughts of it recycled themselves continuously. After long moments, he rose to his feet and in a plodding motion, he went to the desk to talk with the charge nurse. "Has he shown any sign of coming out of his coma?" he asked in a pathetically mild voice.

She looked up at him. "No, he hasn't moved, yet. It's too soon to know if he'll regain consciousness. He was in shock from the loss of blood. That has made it more difficult to predict an outcome. We have him stabilized now. So, all we can do is wait and see how he does. Right now, we're trying to prevent infections in his wound. His burns are some of the worst that I've seen. . . . Dr. Martin is a very good physician. You can rest assured your friend will receive the best possible care."

"Thank you. I'll be going now. Another friend of his would like to see him, too."

"That'll be all right. We'll have to care for him in about fifteen minutes. They can see him until then."

"I'll tell her."

Bill returned to the lounge and allowed Diane a chance to see Peter.

Peter's condition remained unchanged while Bill and the girls kept a vigil of visiting him. Diane and Marie Louise had to work at Fletcher's, but they found it difficult to keep their minds on their dancing. With their apartment destroyed, they had accepted Bill's sister's gracious offer to allow them to stay at her home.

Three days later, in the early afternoon following Peter's hospitalizatin, Diane was in the ICU while Bill and Marie Louise waited in the lounge. Bill inquired of Marie Louise, "What are you thinking about? You've been quiet for some time now."

"I can't help remembering the night of the cursed attack on us. We were lucky that we weren't all killed. I keep thinking about poor Mr. Dudley and his wife dying in the fire. The paper said one of the tenants brought him outside of the building, but he rushed right back in to be with her. He must have really loved her. That kind of devotion is rare these days, what with everyone getting divorced."

Marie Louise's eyes relaxed, and she looked down and twisted her hands together. She focused them again and looked at Bill, saying, "I mentioned to Mr. Gillis, the manager of the club, how I felt about Mr. Dudley's devotion to his wife. All that he said was, 'I wouldn't do that for no woman. I believe that people should get married in the morning. That way, if it doesn't work out, they haven't ruined the whole day.' "

She turned to face Bill. "He's such a callous person, I shouldn't have expected him to show any emotions over their deaths. Mr. Dudley told me they had rented from him for over ten years." Her face took on a disgusted look. "All he valued in them was their money."

Bill gave her a sympathetic look. "Unfortunately, there are many of his kind in this world." Then, speaking about the Dudleys, he said, "Even though I only met him that one time, I felt badly when I read about them dying."

Bursting into the lounge, Diane blurted out, "It's Peter!" Reading the expression on her face as a sign of panic, Bill jumped to his feet. "What about him? Is something wrong?"

"I just don't know! He was making growling noises! It frightened me, so I got the nurse! She didn't know what to think of it either and called the doctor! She asked me to leave and said they'd send someone here when they finished checking him!"

Marie looked at Bill with a mixture of bewilderment and disbelief as she asked, "What do you think it means?"

Bill was equally puzzled. "I don't have the slightest idea of what it could mean." He shook his head, feeling perplexed. "I suppose it could be that he's having a nightmare?" Then, he questioned the validity of his own statement.

They stood momentarily speechless. . . . The silence was broken by the sound of shattering glass.

"My God! What's going on down there? That sounded like it came from the ICU!" Marie exclaimed as panic spread across her face.

A nurse rushed past the lounge doorway in the direction of the noise.

The clang of equipment falling to the floor, followed by the muffled sound of shouts, came from the ICU unit.

Bill and the girls ran to the hallway in time to see a male nurse disappear into the unit.

A look of anxiety and fear spread over their faces as they wondered what was happening in the unit.

Diane shouted hysterically, "It's that cursed thing after Peter again! . . . I've had a strong feeling that it wouldn't leave us alone!"

Taking her by the shoulders, Bill led her back into the room and tried calming her down. "There's no way of knowing, right now, what's happening in there. Try to relax and we'll know soon enough. It may not even be Peter."

Silence prevailed as they stood in the room. Marie Louise remained in the hallway, looking toward the unit, not knowing what to expect. Shortly, the male nurse, his uniform sleeves torn, emerged from the room. He was followed by two nurses and a doctor. She hurried toward them. "We heard the noise! Is Peter Dunn all right?" excitedly, she asked one of the nurses.

"Yes, he's sleeping now. We have him on a sedative. . . . We're not sure what happened. He pulled the IV out and tried to get out of bed. It was so sudden and unexpected it surprised the nurse who was checking him. Some equipment was damaged, but I'm sure that he'll be all right. Don't worry. . . . He won't be able to have any visitors now, but we'll call you when you can be allowed back in."

Bill had come out into the hallway when he heard Marie Louise talking. He walked over to them. His thoughts concerned the girls as he was afraid of how they would take this incident. He spoke to the nurse. "Thank you. . . . Do you think we can get some medication for the girls? This excitement and the apprehension of waiting to hear from you may be very difficult for them."

Diane had followed Bill. Settling herself down considerably, she said, "I don't want anything. . . . Now that I know what happened, I'll be all right. It was the thought of that thing being in there that got to me. I'm sorry. I know I lost control of myself for a while."

138

"I don't need anything, either. I'll be all right, too," Marie Louise, still shaking slightly, assured him. "That was thoughtful, Bill. Thank you for being so considerate of us."

The nurse offered, "Are you both sure you don't need something to help you relax? I feel sure the doctor would order it for you."

"We'll be all right without anything, thank you," Marie Louise said to her.

Unable to visit Peter, they left and went to Bill's sister's home. While Marie visited with his sister, Gwin, Diane and Bill sat in the living room. Diane spoke to him. "I still can't understand what happened to Peter. Even if he was having a nightmare of some kind, you'd think he'd have awakened from it and not tried to fight."

While Diane spoke to him, her mind raced trying to make some sense out of the situation.

Bill looked at her as he lit his pipe. "The mind does strange things. When it's under stress, there's no telling what can happen. He may have awakened suddenly, thinking he was still in the apartment, fighting those things that were attacking us."

"That could be what it was, but it's still scary. These past few days have been a nightmare for me. I'll be glad when everything gets back to normal. . . . Having to keep working, too, is difficult. I can't get into my dancing, either. I'm sure it shows when I'm on stage," said Diane.

Bill had offered to help them out financially so they didn't have to work, but they'd refused. He spoke fatherly to Diane. "Most of the people in there know what happened and are understanding, but, it would have been better if you and Marie had taken time off. You know I'd have helped out."

"It seems like a no-win situation, because then I'd have too much time to think. It may be hard working, but at least it keeps my mind occupied. Besides, we have contracts and Fletcher's didn't have anyone to take our places. They probably could have managed without one, but not without the two of us. Besides . . . I've never had to depend on anyone but myself. It's not that I don't appreciate your offer, but I could never look at myself in the mirror if I did accept your money. . . . You are the kindest person I've ever known and, that includes my parents!"

Bill felt close to the girls, even though he'd only known them a short time. He puffed on his pipe and blowing out the smoke, he looked at Diane and said, "In times like these, people have to stick together. I know that you've had hard times, but that hasn't changed you inside. There are a lot of fine qualities that I can see in you."

Diane looked into his eyes, and tears swelled her eyes. She fought to keep them back. Bill moved closer to her, put his arm around her shoulders, and pulled her close to him.

Producing a shy smile through her teary eyes, she whispered, "If you were my age, I'd ask you to marry me."

Bill released her and saw a few tears starting to flow down her cheeks. "If you were my age, you'd have better sense than to want to get married," he kidded her, as he gave her a loving nudge with his elbow.

She burst out in a full teary-eyed smile. "You know how to get me out of a sentimental mood, don't you?" she said and leaned over and kissed him on the cheek.

At that moment, Bill's sister and Marie Louise entered the room. "We can't leave you alone with a pretty girl for five minutes before you have her under your spell," Gwin chided him. She gave Marie Louise a knowing glance and winked. "He'll never change. He's been like that all of his life. . . . Love 'em and leave 'em."

Diane took the cue and challenged Bill with, "You told me I was the only girl you've ever loved in your whole life! Now I don't know who to believe."

"You'd better believe me. You don't think he got to be that old without having left a string of broken hearts along the way, do you?"

His sister, Gwin, was that way. She didn't care who was around when she'd seize an opportunity to reprove him in a kidding manner.

Bill responded, "Trying to get me into trouble, are you? Can't you see this girl loves me more than life itself? Stop your fibbing to her. Before you know it, you'll have changed her mind about marrying me."

Remembering how she'd had her share of unmerciful teasing whenever he'd gotten the opportunity, Gwin kept the pressure on her brother. "Marrying you? At your age, I'd say she was much closer to burying you."

Bill nudged Diane with his elbow. "Marrying is what I said. We've had the preliminaries, and we're all set to tie the knot. If you keep on talking that way, you won't be invited."

Marie Louise chuckled to herself as she silently observed the family jousting. Then, unable to contain herself any longer, she blurted out, "You're a bunch of crazies, but I love you all!"

Diane also had sat quietly enjoying the jovial mirth. Finally, she said, "I haven't enjoyed myself this much in a long time and I hate to change the subject, but we'll be late for work. I have to shower and get ready now. . . . I'll have to leave you two to kiss and make up." Then she patted Bill's knee before getting up to leave.

Marie Louise looked at her watch. "As much as I hate to admit it, you're right. Time does fly when you're having fun." Then, turning to Bill, she asked, "Can you drive us?"

"I wouldn't have it any other way. Your wish is my command."

Gwin frowned. "That proves my point. Because I'm not young and pretty, he'd tell me to get a cab."

Bill grinned. "Right."

The following day Bill was up early when the hospital called, "Yes, this is Bill LaBark. We've been expecting your call. Thank you," he said and hung up the phone. Then, he called to Marie Louise who was in the kitchen, "That was the hospital. We can see Peter today. . . . Wake up Diane so that we can have breakfast and get there early."

"All right, I'll get her. I'm so glad we can get to see him. How is he doing?"

"I didn't ask. That was a nurse's aide who called. He must be doing all right or they wouldn't allow us to see him."

Later, at the hospital, Bill was in the ICU talking with the charge nurse. In answer to his question about Peter's condition, she said, "His wounds are healing much quicker than we'd expected. It could be the silver nitrate solution we're using, or it could be because he's young. But, you can almost see the new tissue growing and filling in the open area. Dr. Martin was amazed at the progress he's making. He's stirred a number of times, but he hasn't tried to get up like he did yesterday. The doctor has kept him under heavy medication. But, we're baffled by the guttural sounds and what appears to be a deep growling noise that he makes occasionally. I've never heard anyone do that before."

"It does sound strange. Do you think a part of his mind could have been damaged and have affected him in that way?"

"That could very well be. They did an EEG on him yesterday afternoon, which was normal, and they'll be running some tests on him this afternoon that may indicate something."

"Thank you for everything you're doing for him."

Peter lay motionless in the bed when Bill entered the room. As if in response to Bill's thoughts about him, Peter slowly rolled his head over so as to face him.

This sent a rush of hope through Bill. Peter's eyelids opened slowly, revealing rapidly moving eyeballs as they rolled in their sockets. Bill's excitement quickly vanished when he saw this uncontrolled oscillation. He called out, "Nurse, can you come here? There's something happening to him that you should see!"

The nurse came running into the room. "Oh, my God! I'd better call the doctor!" she exclaimed. Then, turning to Bill, she said, "Watch him for me!" and she rushed to the desk.

Bill remained a few minutes with Peter until the nurse returned and gave him a shot. Then he asked, "Do you think this could mean he will be regaining consciousness soon?"

"It's hard to say what it could be," she answered as she inserted a thermometer into Peter's quivering mouth. "He has been unusual in many ways, especially the way that his wounds have been healing so rapidly. It's uncanny. The monitors have been within the normal range, so I don't think this upset is significant. We'll know more if he does regain consciousness. You'd better leave, now. We'll call and let you know when you can return."

Bill went to the lounge where the girls were waiting.

Seeing Bill's face, Marie Louise became concerned and said, "You weren't in there very long." Then she inquired, "Is there something wrong?"

"I hope not. He opened his eyes and they started rolling uncontrollably. They're checking him now and will let us know when we can see him again. . . . Why don't we have a cup of coffee while we're waiting?"

Diane got up from the couch. "That sounds good to me. I could go for something sweet to go with it."

Marie Louise looked at her and asked in surprise, "You've just eaten and you're hungry all ready?"

"Maybe I'm getting to be hypoglycemic. Lately, I've had a craving for sweets."

Bill winked at Marie. "She's still a growing girl, so it won't hurt her to eat a little extra now and then. They say it's not the first one that's bad for you, it's the ones that follow that put the weight on. . . . Besides, with everything that's happened lately, you've been very nervous. You're probably burning up more sugar from your blood than normal. Besides, I'm glad it's you that has the craving because food looks better on you than me."

Looking at him, she commented, "Oh, you!" Then she said, "I hope you're right, that I'm burning it up. I'd hate to think it was all going to waste . . . mine!" She paused. Then, picking up her purse, she said, "I'm ready, let's go."

Once in the cafeteria, they settled into a booth in the corner across from the entrance. The room was comparatively empty, and the waitress came over shortly after they'd seated themselves. Her brown eyes twinkled beneath her blond bangs. "Would you like menus?"

"Not really," Bill responded. "I'd just like to borrow a cup of coffee. If you'd like, you can have it back when I'm through with it."

"No, thanks. I mean, you can have the coffee, but I don't want it back. I know the process." Then, blushing and smiling shyly, she asked, "Do you want coffee, then?"

"Right, cream only."

Pointing, she said, "The cream is right there." Then, turning to the girls, she asked, "What would you like?"

Diane looked at Marie Louise. A sheepish smile developed at the corners of her mouth. "Do you have any rolls with chocolate frosting?"

"Sure. We have cream-filled long johns with chocolate on them."

"That sounds good. I'll have one of those with coffee."

Marie Louise frowned slightly at Diane and shook her head. She glanced up at the waitress and ordered, "Just coffee."

"Would any of you like sugar?"

"Please," Diane requested.

When the waitress had left, Marie Louise looked at Bill and asked, "You always have to come up with your one-liners, don't you, Bill?"

"The time passes faster for people when you make them smile and feel good inside. She may have been a little embarrassed, but she'll get over it," Bill answerd with a grin.

Then his face took on a serious look. "I had a strange dream last night. It started with me being in a basement. The lights kept getting dimmer, and I had the feeling that I wasn't alone. I climbed the stairs and when I got to the top, I looked down and at the bottom, there was black smoke starting to form into something."

He noted by the look on their faces that they'd become apprehensive. "Maybe I shouldn't tell you about it," he suggested.

Marie Louise patted his arm. "It's all right, Bill. We're big girls now."

Diane nodded agreement, so he continued. "I threw what I had in my hands down at it, but it passed right through as it formed into a man. He came floating up the steps toward me. I ran from the doorway and grabbed a chair. When the thing came at me, I punctured its stomach with the leg of the chair. Emerald-green slime oozed out, and he slowly disappeared back down the stairs. I lost my fear and went after him, but the top of the steps was covered with a thick black film. I broke the film, and the room started filling up with soot and plaster dust. Suddenly, I felt I had power over whatever it was, and I started commanding all this dirt and dust to go back down the stairs. An intense wind from behind me started blowing it into the basement on my commands.

"When I woke up, I was saying over and over, 'I command you to go to hell . . . straight back down to hell.' "

Marie, who was listening intensely, said hopefully, "That is strange. Maybe it means you'll have power over whatever it was that attacked us, if it tries to do anything again."

Diane looked at Bill and noticed that his eyes were steel gray as he spoke. "I don't usually take dreams seriously, but this one was too real. I felt when I woke up that it had a meaning. Of course, it could be that what happened has got my mind playing tricks on me," he admitted.

Putting her hand through Bill's arm, Diane said, "I believe what Marie said. You're a wonderful and good man. Maybe God is telling you not to be afraid of that devilish thing."

The waitress arrived with their order. Bill looked up from talking with the girls and commented, "Not much business today, I see."

"Right. It's just like downtown, only not so crowded."

Diane smiled at her. "I like that. It's a cute way of putting it."

She smiled back as she set their order on the table and asked, "Is there anything else that you'd like?"

"Not right now, thanks," Bill answered. Then, turning to Diane, he said, "It's just that I try to keep my life in perspective. I don't expect from others what I'm not willing to give myself. Too many times people want to give of themselves only ten to twenty percent and expect others to give the other eighty or ninety percent. That just doesn't work, and so they may become unhappy with God and blame him. I believe that there is a God and that He has power over evil, so you may be right."

Bill poured his cream and after stirring it, he took a sip. Putting the cup down, he added, "Jesus Christ said, 'Even as I do, you also can do.' So, in a way, we all have power over evil." Then, momentarily thinking about it, he shook his head in agreement. "You could be right about this dream having the meaning of power over that evil."

Diane questioned, "But, how do we really know there is a God? He's never answered my prayers when I needed him."

Bill looked over his cup at Diane, and he sipped more coffee. He put it down and answered, "No one ever knows for sure, but you have to believe in something first before it can become reality for you. No matter what you want in this life, you've got to believe it is possible. If you don't, you'll never try to achieve it. That means having faith in what you believe in. The stronger your faith, the more you believe. But, before, you believe or can have faith, there must be some evidence that it is possible."

He took another drink and continued. "I look at it this way. Everything in this world had to come from somewhere. However it was created, there has to be something of a miracle in each living thing to be able to function so perfectly without conscious involvement. Take people, for example. Either our original ancestors were a hell of a lot more intelligent than we are, if they created our bodies so perfectly, whereas we can't even grow hair on a bald head, or there is a God that created us. I firmly believe in a God Being unquestioningly. A God that is in all there is around us."

Attempting to accept what Bill had said as being true, but being

144

skeptical of God's motives and wondering if He really does exist, Marie Louise asked, "If there is a God that is all-good and perfect, why does he allow hurt and pain in this world? . . . Take innocent babies born with defects, or . . . take Peter, for instance. He is a good person. Why did He allow this to happen to him?"

"That's the part I have the most problem with. I'm sure most people find that difficult to understand. I guess if we didn't have adversity in our lives, we may not be able to recognize pleasure. You have to know one to know the other."

Marie Louise had always questioned God's reasons for allowing the world to be as it is. She was skeptical. "But some people have a lot more pain and suffering than others. Some people have life easy and they're bastards, while others are good but are tormented and plagued with problems. I don't think that's fair."

Bill appeared thoughtful as he paused, packed tobacco into his pipe, and lit it. He looked intensely, first at Diane and then at Marie Louise before speaking. "I know that you've both led hard lives and had many difficulties to overcome. You've drifted from the straight and narrow path of righteousness out of necessity. I also know that you have a beauty within you that you don't want to lose. I believe you've come to a turning point in your lives now."

He paused and pulled hard on his pipe, exhaling a large cloud of smoke. "It may be the shock of the reality of what's happened in the past few days that may have made you realize that you're not immortal and your life could end quickly. I can tell this by the sincerity in your faces. As you know, I don't have all of the answers, but you are right about the disparity in people's lives."

Bill was silent momentarily, thinking of how the world held mysteries that neither he nor they could explain. Again he puffed on his pipe, then he turned to Marie Louise. "You said this life isn't fair. . . . My dear, that's the reality of it all. There is no real fairness here on earth. If you really want to find fair, you have to go to the dictionary to find it. Even though we have the ability to give our lives a certain amount of direction, we are still dependent on fate."

He leaned back and puffed on his pipe. "Many times fate is influenced by the interactions of others. Take the situation where two people collide with their autos. If one of them dies, members of his family may look at his death differently. One member, who strongly believes in God or fate, may believe the road conditions had caused the accident and it was meant to be and, therefore, fate was the reason. Another may blame the other driver for carelessness. Still another may blame themselves for allowing the dead person to go out in poor driving conditions."

Marie nodded her head, agreeing. "I understand what you're saying. Everyone looks at things differently."

Bill relit his pipe and continued. "Yes, that's basically the way we are. The world to us is dependent upon how we perceive it to be. As an example, I may perceive you to be one kind of person based upon what I see in you when you're with me. Because we all interact differently with different people, we give those people a different view of how we are. You are to that person ONLY what they perceive you to be. Their perception of you is totally limited to their contact with you and what you have allowed them to know about you."

Diane asked inquisitively, "Are you saying that we all wear a differnt disguise with everyone?"

"Yes, that's what it amounts to, to a certain extent. Or, we can show the same side of us to different people, and they might all think of us in the same way. The disguise depends upon who or what the other person is like, how well we know them, and how much we like them. It is also dependent upon how the other person is or acts toward us. So you see, there are many variations possible in each of us, and it becomes impossible for us to really know another person completely," Bill said, trying to give the girls some insight on how he believed people were. Then he added, "Or, for that matter to even know ourselves."

Marie Louise joined in. "I know people who say that when stories of their home life are compared to a sibling's, it's like they were raised in different families. I've wondered about that, and now it makes more sense to me."

"As I said, people are to us as we perceive them. If I perceive you to be a certain way, I may get upset if you do something unexpected that I don't like. If you disappoint me, I may also get very upset. It may very well be that you were that kind of person all along and I didn't perceive you to be that way. Or, you may have known that if I knew certain things about you, I would be upset. Then you wouldn't show that side of yourself to me."

Bill took another drink of coffee and continued. "The more a person cares about another, the more upsetting it is when they find out the person isn't as they perceived them to be. That is why a person in a relationship who fears losing their lover may hide a lot of the bad sides of themselves. When they relax in the security of marriage and become themselves, the other person may feel, 'Where is the person I knew? Where did this one come from?' They may feel disillusioned with the person and not trust them anymore because they weren't honest in the beginning. When both people are playing head games, the relationship doesn't have a chance to survive."

Marie Louise nodded in agreement. "A lot of people are like that nowadays. I've known quite a few."

Bill looked at her and said, "Right." Then he continued. "The problem really occurs early in the relationship when it is fragile. Honesty and sharing inner feelings makes a person vulnerable, and the relationship could end because of what they've seen in the other person. That's when they start playing games to hide the real person they themselves are, in an effort to keep the other person. Once they start playing, they can't seem to quit. . . . It is far better to be consistent and sincere with everyone and lose a person because they see things in you they don't like, than to win them with deceit."

Diane added to the conversation. "I've had friends who see the problems they're getting into before they get married. They'd think they can change them after marriage, but they never could. . . . I have a girlfriend who was convinced that she could change her boyfriend once they were married. She's been very unhappy with him because he hasn't changed a bit. . . . She's probably still trying, if I know her."

Marie Louise, who had been quiet, said, "There are some of my friends who got married and just gave up on everything when they found out they couldn't change their husband. Their lives are passing them by, now. They would have been better off if they'd learned, before they got married, to accept the whole person just as they are. I can see that, now."

She leaned back in the booth, feeling a great deal of respect for Bill as she concluded, "You seem to know a lot about people. Did you take psychology courses in college?"

Bill answerd, "I never went to college, just the school of hard knocks. . . . I've found that you don't change people. They only change themselves. You can give them insight as to why a change would be beneficial for them, and that's all you can do. It's like the saying, 'I can't make you do it. I can only make you wish you had.' People always end up doing what they consider right for themselves."

Marie Louise looked at Diane then at Bill. "Not that I want to change the subject, but I've been thinking very seriously about starting to go to church again. I've been in a rut with my life and I want to get it back together. It's been years since I've gone, but I know that I'll feel much better when I do go," she admitted and added, "I really have the feeling this is a good time to make a break in my life-style."

Bill placed one hand over Marie Louise's and looking at the seriousness written on her face, he said, "I'm sure you won't regret making that decision. . . . Peter mentioned to me that you want to go to college. You can be assured that ifyou ever need help, I'll do whatever I can to help you to get an education. In this day and age, it's one of the few ways to be able to earn a decent living."

"Thank you, Bill. I did tell him that I wanted to go back to school. . . . I meant high school. I quit in my senior year. I have to finish that first. I do intend to go to college, though, but I want to make it on my own."

"Whenever it might be that you do, if you need my help, I'll be there for you," Bill said to her and then glanced at his watch. "We should get back upstairs and see if they've finished with Peter."

A short time after they'd returned to the lounge, a nurse came in and said to Bill, "Your friend Peter was conscious for a few moments, and he called your name. Then he lapsed back into unconsciousness. I reported it to Dr. Martin, and he felt it was a sign he may recover quickly. He'll be running tests on him in an about an hour. . . . We don't understand why he makes those unusual sounds, though. At times they're more animal than human, and he does have what appear to be slight seizures."

Bill listened to her attentively, then said, "I guess, all that we can do now is to pray he'll be all right. I've been very concerned about him, but now I've placed his life in God's hands."

"A lot of us have been praying for him, too," the nurse informed him.

"Can we go in to see him?" Marie Louise asked.

"He's resting quietly. . . . One of you can go in, now."

Bill thanked her. Then, turning to Marie Louise, he said, "You girls will have to go to work soon, so you go in first. It's a good thing that he's able to talk. I was worried he might be like some stroke victims who have brain paralysis and aren't able to speak right, afterward."

Marie Louise offered, "It does sound good to me, too. . . . Even though I do want to see him, he asked for you. Maybe it would be better if you're in there with him, when he wakes up again. If he is able to talk, he may want to talk with you first."

"I appreciate your thoughtfulness, but I know that he will want to see you, too. We'll wait. You go in," Bill assured her.

Marie Louise went to Peter's bedside. She found the pillow and sheets wet with sweat, so she informed the charge nurse.

The nurse informed her, "He's been sweating a lot. . . . He's also been very restless at times, thrashing around in bed. We've had to sedate him quite heavily, rather than restrain him, to prevent him from injuring himself. We'll change him when you leave."

Marie Louise took Peter's hand in hers and sat quietly by his bedside. After a while, she spoke softly to him. "Peter. This is Marie. We're praying for you to get better. The nurses tell us your shoulder is healing

148

much more quicky than they had anticipated. That means you will be able to be released soon. We want to have you back with us."

She paused and sighed, squeezed his hand, and continued. "I know that you may not be able to hear me. If you can, please show me some kind of a sign." She paused again and watched him intensely, but there was no noticeable movement. Still holding his hand, she gently massaged the back of it as she remembered their first meeting.

A sense of shame crept over her as she realized the type of person he must have believed her to be. She thought about how callous she was and how his friendship had made her see what she'd become. She thought also about Bill. He was Peter's friend, but she knew he was her friend now, too. The conversation she'd had with him made her realize there were still some kind people in the world. She was glad her eyes were now opened as to how her limited contact with people had narrowed her perspective of them as a whole. She thought about how special a person Bill was and how lucky Peter was to have him for a friend.

As she sat, deep in her thoughts, she felt Peter's hand move slightly. Brought back to reality, she sharpened her awareness and peered intensely at his face. Seeing his eyelids flutter slightly, she spoke to him. "Peter. Can you hear me? It's Marie."

His eyelids continued to flutter. She waited with bated breath for him to speak. Then, she realized his movements were involuntary as they increased in intensity. His hand jerked from hers as both of his arms started to flail the air around him.

"Nurse!" she called out.

The R.N. dashed into the room. Surveying the situation at a glance, she returned to the nurses' station to get an injection. In an instant she was back. "Can you hold his arm while I give him a shot?" she requested.

"I think I can," Marie agreed and held his arm as best she could. Then the nurse said, "He appears to be having another seizure." She quickly checked the syringe and squirted air and a small amount of liquid from it. Within seconds the needle punctured his skin. Deftly, the medication was administered and the needle removed. "He'll rest comfortably now. You can stay with him," she said as Peter's arms began to relax.

"Thank you. . . . I should leave and allow one of his other friends in, if that'll be all right."

"Certainly," she agreed with a knowing smile.

Marie returned to the lounge and explained to Bill and Diane what had happened.

Bill looked downward. "I may have been getting my hopes up too soon. He may not be doing as well as I've persuaded myself to believe. . . . I know he'll need our patience and understanding. When I heard how quickly his wounds were healing, I guess that led me to believe his mind was healing just as fast."

"It's a natural assumption," Marie Louise agreed. "I felt that way, too."

"You'd better go in to see Peter. We'll wait for you." She paused and admitted, "I haven't said so many prayers in years, as I've been saying for him."

Chapter 8

THROUGH THE SANDS OF TIME

Two weeks later, Bill and the girls were continuing to visit Peter. Feelings of disappointment and frustration filled Bill's heart. Peter was not conscious during the times he was at his bedside. The nurses had reported to him that although there were times he would say a word or two, the periods when he appeared to have seizures were getting more frequent. The dosage of the sedatives had to be increased to control his involuntary thrashing as he grew stronger. The guttural, animalistic sounds were also becoming more frequent. Bill was in the hospital lounge waiting to see Peter when Doctor Martin came in to see him.

"Good moring, Mr. LaBark."

Bill stood up and walked over to greet him. "Morning, Doctor." Then he asked hopefully, "How is Peter today?"

"That's what I'd like to talk with you about. Since we can't ask his family about him, I was hoping you might be able to help us. Has he ever had any type of seizure in the past that you know of?"

"He never mentioned anything to me. As far as I know, he's never had any medical problems."

"What about allergies?"

"None, I'm aware of."

"His condition has been bothering me. We've tried all of the known medications to control the seizures, with little effect, so we have to sedate him. Even though there are similarities to seizures, I've come to the conclusion that he is not having them. I'm beginning to think that it's something else. . . . I've had consultation with some specialists, and they agree. They don't know what to make of it, either. At present, his mental condition is very unstable. I would like to reduce his medication, but

I'm afraid that he could injure himself or someone else. A few times we've had problems, and we can't take any chances. His strength is increasing daily, and his wound has healed beyond belief," he said, slowly shaking his head.

"I'd say it has taken less than one-hundredth of the time it would normally have taken, which is unheard of. It's nothing short of a miracle. We had figured that he would need plastic surgery to dress up the scars, but the healing process is so complete that it appears there won't be any visible signs of the wound. . . . I had hoped that you could shed some light on this mystery."

Bill looked at the doctor, then out the window, then back at him. His face mirrored the heavy weight he carried in his heart. "I'm sorry that I can't help you. . . . We've been praying for him. When I heard he was healing so quickly, I was convinced God had heard our prayers and was working a miracle. Now I'm wondering why He would heal his flesh so rapidly and allow his mind to be so troubled."

"We can't keep him in the intensive-care unit any longer, and his condition is too unpredictable to place him in a regular hospital bed. . . . I've ordered him transferred to the psychiatric unit. . . . We felt it would be best for all concerned to have him there for observation. . . . Don't be alarmed to find him restrained. It's for his own protection."

Bill looked down. "I understand. It's hard for me to see him this way after knowing the kind of person he was before he was attacked."

Dr. Martin showed his concern. "Is there anything you might remember from what happened to him that could possibly have something to do with the way he is, now?"

Bill shifted his weight to his other foot before answering. "As I told you before. I didn't actually see it happen. Whatever it was attempted to kill me first. Peter came in and helped me, and that's when all hell broke loose. The whole place came alive. There was something evil there. I don't know why we were attacked. None of it makes any sense. But, there was something half-animal that spit fire from its arm at us when we were leaving. It could have been something like that, that struck his shoulder."

Doctor Martin turned to leave. "Okay, I guess that's all we have to go on, but that doesn't explain his mental condition. . . . If anything does come back to you that may have some bearing on what's happening to him now, I'd like to know. I've been trying to find someone with some experience in dealing with the supernatural, but haven't found anyone as yet. The nurses have reported that sometimes he acts more animal than human. I didn't want to upset you, but it has me baffled."

"It has me stumped, too," Bill said as he felt his heart sink lower in despair over his friend's condition. "Has he been moved yet?"

"No, they will make the transfer tomorrow. You can go in to see him."

"Thank you. I know that you've done everything possible for him," Bill said, and the doctor left.

Bill went in to be with Peter, who was perspiring profusely as he lay unmoving in bed. He walked slowly as with measured steps to the chair in the corner, took it by the back, and slowly slid it across the floor to Peter's bedside. Seating himself, he stared blankly at his friend and drifted off in thought.

Time became Bill's relentless enemy, and it seemed to him like an eternity since Peter's admission to the hospital. Dragging him through restless and intermittent sleepless nights, it kept him tired. Sitting with Peter now, he recalled the times they'd spent together. Times when he'd seen significant changes in his personality while they'd been traveling together.

Blinking back the torrent of tears that threatened to gush from beneath his eyelids, Bill thought about the love that had developed between them. He cursed under his breath. These feelings of love made him a prisoner of hurt. They had ravaged his life, making it unbearable at times. He also thought about the aimless, sequestered drifting he'd been doing since the death of his wife before meeting Peter. He'd had no real meaning then, either. He realized that life was enjoyable only when he had someone to share it with. He cursed again as once more, his eyes focused through their hazy obstructions upon Peter's motionless form.

Changing his point of concentration, his thoughts turned to Marie Louise and Diane. He knew they were good kids at heart. Girls who had gone astray as many do, when they don't have a close, loving family. He thought about the changes he'd seen in them and also about how he'd come to love them, too. In thinking about them, Bill began to feel better about his life. He remembered how they were giving him support when feelings of depression would take over his thinking. He'd tried to help them, and he realized they had helped him, also. He remembered how their canceling the job in Spokane and becoming "house girls" for an additional few weeks at Fletcher's had kept the three of them together. He knew they couldn't stay on indefinitely and eventually would have to leave.

As he thought about this, feelings of abandonment crept over him. *The girls will soon be gone,* he pointed out to himself and thought, *I should go with them. There really isn't any point in remaining here, if Peter remains the same as he is now.* This thought tightened his stomach into a knot.

"WHY ME?" he uttered half-aloud. Then, he turned his focus on the open window.

The soft warbling of a bird in a tree nearby had caught his attention. "You don't know how lucky you are to be free of the pain that love brings," he whispered under his breath.

"Bill, is that you?" Peter asked, exerting much effort as he shook his head in an attempt to focus his rolling eyes.

"Yes, Peter! Thank God you're all right! . . . Thank you, Lord!" Bill blurted out as his heart leaped up into his throat with excitement. "You're awake! I thought I was hallucinating!"

"Bill. I've been worried about you," Peter whispered.

Bill stood up and walked over to his bed. "Worried about me? I've been worried about you, Pete! I thought that you'd blanked out on me!"

"Not a chance," Peter answered softly. Then he asked, "Are Marie and Diane all right? I've been worried about them, too."

Bill's hopes soared to unmeasurable heights fueled by Peter's alertness. He answered, "Yes, they're all right. They've been praying for you. We all have!"

"Thank you. I'll need your prayers."

Bill could see the effort it took for Peter to talk. He said to him in a fatherly way, "Don't try to talk if it's too hard for you."

"I'll be all right. Where are Marie and Diane?"

"They're both working."

"Tell Marie that I want to see her."

"I will. She'll be here tomorrow. . . . She's been worried stiff about you. You're all she talks about."

Suddenly, Peter's face tensed.

Bill reached out and took hold of his hand. "What's the matter, Peter?"

Peter didn't answer. His eyeballs started quivering in their sockets.

"Nurse!" Bill called out.

The nurse responded immediately and arrived with a syringe of medication. "Hold his arm. He'll be all right after he gets this."

Bill complied with her request. Almost immediately, he saw Peter's expression change as his tensed muscles relaxed.

"I could hear muffled sounds. Was he talking?" she inquired.

Bill passed on to the nurse what he'd said.

"That's encouraging. Perhaps he's not as bad as we'd thought. He has a tremendous amount of strength when he has the attacks. We're not staffed in here for that kind of thing. . . . He's being moved to the psychiatric unit, tomorrow."

"Yes, I know. Dr. Martin told me about it before I came in."

"I'll inform him that Peter spoke to you. I'm sure he will be relieved to know he was coherent," she said and added, "Doctor's been very concerned about him."

Bill glanced at Peter's pathetically motionless form, then turned to look at the nurse. "I was pretty depressed before he spoke to me. My heart almost jumped out of my body when I heard him. I thought it was voices in my mind."

"I'm sure it must have been reassuring to you to hear him speak."

"It was. My heart is still racing from it. I would imagine he'll be out for a while. . . . I'm going to leave now," Bill said as he removed his coat from the rack.

"Yes, he will. We'll inform you if his condition changes."

"Thank you. I may be back in a few hours, if that's all right."

"That'll be fine."

Bill turned to leave, then asked, "By the way, are there any visitor restrictions on the psychiatric unit?"

Smiling pleasantly, she informed him, "No. You can all visit him together, there."

A few hours later, that afternoon, Bill was a few blocks from his sister's home. The sun was shining through a haze of light fluffy clouds. His day had turned around for him and instilled a new purpose in his remaining in town. The shadows that clouded his future were replaced by a jubilance over the fact that Peter appeared normal in the short conversation they'd had. He felt as though the anchors on his life were being lifted. As he walked along the edge of the city park, his spirits soared. Now he was able to see the world from a different perspective.

A black squirrel scrambling along an overhead tree branch caught his attention. "A few hours ago, I wouldn't even have noticed you," he remarked aloud.

His thoughts turned to how wonderful it is to be emotionally free.

Although he'd tried to shake it, the burden of fear for Peter's recovery had weighed heavily on his mind. It was his constant companion. Now, Bill was excited in believing Peter would recover, but he was still concerned about the seizures. He realized Peter's having spoken to him wasn't a complete reassurance that he wouldn't have mental problems. He believed the seizures, or whatever they were, might inhibit his progress. Walking over to a park bench, Bill seated himself on one side.

A second black squirrel joined the first. They sat on a limb a few feet apart, chattering at each other. Smiling, Bill said to them, "A family squabble, eh?"

One of the squirrels looked down in his direction and chattered as if to say, "You keep out of this! Mind your own business!"

Bill chuckled to himself and muttered, "Guess you told me."

He noticed a woman trying to teach her small child to hold onto the ropes of a swing, which she gently pushed. Fascinated, he watched her coaching the young girl.

So engrossed in watching the woman was Bill that she commanded all of his attention. He was startled by a rustling noise beside him on the bench. He had not heard anyone approach and tensed against attack. Turning his head slightly, he saw an old woman who appeared to be in her late seventies. She had seated herself at the far end of the bench. His first reaction to her was a feeling of empathy, because of how pathetic she looked.

Sallowed skin stretched tight over protruding cheekbones identified her plight. *A bag lady,* he thought. She looked straight at him, with obvious interest, while he sat quietly studying her through the corner of his eye, expecting to be asked for a handout. Moments that seemed like hours passed between them without the advantage of speech. He turned to look directly at her. Pale-green eyes peered back at him from beneath a faded light blue scarf she wore on her head. Her bleak attire and frail body was heart-rending and tore at his sensitive inner feelings.

"Isn't this a beautiful day we're having?" he volunteered.

She did not respond. Her eyes fixed themselves on his. Silence once more prevailed.

He looked away from her gaze and unable to resist, he looked back and asked inquisitively. "Is there something that I can do for you?"

She answered in a weak voice. "I wonder if you would be kind enough to carry my grocery bag for me? It isn't very far to my home, but I don't think I can make it the rest of the way on my own. . . . I would be able to pay you."

"Certainly, I will. Are you able to walk all right? I don't live far from here. I could get my truck and give you a ride," he volunteered.

"No, that would be too much bother. I don't want to cause you any trouble. I'm sure that I can make it."

"Would you like to rest a while, first?"

"Yes, for a few moments. I suppose that I should introduce myself. I'm Angeline Karsti. You can call me Angie. . . . What's your name?"

"Bill LaBark. . . . I'm pleased to meet you, Angie."

"I don't have the energy that I once had. This old body of mine has seen better times, but that was long ago when my husband was alive," she said in a pitifully sad voice that was just above a whisper.

Finding it hard to hear her, Bill moved closer. "I would imagine that life has been hard on you," he said.

"Yes, it has. But my husband and I did have a good life together,

156

when he was alive. We had a new home, a car, and everything we wanted. John owned a hardware store here in town." She appeared to Bill to want to talk, so he let her continue. "We had everything going for us when he died."

"How long ago was that?"

"He died eight months after our son was killed in 1944 during World War II. His ship was torpedoed off the coast of Japan. It broke John's heart when they told us about it. The doctor said it was a heart attack, but I'm sure he died from grief."

Bill could see tears in her saddened eyes. She held a slight smile at the corner of her mouth in evidence of the pride she carried inside of her. She went on, "He didn't want to be insurance-poor, so he had only a small life-insurance policy. It all went for the funeral and only part of the doctor's bill. I had a little savings that I paid the hospital bills with. I know now that I should only have paid them a little at a time, but I didn't want any bill collectors hanging around my door. I should have used the extra money to keep the store going."

She paused and breathed deeply. "I was a housewife, not a business person. I couldn't afford to hire anyone to run it for me, so I lost that too. But, that was years ago. I've been dragging this bundle of bones around for too many years now. . . . God willing, it will all be over soon."

She sighed, as she paused to catch her breath. Bill's heart went out to her. He realized she was another one of the Great Society's rejects, who had been forced into a meager existence.

Bill felt a flow of pity pass through his body, as he expressed his honest feelings. "I'm really sorry to hear that you've had such difficulties."

She looked beyond him as she struggled to breathe. "The hard times are almost a thing of the past for me now. . . . I can still hear my mother preaching to me that I should get an education before getting married. I was full of pride once and struggled to live proper. I couldn't get decent-paying work, so I slowly lost that, too."

She breathed deeply. "I had to move a lot. . . . Each time to a smaller place. Pretty soon, my arthritis got the better of me, and I couldn't even get the small jobs that I lived on."

Bill couldn't resist asking, "How did you manage to survive?"

She wheezed, "My sisters helped me out some, for a while. But, even they're gone, now. I'm on a small pension. Social Insecurity, I call it." She breathed deeply, having exerted much of her energy in talking.

Feeling concerned about her health, Bill asked, "Are you all right? . . . Have you seen a doctor lately?

"I know that I'm not healthy, but I'm surviving. I wouldn't be caught dead in a doctor's office. They're all the same. . . . All they can see is dollar signs in front of their eyes when they examine you," she wheezed in short breaths.

Bill offered, "Look, I only live a couple of blocks from here. You wait here and I'll be right back. I'll give you a ride to your home."

"Maybe you're right, son. All of this tongue-wagging has got me tuckered out." Her breath came in shallow spurts. Bill noticed a flicker of gratitude appear in her eyes.

He hurried back with the pick-up. Then, following the directions Mrs. Karsti gave him, he found himself in front of her home. They entered from the alley into her small, duplex apartment. The smell of enclosure hung dank in the air. A thick, musty smell attacked Bill's nostrils, filling his senses with the memory of his grandfather's cellar. He looked around the dimly lit, shabby, dust-filled room. One corner of the dirty, faded ceiling paper hung downward. The loose end rested on the top of a shelf piled high with old papers. In other places, long strips of white tape held large bulging sections suspended. The walls were a barren, faded, calcimine green. Huge sections had chipped away, revealing multi-layer colors along the edges. A small, open sink resting lopsided in a corner, Bill noted, was a relic of the past, just as she was. Small chips in the porcelain were partially covered by a gray-green ragged dish towel. A few mismatched dirty dishes and some silverware cluttered the small kitchen table.

"Please, come in," she invited. "I want to pay you for your kindness."

"Thank you. . . . But I couldn't accept any money," Bill said, as he seated himself on one of the two straight-backed chairs that stood near an old, white painted table.

"You are a kind person. . . . Please, excuse me. I have to go to the bathroom. I'll be right back. . . . Please don't leave," she requested. Then, looking at Bill, she appeared to be afraid she would lose her newfound friend.

He reassured her. "Go right ahead. I'll wait."

As his eyes adjusted to the subdued light, he noticed a shelf over the small stove. It appeared to be her only food storage area. His eyes passed over the items, which were mostly cans. At the end of the row were a dozen cans of dog food. He doubted that she had a pet and found it hard to believe the only other alternative. To his right was her bed. A lumpy, disheveled menagerie of clutter. An indentation identified where she had been sleeping on top of various items that lay on it.

Before long she returned and removed her scarf, revealing thinning hair at the top center of her head. Her remaining dirty, gray hair was cropped short at the sides. If her mannerisms didn't belie her appearance, he might have believed that he'd been lured into a witch's lair.

Not sure how he would accept what she had to tell him, she looked into his eyes as she urged, "Please don't be upset if I tell you something."

A sudden interest showed on Bill's face. "I don't understand. What is it that you think might upset me?"

"I couldn't take my eyes off of you when I first saw you in the park. It was because I've seen you before."

Surprised, Bill asked, "Where have you seen me before.?"

Cautiously watching his reactions through piercing eyes, she replied, "In my dreams."

He allowed himself to be captured by his curiousity. "Tell me about the dream."

"Not just one dream, but many. They've been haunting me for over a week now. Until I saw you, I was confused by them."

"What were they about?"

She answered him almost apologetically. "A very close friend of yours is in very grave danger."

Immediately, Bill thought of Peter and his heart started pounding into the inside of his rib cage. *What can she know about Peter?* he questioned himself. "What kind of danger? Please tell me everything that you've dreamt about us."

She breathed deeply. "They don't make any sense to me. The first one was a very short dream. I remember seeing a young girl in her early twenties. She was dressed very pretty in a white gingham dress. And, she had long blond curls trailing down her back. It was in the springtime, with apple trees in blossom. You were walking down a wooden sidewalk with her. You stopped to pick blossoms from a branch and gave them to her. That's when I woke up. I felt very warm inside to see how very much you loved her. I know the young girl was your daughter." She paused and breathed deeply.

Bill sat with his arms resting on the table as he attentively listened to her. The dream didn't make any sense to him, either. He'd never had a daughter, unless it had something to do with Marie. He wondered if this woman was wrong about him being in her dreams.

When he felt she was able to go on, he stated, "You must be mistaken! Are you sure it was me? . . . Besides, I don't really believe dreams relate to the real world."

Her face grew serious. "My dreams tell me many things. When I smell fresh flowers in them, it means death is in the air. I could smell the blossoms and the sweet honeysuckle, so I knew someone was in danger."

Bill wasn't sure what credence he should put on what she was telling him. "Tell me the other dreams you've had," he prompted her.

She paused, took a few short, deep breaths, then continued. "In a second dream that is still clear in my mind, you were with a young boy and two young girls. It was a bright sunny day, and the four of you were outside. Suddenly, there was a heavy black cloud that formed above the boy's head. It became thicker and dropped down, completely surrounding him. He struggled to free himself, but the outside was made of a strong film that his arms couldn't penetrate. You and the girls tried to help him, but you couldn't break through to him. There was a strong odor of sulfur I could smell," she finished telling him, then wheezed as she breathed deeply once more.

Angeline Karsti consumed Bill's entire interest as he sat watching her. He looked away momentarily. When he glanced back at her, he grimaced slightly. In the dim light, Mrs. Karsti's hollow cheeks and prominent nose gave him the distinct impression he was face to face with a real witch. His interest being too keen to allow anything to upset him, he curbed his distrust before she noticed his reaction. He asked her, "Were there other dreams you can tell me about?"

"There were many other dreams. Those two are the only ones I can remember. My memory isn't too good anymore. I wrote down what I could remember from some of them, but I've lost that paper, too. I didn't expect to meet anyone from in them, anyway, so I don't know why I wrote about them in the first place."

"What do you think these dreams mean?" Bill asked, having been convinced by the second dream that in some strange way they might have something to do with what had happened to Peter.

"In all of the dreams, you looked the same as you do now. That's why I recognized you quite easily. Some of the dreams were from a time long past. . . . .I'd say around the late 1800's or early 1900's. Most of those dreams had something to do with your daughter and you, but there were other people in them, too. The rest of them have to do with the present." She paused and leaned over the table as she breathed deeply.

Bill became concerned about her. "Are you all right?"

"I've had this condition for many years, but I'm not used to talking, since I don't get company anymore. I hope it doesn't bother you that I stop to catch my breath somewhat from time to time."

"Not at all. . . . I can come back another time, if it would be better for you."

"No. Please stay," she requested. Then she paused again to catch her breath. After a few moments, she reached for the small bag of groceries she'd left on the table where Bill had placed them. She reached inside and produced a small bottle of instant coffee. "Would you like a cup of hot coffee?" she inquired of him. "I could heat some water."

"No, thank you," he answered, wanting her to continue. He couldn't help wondering if she might be able to shed some light on what was happening to Peter. Hearing her now renewed his anxiety over his condition. He wondered if she could tell him if Peter's seizures were connected with the demon that had attacked them.

She looked down at the table, then focused her pale eyes on his. "All right, then I'll get back to the dreams. . . . Your daughter in the first dream I told you about is the same person as the young boy in the second one." She watched his reaction intently as she mentioned this.

"Are you telling me that Peter was my daughter in a previous life?"

"Peter. Yes, that was the name of the boy. HE IS the reincarnation of your daughter," she confirmed. "I do remember though, that one of the girl's in the dreams you called by the name of Marie. I don't remember the other girl's name."

Shocked, Bill sat up suddenly. He wanted to continue questioning her to obtain clues that could unravel the developing mystery, but he was hesitant about forcing her to do too much talking for fear she might die from the effort. Questions developed in his mind, now that he was convinced of her authenticity. Knowing she may have information that could help in Peter's recovery, Bill was in a quandary as to whether to continue or to leave and return.

"Why do you think Peter and the girl you say is my daughter are the same person?" he couldn't help asking.

"I just know they are," she explained further. "For many years, people would come over and have me interpret their dreams for them. I must say that I did very well at it, because they could relate them to real events in their lives. They would pay me, and that helped in surviving the hard times."

"Do you know anything else from the dreams that you can tell me?"

"I will think on it. If any thoughts come to me, I will write them down."

"I would appreciate knowing anything at all. Please try to remember any new dreams you have, also. I would be willing to pay you for any information you can give me. Maybe your dreams will tell you if Peter's life is still in danger."

He wanted answers and would do just about anything to protect Peter from continued danger. And, she appeared to be his only hope at the present.

Angeline looked at him thoughtfully. "I don't need much money at this time in my life. Now that I know how important my dreams are, it will be payment enough if I can help to save that boy's life." Then, using her reserve energy, she emphasized, "HE IS STILL IN VERY GRAVE DANGER."

Bill became more upset. The feelings that had warmed his body in the sunlight were gone. His high hopes for Peter's recovery were now shattered. He looked away from the source of his present despair. Fidgeting, he rubbed his hands together while considering her revelations.

Slowly he turned and, looking back into her solemn eyes, he asked, "Is there anything that can be done to protect him?"

"Much will depend upon the boy's own ability to resist the evil force that is trying to destroy him," she wheezed through emphysema-laden lungs. "Please, do not ask any more questions now. I must get some rest. If you can return tomorrow evening, we can talk some more. Maybe I will have rememberd more from the dreams by then," she said. Then while breathing deeply, she grasped hold of the edge of the table.

"I'm very sorry to have put you through all of this. Is there anything I can do for you?" Bill asked, hoping she would not breathe her last breath before he could return.

Sensing his tension and concern, she answered, "No, Mr. LaBark. I have been like this for many years now. Don't be worried about me. My heart is as strong as an ox."

"I'll leave you to get your rest. . . . I really do appreciate your help. . . . Thank you for everything." He stood up to leave. "I'll see you tomorrow, then."

While pulling herself erect, using the table for support, she said, "Yes, please do come by."

Bill left her home and walked to his truck, feeling very down. He pulled himself in behind the steering wheel and sat there thinking. After a few moments, feeling the need for support, he reached behind the seat and brought out his bottle of brandy. He paused and rested the bottle against the wheel. Then looking at Mrs. Karsti's dimly lit curtainless windows, he shook his head.

Uncapping the bottle, he threw down two quick gulps, wiped his lips with his sleeve, and slowly turned his head from side to side. Quickly he swallowed another stiff belt. The warm liquor burned his dry throat and rose up into his nostrils, matching the burning fire his mind had become. Recapping the bottle and setting it beside him on the seat, he started the motor. His first thought was to drive over to Fletcher's to talk with the girls, but he quickly rejected it. He realized the club was no place to be talking about evil spirits. Besides, he reasoned, they don't need this added burden at work. Instead he simply drove through the city, trying to straighten out his own thoughts.

"Isn't that the way life is? The minute you think things are getting

162

better, something comes along to ruin it," he thought out loud in disgust, slowly shaking his head as though trying to understand what was happening in his life. He had always prided himself on his ability to think things through clearly. But, as he drove, he realized how intricate life can become when other people are involved.

"Reality is simple to deal with, compared with the supernatural," he mumbled to himself.

"What you can't see and don't understand seems impossible to deal with," he said aloud.

When problems weighed heavily on his mind, Bill often talked to himself. He pondered the thought of washing his hands of the whole mess and moving on by himself. "It may be a lonesome row to hoe," he thought out loud, "but there's less heartache that way."

Even as he thought this, he knew he couldn't leave his friend alone with his life in danger, especially since Mrs. Karsti had indicated that Peter might be a reincarnation of his daughter from a previous life.

Bill took another swig from the bottle and mumbled, "Funny, I've never believed in that stuff. Now, I'm not even questioning its possibility."

A flashing red neon sign caught his attention. It read "Barnie's Bar." Having driven past it by the time he'd decided to stop, he drove around the block and into the parking lot. He entered the bar with only one thought on his mind. To get so shit-faced drunk that the supernatural and reality would blend into one big nothingness.

"Bartender, I'll have a shot of brandy and a beer for a chaser," he ordered with determination.

The following morning, he felt his bed suddenly shift to one side. Awaking, he realized it wasn't the bed moving; he thumped to the floor.

Bill's sister, Gwin, stood over him. "You big lug! Mother cleaned up after you at home, but don't expect that of me! If you're old enough to get drunk out of your mind, you're old enough to clean up after yourself!" she snapped. "Get your carcass up and clean up the mess you've made in the bathroom and down the hallway!" She was burning mad and had no sympathy for Bill's huge, throbbing head.

He opened his bloodshot eyes one at a time and stared up at her. Rubbing the side of his face, he made an effort to get up. Suddenly, he sank back to the floor, eyes closed.

Muttering under her breath, she left the room. Bill was snoring when she returned. "I'll fix you. . . . This won't happen again, if I can help it," she muttered, half out loud.

Standing over him with a half-smile on her face, she poured the contents from the pitcher—she'd gotten it from the kitchen—onto Bill's head.

Immediately, he came to life. With reflex action, he leaped to his feet in a flash, with water and ice cubes flying in all directions. After shaking his head to throw off the cold water, he glared at Gwin.

She stood mute, stone-faced.

Wiping his unshaven face off with his hand, Bill caught the impact of the situation. He knew from experience she wouldn't back down. "What the hell was that all about?" he demanded.

"I told you when I woke you up! I don't intend to clean up after a grown man! Since you had the pleasure of drinking that rot-gut half the night, you can have the same pleasure in cleaning it up from the bathroom and hallway!"

In slow motion, the reality of the previous night returned to Bill. Knowing he was responsible for the mess, he didn't question the authority of her demand. His glare changed to a sheepish look. "Guess I was sloshed and pretty damned sick last night when I got home. . . . You're right, as usual," he admitted. "I'll clean it up."

Looking like a dog with its tail between its legs, Bill dragged his uncooperative legs along the trail of puke down the hallway toward the bathroom.

The puddle of half-dried barf in front of the toilet made his stomach retch. He knew how particular his sister was about men missing their aim and spraying the surrounding area. So, he raised the toilet seat, and with great effort, straddled the mess, bent his knees, leaned forward, and put one hand onto the toilet tank to steady himself. Attempting to be very careful not to miss, he urinated. The spark knock in his head hammered, as he felt the relief he gained by tapping his bladder.

Watching the never-ending deep yellow stream flowing, Bill muttered, "God, I must have drunk a lot."

While he was still urinating, his left leg suddenly crumpled, twisting him sideways. He fell to the floor, spraying the toilet seat and wall. "Son-of-a-bitch," he cried out, as he struck his elbow against the corner of the sink on his way down.

Marie Louise was in her bedroom fixing her hair when she heard the thud as he struck the floor. Rushing into the bathroom, she was the first one to reach him. Looking down and seeing this half-dressed man struggling to close his zipper, struck her funnybone. She burst out laughing.

"Ouch!" he yelled. In his excitement, he'd forgotten to tuck his penis back into his pants and got it caught in the zipper.

"Want me to help you with that thing?" she offered kiddingly, as she tried to contain her laughter.

"Stop your damned grinning! That hurt!" Embarrassed, Bill tried to control his anger and make light of the situation. "Now I've probably ruined it for life!" he spit out.

Finally, he released the piece of skin that was held fast in the zipper. Marie Louise felt a pang of pity when she saw it bleed like a stuck pig.

"Ah. . . . You poor little thing. Do you want me to kiss you and make the hurt all better?" she offered, still trying to sober her face as she watched him attempt to control the bleeding by applying pressure.

"Get the hell out and close the door!" he commanded. "Do you think I want to be a monkey in a sideshow? Next thing you'll want to sell tickets!"

Wheeling around in time to see Gwin withdraw, Marie Louise left the room, closing the door behind her. Through the door, they could hear muffled cussing. Gwin had not been able to see around Marie Louise, so she asked, "What happened to him?"

Marie Louise grinning, answered, "I don't think he hurt himself very badly. He's just embarrassed more than anything. He caught part of his plumbing in his zipper and it bled a little, that's all."

"Serves him right!" Gwin said sternly. "That ought to be a lesson to him. Maybe now he'll realize that he's not as young as he used to be. . . . I wonder what got into him? He hasn't gotten that pie-eyed in years."

Diane, who had been asleep and was awakened by the commotion, opened her door and peered out. "What's going on?"

Still grinning, Marie Louise explained, "It's just Bill. He got schnookered last night and lost his cookies. I'll tell you about it later."

Bill, embarrassed by the incident, avoided immediate ridicule from the women by taking the back stairs to the kitchen. He got the scrub brush and cleaning supplies and returned to the ordeal of cleaning the rugs. The more the stench of the mixture of beer and half-digested pizza retched his stomach, the more determined he became to never have to clean up such a mess in the future. At first, he'd thought he could blend the cleaned area with the rest of the rug coloring, but when he stood back and surveyed the results, it became obvious he'd have to clean the entire rug. When he finished, his stomach tossed like a goldfish in a jar that had been suddenly overturned. His back ached and his head still attempted to explode, so he fortified himself with antacid and aspirin and headed back to his bed.

Two hours later, Bill entered the living room. His face was bleak, and he was tired.

"Well, well, look who's here, Gwin chided, shaking her head, "Was it worthwhile? . . . You look like death warmed over."

"Go ahead and have your fun," he answered.

Gwin's eyes sparkled and danced. "I thought it was you who had fun last night. . . . When I heard you come in, I was going to come down and have a cup of coffee with you. But, by the time I got my robe on, you were already on the stairs. . . . I almost burst out laughing." Smiling from ear to ear, she paused.

Bill interrupted, "What the hell's so funny?"

"Nothing," she replied, "if you think seeing a grown man crawling up the stairs is normal."

"I don't remember that. You're just trying to make fun of me in front of the girls," he retorted, paused, then added, "On second thought, you could be right. . . . I don't remember much of anything from last night."

Sympathizing with him, Diane offered, "You've had a lot on your mind, with all that's been happening the past few weeks. . . . It was probably good for you to get it out of your system that way."

Remembering the events of the previous day, Bill, looking at the floor and feeling down, said, "It wasn't that so much, compared to what happened yesterday."

"What happened?" they asked, almost in unison.

Bill explained to them what had happened with Peter and then with Mrs. Karsti.

Later that morning, before going to see Peter, Bill brought the girls with him to see Mrs. Karsti. He rapped on her door a number of times, but there was no answer. Becoming worried that she had died during the night, he shaded his face and pressed it against the window, attempting to look into her room. Squinting his eyes, he saw that her bed, which was directly across the room, was empty. Puzzled by her absence, he rejoined the girls in the truck.

"I doubt if she would have let anyone know, if she did have problems," Bill said as he started the engine, "so I don't think she was taken to the hospital."

As he started toward the hospital to see Peter, he added, "We can check, to see if she was admitted. . . . There has to be an explanation to all of this, and she seems to have the key. . . . I hope Peter will be able to tell us something, too."

When they arrived at the hospital, Bill checked with the admitting office to see if Mrs. Karsti had been brought in during the night. He was informed that she was not listed as a patient, so they went to see Peter.

At the nurses' station, Bill asked the nurse in charge, "How is Peter doing today?"

"He ran a temperature last evening, but it's normal now. His wound has stopped draining and is still healing very rapidly. There's only a slight evidence of any injury remaining. That boy's recuperative powers are unbelievable. It doesn't appear that he'll even have a scar, which is truly amazing to me."

Then, glancing at his chart, the nurse continued, "He was restless last night and was awake periodically. Sometimes he would relax and speak a few sentences, but then, it's as though something comes over him. He becomes very agitated, and his voice turns to guttural mumbling and hissing."

She paused. Her face becoming sober, she added, "If I didn't know better, I'd say he has a demon in him . . . The psychiatrist examined him yesterday afternoon and believes that he is developing a split personality. She thinks the mumbling and hissing may be the second one trying to surface."

The telephone rang. Before turning to answer it, she finished, "Please, let me know if anything unusual happens when you're with him."

"We'll do that," Marie Louise answered. Then, looking at the nurse, she asked, "Can the three of us go in together?"

"Yes, there are no restrictions on the number of visitors."

Bill thanked the nurse, and they went to see Peter. He was in a private room that could be used for detention patients. Bill looked into Peter's room and noted the windows were barred, giving the impression of a prison. He realized that when Peter became aware of his circumstances, this would upset him. He remembered the anguish on Peter's face when he had told him of the difficulties he'd had in jail, after the school fire.

When they entered, Peter was lying on the bed asleep. They spoke softly.

"Peter doesn't deserve to have this happen to him," Marie said as she looked at him. "He looks so relaxed. It's hard to believe he's still having problems. I sure hope that old woman is wrong about his life being in danger."

"I'd tend to agree with you if she hadn't mentioned your name. You WERE in one of the dreams, remember?" Bill pointed out.

"Yes, that's been on my mind, too. And, her disappearance makes it even more strange."

Diane spoke up. "There's probably a logical explanation as to why she wasn't at her home."

"We'll stop by on the way back and see if she's there," Bill said.

Peter moved his arm and Marie, seeing this, went over and took his hand in hers. "Peter . . . are you awake?" she asked with anticipation.

He opened his eyes, looked at her for long moments, then smiled. "Marie. . . . It's so good to see you." Then, looking at Diane, he said, "You too, Diane. I thought you girls had left town. You were almost finished working before I ended up here. Bill, are you helping them, too?"

Bill responded, "No, Pete. I would've if they'd let me. They stayed over and are working at Fletcher's, waiting on tables and dancing." He walked over and stood close to Peter's bedside.

Appearing to be quite strong, Peter said, "That's great!" Apologetically, he added, "I haven't been awake very much. . . . Bill was in one time that I can remember, but I've been wondering about you girls. . . . If I'd ever see you again."

Marie Louise asked, "You know that we wouldn't desert you, don't you?"

"I guess I really did, but I've had a lot of dreams about you, Marie. Each time I try to talk to you, you're either too far away or you're too busy talking with someone else, or you've gone away and I'm looking for you everywhere. . . . I can't wait to get out of this place." He glanced around. "This room is terrible. It gives me a horrible feeling of claustrophobia with those bars on the windows. They really get to me. It's almost like I'm back in jail."

Bill tried reassuring him. "I'll talk with the doctor about that and see if we can have you moved."

"Thanks, Bill. . . . How long have I been here?"

Marie answered, "A little over two weeks."

Throwing back the sheet, he exclaimed, "I feel good enough to leave right now!"

Pulling the sheet back onto Peter, Bill said, "Your injury has healed so rapidly that the doctor couldn't believe it, but they still aren't sure if you're having seizures, or if there is something else wrong. When I was talking with you yesterday, something happened. Do you remember that?"

"Yes . . . something took over my body."

"What do you mean 'took over your body'?" Bill asked quickly.

"I get strange feelings when I'm dreaming that there's something inside of me, trying to take over my body. Yesterday, I think something actually did take it over. I could feel the pressure on my skin. It felt like it was going to burst apart. It has the same form as me, but is much larger, and my body isn't big enough for it."

Trying to understand what Peter was having to deal with, Bill asked, "Are you sure that it's something in you?"

"No. . . . I'm not sure what it is. . . . When it happens, it comes on

168

quickly, then I can't remember anything after that. . . . I've been trying to fight, but I don't know what I'm up against and I'm not sure what to do. I don't like the feeling I get just before it tries to take control."

Marie's face grew tense. Scrunching her eyebrows down, she asked, "What kind of feeling do you get? Can you describe it?"

"It's really weird," Peter explained. Then, his eyes tensed up as he continued, "When it starts, it's like I'm talking to myself. Something inside of my head says, 'You don't deserve to live! I'm taking control over this pitiful body. I'll do more with it than you've ever done. You owe me this chance to live again. You will die and I will live.'

"Then I get all nervous inside, and it feels like I'm losing my mind. I see hundreds of colored lights, like lightning flashing in my mind. My body feels like it's tearing apart in all directions. I feel tremors crawling over my entire body. I try to fight off the feeling, but I—like pass out and can't remember anything after that."

Peter pushed himself up onto his elbow. He looked at Bill as though expecting him to have the answers.

Trying to get as much information as quickly as possible before anything happened to make it impossible for Peter to explain, Bill asked, "Does this other person identify itself? Does it have a name?"

"No. It's almost like it's trying to impress on me that I'm not worthy of living. It did say once 'I healed this body of yours for myself. If it had been up to your worthless system, this body would have died.' "

"Have you told any of the hospital's staff about this?" Bill asked.

"No. . . . I haven't had a chance to talk like this before. It has always started taking control just as I begin to wake up. Sometimes I feel like I'm drugged and can't think clearly."

"The nurses have told us that they're giving you medications because you're having seizures. . . . Have you ever had them?" Bill inquired.

"No. I've never had any problems like that in my life."

Diane asked, "How do you feel now?"

"I feel great. Like nothing happened, except that my shoulder feels itchy."

"That's probably the new skin where your wound is healing," Marie Louise offered, Then she asked, "Can we see it?"

"Sure," he responded and then he requested. "Bill, can you help me to remove this pajama top?"

Bill assisted him and they looked at the area in amazement. His shoulder was without bandages. Where a couple of weeks earlier there was a gapping deep, blackened, bleeding hole down to the bone, now the area was a deep red and completely healed over.

Bill was filled with amazement and said, "They told me you have super healing powers, but I wouldn't have believed it if I hadn't seen it myself."

"I can't believe it, either," Peter answered. Then he said, "Now, I'm starting to get that enclosed feeling again. Bill, you know the problem I have with that."

"I sure do, kid. I know you've had it really bad, but you were starting to get over it as we traveled together."

"I know I was starting to lose it. . . . But, when I wake up in here, after a short time, I become restless and want to get out into the sunshine and fresh air. I need to be free of this place. . . . Please do something to get me out of here as quick as possible!"

Marie Louise felt sympathetic and said, "I can understand that. I don't like hospitals any more than you do. When I had my tonsils out, I was only five years old and I tried to get out. They found me in the lobby and brought me back."

"They've sent a psychiatrist in to see me a couple of times, but each time she was here, that thing took over my mind. I don't know what happens after I lose control. . . . I think she believes I'm a head case."

"I'll talk with her. They had some concerns that you've developed a second personality," Bill mentioned and immediately had second thoughts about it being the right thing to tell him. To him, Peter seemed very normal, now. He didn't want to say anthing that might upset him, or give whatever it was that was trying to get control of him, any reason to stop Peter from talking to them. It pleased Bill that for the first time, they had a chance to talk with him at any length. But his thoughts drifted back to the absence of Mrs. Karsti, and it bothered him. And, what she'd told him about her dreams fit in too well with what Peter was telling them now, about his possibly being possessed. The fact that Peter's rapid healing could be explained by the thing inside him, having the power to heal his body for its own purposes, worried him, also.

Peter felt a flow of determination. "Whatever it is, I'll beat it. Life is too important to me to allow anything to ruin it."

With her mind at a loss as to what they could possibly do for him, Marie Louise tried encouraging him. "That's the way, Peter. We're all for you. . . . We'll help you fight it."

"You bet, Peter. We want you out of here and back with us. We've got a lot of living to do." Diane paused, turned, looked at Marie Louise and Bill, then back at Peter, "Marie and I talked it over and, if it's all right with you and Bill, we'd like to be a part of your lives. We know the two of you had planned on going to Seattle. . . . We could go with you and get respectable work."

Peter's eyes lit up, "That'd be great. What do you think, Bill?"

"Sounds good to me, too. First we've got to get you out of here."

Marie Louise felt an urge to cry, but she supressed it. She squeezed Peter's hand. "It's good to see you getting so much better. The doctors told us you might not make it. I was so worried that I couldn't sleep. I thought about you all of the time. . . . I guess that's what made me realize how much I cared for you. Now I can hardly wait to be with you again. You'll see a changed girl in me. We can have a good life together, you'll see." She paused, looked at Peter, and continued, "That is, if you want me."

Peter was momentarily silent, while thoughts rolled through his mind. He recalled his first love, Maggie, and how much he'd hurt inside when they were abruptly separated. He remembered the poem she'd written and given to him on the last day they were together. How he'd read it so many times that the paper became ragged. Now, he was being asked by a girl he cared for, but didn't love, to share her life. He knew he wanted to be with her. And, also, it was an opportunity for the four of them to be together again. There was a need in him to be loved and to show love in return. He wondered if any girl could ever replace Maggie's love.

Not hearing an immediate response, Marie Louise asked, "Did you hear me, Peter? I said that I want to live with you when you get out. We can have a good life together."

Reaching out and taking her other hand in his, he answered, "I know we'll have a good life together. I like being with you, too. It'll be good to be out of here, so the four of us can be together again. . . . We'll have our whole lifetime to be together, and we can learn to love each other."

They visited with Peter as long as possible before the girls had to leave for work. Peter appeared so normal that Bill found it hard to believe he wasn't—that Mrs. Karsti could be right. He hoped whatever it was that loomed over Peter's life, he could succeed in beating before it took control of him forever.

Bill was in good spirits when he left the girls off at Fletcher's and drove to his siter's home. He thought, *Still some time for a round of golf. Maybe Sam Engles will go with me.*

As he drove past the park, he suddenly had an urge to check on Mrs. Karsti. He drove to her home and, passing her window, noticed movement inside. She answered his knock. Her voice had more volume to it. "Mr. LaBark, how nice to see you. Please, come in."

"It's nice to see you, too, Mrs. Karsti. I stopped by this morning, but you were out."

"Oh. That must have been you I heard. I was in the bathroom at the time. When I got out, you had left. I'm sorry I missed you." She smiled and offered him a chair. She wheezed slightly. "How is your friend who's in the hospital?"

"He's doing much better than we'd expected. We visited with him for a long time today, and he was completely back to normal."

She shook her head slowly and breathed deeply. "You mustn't let that fool you. He's a sly one that you're dealing with."

Bill was determined to get some answers. "Do you know any more than you told me the other day?"

"After you left, I remembered some of the other dreams. I wrote them down on a piece of paper and put it in a place where I'd remember where it was." She paused and stood up. "Now, where did I put it? It's hell to get old. My forgetter works better than my rememberer."

Smiling slightly, Bill commented, "You don't have to be old for that to happen. We all have that problem."

While rummaging through the pile of envelopes and papers on the foot of her bed, she commented. "But, it gets worse."

Bill looked around the room, hoping to spot its location. His eyes came to rest on the shelf with her food. Protruding from beneath the dog-food cans was the corner of a piece of paper. He pointed. "There's something on the shelf with your canned food. Could that be it?"

She straightened up and looked at Bill, her eyes twinkling. "My gosh, sure enough. I put it with my food, so I'd see it when I eat."

She laboriously hobbled to the shelf and returned. Seating herself she rested her elbows on the table, and wheezing, breathed deeply. After a few moments, she put on horn-rimmed glasses and read her notes. "Your daughter caused this entity much grief and heartache. It seeks revenge now. It has already caused this boy much unhappiness and wants to control his spirit."

Bill didn't want general information. If he was to help Peter, he knew he had to have as many facts as possible. "Can you tell me specifically what you're referring to?"

"It caused a school to burn and the girl he loved to be taken from him, to destroy his will to live. She was a pretty girl, too, with auburn hair."

He shifted on the chair uneasily. Recognizing the accuracy of what she was telling him, he plied her, "Go on and tell me more."

She looked at him. His face was drawn, and he fidgeted with his hands. Sympathy shone in her eyes. "It tried to destroy him a few months later when it burned the place where he was living."

"That would be the house in the Ozarks," Bill mumbled to himself. He found it unbelievable this haggard old woman could be so accurate in her description of significant events in Peter's life.

Mrs. Karsti sat quietly, breathing deeply, while the rasp of congestion rattled in her chest. Wheezing deeply, she continued, "Now it is trying to control his spirit. If it can't do that, it will destroy his life."

She wheezed again, trying to breathe deeply. Using the table for support, she pulled herself to her feet.

Leaning on the table edge, she said, "I'm feeling rather poorly and need my rest. Please, do come back to see me. I want to help you save your friend from destruction."

Bill stood up to leave. Wanting more information, he asked one more question. "Can you tell me anything else that could help us to stop this thing from destroying him?"

Fighting to breathe, she said, "You know more than you're aware of . . . You've seen the baby."

This revelation caught him off guard. "What baby?" he blurted out instinctively.

"It's mother was your daughter."

Bill was confused. The only baby he could think of was the one he and his wife had had. It was a girl, who had died six months after birth. The doctors hadn't given them much hope of her living into adulthood because of a heart defect. He wondered how she could have had anything to do with what was happening to Peter, now.

Bill needed more information, but he didn't want to press her now. He knew he'd have to return and ask more questions then. He smiled and said. "Thank you, Mrs. Karsti. Please, take care of yourself. I know that you're a good person and God loves good people."

A tear swelled beneath her eyelid, ran to the corner of her eye, and down her cheek. "That's the nicest thing anyone has said to me in years. Thank you for being so kind."

"I meant it. I'll let you get your rest now and will be back again. . . . Good-bye, for now."

"Good-bye, Mr. LaBark. I'm sure God loves you, too. Do what you can to help your friend. Don't be fooled by this entity. . . . It will NOT stop at anything to accomplish the evil it has cast on your friend's life."

The following morning Bill had an appointment with the psychiatrist assigned to Peter's case. Since her office was in the north wing of the hospital, he brought the girls with him. While they visited with Peter, he met with her.

Bill explained to her as much as possible. The tall, platinum blond,

173

her face void of expression, said to him, "From what you've been telling me, Mr. Dunn has not had any mental problems in the past, but he's had a lot of stress in his life."

"I agree. He has had his share of stress in his life," Bill admitted.

"Sometimes this causes latent effects on a person's mind. When the conditions are right, the mind can't handle reality and, as a result, there is a splintering effect that causes a second personality to come forth. The original personality many times is not aware of these other multiple personalities that control a part of their life. Sometimes it slips into the background. In Peter's case, the near-death situation would be enough to trigger this reaction."

Bill couldn't help asking, "Has anyone told you the circumstances of his injury?"

"I've read his chart and had a long interview with him last night. Of course, I've discounted the supernatural part of the incident. I deal in reality and have attributed his version of what happened to a form of hallucination. I think that he's confused the facts with some dreams he may have had while he was unconscious."

"Then you apparently don't believe in the supernatural."

"I think it's a whole lot of rubbish dreamed up by fictional writers trying to make a buck."

"Then you don't believe dreams can have meanings about the past or future, either."

"On the contrary, they do have a lot of meaning. They can help us to understand what is going on in a person's mind. But, mostly they deal with the happenings of the previous day." She paused and looked at Bill matter of factly. "I don't believe you've come to see me about my beliefs, though. Let's talk about your friend, Peter."

"Do you think he has what you call multiple personalities?"

"He has the possibility of having a second personality, judging by the way he describes something trying to take over his body and control his mind. We're going to keep him in the unit for a couple more days to be sure that it is safe to release him. I should know more after we've completed some tests with him tomorrow. If everything checks out, I can see him on an outpatient basis."

"What kind of tests?"

"We'll be giving him an MMPI, for one thing."

"Might I ask what that is?"

"That's a Minnesota Multiphasic Personality Inventory test. It covers a large variety of potential areas we may want to look at in treating him."

"You mentioned there are more tests. What are the other ones for?"

"He has agreed to hypnosis. Sometimes we can reach the second personality in this way."

"Will you keep me informed of anything of importance that you find out from him?"

"He has requested that we release this information to you. Therefore, I will be most happy to keep you informed."

Bill stood up to leave. "I thank you for seeing me. I visited with him for a long time yesterday. He seems normal to me. I hope you can release him as quickly as possible. He does have problems with being in enclosed places, but I'm sure he must have told you that."

"Yes, he did. We've cut his medications down to a light sedative and an antidepressant. These should help to ease his anxieties." She paused, then asked, "Do you have any further questions?"

"No. I can't think of anything else right now, except that I would appreciate it if you could move him into a room that doesn't have bars on the windows."

"I'll see what I can do. Is that all?"

"Yes. Thank you, again."

It seemed obvious to Bill that she fit his opinion of psychiatrists. "They all have a screw loose." As he left her office, he mused, "I guess, you have to be crazy to recognize another one who is."

Bill visited with Peter and the girls and tried to obtain additional information from him without allowing the entity to know that he was aware of its existence. He told them what the psychiatrist had said about a second personality and made it appear that he believed this could be true, not wanting to let the entity know what he really believed.

Later, he drove Marie Louise and Diane to work. Once they were alone in the truck, he felt free to discuss what Mrs. Karsti had revealed to him. After filling them in on all of the details as he knew them, he said, "The accuracy of what Mrs. Karsti knew was uncanny. Although Peter appears completely normal, I believe his life is still in danger. I think it realized that its attempt to take control of him in the hospital resulted in increased medications and a longer hospital stay. Once he is released, it might make a stronger attempt at possession of his body."

Marie Louise listened with keen interest. When he finished, she said, "If it can't overcome his will, Mrs. Karsti said it will destroy him. . . . We'll have to arrange our schedules so that one of us is with him at all times, once he's released."

"That's a good idea. It seems as though this entity has come back through the sands of time to avenge something that happened in a previous life." Bill paused, took his eyes off the road, and looked at the girls. His face was drawn with concern. He looked back and continued. "I've thought a lot about what that old woman said. She may hold the only clues there are to the reason that thing has come here now and how we can free him of it."

Bill drove in silence, deep in thought. A while later, he spoke. "I must admit, this whole thing has me completely baffled," he concluded. "None of it makes any sense."

Diane agreed, "There doesn't seem to be anything she said so far that will help us."

Trying to jog his memory, Marie Louise prodded, "What about the baby? . . . That must be a clue of some kind. She said you know something that has to do with a baby."

Bill responded, "That's the most perplexing part of it all. First, Peter and I are related in some previous life. Now, there's something about a baby that I'm supposed to know about in this life, that's involved with Peter in some strange way."

"It's too deep for my mind to grasp," Diane admitted.

Marie Louise offered, "Mrs. Karsti may have more information than she has given you, or maybe she has forgotten something important. She did write those things down to tell you. Maybe by now she has written more."

"Yes. She does have the only possible answers to this puzzle," Bill admitted. "If she wasn't so fragile, I might have been able to stay longer. Maybe then, we'd have more answers, now." He paused, then added, "I'm sure she knows more about the baby that would help me to re-member what it is she's referring to. After I leave you two off, I'm going right over to her place."

Marie Louise agree, "That sounds like the thing to do."

"The only problem is, I hate to keep pestering her every day. The poor woman hardly has enough energy to get through the day without me draining it from her. Her situation is so pitiful, I feel sorry for her. She's one of the people that the GREAT SOCIETY has forced into humility."

Marie Louise agreed, "It does seem that way. Judging by what she says, she's the only hope that we have to save Peter's life. If she dies without helping us and that demon is in him, he has no chance whatever."

"You're right, Marie. We have to know more about this thing before we can help him fight it."

After leaving the girls off at Fletcher's, Bill went straight to Mrs. Karsti's home. As he drove up, he noticed the door was partially open. Fearing something had happened to her, he quickly jumped from the cab and ran to the door. He called out her name, but she didn't answer. His mind processed unlimited possibilities about her welfare.

A dank odor of mildew and fungus exuded from the doorway, which was repulsive to his nostrils. He hadn't noticed the smell the previous day, and it surprised him. Pushing the door open wide enough, he slipped inside. The place was a shambles. The chair he'd sat on the previous day lay in the corner broken. The table was split down the middle, laying on its side. He looked at her bed. The mattress was torn open, with the contents spread onto the floor in clumps. A thick coat of dust and dirt that had blown in, covered everything. Remembering where she had put the paper on which she had written her dreams for him, he turned to look at the shelves. They were empty!

"My God! What's happened here?" he thought out loud. "Has the entity become aware of her helping me and is trying to prevent me from unraveling this mystery?"

Mechanically, he walked back out into the sunlight, dazed by what he'd found. *Someone must have heard something*, he thought. "What's happened to her? How are we going to find out about the entity now?" he questioned.

Slowly he walked down the alley, then across it to the closest house. His knock was answered by a woman in her late fifties. "Yes, can I help you?"

While pointing, he said, "I'm inquiring about the woman who lives in that house. Something has happened to her, and I thought you might have heard some noise there, last night."

Looking at him blank-faced, she stated matter of factly, "No one lives there."

Controlling his voice to keep from shouting, he asked, "What do you mean, 'No one lives there'?"

She looked at him in his frenzied condition, as though wondering what kind of madman she was dealing with. "No one's lived there for many years!"

Bill thought he was dreaming and wanted to pinch himself to wake up. "But, I talked with a woman in that house several times. The last time was yesterday!"

Determined to bring her point home to him, she stated, "I tell you that house has been vacant for the past five years! I ought to know! I was the one who found the poor old woman who lived there. She had died in her sleep!"

"You found her dead? How did it happen?" Bill couldn't help asking.

"I used to look in on her to be sure she was all right. She had gotten to feeling poorly, and no one else cared about her situation. I still say she died from eating that dog food."

Wanting to confirm in his mind that it was her home, Bill inquired, "Was her name Karsti?"

Reaching over and leaning against the door casing, she answered, "Yes. That's the name. Angeline Karsti. She was a sweet old woman that the world had passed by. I couldn't help feeling sorry for her, the way she lived. I wanted her to see a doctor for her asthma, but she wouldn't hear of it."

Her voice softened. "I'm sorry if I've upset you, but you couldn't have talked with a person yesterday who's been dead for years!" Suspecting that he'd had a lapse of memory, she asked, "Are you all right? Were you in an accident?"

"No. I'm all right. Maybe it was only a dream I had. Thank you for your information." *A bad dream, would be more like it,* Bill thought.

"You're welcome. Are you sure you're all right?"

"Yes, thank you," he answered. Discouraged and questioning his own sanity, he turned and walked back to his camper.

Bill had a lot of thinking to do. Because he felt that his mind would be sharper, he awoke early the following moring. The episode at Mrs. Karsti's home seemed more like a dream than reality. His first thought was that, if he went back, she might be there. Then he wondered if it may have been a warp in time that had placed her five years into the future. To him, it seemed just as logical as to believe he'd been talking with someone who'd been dead for five years. Finally, he decided neither one was logical. He knew that he should clear his mind of unrelated information first, then sort out the facts. Believing that he should get the girls's opinions, he hoped that between them they could piece together enough information to give him some direction in which to proceed.

It wasn't until some time later that Diane appeared in the kitchen doorway. Bill was sitting at the table, sipping his coffee.

Entering the kitchen and bathrobe-clad, hairbrush in hand, Diane greeted him. "Good morning, Bill. I see you're up bright and early. How'd it go with the old woman?"

Marie Louise was right behind her. "I hope she was able to give you more information," she inquired then added, "I thought about it a lot last night and didn't come up with anything worthwhile."

He turned around to look at them and shook his head from side to side very slowly. They read the disappointment written on his face. Marie Louse was concerned and asked, "What happened?"

"She's gone! Disappeared!"

Marie Louise tried making sense out of what he'd said. "That's what you thought the last time. Were you able to get in?"

"Yeah, and check in the bathroom?" Diane added, trying to be helpful.

He looked at them and wondered how they would accept what he was about to tell them. Since he was the only one who had actually seen or talked with her, he couldn't blame them if they didn't believe him.

The high anticipation Marie Louise had when she entered the kitchen changed to feelings of despair, and his momentary silence caused her to ask, "What's wrong, Bill? . . . Something happened to her! She's dead, isn't she?"

Nodding his head, he agreed. "For five years!"

"Five years?" they echoed in unison.

"Yes, five years. That's what I said. The place was wrecked inside. No one has lived in her house for five years! It was her home once, though. The woman across the street confirmed that. She was the one who found her dead." He paused and studied their faces. "I wouldn't blame you for not believing me. I hardly believe it myself. I've even thought I'd dreamt it, or been cast back into the past. . . . I really don't know what to make of it."

Diane interjected, "It could be that thing playing games with us. Maybe it knows we're onto it, and it's trying to throw us off the track by having that woman tell you what she did."

Looking bewildered, Marie Louise agreed, "That could be it, all right." Then she asked, "Now what do we do?"

I'm fresh out of ideas, myself," Bill admitted. Then he continued, "I got up early to try to think this thing through clearly, but I'm no further ahead now then I was yesterday."

"At least then we had hope of learning something from that woman," Diane concluded.

They were interrupted by the ringing of the telephone. Bill answered it and heard a woman ask, "Is this Mr. LaBark?"

"Yes, who is this?"

"This is Tammy Duncan, the charge nurse of the psych unit at West Memorial Hospital. Your friend Peter Dunn has disappeared from our unit. We've checked the entire hospital, but he's nowhere to be found. We thought he may have gone to your home. . . . Is he with you?"

Panic flowed through Bill's veins, "No. This is the first I've known about it. Have you contacted the police to have him picked up?"

"No, we haven't. He wasn't committed to our facility. We were going to have him sign a voluntary commitment today for a few days of observation. I've talked with Dr. Preskins, the psychiatrist in charge of his case, and she feels he is harmless, so we can't call the police in."

Bill pressed her to take some action to find Peter. "He left without being released, didn't he? Isn't that enough reason to have the police search for him?"

She became defensive, "That's not a crime. Every so often a person leaves without doctor's orders. If we don't have a legal right to hold them, they are on their own. The hospital can't be responsible for what happens to them after they leave. I wouldn't worry about him, though. He seems like a sensible boy and is probably headed for your home right now."

Bill wasn't sure what would happen once Peter was free. Realizing he would receive no help from the hospital, he thanked her for calling and hung up.

"He's gone, isn't he?" Marie Louise blurted out, "I had a strong feeling something else terrible would happen today."

"Yes. He left without permission. . . . The hospital won't do anything to find him." Bill knew that if he didn't do something immediately to find Peter, and the entity had taken control of his body, they could lose him forever.

"Get dressed! We're going out looking for him! He may still be close to the hospital!" Bill cried out in desperation. "He doesn't have any money, so he may be trying to hitch a ride!"

Marie Louise called over her shoulder as she ran from the room, "It won't take us long to get changed. You get the camper backed out, and we'll be right with you."

Bill and the girls drove the streets near the hospital and gradually increased the circle until they'd covered a ten-block radius. From there, they checked the expressways on the edge of the city.

In frustration, Bill finally gave up, "It's no use. We've been driving around for over an hour, and there's no sign of him."

Marie Louise suggested, "Why don't we check around the hospital once more before giving up? If that thing has him in its clutches, it may have seen us coming and hidden until we passed by."

Bill turned the camper around and headed back. "Good idea. Diane, you're in the center, so you watch as far ahead as you can. Marie, you check the alleys on your side, and I'll check those on mine," Bill instructed.

After another half-hour of looking, there was still no sign of Peter.

Diane inquired, "Now what do we do?"

Feeling badly because he'd failed his friend and being disgusted with himself, Bill said, "I guess all we can do now is to go home and hope that he shows up."

They waited at Gwin's home for an hour to see if Peter would walk in, but they didn't hold much hope of it. Bill sat quietly thinking. Finally, he said, "Peter doesn't deserve to be going through this sort of thing."

Diane commented, "That's right." She paused. Then, looking at Bill, she added, "There must be some way we can find him. I know we're overlooking something important."

At a loss, after having exhausted every possibility in her mind, Marie Louise asked, "But what?"

Diane asked, "What if that old woman came back to this life because she knew that entity in the spirit world?"

Bill didn't understand what she was leading up to. "Go on. What would that have to do with her telling me what she did?"

Diane continued, "Well, if she knew the entity, she would know why it was after Peter. What she told you weren't dreams at all. They were facts she was aware of."

Marie Louise interjected, "And, if she was aware of what had happened to Peter, she knew you wouldn't believe her unless she made it seem like they were dreams."

"You both could be right. But why didn't she stay around long enough to tell us all of the facts? It seems almost like a game someone is playing with us. . . . It still could be the entity using her to throw us off the track like you said, Diane."

Diane answered, defending her idea, "But, what if it didn't know about her and that she intended to help you? Then for some reason she couldn't stay or that thing found out about her, after she tried to help and did something to prevent her from helping us further."

Marie Louise agreed, "Diane could be right. Maybe she brought you to her house because there's something in it that might help us."

Bill cried out, "Then, what are we waiting for? Let's get over there right away and check the place out!" Picking up his camper keys from the table, he ran to the front door.

Within minutes, they were at Mrs. Karsti's house. Finding it in the same condition as Bill had left it, they entered and began looking around.

Wrinkling her face in disgust, Diane said, "It smells terrible in here. It's so acrid that I don't know if I can stand it for long."

Bill advised her, "Do the best you can. If it gets too bad for you, go out in the fresh air."

The room that Mrs. Karsti had lived in was small. From the appearance, Bill guessed it had been the kitchen of the much larger home to which it was attached, and had been converted into living quarters for her. Within a short time, they had searched every conceivable place in it.

"What about under the mattress?" Marie Louise suggested.

Bill answered, "I've looked under it already."

Intent on finding some clue as to where the entity might go, Marie Louise suggested, "I know, but you've only looked under the edges.

Maybe we should take it all the way off. A lot of older people put things under their mattresses."

"The dust from that thing will kill me," Diane stated, "I'm going outside for a while."

Bill agreed, "Go ahead. We'll be out in a couple of minutes."

He slid the mattress off the spring onto the floor, raising a cloud of dust. Eagerly they looked for something, but there was nothing beneath it. He rolled it over, thinking there might be something stuck to the underside, but he couldn't find anything there, either. Disappointed, they walked out.

By the look on their faces, Diane could tell they'd found nothing. She advised, "I walked around the side of the house and looked in through the windows. There doesn't seem to be anyone living in the back half of the house, either."

Marie Louise inquired, "Do you think she owned the house and when times got hard she moved into this one room?"

Diane suggested, "Let's check the entire outside to see if there's some way to get in."

Being a law-abiding person, Bill cautioned, "That would be breaking and entering."

Marie Louise looked at him tight-lipped. Then, defiantly, she stated, "I've been in a lot of places where I didn't belong. If you're afraid, we can go in. You sit in the truck and blow the horn if someone comes and we'll hide inside." Starting to walk toward the back of the house, she said with determination, "It's Peter's life, and I don't intend to leave until I've checked this place out completely."

"You're right," Bill conceded, realizing that time was important and this was their only chance of finding something. "I wasn't thinking clearly for a second. . . . There may be an easy way in. Let's have a look."

Marie Louise suggested, "The inside could be irritating to you, Diane. Why don't you warn us if anyone comes around."

"Sure, I'll do that," she agreed and headed for the camper.

Bill and Marie Louise walked through the tall grass and long weeds beside the old house, carefully checking the windows and doors for entry. At the rear it was butted against another building, so they walked around to the other side and began checking there. Bill spoke, "This window isn't locked. It looks like someone has gotten in here before." He pushed it open. "You get in first," he instructed Marie Louise, "I'll boost you up, then I'll follow you in."

Once inside, they found the house littered with broken furniture, picture frames, shredded clothing, and scraps of bedding. The evidence of children having broken in was everywhere. Ceiling plaster hung loose in many places. In others, it had fallen to the floor and scattered around. Sags in the floors from years of water leakage made their progress treacherous.

"You take the front, and I'll check the back. Be sure to look everywhere. And BE CAREFUL," Bill cautioned her.

Carefully, they searched the house room by room, looking into and under everything. When they'd finished, they met back in the room where they'd started. Bill felt down in the mouth. He shook his head in disgust, saying, "I've looked everywhere, and there's nothing useful here."

Marie Louise felt the same as Bill as she informed him, "I've looked through all this crud, too. All I found that might have some information is a couple of boxes with old newspapers stacked in a closet. Most of them are scattered around the floor, though. It looks like a lot of parts are missing from them."

Bill felt hopeful, "They may have some information in them." But he believed he was grasping at straws as he said, "We'll pick them all up and put them in the boxes. I'll go through them while you and Diane are at work." He paused, "I wish I knew what we're looking for. It's going to be easy to overlook anything of importance, but it's worth a try."

Marie Louise looked at him and suggested, "We're not going to work today. This is more important. We'll call in and tell him we're both sick."

"He'll never believe you're both sick."

She became irritated. "To hell with him! He can believe what he wants! We're not going to work!"

Bill nodded his head in agreement, "Let's get those papers together and get the hell out of here!"

A slight shiver came over her as she said, "Let's hurry. This place is creepy, even in the daylight."

Later that evening, at Gwin's home, they were in the basement poring over the newspapers, which dated from the late 1800s into the 1930s. Bill and Marie Louise read the headlines of each article and inscriptions under the pictures, hoping to find something that had meaning. If the items dealt with unusual circumstances, such as a murder or suicide, they read the entire article. Those papers that had follow-up articles they placed together. Diane catalogued the dates of these papers and the titles of the articles for future reference.

Finally, Marie Louise said in exasperation, "This is frustrating. We've spent hours on these papers, and we're no further ahead now than when we started. My eyes are starting to see double from all this concentration."

Diane agree, "I know the feeling. I'm for taking a break and having a cup of coffee."

"Sounds good to me, too . . . I'm taking this photo album with me. Maybe there's something in it that we've overlooked," Bill said, as he picked it up and flipped through the pages.

"I doubt that we can get any more from those pictures. We've looked them over carefully when we first found it," Diane said, as they started up the stairs.

When Bill had reached the top of the stairs, he deduced, "It smells like Gwin's been baking apple pie. It'll feel good to get on the outside of some of that." Then he added, as he saw his sister, "Looks like you've been cooking up a storm. . . . Is there any pie cool enough to eat?"

"Sure enough, but you'll have to wash up first. It looks like all that dust from the papers has found a home on you."

Marie Louise grinned and looked at her through dirt-covered eyes. "I feel like I've eaten a ton of it, too."

"Has your prowling through all of them done any good?"

"Not so far, but we have a whole lot more to go through," Bill answered. Then he continued, "We found this photo album, but there's nothing in it either that's of any help. I brought it up to check it over once more. There are a few pictures with babies, and Mrs. Karsti did tell me that a baby had something to do with that thing and Peter."

"Give it to me. I'll look through it while you three clean up."

Bill handed the album to her. "I doubt that anything in it will mean anything to you, either."

"That woman said you had seen a baby. It's possible that we had both seen it when we were young. It can't hurt for me to look. Nothing to lose 'cept a little time, and I have plenty of that."

Bill was drying his hands when Gwin called to him, "Bill, come here. Maybe this will help. There's writing on the backs of most of these pictures."

Bill hurried into the living room, with Marie Louise and Diane close behind. Gwin had some of the pictures removed. Bill read the inscriptions as she removed the rest.

Bill stopped on one that caught his attention, "This picture has the date May 8, 1923 and has the names Martha Daget and her daughter, Lynn! It's the only one that has any vague semblance of meaning! The name of the town is Far Rockaway, New York! That's where Emily and I lived!" He turned the picture over and examined it. "It may be the baby we're looking for, but I don't know the woman. I'm not rushing to New York before we're sure. We still have more pictures and a lot of papers to go through."

"Did you say Martha Daget?" Marie Louise asked excitedly.

"That's what it said. Why? Does it mean something to you?"

Her excitement heightened. "There was an article I read about a woman by that name who was found dead in her home! The baby's crying got the neighbor's attention! They found her strangled and were looking for the man who she'd lived with, for questioning!"

Bill felt energized and was beside himself with a surge of excitement he could not contain. Here, at last, seemed to be the scrape of information they'd been searching for. "Did it give the address of the woman?" he asked.

"I think it did. We'd have to check!"

Diane headed for the basement. "Do you remember the title of the article?"

"It was on the front page of one of those papers. It just said, 'Woman Strangled'!" Marie Louise yelled out excitedly as she joined Bill and Diane, who were running down the steps. Diane quickly thumbed through her list of articles, "It's in that pile!" she pointed, "The date on the paper is August 27, 1923."

Marie Louise hastily searched through the pile. "Here it is!"

Reaching out, Bill took it from her. "Let me have it!"

Quickly, he scanned the article, "Number 4726 Finger Island Road! That was our address!" He took the picture from his pocket and looked it over carefully. There was a slight recognition.

"That woman's face rings a bell from somewhere, but I can't put my finger on where I've seen her before. I couldn't have known her. She died in my house long before we lived there." His face showed concentration as he tried to make a connection.

Marie Louise dropped the papers she was holding and looked at Bill. "That house must have something to do with that thing in Peter. He must be heading there right now!"

"You're right. If I fly out there, can you two girls manage to drive the camper across the country?"

Marie Louise was in agreement. "We can handle it. We both drive."

"I'm taking this picture and the article with me," Bill said, as he hurried up the stairs.

Diane followed close behind. "We'll drive you to the airport. Then, we'll come back and get the rest of these papers, in case there's something else in them of importance."

"It looks like you've found something to help you find Peter," Gwin commented as Bill hastily emerged from the basement.

"You know the house Emily and I owned in New York? An article from those papers says a woman was killed in it in 1923 and she had a baby! She may have something to do with what's happened to him! That picture helped us find it! I know it's a long shot, but I'm going up there!"

Shaking her head in disbelief, Gwin commented, "It all sounds weird to me. I've never believed in these kinds of things happening in real life."

Bill paused a moment to talk with her. "I can't believe this is happening, either, but I've got to check it out. It's the only thing we have to go on, and his life depends on us helping him."

"I know how important it is that you not waste any time, but I've set out the pie and I have ice cream to go with it. There's fresh coffee in the pot, too. You'll need the energy. Best you have some before you leave," Gwin offered.

"Maybe I'll have some when I've finished packing," Bill said, trying not to hurt her feelings as he headed for the stairs.

Gwin called after him, determination in her voice. "There's no maybe about it. You'll eat if I have to stuff it down your throat. I know how you are when you've got something on your mind. Eating is the last thing you think about."

While Bill packed, Marie Louise wasted no time in scheduling him a flight out. She looked concerned as she turned to Diane and Gwin. "We've only got half an hour to make his flight. Traffic is bad this time of night, too. Bill can eat on the way, and I can drive. Gwin, why don't you get some ready to take with us? Diane and I can have some when we come back." Then she ran up the stairs, yelling, "Bill! You'll have to hurry! We don't have much time! Just take what you need 'til we can bring the rest with us!"

Arriving at the airport, Bill picked up his ticket and checked in his baggage. "I almost forgot. Here's my credit card. Use it for whatever you need on the trip." He handed it to Marie Louise.

"This won't be any good to us. It has your name on it. So does the camper. You'll have to give us the registration and permission to use it, too. We have some money. Maybe it'll be enough. There isn't time to get any from anywhere now."

"You're right. I wasn't thinking straight. I'll write you a note giving my permission to have the camper." He wrote on the back of a deposit slip. "Gwin has her name on my checking account. Tell her to give you enough, so you don't run short. Here's the registration. I've got to go. I'll see you at the house when you get there. You have the address. Don't rush and get into an accident."

186

Diane checked and found the paper Bill had written the address on. "I've got the address. Don't worry about us. You be careful and don't take any chances." She paused, then added, "That thing is evil and may have more power than we're aware of."

"I will. I'll see you there, then. Good-bye. I love you both and appreciate your helping me."

"We love you, too, Bill," they replied in unison. "Good-bye and be careful."

Waving, they watched as he boarded the plane. Then they headed back to Gwin's home.

Chapter 9

NEW YORK

AFTER landing in New York, Bill rented a car and drove to his old home in Far Rockaway. It was dark when he shut off the lights and drove the last block to the house in the dark. He parked a few houses down from the home, not wanting to arouse Peter's attention if he was there. Reaching for the bottle of brandy he'd bought at the airport, Bill downed a couple of quick gulps to stabilize his nerves. Not knowing if he'd find Peter possessed by the entity there, skulking around nearby, he resolved to be very careful.

Making his way along the tree-lined road, Bill noticed that the house was dark inside. It appeared not to have been lived in for years, he judged, as he walked through the overgrown yard and peered in through the broken windows. With no sign of life to be found, Bill decided to find a motel and bed down for the night. He'd remembered seeing a few on the other end of the town and decided to check them out first. As he drove down the main street, a sign, "Hypnotic Therapy," caught his eye. Thoughts popped into his mind. *I wonder if I can recall under hypnosis why the woman in the picture seems familiar. It may be worth a try. If Peter doesn't show up at the house and the hypnosis works, it may be the only possible lead I'll have.*

A blue, neon sign, "Nameoke Motel, Vacancy," flashed an invitation to Bill's heavy eyelids to stop and lose his weary mind in peaceful rest.

A bell rang as he entered the office. Within minutes, a bathrobe-clad woman in her mid-forties appeared in the doorway that led to the back. At a glance, he noted she wasn't married. Normally, this would signal his brain to turn on the charm. People who knew him insisted he never passed up an opportunity to flirt with a pretty woman. This night would have to be an exception, he told himself.

Her hair was long and blond and partially covered one eye. She smiled through tired eyes.

"I'd like a room for the night," said Bill.

"For how many people?"

"A single will do. Make it a ground floor, if that's possible."

"The only one I have is a small room next to the office."

"That'll be fine. I'm not fussy, just tired." He signed the registry card.

She yawned and smiled slightly. "It feels like a tired night to me, too."

"You've got that right. I'd like to sleep late. . . . What time is check-out?"

"It's at twelve noon. I'll tell the housekeepers to do your room up last."

"Thanks."

Sleep didn't come easily for Bill. After a couple of healthy swigs of brandy, he tucked himself in. But his brain raced on fire with questions for which he had no answers. He tossed in an uncooperative bed. Each ripple in the sheet beneath him protruded into his tired body, as though they were dead branches spread across his bed by the devil. He became aware of the sensitivity of his body hair touching the sheet and it drove him crazy with itching, which was only temporarily relieved by scratching.

In disgust, he sat on the edge of the bed and tippled the remains of the fifth of brandy. His mind became a haze, and he slumped back onto the bed crosswise. He had one more thought, *That blond could have taken my mind off of all this. Wonder what she's like in bed?*

An insistent knocking shattered his dreams. He laboriously raised one heavy eyelid and glanced at his watch. "Only nine-thirty. what's going on?" he grumbled to himself.

He heard a key turning in the lock. Suddenly, the door swung open, followed by a young black girl, wide-eyed with surprise. Bill lay naked, sprawled on the bed the way he'd fallen asleep. He grabbed for the bedding to cover himself and caught hold of the foot-end that was still tucked in.

Realizing it was too late to protect his jewels from observation, he made no further effort. He was caught, exposed where the sun doesn't shine.

"Oh! U'm terr'bly sarry, sur! Ah knocked and, when yoo didn' answur, Ah taught yoo'd left." Filling her eyes with his manhood, she quickly pulled the door closed behind her.

Bill sat on the edge of the bed, rubbing his red eyes, in semi-shock from the intrusion. His head bobbed as he thought, *Too dumb to put the chain on the door. Serves you right. . . . She's probably had so many stuck in her that she'd look like a porcupine if they were all sticking out of her.*

His thoughts turned to the night before. *That dumb blond must have forgotten to tell them.*

189

Failing to get back to sleep, Bill dressed. Quickly, he rejected his first thought of checking out and telling the blond off. He decided to keep the room until the girls arrived with the camper.

Bill stepped out into the morning sunlight. Driving he turned right and headed for "Tubby's Cafe," which he remembered was around the corner. He looked up the road and muttered, "Same old town. Just a wide spot in the road. Blink your eyes while driving through and you've missed it."

He sat up to the counter and ordered their breakfast special of ham, eggs, toast, and coffee. His stomach growled, protesting the past day of fasting, as he stood up to look for a telephone. Upon starting to walk toward it, he felt a hand on his shoulder and glanced around.

"Bill! Bill LaBark, you old girl-chaser. What are you doing back in town?"

Bill's eyes settled on a tall, slim man with his hand out stretched. Smiling broadly, the man spoke. "As I recall, you and Emily were chased out of town by some ghosts in that house you had up on Finger Island Road."

Bill squinted, then recognized him. "You son of a sea horse!" he said, extending his hand. "Jim Switzer. If it isn't the living dead. I never expected to see you this soon. I know you're all over like shit in a cow pasture, but I thought it'd be later rather than sooner, that I'd run into you."

"Where's Emily?" Jim paused and looked around, then stated kiddingly, "The wife and I were just talking about you two last week. I didn't expect them to resurrect you this soon."

Bill's expression changed to a slight frown. "She died a few years ago."

Jim's eyebrows raised. His face showed his concern. "Gee, I'm sorry to hear that. Gin will be too. They were pretty tight when you lived here."

"I know they were close. . . . When we moved, we had every intention of staying in touch, but we bought a hardware store in Rockford and got busy setting that up for business. I guess we put in too many hours on it. . . . You know how it is when you're starting out. Money is short and you try to do it all yourself. . . . The doctor told her she had heart trouble, but she kept it to herself. A couple of years after we moved there, she died in her sleep. . . . I guess that's the best way to go, though."

"That must have been rough on you. You two were very devoted to each other," Jim commented, then added apologetically, "I didn't mean anything when I called you a woman-chaser a minute ago."

Bill looked him in the eye. "I wouldn't have recognized you so quickly, if you didn't act like yourself. Anyway, I knew you didn't mean

190

it." He paused and became serious. "It's good to see you, Jim. I've had a lot on my mind lately, and it's good to relax and banter around a bit."

"Some heavy thinking, eh?" Jim paused. "Judging by the look on your face, you're carrying some heavy baggage around in your mind. Care to talk about it?"

"I've got some brreakfast ordered, and my guts are protesting. If you've got the time, we can talk right here. . . . Can I buy you something to eat?"

Jim slapped Bill across the back and agreed. "Why not? That's what I came here for, and I've got some time to lose."

Bill filled him in on the details that led him back into town.

Jim was quiet, then he admitted, "I was kidding you about being chased out of your house. No one around here believed it was haunted when you left. Although, since then a number of people tried to live in it and they made the same claim. The place is a disaster now and should be torn down."

"I've been there already and I agree, but, I'm glad they haven't destroyed it. That house is my only link with what's happened to Peter. I'll be going up there when I've finished here. If you'd care to come along, I could use someone to keep an eye out for me." He paused and Jim could read the anxiety in his friend.

"I guess I could dump a shift from the mill. Sure, I'll go with you, since I can see how important it is to you."

Bill asked, "Do you know anything about the hypnotist? I saw a sign on the main street. It wasn't there when I lived here. . . . I was heading for a phone to call for an appointment when you stopped me."

"Not much. Gin had mentioned that he works with the doctors at the clinic."

When Bill finished eating, he turned to Jim and said, "I thought if I were hypnotized I would remember something about the baby I'd mentioned about to you."

"Judging from what you've told me, I'd say the woman and child that you and Emily saw when you lived in that house could be the same people in the picture you found."

Bill felt encouraged and produced the picture. "You could be right. I hadn't thought about that. Guess I couldn't see the forest for the trees," he muttered, while examining it. Then he added, "We'll have to be careful at the house. If Peter is there and he's possessed, there's no telling what could happen."

Jim asked an obvious question that struck his mind. "What if he's there and attacks you? Are you prepared to fight back?"

"I have a pistol with me," Bill responded instantly.

191

"Will you use it, knowing that your friend could be seriously injured or even killed?"

Bill looked beyond Jim, his eyes losing their shine. "That's the question I've asked myself a thousand times, if I asked it once. I really don't know."

After leaving the restuarant, they drove directly to the house on Finger Island Road and parked a few hundred yards down the road from the house, so as not to draw attention to their activity.

Set back from the road some twenty-five feet, desertion was evident. Tag elders and ragweed replaced a well-kept lawn. Weed-choked flowerbeds produced scraggy roses and other perennials that had been the pride of his wife, Emily. The sight of the condition of the home, combined with the potential of doing bodily harm to his friend, drew Bill's stomach muscles up into tight knots. Although windows were broken throughout the house, his former home appeared to him to be less desolate and foreboding in the daylight.

Bill posted Jim with a hidden view of the road before he gained entry through a loose basement window. Running his hand over his face, he cleaned off the collecting cobwebs. Upon remembering there were two rooms in the cellar without windows, he cursed himself for neglecting to bring a flashlight with him. Because of poor lighting, he decided to go directly to the upstairs and return later with a light to investigate the basement, if need be.

The stairs ended at the kitchen door. Bill attempted to open it quietly, but he found it jammed tight. His shoulder provided assistance, and the door creaked open. A sudden movement to his left caused him to duck in reflex action as a bat swooped near his head. "Damned bats," he muttered under his breath. Regaining his composure, he evaluated the room. It was completely devoid of furnishings. He checked the pantry and fount it empty. Disappointed at the emptiness, he walked into the living room. He noted the wall-coverings were the same as when he'd left. The entire house produced nothing. The barrenness was overwhelming. He pushed the front door open and walked out into the bright sunlight.

Jim estimated the situation. "You look down in the mouth. I take it you didn't find anything."

"That place is as bare as a newborn baby's ass. I thought for sure I'd find something that could shed a little light on the situation, but there was absolutely nothing." He looked thoughtfully off into the distance. Then he chewed his words in disgust. "There are a couple of rooms without windows in the basement. If I'd have thought to bring a flashlight, I could check them out, too."

After standing in the yard and gazing at the house, Bill turned to leave when Jim offered, "I'm sure I must have a flash in the car. I'll be right back."

Jim returned swinging a three-cell light. "This ought to do the trick," he said, handing it to Bill.

"Thanks. You've saved us some time," Bill said. Then turning, he returned to the house.

Later, while Jim stood watch on the road, he caught sight of movement near the house through the corner of his eye. Facing in that direction, he recognized Bill. "Find anything?" he asked.

Bill shook his head slowly with precision.

"Was there any sign of anyone being in there?"

"No one's been in that place in years. My bootprints are the only ones in the entire house."

Jim asked, "What are you going to do now?"

"I'll keep an eye on the place, while I figure out what to do next, just in case Peter shows."

Jim reflected on the situation, then stated, "It seems to me there must be something more productive you could be doing with your time than watching an empty house."

His face tight with disappointment, Bill confronted his friend, "You're the pillar of logic, aren't you? . . . All full of ideas as to what to do, I suppose!"

Jim, lips white with anger, snapped, "So, what do you want from me? I can see there's no use talking to you now! You wouldn't listen anyway!"

Bill relaxed somewhat. Realizing that he was taking his restrained anger out on his friend, he offered, "I'm sorry I turned on you, Jim. You've always been a good friend to me."

Jim had always been somewhat of a laid-back person who could take most situations in his stride. His thinning, red hair and white beard gave evidence of a tendency for a quick temper that flared and subsided all within a matter of moments. Bill admired in him his consistent, no-nonsense approach to problems, in days past.

A level-headed man who weighed his thoughts, Jim responded, "No apology necessary. You know me, Bill. I say what I think and sometimes it gets me into trouble. But, what the hell? That keeps life stimulating. . . . I just meant there is always more than one option, and you should try for more alternatives. For instance, that hypnotist might give you a lead to follow up on. You don't need him to identify the woman, if it is Martha Daget, but he may be able to regress you into the previous life where Peter was your daughter. I've heard they can do that. You may get something to go on, if he can get you back there."

Jim slapped his hand across Bill's back, pulling him forward. "Come on," he said. "There's nothing here now. . . . Let's get a cup of coffee. Maybe we can toss some ideas around and come up with something. Besides, if it's as you say—your friend doesn't have money and is hitch-hiking across the country—it may be a while before he gets here. By then the two girls should be here, too."

"You're right, again." Bill paused and turned to him. "You are something else, Jim. You're a good stabilizing force that I need in my life right now. . . . Coffee sounds good to me. Let's go."

"There's the Crimson Chicken down the road. It's a nice place," Jim mentioned. Then he added as a second thought, "Or, we can go to my place, if you want privacy. There's no one at home now."

"Your place may be the best bet. Too many flies on the walls in public places. . . . We don't want to start any rumors."

At Jim's home, the hours passed swiftly as they sat in the living room talking. Bill stood up as Jim brought out a third pot of coffee. "My back teeth feel like they're floating. As I recall, the bathroom is to the right off the kitchen."

Jim chuckled under his breath. "Your fluid drive never did hold up too well. Hope everything comes out all right."

Bill turned his head and spoke over his shoulder. "You're no iron kidneys, yourself. . . . Just slightly better than me."

Bill returned a short time later. "I'd better give Gwin a call and see if Peter might have showed up there. . . . I'll have to let her know I'm at the Nomeoke Motel, in case she has to get in touch with me."

Jim refilled their cups. "Good idea, but why not stay here? My daughter's room is empty. Gin wouldn't mind."

Bill took a drink. "I don't want to put any extra load on her. When she gets through with work, I'm sure she wants to relax and not have to fuss with company."

"It'll be okay by her. Besides, you and Emily were like family."

Bill thought a moment, then said, "Agreed then." As he walked over to the telephone, he said, "I'll give Gwin your phone number. Let me know what the charges are when you get the bill."

Bill dialed the number and reacted to a busy signal. "I should have expected it to be tied up. Her telephone chair is the only piece of furniture she's had to have recovered about a dozen times."

Jim smiled. "Sounds like you're trying to tell me something unusual about her. . . . She sounds like a normal woman to me."

Bill pushed a button on the phone and a cover flipped up. He turned toward Jim. "What are the cassettes for? Do you record your conversations?"

"You didn't know that I work part-time for the FBI, did you? That's for my cloak-and-dagger work," he said, before clarifying its purpose and while watching his friend's expression change.

Surprise exaggerated itself on Bill's face as he asked, "How did you get into that?"

"I'm just kidding you. Actually, it's an answering machine. It records messages when we're not home. It has a re-dial on it, too. Just press the star to re-dial."

Bill pushed the star. "Amazing. What'll they think of next?" he exclaimed as he waited for his call to go through.

Gwin answered and he talked with her for a few minutes, then hung up. "No sign of Peter back there, and she hasn't heard from the girls since they left," he reported, somewhat disappointed, having hoped Peter had returned and he was back to normal.

Walking to the couch, Bill said, "Marie and Diane are bringing the boxes of newspapers with them. When they get here, we'll spend some time going through them carefully. It's possible we've missed something important."

An inspiration crept into Jim's mind. "Why don't we check the records at the courthouse, starting with the date on the picture and working backward? The baby appears to be only a few months old, and chances are it was born here in town."

Bill's eyes brightened. "Great idea. When the girls get here, if we can find the birth date and check the newspapers around that date, we may be able to piece this thing together."

Around four in the afternoon, they returned. Bill's face was drawn. "I had thought your idea was brilliant." He paused as he turned toward Jim, who was seating himself in a chair. "It doesn't make any sense that they wouldn't have a record of the birth at the courthouse. The suggestion the clerk made about church baptismal records made sense, too, since many births were recorded by the churches in those days. I was sure we'd find a record in one of them."

Jim suggested, "It's possible they hadn't gotten it baptized by the time the mother was killed."

Bill felt agitated. "So where does that leave us?"

"Back to 'start,' I'd say."

"There's got to be something we're missing." Bill spoke with determination.

Jim looked at him, wanting to be helpful, but not knowing how. "Gin will be home soon. She'll be mighty surprised to see you." He picked up the daily paper and opened it to the sports page. "Take a load off your feet. Sit down, relax a bit, and rest your mind. We can talk this over after we eat. By then, we may have a fresh outlook."

Bill's face changed expression. "I'd completely forgotten about checking out at the motel. How about if I do that now? I could look over the house again at the same time and be back shortly."

"Can't stop driving yourself, eh? Okay, I'll have Gin set you a place, so don't eat out," Jim directed.

"I wouldn't think of missing her home cooking. I'll be right back."

Bill left, intending to go to the motel first, but an inner feeling pushed him to drive to the house. Once there, he had a strong sense of a presence. As he carefully checked it over, he realized the overpowering anxiety developing in his system was playing tricks on his sensibility. After assuring himself the house was empty, he drove to the motel.

Upon his entering and responding to the bell, the blond looked up and smiled. "Can I help you with something, Mr. LaBark?"

He returned her smile. "You remembered my name. . . . I'm impressed."

She brushed the hair back from over her eye. "We don't have a lot of customers this time of year, so it's easy. Besides, you were in not too long ago, when you extended your room."

"That's right. Now I'm checking out. I know I'll have to pay for tonight. . . . I should have called earlier when I found I wouldn't need it."

"How was everything?" she asked matter of factly, as she looked for his bill.

With an impish look on his face, Bill answered, "All right, so far."

Holding his bill, she looked confused, not sure of what to do. "What's that supposed to mean? Are you expecting something else? You did say you're checking out, didn't you?"

Bill grinned and laughed to himself. "Just kidding. I wanted to see if I could get a rise out of you."

Her expression changed to a broad smile. He continued, "Yes, I'm checking out."

"If you didn't use the room since noon, I won't charge you for today. We still have time to fill it tonight."

Bill looked surprised. "I have my things in it and will get them out right away. . . . That's mighty gracious of you."

"Cash or charge?" she asked.

Bill produced his credit card. "Plastic money," he quipped and handed it to her.

Looking down at the machine, she ran it through, then glancing up at him, she said, "I can tell by your eyes that you're the kind of person who would do the same for me, if the shoe was on the other foot." She winked coyly at him. "Sign here," she said, pointing to the charge slip and sliding his card onto the counter.

Apologetically he replied, "I expected to stay here, but I ran into a friend and I'm staying with him and his wife."

She looked up back into his eyes. "I know most people in town. If you don't mind telling me their names, I might know them."

"Sure. Jim and Ginny Switzer."

"They're good people. I did nursing with Gin at the hospital a few years ago. They live over on Bath Walk," she said, twisting her head in a quick jerk to throw back the hair from over her eye.

Bill agreed, "Right you are. They don't come any finer."

She smiled. "I'll second that notion. I get over to their place once in a while."

Approvingly, he returned her smile. "Maybe I'll see you there sometime."

"I'd like that." Her smile broadened. "You seem like an interesting person. I'd like to get to know you better."

Bill winked. "What's your name? I'll tell them I met you."

"Ellie Sue Carling."

"I've got to be getting back to eat. Don't want to ruin my welcome. I'll leave the key in the room." He picked up his credit card to leave. "Nice meeting you, Ellie Sue."

"Same here. . . . Take care now."

The following day, Bill was up early. His head felt twice its size. He allowed his feet to guide him to the kitchen. Jim looked up from his breakfast. "You look good for a man who tried to drown himself in brandy."

Bill stood, knees bent, rubbing his tired eyes. Slowly, he lowered his hands and looked at Jim. "The last time I tried, I puked all over my sister Gwin's rugs. By the time I finished cleaning it up, I was wishing I HAD drowned in it."

"It was mighty considerate of you not to do that here," Jim chided him. "Gin can be a tiger when it comes to that sort of thing."

Bill walked over and joined him at the table. "I'll have to remember that. If I get that bad off, I'll just get a room."

He paused to sip the coffee Jim had pushed his way. "You're the one with the clear head this morning. Got any fresh ideas as to how I'm going to find Peter? . . . And while you're at it, try and figure out what I should do about him when I do."

"I've been giving that some thought, too, but so far I don't have a solution. . . . I'll have to work today. In fact, I should be leaving shortly. You might try the hypnotist for openers."

Bill propped his elbows on the table and slouched over, his head cradled in his hands. Then he answered Jim, but he chewed his words and they came out incomprehensible.

Jim was annoyed. "If you're so hungry you're eating your words, why don't you put some food in that paunch?" He paused, then continued, "Either that or speak so I can hear you."

Bill raised his tired head. "I said, that's all I was able to come up with, too."

Jim's eyes lit up slightly. "You know, the baby could have been adopted. You might try checking to see if the Probate Court has some records on it."

Bill finished his coffee and poured himself another cup. "Good thinking, Jim. I'll check that out, too."

Jim stood up. "Got to leave now. Gin'll be up soon. She has to be to work by nine. I've told her about your friend. Maybe she'll have some ideas that might help."

"Marie and Diane should be here pretty soon, too. They were going to try to drive right through. Between all of our heads, we should come up with something. Meanwhile, I'm going to keep an eye on that house. So far, it's our only link." He paused and walked with Jim to his car. Then he said, "Thanks for everything, especially for taking yesterday off."

"What are friends for?" Jim closed the door to his car and rolled down the window. "Good luck. See you tonight. Remember, I've got tomorrow off. I can help you then."

"See you later and thanks again." Bill walked slowly back into the house, not sure what he should do to effect progress in finding Peter.

He poured himself a cup of coffee and while he processed his possible options, Gin walked into the kitchen. "Good morning, Bill. You look like you're trying to unscramble a can of worms. . . . Jim explained the situation to me. I'm sorry to hear of your bad luck."

"Morning, Gin. . . . You're right, my mind is a mess. The more I think about the whole mess, the more confused I get. I keep coming back to the house Emily and I owned, but there's nothing there except a thick coat of dust."

She walked over to the stove, poured herself some coffee, and tried to be understanding. "I know how frustrating it must be. I'd probably have given up long ago."

"Did Jim mention to you that I won't need to stay on when my camper gets here?"

"He said that a couple of your friends are bringing it out and they should be here any day now." Then she invited, "But, we have plenty of room, and you can all stay here as long as you like. It'll be much more comfortable than trying to live in the back of a pickup."

"I appreciate your allowing me the hospitablity of your home, but I don't want to take advantage of you and Jim."

Gin smiled. "Nonsense. We enjoy company. Besides, you've already bought enough food to feed an army. You'll have to stay and help us eat it."

She pulled out a chair, sat down, and set her coffee on the table. "You know, Bill, I have a hard time believing in the supernatural. If I didn't know you better, I'd say you have a screw loose." She looked at him over her cup as she sipped. Finding it hot, she put it down and continued, "I remember when you and Emily told us about your place being haunted. I must admit, we didn't believe you. It wasn't until others tried to live in the house after you left and strange happenings were reported that Jim and I actually believed what you told us. We felt very badly about it and wanted to apologize to you and Emily."

Bill glanced at her. "We didn't expect you to understand. If we didn't see it with our own eyes, we wouldn't have believed it either."

Gin raised her cup, looked across the top of it at Bill, and blew to cool it. After taking a sip, she set it down and spoke. "I've felt guilty about it ever since. Now Emily is gone and I can't tell her, so you'll have to accept for the both of you. I am truly sorry you both left here knowing that not one of your friends believed you."

Bill knew she spoke sincerely. "You don't have to apologize. That was a long time ago and would have been forgotten, except for this nightmare. Somehow, the beastly thing that has enslaved Peter is tied to the both of us from some previous life."

Gin's expression showed concern. "Jim didn't tell me about you and your friend being connected in that way."

"He may not have completely understood all that I was telling him at the time. Supposedly, Peter was my daughter."

He could see a look of surprise in her eyes as she spoke. "Why don't you tell me everything about it? That way I might be more able to help."

Bill explained the entire situation to Gin. They talked until she had to leave for work. A short time later, he drove over to the house. Finding nothing had changed, he decided to stop at the hypnotist's office on his way back. The receptionist informed him that the hypnotist, Dr. Meyer, would not be in until after lunch and made an appointment for him at four o'clock.

Remembering what Jim had said about the Probate Court records, Bill decided to try there first. At the courthouse, he was unsuccessful in persuading the Probate Judge to allow him access to the old records. "You may not understand, Mr. LaBark, but Probate records on adoptions are sealed for the good of the children who are placed in adoptive homes."

Bill wanted to explain the reason he needed the records, but he held back in fear of disbelief on the part of the judge. "But this child has probably died many years ago. I need the names of the placement parents."

"The law doesn't set a time period. There's no telling the disruption you could cause in these people's lives, if you had access. It's also for that reason the law was written."

Bill's first reaction was to contact an attorney, but immediately he dismissed the idea, realizing the time and expense might be fruitless. Nodding his head in agreement, he turned to leave. "I guess you're right. There probably isn't anything I need in them, anyway."

Disappointed, Bill decided on having an early lunch. After eating, he drove to a roadside park on High Point Road, hoping to relax and collect his thoughts. The park was empty, and he was thankful for the solitude. Remembering a natural seat, which was carved into a rock by the ocean in past millennia, he headed for it. As he walked, he thought about how he and Emily had spent many pleasurable hours there, quietly listening to the banter of the waves lapping their way through the jagged, rock-strewn shoreline.

As Bill picked his way between the rocks toward his secluded refuge, a sound of droning engines drifted into his awareness. Turning his head he looked over his right shoulder out into the water. Standing motionless momentarily he scanned the horizon and became entranced with the peaceful feeling that crept through his soul. At first he saw nothing. Then, a fishing trawler, slowly churning its way toward him, appeared around the treeline and headed into the large cove adjacent to the park. He smiled to himself, then continued his way along the shore.

By the time he'd settled into the comfort of the seat and learned back against the rock back-rest, the trawler had come to a stop at an underwater reef a few hundred yards offshore. Releasing all conscious thoughts, Bill fixed his attention on the attraction.

Watching the yellow-clad men bring in their nets and hearing the steady drone of the motors tranquilized him into a hypnotic state of being. A single thought drifted slowly through the chasms of his mind.

How very good it feels to be totally relaxed.

It seemed to Bill now like an eternity since he'd allowed himself this luxury. As he watched, eyes half-closed, a lone seagull appeared on the horizon, and within minutes the trawler was surrounded by squawking, darting birds.

A slight sea breeze rustled the leaves on a small elder directly behind him, further relaxing him as he slowly drifted off into la la land.

Bill's dream of Mrs. Karsti was suddenly interrupted by a splash of water. His head jerked to awareness. Through his water-filled eyes, he caught a glimpse of a jean-clad teenage girl with long, flowing, red hair disappearing behind a clump of small trees. She carried a water pistol and was laughing loudly. He sat upright, slowly wiped the water from his face, and flipped it from his hand. Failing to see the humor in the act, Bill grumbled, "Damn kids!"

Feeling a slight chill crawl over him, he shivered slightly. The warm, sun-heated day had given way to a light fog that was rolling in from the ocean.

Realizing it might be late, Bill glanced at his watch and read three-thirty. Standing up, he yawned, stretched, and muttered to himself, "Better get your ass in gear. Can't be late for the appointment with the hypnotist."

At a half-run, Bill wound snakelike down through the rocks to his car. Having been quite some time since he'd had this kind of exercise, he panted deeply as he ran. His tight shirt stretched in rhythm with the incessant pumping of his overworked heart.

As Bill drove back into town, he tried desperately to recall what Mrs. Karsti had revealed to him in his dream, without success. He knew it might have been meaningless, but he kept hoping that she had actually given him some clue to Peter's whereabouts.

At five of four, Bill approached the hypnotist's receptionist. "I have a four-o'clock appointment," he announced.

The pretty brunette looked up from her desk. With her light-green eyes wrinkled into a smile, she said, "I'm sorry, Mr. LaBark, but the doctor won't be able to see you today. He had an emergency at home and had to leave. We can get you in at ten tomorrow morning, if that will be all right?"

The smile he'd presented upon entering quickly changed to one of annoyance as Bill's face reflected his disappointment. Knowing he was losing valuable time, which could mean the life of his friend, he curtly agreed. "I'll take it!"

Turning to leave, he heard her say, "See you in the morning. Have a nice day."

Bill left without responding. Once outside, he muttered to himself, "Sure, I'll have a wonderful day."

Disgusted and feeling mixed up inside, he drove back to the house he'd once owned and found no evidence of anyone having been there. On his way back to Jim's house, he glanced up a side street and noticed a sign that read "Psychic Readings." He'd never believed in these people, but he was willing to try anything. He turned the car around and drove up to the house.

A short, plump woman in her mid-fifties answered his knock. She wore a bright red, ruffled, felt skirt and a white blouse under a gold-fringed, red, felt jacket. Her round overpainted face and outfit immediately gave him the impression of an aged pixie, complete with a gold-fringed red felt hat. Bill found himself staring at her in amusement. Smiling, Bill said, "I was driving by and saw your sign."

She invited, "Yes, come in." Leading the way into her studio and offering her hand, she said, "My name is Ann."

Such a plain name for a psychic, Bill thought. While shaking her hand, he introduced himself. "Bill LaBark."

"Well, Mr. LaBark, what can I help you with? I do everything but seances."

"I'm not quite sure what you can do for me."

She offered, "Why don't you sit down and tell me what's on your mind."

"Thanks," Bill replied while seating himself.

"Would you like some tea, . . . or maybe coffee?"

"Coffee'll be fine," he answered.

She turned to leave for the kitchen. "Be right back."

Bill looked around the room while he waited. It was a small room with half-closed drapes that gave an eerie appearance. The furniture appeared to be antiques and consisted of three upholstered chairs with floral patterns in need of recovering. A few folding chairs stood in one corner. He noticed a large number of photographs and paintings, hung in groupings that gave it a cluttered appearance. He was studying them when she returned.

She handed him the cup of coffee and said, "I brought along cream and sugar, because I forgot to ask when I left, if you use them."

"Thanks, but black is the way I like it. By the way, how much do you charge?"

"By fifteen-minute increments, at twenty dollars each."

Bill considered this a while thinking, *A little steep, but if she can help, it'll be worth it.*

"Now, what is it you'd like me to do? Predict the future? Maybe you'd like me to read your aura and tell you what the colors represent. I don't act as a channel for spirits, but I can see into past lives," she offered.

Bill felt a bit encouraged, but he was still skeptical. "It has to do with a past life."

She set her cup down and asked, "Was there something in particular that you want me to search for?"

Bill took a sip and held his cup on his knee as he answered, "Yes. I'm searching for a friend who has disappeared. He may have been related to me in a past life that occurred around the turn of the century."

Scrunching her face into a half-smile and in a monotone, high-pitched voice, she replied, "Good. That's a starting point."

Bill lifted his cup and took another sip of coffee. In doing so, he realized he was getting hungry and hoped this wouldn't take long.

Leaning back in her chair, Ann began to stare off into space, while Bill studied her like a cat eyeing a bird in a tree.

Her eyes glazing slightly, Ann began to speak. "I see a large, sailing ship that I am told is somewhere off the coast of Spain. It is an English galleon, carrying freight. Now I see another ship approaching it from the side. It's flying a pirate's flag. They're going to attack the English ship. It's alongside now, and they are boarding it. There is much fighting all over the ship. Now I see you. You are standing on the side of the ship with a sword and you're fighting with one of the men. Now, I see you being knocked overboard and you are drowning." She sat upright. Looking Bill squarely in the eyes, she stated, "My God. You're deathly afraid of water, aren't you?"

Even though she had revealed nothing concerning Peter that he could relate to, he was stunned by her statement. "Yes, I am. I've never understood why. . . . You could be right in what you saw."

"That life had nothing to do with your friend, so I'll try again."

Disappointed, Bill agreed. "Right."

"What is the name of the person you are looking for?"

"Peter Dunn."

"Do you have a picture or anything that belonged to him, so that I can be more accurate?"

Wistfully, Bill answered, "No, I don't have anything."

"Then I'll do my best to find this boy in a previous life you may have shared together."

Bill relaxed a bit as she tried a second time.

"I see you looking out into the water. I am told it is the English Channel. There is a steep embankment to your right, covered with trees. You are in a wooded area. You have disguised yourself as a monk, and you're waiting for someone to come in by boat. It is nighttime, there is only a slight amount of light, and the water is hazy. Now I see three small rowboats appearing from around the embankment."

Suddenly her body shook slightly, and she adjusted her position. "Now, I hear cannon and rifle fire, too. Someone is blowing the boats out of the water. On your left, I hear people running in the woods and they are shouting, 'Get the traitor. Kill that traitor.' You turn and run off into the trees just as soldiers appear. I see them shooting at you. I can see you falling to the ground. They've shot you. Now I see them crowding around your body. One of them is leaning over your body and I can her him telling the others that you're dead."

She came out of her trance. Following his earlier encouragement, Bill now felt a flood of disappointment.

Ann said apologetically, "I'm very sorry that I haven't been of any help to you. . . . This is very strenuous for me. I'll need some time to regain my strength before I can try again. If you can come by tomorrow, we may have better luck."

Luck, Bill thought. *I guess that's all it is to her.* He set his cup down, saying, "That was all very interesting, But you're right, it hasn't helped me any."

She offered with a smile, "Perhaps, if you'd like to have me try again, you could tell me more about this boy and why you're looking for him. I could then more easily locate the past you are looking for."

Bill, his face void of expression, said simply, "It's a long story."

"I wouldn't charge you for the time you spend telling me what you might know and why you're looking for him. Or, why you think he has something to do with your past. Then I would have a better chance of locating just what it is you're looking for."

"I'll try to drop by tomorrow sometime. Is there any special time I shouldn't come?"

"No, not really. Anytime will be fine. I'll be here all day."

"How much do I owe you?"

"That'll be forty dollars."

Bill wondered if he could be wasting valuable time, by returning. His second thought was, *If I do tell her everything, she might be of help.* Handing her the money and turning to leave, he thanked her.

Reaching for the front door knob and with uncertainty in her voice, Ann said, "I'll see you tomorrow, then?"

Hoping the hypnotist could supply his needed information, Bill replied, "Perhaps. I'll have to see what else might turn up in the meantime."

Disappointed, Bill drove to his friend's home. When he arrived, the aroma of meat cooking on a grill greeted him as he stepped out of his rented car. He followed his nose to the back yard and found Jim cooking steak. "Smells good. Caught a whiff of it all the way out front."

"It'll be superb as soon as I'm finished with it. . . . Steak is hard to cook up right on these things, but I've got it down to a science. I do it by time." He paused, then added, "Gin has everything all set inside, so we can eat in a few minutes."

"Good. It's been a wasted day. . . . I didn't realize how hungry I was until I smelled this."

"You didn't find out anything worthwhile, I take it?"

"Right, and it's really getting to me, too. I'm no closer now than I was when I came here."

Jim looked at Bill and, giving the steaks a final turn, he inquired, "The hypnotist was a fraud, I take it?"

"That's part of the problem. I didn't get to see him. He had some family problems and canceled the appointment. I have to go back in the morning."

Jim dipped his hand into a cooler, pulled out a beer, and tossed it to Bill. "Here, have a cold brewski while you're waiting. These'll be finished in another minute."

He caught the can and popped it open. Tilting his head back, Bill took a long draw from it. "That does go gooood," he emphasized as he walked to a lawn chair and seated himself. Brushing back his tangled hair with his hand, he watched Jim momentarily. After guzzling a quick one down, he commented, "It's sure ideal weather for a cookout."

"That's one reason why I decided on it. It's too damned warm for cooking indoors."

Bill sipped his beer, then stated, "The girls should be getting here soon. I think I'll give Gwin a call tonight and see if she's heard anything from them. They're supposed to check with her when they arrive, so she can tell them where I'm staying."

Jim sipped from his can and said, "I'm glad you mentioned that, or I might have forgotten to tell you. There was a message from her on the answering machine when I got home. She wants you to call her as soon as possible."

An anticipatory rush filled Bill. Excitedly he said, "They must've gotten into town and contacted her. I'd better call right away and find out where they are."

Jim, his face broadening into a smile, suggested, "Invite them over to eat with us if they're here. We have plenty of food for them. . . . It'll be refreshing to have some young chicks around the place."

Hurrying toward the house, Bill replied, "Thanks, I will."

Feeling good inside and thinking about seeing the girls again, Bill dialed his sister's number. He listened intently to the clicking of the phone making the connections. His anticipation dwindled with the endless ringing of the phone. "Damn women. Never at home," he muttered to himself. After allowing it to ring a few more times, he decided to hang up and call later.

As he was about to replace the telephone, he heard, "Hello."

Quickly, he returned the phone to his ear. "Hi, Gwin. This is Bill. Jim said you'd left a message on his machine. Have you heard from the girls? Have they gotten here yet?"

Silence met his ear. Finally she said, "I don't know how to tell you this, Bill."

Bill's heart jumped, his mind went beyond his control. "Tell me, what's wrong? For God's sake, woman, spit it out! Has something happened to the girls . . . or Peter?"

"It's the girls. They got into an accident in New Jersey. They're both dead."

Bill's heart fell into his stomach. "Dead!" he exclaimed. "What happened?"

"They went off the road, and the camper burned with them in it. The police got your license number from it and finally traced you here."

His voice quavering and filled with sudden emotion, Bill exclaimed, "My God! I—I just don't believe it."

Gwin, trying to explain, said, "They said there was no question about it. It was a camper with two people in it that burned. I know how you must feel about this, Bill. I just don't know what to say."

Depression set into Bill's mind as his hopes ebbed from him. He answered, "I guess there isn't anything anyone can say! . . . I'll be in touch!"

Gwin tried to be consoling. "I'm very sorry, Bill. I know this is going to be hard for you to accept. . . . I'll be saying some prayers for you. . . . Please take care of yourself."

Bill's eyes blurred. "Thanks, Gwin. I'll be all right." Holding the receiver he stood in shock as he paused a few seconds, then he added, "Good-bye."

Shuffling his way to the nearest chair and with tears loading his eyes, Bill dropped into it. Feelings of aloneness he hadn't felt since the death of his wife swept through his brain. With water from his eyes flooding down his face, he covered it with his hands and openly wept uncontrollably. A sudden ominous deep feeling of depression swept through his entire being. Memories of his wife dying swiftly in the night while lying beside him in bed flooded his mind and eroded his ability to think clearly. The mixture of anger he'd felt toward her for having left him alone and the all-consuming emptiness that filled his soul for many months afterward, which he couldn't tell anyone about, had now returned. The terror of these feelings filling his life again seemed unbearable to him in his present altered state of mind.

He knew he'd told many people that the past couldn't be changed and therefore has the same value as a dream, but this wasn't of any value to him now. He knew the past, like a dream, can be remembered, enjoyed, but since it can't be changed, it shouldn't be dwelled upon. Now the idea was not consoling to him as his memories and accompanying thoughts gnawed his mind raw with despair. Visual images of the girls and Peter appeared and quickly vanished in a flurry of memories of the recent past.

Noiselessly, Jim's wife, Gin, appeared beside him. Stunned in disbelief at how she found this burly man reduced to tears, she exclaimed, "Bill! What's happened?"

Slowly, Bill lowered his hands as he returned to reality. Reaching into his pocket for his handkerchief, he pulled it out, wiped his eyes, and before answering her, he blew his nose in a loud snort. Looking up at her and exerting much effort, he related, "It's the girls. They were killed in an accident."

Involuntarily, her hands flew to cover her mouth. "My God, no! How did it happen?"

Bill wiped his eyes again. "Gwin didn't know many of the details. The camper went off the road and burned. They didn't get out."

Tears swelled his eyelids and erupted in a waterfall. He quickly looked downward and covered his eyes with his hankie.

"Jim!" Gin called out. Excited, she immediately called again, "Jim, come into the living room!"

Jim, who was in the kitchen, appeared in the doorway, a questioning look on his face. With a glance, he caught sight of Bill and inquired, "Something's happened to the girls, hasn't it?"

Gin's face reflected the compassion she felt for Bill and moving behind him, she put her hands on his shoulders, saying to Jim, "Yes. They're both dead. They were killed in a car crash."

With surprise written on his face, Jim asked, "They hit a car?"

Bill wiped his eyes, got control of his emotions, looked across the room at his friend, and corrected Gin. "They were almost here when they went off the highway. The camper burned with them in it."

Jim's face muscles tightened. "Geeze, I'm awfully sorry to hear that, Bill. I know how close you were to them." He walked over and stood by Bill.

Teary-eyed, Bill made an effort to speak. "I—I don't know how good they were at driving." He paused; a lump rose up into his throat.

He cleared it and continued, "But they'd assured me they'd be careful and not take any chances. . . . I've got a feeling that thing had something to do with it."

Jim looked down at Bill. "I guess we'll never know." He paused, then commented, "I don't know much about that sort of thing, but I do know how much you were looking forward to their getting here so they could help you to find Peter."

Bill wiped his nose on his sleeve. "Yes. We'd gotten real close. They had their problems, but I respected them for the way they stuck by Peter and me through all of this." Then, with an instant flash of memory, he added with a swell of tears, "They were fun to be with, too."

Feeling compassion for Bill, Jim moved in front of him and inquired, "I know this has been a sudden shock to you, Bill. Do you feel up to eating?"

Having regained his composure somewhat, Bill looked at him through misty eyes, his nose dripping slightly. With a half-smile on his face, he turned to face Gin and said, "Those steaks looked really good on the grill. I know I have to go on living and I'll have to eat to live, so I might as well start now."

Jim nodded his head. "That's good. I'm sure you'll feel better, when you've finished eating."

Gin turned to go into the kitchen. "I made some good potato salad to go with them."

Bill wiped his eyes and blew his nose. "I like the way you make it, Gin. There's none better!" He paused and looked toward her. "I'm sorry for upsetting everything. You people have gone out of your way to make me feel welcome. I hope someday I can repay you for all your kindness."

Offering his hand to Bill, Jim helped him up from the chair, saying, "We wouldn't have it any other way. You know you're always welcome with us. Right, Gin?"

Walking toward the bathroom, Jim added, "Let's get cleaned up. The steaks won't wait too long."

Reaching the doorway to the kitchen and her eyes twinkling, Gin responded, "For sure, Bill, you've been more than paying your way with all the groceries you've been buying. You know we haven't wanted you to do that, either." She paused and added, "Give me a couple of minutes to get the food on."

Bill felt very lucky to have friends like them and walking out behind Jim, he answered, "Guess it's my way. . . . I do appreciate having a place to stay. If I had to stay at that motel, it would have cost me a hell of a lot more."

During the meal, Bill's mind became mired with thoughts of the past. Pictures of Peter, the girls, and his dead wife popped in and out of his mind, blocking out parts of the conversation. With their understanding he suffered through the supper meal.

When he was finished, he excused himself. "I think I'll take a walk. I know that I won't be good company, and I have some heavy thinking to do."

Jim responded, "We understand. . . . That's probably a good idea. If you'd like to go out and have a couple of brews when you get back, let me know. I wasn't planning anything special tonight, so I'll be around."

Bill slouched as he left the kitchen. "Thanks, Jim. That might be what I need."

Before leaving, Bill went to his room and retrieved a new bottle of brandy from in his dresser drawer. Raising it to his lips, he let the warm liquid flow down his throat in a steady stream before lowering it. The vapors permeating his nostrils anesthetized his brain somewhat, giving him a false sense of stability. Then, placing the bottle in his right hip pocket, he left, walking dazedly along the sidewalk and wandering without awareness of any specific direction.

Swirling, his mind was like seaweed-filled water along the shore that had been torn from the bottom of a lake by a sudden summer storm; he couldn't have cared less where he might be heading. His thoughts became jumbled, and his mind vacillated with questions that remained unanswered.

After meandering doglike and swigging from the bottle for an hour, with no settling of his mind, an incessant sensation caught Bill's attention. He glanced up and his half-open eyes read the sign, "Silver Nugget Bar."

Unconsciously he turned in and pushed open the large oak door. His eyes adjusted themselves to the change in lighting as he shuffled to the bar and seated himself.

The young, male bartender looked to Bill's left down the bar as he directed his question at Bill. "What'll you have?"

Bill answered, "A double shot of brandy and a draft beer." Then he muttered, "It doesn't matter what kind."

"That'll be two seventy-five," the bartender announced while changing his gaze and looking steadily at Bill with closely placed, beady eyes.

Bill tossed the money onto the bar, downed the shot, and then gulped half the glass of beer.

"Give me another double shot of brandy."

Hearing a woman to his left talking, Bill slowly turned and raised his eyes to look at her. Seeing a small redhead, about thirty years old, seated alone one stool away, prompted him to ask, "Did you say something to me?"

After noting that she was ignoring him and concentrating instead, on her bottle of beer, he started to turn back around. While he was in mid-turn, she mumbled something he couldn't understand.

The bartender served the brandy, and Bill produced more money. Bending over to pick up a fallen bill, he noticed the man to his right. He appeared to be a mountain of a man who began drumming his fingers on the bartop and staring in Bill's direction. He knew he'd seen this kind many times before. A rowdy screw-loose type who was not playing with a full deck.

Looking down the bar past Bill, the brute hollered to the girl, "Hey, kid."

She didn't respond.

Loaded to the gills, he made a halfhearted effort to smile, then he looked down and yelled again, "Hey, kid."

Ignoring the huge man and looking at Bill, she asked, "What's wrong with me? What am I doing wrong?"

Bill continued to observe without answering.

"How about you and me?" the ugly guy queried.

She looked down at her bottle, with no reply.

Bill became intrigued by the drama unfolding before him as he attempted to appear disinterested. The drumming of fingers started again as the big guy stared at the redhead. This continued for a few minutes before he gave up on her and moved farther on down the bar, where he attempted to hustle a drink.

Bill finished his shots and beer and had them refilled while he periodically glanced in the girl's direction. She sat quietly, clutching her bottle like it was her only friend. Finally, he offered a smile and asked her, "So, how you doing tonight?"

She spoke in an intoxicated manner. "It's all their fault across the street. I don't know what I'm doing wrong. What's the matter with me?"

"It doesn't look to me like anything's the matter with you," he answered and then added, "Who's across the street?"

"Joe, my husband, and the others."

Bill had finished his third set of double brandies and was finishing his beer. "Can I buy you a drink?" he volunteered.

"I was going to go, but sure you can. I'll have a Harvey Wallbanger." She smiled at Bill and signaled the bartender, who took their order.

"I think he wants me to find a boyfriend. Do you think he wants me to find a boyfriend?" she asked.

Seizing an opportunity to make an advance, Bill replied, "Could be. What happened?"

"Oh, he's changed. He used to be so nice, but since we got here, he's changed."

Forgetting his own problems and becoming intent on encouraging her to talk, figuring she would be a good lay, Bill asked, "How long have you been here?"

"About six months. It's all those others. He don't want me anymore." Long-faced, she questioned, "What's wrong with me?"

Bill moved to the bar stool next to her. "You look good to me. Is he looking for someone younger?"

"I guess so." Attempting to smile, she asked, "How about some nice music? I have some change. Will you play some nice music?"

Bill stood up. "Save your change, I have some. I'm not sure what I select will be what you want."

"I like Willie Nelson. I like cowboy music."

"Okay, I'll play Country and Western."

"Oh, I'm sorry. It's not cowboy, it's Country and Western."

Smiling, Bill remarked, "That's nothing to be sorry about. . . . I'll be right back."

As he moved away toward the jukebox, he heard her say, "I like you." Then she emphasized her feelings. "You're nice, real nice."

When Bill returned, she ordered another drink for them. "You're a nice person," she commented and continued, "I like you. Let me pay for these. I have lots of money. I was once married to an undertaker. I don't ever have to work."

Bill winked at her and smiled. "No, let me buy this round. Maybe the next one, okay?"

Propping her head up with her hands and looking at him, she spoke, "Jake tears my purse apart when he's drunk and looking for money. I should have my own money. I should put it all in checking and savings accounts with only my name on it. What do you think?"

Bill put his arm around her and answered, "I really can't say. I don't want to influence your decisions."

She flashed a big smile, then puckered her mouth. Bill leaned over and kissed her. She put her hand onto the back of his head and pulled him tight, while she darted her tongue into his mouth and lingered in the kiss.

Wrinkling her nose and smiling, "I love you," she said.

Feeling a sense of progress, Bill looked intently into her eyes, "You have beautiful eyes."

"I'll know you tomorrow if I see you, or anywhere, if I see you again. Do you love me?"

Still looking into her eyes and smiling, "I like you," he answered.

She leaned over and kissed him with intensity.

Bill suggested, "Why don't you and I leave here and go some place where we can be alone?"

211

She looked at her drink, then at Bill. "I'm going to sit here. I'm staying here."

Bill looked into her eyes, again. "Sure. . . . Can I buy you another drink?"

Looking down and noting her glass was almost empty, she agreed, "Okay. I'll have another."

She leaned forward and kissed him. Then, she sat back and wrinkled her nose. "I love you," she said and paused then added, "I have a nice house here in town. Why does Jon treat me like this? I'm just a mother living in a ghost house. I've got a real nice house full of plants. . . . Across the street. They're all over there."

Realizing she was saying different names, Bill asked, "Who's over there?"

"My husband and the others. He treats me this way. Why does he treat me this way?"

"What do you mean? How does he treat you?"

She looked at her drink. "He's only with the others, wants to be with the young ones."

She turned to look at Bill. "Jon, you lied to me down the street. They followed you."

Bill, trying to tell her he wasn't her husband, was being ignored in his halfhearted attempt to snap her out of confusion. He reminded her, "I'm not Jon. Jon's not here."

"I don't care. I know you're not Jon. Are we going to go home together? Are you going to take me home with you?" She leaned over and kissed Bill. "Do you love me, Jon? I love you. Do you love me, Jon? Let's go home to bed."

What does it matter that she thinks I'm her husband, Jon? Bill found himself thinking, *as long as she's willing to leave with me.*

She blubbered, "Let's go home to bed. Are we going now?"

Looking into her eyes, Bill suggested, "Let's go, honey."

At that moment Bill became vaguely aware of movement behind him and felt a tap on his shoulder. Thinking that it was her husband, he prepared himself for a fight. While wondering if he should turn around, he heard a voice behind him. "Better be careful, buddy. Her husband is in the bar across the street."

The anticipatory juices flowing through Bill suddenly subsided as he thought, *Someone in here knows her.* His mind felt dulled by the alcohol, but it wasn't enough to prevent him from the realization that he'd better leave before her husband came in.

She looked at him. "Are we going to leave now, Jon?"

"I'm not Jon," Bill answered, now somewhat frustrated by the turn of events. "Can I buy you another drink?" he suggested.

"Sure, why not? I don't care if you're not Jon. I love you. Do you love me, Jon?" she repeated.

Bill ordered another round while trying to decide what to do about leaving with her.

"I like Waylon Jennings. Do you like Waylon Jennings? . . . Play some music on the jukebox. Whatever you like," she requested with a half-controlled smile.

Bill slid from the bar stool and moved slowly over to the jukebox. When he returned, she was waiting for him with a relaxed smile on her face. As he seated himself again, a large, heavy-set man with black, curly hair stepped up to the bar. He stood between Bill and the woman, facing her and ignoring Bill. He talked to her cruelly in low tones, and Bill was unable to make out what he said to her.

She yelled, "You're lying, Jon! I'm not crawling all over the bar like a wild animal!"

She then poked her head forward to see around her husband and asked Bill, "Hey, guy! I'm not hanging all over the bar like a wild animal, am I?"

Realizing he might easily become involved in a fight over a family squabble, he answered, "I didn't think so." Then, getting up to leave, he tapped her husband on the shoulder and added, "Take it easy. She didn't do anything wrong." But the man ignored him.

Moving unsteadily out the door, Bill heard the man yell at her in a commandingly cruel voice, "Get your ass home!"

The next morning came early for Bill. He glanced at the clock, which read eight-thirty. Getting to the edge of the bed was a difficult task, which he accomplished with much effort. His mouth tasted to him like he'd been eating pure shit. He sat there a few moments while he rubbed his eyes and yawned deeply. A familiar aroma teased his senses. Getting up, he walked over and picking up his pants, he examined them. A few small pieces of glass fell to the floor. "Son of a bitch, I must have broken it when I fell last night," he muttered.

Reaching around to the right cheek of his butt, he found that his shorts stuck to his skin. Pulling them loose, he felt a slight pain where a scab that had been forming, opened a wound.

At ten o'clock sharp, Bill walked into the hypnotist's office and was greeted with a bright-eyed smile. "Good morning, Mr. LaBark. If you'd like to have a seat, the doctor will be with you in a few minutes."

"Thank you," Bill answered, returning the receptionist's smile. He hadn't had time to think about his problems and as he waited, the thought of the girls's deaths returned. Visual images of them danced in his brain.

213

"You can go in now," the receptionist announced.

Bill entered the door she had indicated and found the room empty. He glanced around, expecting to find a couch, but there were only three comfortable chairs in addition to the doctor's desk. The walls were bare except for a few framed diplomas. He noted that one of them proved the hypnotist to also be a medical doctor. "Good. He's probably not a quack," he mumbled as he seated himself directly in front of the desk. A side door opened and turning, Bill saw a large, well-dressed man in his mid-thirties step into the room. Something about him appeared vaguely familiar to Bill. In a fleeting thought, he wondered if he might be the man whose wife Bill had been hustling in the bar the previous night.

"Good morning, I'm Dr. Meyer," he said, extending his hand.

Bill rose and, turning, he greeted him, "It's nice meeting you. I'm very glad that I was able to get to see you this morning."

"There seems to be some urgency in the way you said that."

"There is. Maybe it'll be best if I explain to you why I'm here."

"Why don't you do that? It may help me to do a better job for you."

Bill explained what had happened and why he thought hypnosis might help.

"That's facinating to me. I've never run into anyone with those kinds of experiences before. They'd be a basis for a good novel," said Dr. Meyer.

"Sometimes I find it hard to believe myself, but I swear it's all true."

"I'm not doubting you." He paused and looking at Bill, suggested, "What do you say we get started? Have a seat." He motioned with his hand as he seated himself.

Seating himself and not sure of what was expected of him, Bill asked, "What do you want me to do?"

"Suppose I explain a little about hypnosis to you first."

"I've been curious about it. How does it work?"

"It depends upon the individual. Everyone reacts differently under it. It is merely an altered state of consciousness, the same as sleep. You don't have to be afraid of not coming out of it. Even if something happened to me, you would awaken the same as you wake up in the morning."

He paused, watching Bill's reactions. "Since it's a deeper form of sleep, you have more of a feeling of being completely rested."

He paused once more, then continued. "A lot depends upon your ability to concentrate. How do you feel about yours?"

Bill rubbed his chin while listening. He answered, "I think I'm better than average."

"Good. The first thing I want you to do is to take about a half-dozen deep breaths. Then, I'm going to have you visualize something. After that, I'll have you count backward down to one. How does that sound to you?"

"No problem. I'm good at visualization, but I'm not sure what you mean by deep breathing. Is there some special technique to that?"

Dr. Meyer instructed, "You breathe in through your nose to the count of three, expanding the lower part of your lungs. Don't be afraid of allowing your stomach to expand. Then breathe out through your mouth to the count of seven. . . . You may have to force the last of the carbon dioxide out. As you breathe out, say the word 'relax.' Sort of dragging it out for the entire count of seven. . . . Why don't you try a few of them?"

Bill followed his instructions and found that it made him feel very relaxed. "It seems to me this may be a good way of getting into a relaxed state very quickly."

Dr. Meyer looked at Bill from across his desk as he agreed and instructed, "Right. I can see that you won't have any trouble with that part. Now, let's go on. Put both of your feet flat on the floor and find a comfortable position. Also, close your eyes and begin the deep breathing. Do at least six of them."

Bill began deep breathing and when he'd finished, the doctor spoke in a monotone. "I want you to imagine that you're on an ocean beach. It's a very warm day, and you feel the sun's rays warming your entire body. Overhead, there's a lone cloud drifting slowly across the sky. A seagull appears to your right and floats effortlessly above you. The heat of the sun is making your body go to sleep. It begins with your feet. You feel a slight tingling in them, and gradually they're getting numb so that you can no longer feel them. Your body is now going to sleep. First one leg, then the other. Now your hips and abdomen are asleep."

The doctor's continued monotone voice had its effect on Bill, and he felt his awareness slowly leaving his body. "Your hands, arms, shoulders, and head are now asleep. You are going into a very deep sleep. I want you to count to yourself with me as I count from ten down to one. When I reach the number one, you will be completely hypnotized. We'll begin counting now. Ten, you are going deeper and deeper into sleep. Nine . . . eight . . . seven, you are going deeper and deeper into sleep. Six . . . when I say that number, you will be completely hypnotized. Five . . . four, deeper and deeper in sleep. Three . . . you want me to say that number so you will be completely hypnotized. Two . . . deeper and deeper in sleep. You want desperately for me to say that number now, so you'll be completely hypnotized . . . ONE. You are in a very deep sleep and are completely hypnotized now. Do you hear me, Bill?"

"Yes," he responded.

"I want you to clasp your fingers together as tightly as you can."

Watching Bill clasp his fingers, he instructed, "Good. Now, you won't be able to pull them apart, no matter how hard you try. Now, try to pull them apart," he commanded.

Trying with much effort, Bill found he couldn't get them apart until he was instructed, "You can release them now and open your eyes."

Bill brought his hands to his sides. "You are in a very deep sleep and completely hypnotized. I'm going to take you back in time to a previous life. I'll be recording what you tell me, so that later, we may be able to find something that relates to your current situation. This may be very stressful for you at times. I want you to mentally prepare yourself for anything that might happen. I want you to tell yourself in a very powerful way what I am going to say now. . . . I AM IN CONTROL. . . . THIS IS NOT REALITY, AND I WILL BE AWAKE SOON. . . . I WILL REMEMBER EVERTHING OF IMPORTANCE. Now, Mr. LaBark, you say it three times with as much feeling as you can put into it."

Bill repeated what Dr. Meyer had said and emphasized it, using his hand to punctuate each word.

Keeping his voice in a controlled, low monotone, the doctor continued. "Now, I want you to close your eyes and relax. You are going backward in time. You are progressively getting younger and younger. Back further and further. Back through your mother's womb to a time before you were conceived in this life. Back to a life that you lived around the turn of this century, back to when you were young. You are there now and your age is fifteen. Can you tell me where you are living?"

"I live with my parents and two sisters in an apartment building on Starling Street."

"Can you give me the address of the street and the name of the town?"

"The address is 1492, and I live in Boston."

"Very good. Now, I want you to tell me everything that has any meaning to you as you live your life. Tell me about your family, friends, girlfriends, parties, unusual things that happen. Nothing is to embarrassing to tell. I want to know everything, especially names and addresses of all the people you know, even casual friends. Tell me about any fights you got into, what they were about, who they were with, including addresses. Do you understand? I want to know everything."

"Yes, I understand. It's my sixteenth birthday, and my friends are going to have a party for me."

"What year is it?"

"It's 1892."

"Describe to me what happens at your birthday party, then go on. Remember, I want to know EVERYTHING." He emphasized this, hoping that Bill would make an extra effort to tell even the smallest details that might not seem significant.

Dr. Meyer listened intently and asked questions for more than three hours before removing the hypnotic trance. "When I count to three, you will no longer be hypnotized. You will come out feeling extremely relaxed. One—two—three. You are no longer hypnotized. How do you feel?"

Bill shook his head in amazement. "I can't believe how relaxed I feel. Like I've just awakened from a hundred-year sleep. . . . Tell me, Doc, was I able to remember anything that will help me find my friend Peter?"

"We'll have to evaluate it together. My experience with previous lives is limited. From what you've told me, time is of the essence. You did give a lot of very detailed information that might be helpful. Do you have a tape recorder?"

"No, but I can get one. Why?"

"I'll make a copy of the tape and give it to you when we've finished reviewing it. That way I can study it here, and you can take a copy with you."

Bill felt anxious and stated, "Good idea. Let me hear it now. I want to get moving on it. I've already wasted too much time."

Sympathetically the doctor said, "I understand. The longer the entity is in control of his body, the stronger it will get and the harder it will be to free him from it." About to leave, Bill turned to the doctor who said as an afterthought, "If you find him, try to bring him here to me and I'll see if I can help him."

Arriving at his friend's home, Bill noticed Jim, who was walking on his front lawn. Pulling into the driveway, parking, then getting out, Bill called, "Jim!"

Jim turned and smiled broadly. He felt encouraged to see his friend in good spirits while the night before he'd had his doubts. "Hi, Bill. Looks like something good has happened for a change."

"I'm not sure how good it is, but at least I have some leads to follow up on."

"Come on in and have a cold brew. You can tell me about it while we wait for Gin to make supper." Jim paused, then added, "Gin invited her friend Ellie Sue Carling over to eat with us. You probably remember her. The woman from the motel you stayed at the first night in town."

Bill acknowledged, grinning, "Sure. The buxom blond."

Walking into the kitchen, Jim went straight to the refrigerator, took out two beers, and tossed one to Bill. "Last night, Gin was very worried about you with the way you were feeling. She thought that it might help you if you had a girlfriend. Ellie Sue has been divorced for years and hasn't been dating much . . . Hell, I know it's matchmaking, but it wouldn't hurt to get to know her."

Bill popped his can open and unable to bridle his need to find Peter without delay, he stated matter of factly, "I planned on leaving for Boston tonight."

Feeling concern for Bill, Jim suggested, "I know how much this means to you, but, you'll have to eat somewhere, so why not here? Besides, Ellie Sue told Gin that she thought you were a fox. It appears that she likes you. Don't make any decisions until after we eat. She's good company. I know you'll like her."

Bill reached into his pocket and withdrew the tape. "I'll think about it. . . . Do you have a tape recorder?"

"Did he tape your session?"

Bill sucked on his beer, then answered, "He sure did. That guy is no fool. We listened to it together and talked about it for a long time. He made some notes on what we thought might relate to this mess, and he gave them to me."

"Good," Jim agreed and putting his beer down, he said, "I'll get the recorder, and we can listen to it. Sometimes, when you hear something a second time, you can pick up what you've missed the first go 'round."

Bill lit his pipe, settled back into a chair, and setting his beer aside, he listened to the tape with Jim. After hearing it they discussed it while consuming a few more cans of beer. Bill noticed Jim quickly glance up as he looked on past Bill. The suddenness of it startled Bill, and he whirled around in his chair. With his mind cluttered with the intensity of the tape on his previous life and his preoccupation with the entity, he half-expected to see a ghost.

Ellie Sue Carling stood in the doorway leading to the kitchen, looking more beautiful to Bill than any woman had in a very long time. Her golden blond, shoulder-length hair flowed down over her left eye in a large curl. When he'd first met her, he hadn't noticed how pretty her large, soft-brown eyes were. But then, she was bathrobe-clad and her hair, tossled from sleeping, covered most of her face.

She smiled. "Hi, Jim." She paused and glanced at Bill. "Thought I'd look in on you and say Hi before I help Gin in the kitchen."

"Hi, Ellie Sue. Do you remember Bill? He checked in the motel a while back."

"Sure do. It was late and I was still half-asleep, but I'm pretty good with faces. Now, names—that's a different story." She looked directly into Bill's eyes. "Hi, Bill. It's nice seeing you again. I'd thought maybe you'd left town."

Feelings stirred in Bill. Smiling, he answered, "Nice seeing you again, Ellie Sue. Jim was good enough to put me up." Then he added, "Or, should I say, put up with me?"

Momentarily Bill studied her. Regret at having to leave that night crossed his mind.

She laughed. "Well, I'll see you both later. I'm sure Gin can use my help." Turning, she disappeared through the doorway.

Bill glanced at Jim and nodded his head approvingly.

Jim, seeing a pleased look appear on Bill's face, commented, "Some looker, isn't she?"

Bill answered regretfully, "She's a winner. All the time I spent here without accomplishing anything and having nothing to do in the evenings and now, when I have to leave, you indulge my curiosity with this chick."

Jim laughed. "I knew you'd like her. What I don't understand is how she's remained single."

"Maybe she's a dyke or is frigid," Bill responded in a hushed voice, not wanting to believe what he'd said.

"I doubt that. I know she's not a dyke. She's not that kind of person."

"I was only kidding," Bill quickly answered, paused, then added as a second thought, "Guess you're right. One more night here can't hurt. Besides, I can get an early start in the morning."

During their meal, Bill carried most of the conversation, which inevitably turned to his explaining to Ellie Sue the events that lead to his being in Far Rockaway. "Maybe I'm crazy trying to help someone like this, but there was something about Peter that grew on me. Now, since that old lady told me we'd been related in a previous life, it sort of makes sense, but I didn't believe her at the time."

He paused and his eyes brightened. "Speaking of her, I was asleep at the ocean the other day and she appeared to me in a dream. She was telling me something, which seemed important, when a young girl squirted me in the face and I woke up suddenly. I just now remembered that she had mentioned Boston."

Jim's ears perked up. "That's where you lived in that previous life."

"Right, and that's probably where Peter is now."

Ellie Sue, who had been listening attentively to Bill, spoke. "All this talk about entities and previous lives gives me the chills. I've never really believed in that sort of thing." Looking at Bill, she paused and his eyes locked on hers. She continued, "I remember my uncle telling me once about a white form that he'd seen by a swamp. It frightened him and he ran to his car and cut out of there full blast. But the thing stayed right alongside of his car. He said he'd tried stopping a couple of times, and the thing stopped, too. Finally, it left him. He told a couple of people about it and a few days later when he took a friend down there, the place was full of people, some of them shooting. . . . They didn't hang around there. He'd said the police closed the place off, and I don't know if anyone else saw it after that."

Gin spoke up. "This sure is a strange world. So many things that boggle the imagination." She looked at Jim, then at Bill and Ellie Sue. "Anyone for dessert? We've got shortcake with fresh strawberries."

"Have any vanilla ice cream?" Jim inquired. "I could go for some on the top if you have it."

"We've got something better—fresh whipped cream. How does that sound?"

Ellie Sue glanced at the men. "Judging by the smiles on their faces, they'd like some." Getting up, she said, "I'll help you, Gin."

Bill studied Ellie Sue, trying not to be obvious about the interest he had in her. He deduced that she was not a shy person. Whenever their eyes met, she looked deep into his eyes in more than a fleeting glance. Her tight-fitting red blouse revealed cleavage that left no doubt of the well-formed body it concealed. The short, yellow, cotton skirt she wore with it, allowed Bill to notice that her entire body was proportioned in the right places.

When they'd finished eating, they retired to the living room. Jim and Gin deliberately sat in the two empty chairs, leaving the couch for Bill and Ellie Sue. They continued to talk about Bill's circumstances until Gin finally said, "Bill, I know how important all of this is to you, but I think it would be good for you to relax and forget about it for the remainder of the night. What do you say we all go out bowling?"

Bill responded, "I haven't bowled in years, but it would be good to get out." Then, turning to Ellie Sue, he asked, "What about you, Ellie Sue? Can you come with us?"

"Sure. I'd like that," she responded with a smile, partially showing her bright white teeth.

Jim volunteered, "Then it's settled. There's a new alley over on Dinsmore I think you'll like."

Ellie Sue nodded. "Yes, I've been there. It's a really neat place."

They went directly to the bowling alley. As they walked in, Bill said to Jim, "Why don't you and Gin bowl? Ellie Sue and I can sit at the bar for a while and join you later, if that's all right." He turned to look at Ellie Sue. She nodded agreement.

Gin commented, "Sounds all right to me. We'll have a few drinks with you first, before we get into bowling."

The decor of the barroom surprised Bill. A full-sized stagecoach hung suspended from the ceiling over the bar. The walls were loaded with a large variety of remnants from the past. Jim asked, "What do you think? Some place, isn't it?"

"Quite unique, to say the least," Bill agreed, then he inquired, "Mind if I wander around a bit, just to look at some of these things?"

"I'll go with you," Jim said. Then, pointing to the antique guns that were suspended from the ceiling, he continued, "I don't think the girls get off on these things. They've seen it all before, anyway. . . . Let me get some drinks first."

Gin encouraged them. "Go right ahead. We'll be fine here at the bar."

Carrying their beer with them, Bill and Jim moved around the barroom, examining the array of swords, pistols, rifles, stuffed animal heads, and other relics of the days gone long past. Complete car radiators with their ornaments hung helter-skelter. Auto spoked wheels and steering wheels were mounted on the walls along with other antiques. While walking through the bar, Bill's thoughts briefly turned from his problems and were quickly replaced by the intrigue of the items of yesteryear. An old hand-pump fire wagon caught his attention. Without saying a word, he grabbed hold of one of the handles and began pumping.

He shouted to Jim, "Give me a hand, Jim. We've got to get this fire out before the whole town burns." Running to the other side, Jim began pumping.

Lost in pretending, Bill was suddenly snapped back to reality when his glass of beer he'd placed on the wagon, shaken to the floor, smashed to bits. All heads turned in their direction. A large man moved from the bar and strutted over to them. In no uncertain terms, he reprimanded, "Can't you read? You're not allowed to handle these things. Settle yourselves down or I'll have to ask you to leave."

Bill and Jim walked toward the bar. As they approached the women, Ellie Sue flashed her eyes and smiled at Bill. "Still a kid at heart, I see. . . . I like that."

Grinning, he answered, "The world is too serious a place. . . . A person has to have some fun, too."

Catching the way they looked at each other, knowingly, Jim smiled to himself, saying, "Why don't we bowl now, Gin?"

"Okay," she agreed, then she coyly asked, "Are you going to give me a handicap?"

Bill was about to kid Gin, but he thought better of it. Walking toward the bowling alleys and chuckling, Jim answered, "Sure! If anyone knows about your handicap, I do."

Bill and Ellie Sue sat up to the bar talking while their friends bowled.

An hour had passed before Ellie Sue ventured, "You are a very interesting man. I like you."

"I think you're a cute person," Bill responded. Usually, he was very forward, but she was a different kind of woman than he'd grown accustomed to being with.

She lowered her eyebrows. "A cute person, eh? What's a cute person?"

"It means that I like you, too. . . . I wish we had time to get to know each other better. If this darned thing wasn't so important to me, I'd stay here, but I have to leave in the morning."

"I understand you have a lot on your mind with your concern for your friend's life, and I wouldn't want to interfere with that. We still have a lot of time left tonight to get to know each other." Then, not caring how obvious she was in showing that she liked Bill, Ellie Sue invited, "I live alone at the motel. You can come over to my place, and we can have a few drinks together. There's a rec room in the motel basement with a pool table. Do you play pool?"

Bill answered in anticipation. "After sorts. . . . That sounds good to me."

Ellie Sue's eyes glistening, she continued, "I don't think Gin and Jim would mind if we left while they're still bowling. She told me a lot about you and the kind of man you are. I'd like to help you get your mind off your troubles."

Bill responded, "Thanks. . . . Relaxing with a beautiful woman is like a dream and something I haven't done in a very long time." Then he agreed. "I accept. . . . Let's go over and see how they're doing with the bowling, then we can leave."

Approaching Jim and Gin, Bill asked, "How's the bowling coming?"

Sporting a sly grin, Jim answered, "She's up on me by two games. Even without the handicap I gave her, she's beating my butt. But, I'll get even."

Gin looked toward Bill and with an ear to ear grin, she stated, "I guess it's just not his night. Call me Miss Lucky. It isn't often that I can beat him, so I'm going to glory in it while I can."

Ellie Sue's face beamed with enthusiasm. "Good going, Gin. Make him squirm."

Gin grinned and answered, "You can bet I will."

Ellie Sue informed them, "We're going over to my place and have a few drinks and maybe shoot a little pool."

Later, at Ellie Sue's apartment in the back of the motel, she and Bill were sitting on her couch and after they'd spent a couple of hours making small talk, getting to know each other, Bill's curiosity finally got the better of him. He asked, "How did a good-looking woman like you manage to remain single for so long . . . if you don't mind my asking?"

She responded, "No, I don't mind. A lot of men have asked me that." Her eyes drifted and she looked off into space as she spoke further. "I've had such a hard time with my first marriage that I decided I'd wait a while before taking the plunge again."

Ellie Sue looked down at her lap where she was twisting her hands together. Then she continued, "He was very domineering and extremely jealous. I've had a lot of time to think about it, and I believe it was because he was very insecure. Anyway, I've tried to find Mr. Right and haven't succeeded, yet. Maybe I never will, because I want him to be more than just any man." She looked up into Bill's eyes. "I've dated a lot and they seem to have some of the qualities that I'm looking for, but most of the time, the relationship bogs down into routine mumbo-jumbo."

Her eyes brightened and she looked past Bill, continuing, "It would be great if a person could pick and choose the good qualities from each of the men and make one that is the right combination. It's not that I want too much from them, but I like to be treated like a lady."

Reaching out to her, Bill turned her face toward his. "I can't say that's too much to ask."

She looked into his eyes, saying, "I'm not saying that I'm perfect, either. A lot of the guys have said that I'm a bitch. Either they fight back and we end up not able to stand each other, or they're wimps and I lose interest in them."

Bill felt a glow of empathy for her. "I've heard a lot of men call women bitches, but there are always two sides to every situation. The women they say this about are the kind who are usually honest and have very high ideals and goals in life. They are usually the types of persons who are straightforward and speak their mind. They let you know where you stand with them, which I think is a good trait. I like that in a person, male or female."

Winking impishly, Ellie Sue stated, "I'm beginning to like you even more. You're my kind of man."

Bill shifted his position on the couch so that he could focus on her more clearly. "If someone treats me with sincerity and tells me what I've done wrong or shows me my error, I'm man enough to admit it. I'm not the kind of a person who backs down easily, but if I know I've made a mistake, I can reckon with the consequences."

Changing her position so as to look directly at Bill, she responded, "Now that's one trait I like in a person. One who can admit when they're wrong. I'm the same way. I know it isn't easy sometimes, but the only way a relationship can be meaningful is for people to admit when they're wrong. . . . I may be a bitch, but I get over it quickly if the other person is being truly honest with me. I didn't used to speak my mind when I was married, but instead, I kept it all locked up inside until I thought I'd burst wide open . . . I do speak my mind, now."

Ellie Sue reached over and gently brushed Bill's hair with her hand while speaking. "I don't bitch unless I'm provoked, either." She giggled impishly. "But I guess sometimes I'm easily provoked. . . . Stupidity I hate. . . . When someone treats me like I'm stupid, I resent it and react. If they do stupid things, I also react by bitching. I know I need to be more understanding, but sometimes the things people do, crawl under my skin, and I let them have it with both barrels." Blushing, she looked down before finishing with, "True confessions, eh? I guess I've said too much. Now that you know the real me, you won't like me."

Lifting her head up to meet his eyes, Bill responded, "On the contrary. I do like you for being so honest with me." Then, looking deep into her eyes, he remarked, "Such beautiful eyes you have. They're even more beautiful when you become inflamed in your convictions."

Suddenly, feeling a warm flood of emotions fill his body, Bill threw his arms around her and pulling her to him, he exclaimed, "Oh! Ellie, you're a wonderful girl!" and he held her tightly to him before releasing her.

Then, leaning back and looking at him intently, she was silent. Leaning forward and looking unwaveringly into her eyes, Bill pressed his lips against hers. She responded by putting her arms around his neck and pulling him to her in a full kiss. Slowly releasing her kiss and continuing to look into her eyes, Bill kept his head close to hers, whispering, "Ellie Sue, you really turn me on to you."

She pulled back slightly, requesting, "Can you move back a little? I want to look at you when we're talking."

Withdrawing a little and putting his hand onto her neck beneath her hair, he began gently rubbing it. Whispering, he asked, "How's that? Feel good?"

"Yes. Thank you, it does."

Reaching forward slightly and brushing his hair with her hand, she remained silent.

A few moments later, she withdrew her hand and her face took on a serious look as she spoke. "I know you're a true person, and I like that about you. . . . I don't like game-playing. . . . Too many people don't show their true selves when they first get to know each other, and later there's problems."

Bill relaxed as he got to know Ellie Sue. "I agree wholeheartedly. I don't like game-playing either."

He continued looking into her eyes as he spoke. "A while ago, we were talking about bitching. I believe that a woman who has something to bitch about is a woman who is forced into doing so. Some women are provoked by their men more than others and so they have more reason to be bitchy."

Stroking Bill's hair, Ellie Sue nodded her head in agreement.

Then, sitting back on the couch, Bill placed his hands behind his head and stretching, he continued. "A man who will not do what is expected of him in a relationship, especially a marriage, is the man who gets bitched at the most. Many times this is because of immaturity, but mostly it is because they are uncaring, grouchy, or selfish."

Lowering his hands and pausing, Bill unconsciously began twirling Ellie Sue's hair with his fingers, concluding, "I also think that being a bitch can become a habit. The more bad situations a person has to put up with, the more likely the woman will get to be a constant bitch. Sometimes, obligations and joint goals that involve the man are ignored or family needs are not being met. The woman, then, has to bitch in order to get them accomplished."

Ellie Sue pulled her feet onto the couch and slid them underneath her. Then she spoke softly, "Sometimes, the woman is passive, like I was and things build up inside of her. She feels trapped in a situation she has no control over. . . . When she finally tells him that she wants out, it comes as a shock to the guy. He honestly doesn't understand how, or why she feels that way." She paused, picked up a bobby pin from the end table and spreading it with her teeth, she pinned back the curl of hair that hung over her eye. She smiled at Bill and continued. "It's usually because he never cared about her feelings in the first place. . . . Mine only wanted someone to take care of his house and kid, calling it love. I guess he may have actually believed it was love, because that's what he called it when his house services were threatened to be taken away by divorce." Finishing, Ellie Sue laid her arm across Bill's chest.

Bill, who had listened attentively, spoke. "I also believe any relationship will fall apart if people are taken for granted. This is especially true in marriage, where responsibilities must be shared. There can be too much taken for granted when you're married. It's like when you have papers on someone, they are your possession and you no longer have to try to hold that person's love and respect. When two people love each other and they live together without marriage, they are more likely to continue to show their affection and love."

He picked up his glass of beer and took a drink, then continued. "Sure, there may be a little less security, but that keeps it interesting. When you're dating, it's a challenge not to lose the other person's love. Unfortunately, that disappears in most marriages. Kindness, consideration, and understanding are the keys to keeping it exciting. They are even more important in marriage. If you live together and lose your lover, it's a whole lot better than losing love and being locked in a marriage where the goal is to see who can make the other person the most miserable." Bill paused and then added, "Well, enough said on that subject. Sometimes I get carried away and have diarrhea of the mouth."

Ellie Sue, who had been listening intently, spoke up. "No, Bill, I can see you're a very intelligent person. And, you are right. . . . Many times married people treat their friends better than their spouse." Smiling at Bill, she paused.

He nodded his head in agreement and moved his hand so that his fingers gently touched behind her ear. Noticing her gazing into his eyes and seeing hers relax, he wondered if she would be receptive to love-making. He was about to kiss her, when she spoke, "I see your glass is empty. Would you like some homemade wine? I have a bottle my father gave me."

"I've never been much for wine, but I have some now and again. What kind is it?"

"I think you'll like it. It tastes sort of like Asti Spumonte." She grinned a sheepish grin and added, "I call the stuff spaghetti wine."

A slight smile broke across Bill's face. "I guess it could be pronounced that way."

Ellie Sue picked up his glass and headed for the kitchenette. Returning with two glasses of wine, she handed one to Bill and remarked, "My dad said he put strawberries and blackberries, with a dash of lemon, in it. I like it."

Bill tipped his glass up to take a sip. Misjudging the location of his mouth, he spilled a little that trickled down his chin. Instinctively, he wiped it off with the sleeve of his shirt. "Looks like we'll have to break you of that habit." Ellie Sue chuckled the words out.

"I have a lot more wicked habits that sneak up on me when I least expect them," he kidded.

She grinned. "It seems to me you're like the dog we had when I was a kid. We decided to paper-train him by covering the entire kitchen floor with newspapers. Each day we'd remove a few, gradually working to the center of the room." She paused and grinning, she looked at Bill, who had taken a drink of wine and was observing her over the top of his glass.

He interjected, "Sounds like a reasonable way to do it."

Intensely watching Bill's reaction, she continued. "We thought so. That is, until we got him to only go on the paper in the center of the room and after we removed that paper, the only place he'd pee was in the center of the room." She tried to hold a sober face, but a slight chuckle slipped out.

Bill had just started taking a drink, as she finished her story. Not that it was so funny, but to Bill, visualizing her every word and getting the image of the dog peeing in the center of the floor while everyone watched, exasperated, was amusing. Grinning, he sucked the wine in with his breath. Coughing, sputtering, and leaping up, he spilled his glass of wine across the front of his shirt and onto the floor.

Jumping to her feet and with a suddenness that instantly burst from her, Ellie Sue exclaimed, "Are you all right?" as she patted his back.

Coughing, then catching his breath and glancing down, Bill spit out his words. "Another bad habit I have, ruining people's carpeting, not to say anything about the evening. . . . Now, if you bitch at me for it, I'll understand. . . . You were provoked."

She looked at Bill, who with wine across his front, stood looking very embarrassed. Unable to constrain herself, she burst out laughing. "You have a weird sense of humor. I'm not that much of a bitch. . . . It was the accident that 'I' provoked."

He volunteered, "I'll help you clean it up."

Still grinning, Ellie Sue, surveying the spill, remarked, "Don't be silly. I'll just pour a little water on it, then soak most of it up with a towel. A little dish soap will take care of the rest. Besides, it's almost the color of the carpet, so it won't matter if I can't get it all up." Glancing up at Bill, she added, "It's your white shirt that I'm worried about. . . . The wine might stain it."

Laughing, Bill responded, "No problem. I'll just buy some cheap wine and dye the entire thing."

Laughing with him, she instructed, "Take it off and I'll soak it in cold water."

Bill obliged and removed his shirt.

Glancing at his bare chest, Ellie Sue commented, "Look at those muscles."

He kidded, "That's only a small part of the whole. I left most of them in my shirt."

After momentarily looking into Bill's eyes and smiling, Ellie Sue took his shirt and headed for the kitchen.

227

Shortly, she returned with a refill on his wine, a large glass of water, and a towel. After poouring the water on the spot on the floor, she placed the towel down and walked on it while Bill went to the bathroom. Finishing with the rug, she walked over and turning on her stereo, she returned to the couch waiting for Bill.

Upon his return, Ellie Sue, patting the space beside her, invited, "Come snuggle with me. . . . I want to feel those bulging muscles wrap themselves around me."

In agreement, Bill settled beside her and with an arm around her shoulders, he pulled her to him. "Ummmm, but you smell good. . . . Good enough to eat," he whispered.

Laying her head on his shoulder, she whispered, "Thanks. . . . You do, too."

After talking for a while, Ellie Sue changed position and with her hand, she softly caressed Bill's naked torso. She ran her hand across his arm, onto his bulging muscles, onto his chest, and lingered there, playing with his thick dark hair. Leaning forward she kissed his lips with a gentle kiss that sent shivers up his back. He pulled her close and kissed her in a long and desirous kiss. A feeling of warmth rushed through his body as she spread his lips and inserted her tongue into his mouth and moving it slowly around, she found every sensitive area.

Instinctively, he reached over and cupped her breast, gently massaging it through her blouse. Relaxing and moving back from Bill, while looking deep into his eyes, she whispered, "They say the eyes are the windows to a person's soul. I can see that you have a pure soul."

Unable to contain himself any longer, Bill whispered, "I want to make love to you, Ellie."

Looking into his eyes understandingly, she whispered, "I know, but I don't want to get pregnant. . . . I can't take the pill."

"I've had a vasectomy," he offered.

Feeling a little apprehensive, Ellie Sue questioned, "You won't tell anyone, will you?"

"I won't tell anyone," he reassured her.

"I know you've thought about it," he stated, then asked, "Haven't you?"

Smiling coyishly, she whispered, "Yes."

"Ellie, I want to make love to you now, and I want to do it more than once. The second and third times are the best. Do you like to make it more than once the same night?" he queried.

"Yes, but I haven't done that since I was eighteen," she answered, smiling and relaxing.

Placing his arms around her neck and looking into her eyes, he pleaded, "I want to feel myself inside of you."

Still feeling hesitant, she inquired, "You won't tell Jim, will you?"

Bill encouraged her, trying to set her fears aside. "I won't tell Jim. I won't tell anyone. It will be our secret."

Still hesitant, she asked, "Will you respect me tomorrow?"

Bill looked deep into her soft, brown eyes, reassuring her, "I'll respect you tomorrow. I'll always respect you."

"I want to do it, but it's been a long time since I did." She paused blushing, "I get embarrassed. It took me a month before I could get naked with my husband."

Bill leaned over and closing his mouth over her long, pendant earring, he mibbled on her earlobe. Then, leaning back, he looked at her, saying, "I'll be gentle with you. You've really turned me on to you." Then he offered, "We can turn the lights down low."

"Okay, we can do it, but I have to go to the bathroom first."

Upon her return, Bill picked her up and, carrying her into the bedroom, he placed her sitting on the edge of the bed.

She lay back on the bed and making no effort to undress, she remarked, "I can't believe I'm doing this!" With her feet hanging, extending over the edge of the bed she added, "I've never done it before on the first date."

Bill paused, looking at her. Feelings of concern and frustration filled his mind. *Would she turn him down now? he wondered.*

Reaching over, he fumbled with the snap on her skirt, then finding it to be a button, he undid it and opened her zipper. Ellie Sue made no effort to resist. Gently, he slid her skirt down onto her hips, pulling down her panties with it.

Bill stood momentarily silent, staring at the tips of her long black public hair protruding from the upper laced edges of her panties. Staring at Bill, she did not move.

Searching Ellie Sue's eyes and seeing them change from doubt to agreement, Bill moved slowly, and she raised her buttocks, allowing him to slide her skirt and panties all the way off. Then with her feet, she pushed off her shoes.

With excitement circulating through his veins, Bill removed his clothing while watching Ellie Sue remove the remaining item of clothing obscuring his view of her entire nude body. Pulling her blouse over her head, Ellie Sue revealed her white breasts surrounded by a slight tan.

Lying on the bed naked, with her legs hanging over the edge, she looked exquisite to Bill who gently lifted them up and swung them onto the bed.

Questioningly, she asked, "Aren't you going to take my stockings off?"

Reaching down, Bill removed them carefully while she removed her earrings, placing them on the bedside stand. Then slowly she lay back, completely naked, her blond hair standing out in contrast to the long, dense, black hair covering her genital area. Bill couldn't help looking at the beauty of her body stretched out before him. As he lay down beside her on the bed, she suggested, "You don't know if I'm any good."

Smiling, he kissed her earlobe. "I'll bet you are very good."

Then, smiling broadly, she stated, "I AM GOOD."

Bill snuggled up close to Ellie Sue, kissed behind her ears, and nibbled at her earlobes.

"They're dead," she kidded.

Moving his mouth down, he surrounded the nipples of her breast, gently sucking them. Ellie Sue reached over and moved her fingers through his hair.

"They're dead, too," she continued to tease.

While moving his hand across her body, he kissed her lips in a long and sensuous caress. Then, slowly moving his mouth downward along her entire body, he placed small, lingering kisses.

Before he reached her pubic area, she stopped him. "If you kiss me there, I won't let you kiss me anymore, or I'd throw up! I don't let anyone kiss me there!" she protested. "I've never even let my husband do that!"

Understanding and not wanting to upset her, Bill moved back up and while kissing her on the lips, he placed his hand down onto her large mound of pubic hair, playing with it teasingly. Spreading her legs in anticipation, she allowed him to insert his finger into her vagina.

She moaned in response and moved her hips forward. While pressing his hand tightly against her, he felt her quiver slightly. Noting a positive response, he caressed her lips and worked his finger all the way into her.

An urgency, caused by the way Ellie Sue moved her hands across his naked body, built up in Bill. He knew by her moaning that the same urgency was growing in her, also.

"I want to make love to you now, Ellie."

"Ummmm. Good," she breathed hotly. Then, sitting up, she directed, "Lie on your back."

Straddling him and with accuracy, she leaned backward, letting her orifice consume the entire length of his manhood. Then, slowly she moved her body to the point that he exited her and swiftly she reenclosed him deep into her internal organs, quickly contracting her powerful muscles around him.

While she moved back and forth above him, Bill passed his hands over her breasts, across her body, and down onto her hips. Ellie Sue set

Bill's emotions on fire, and they rippled through his entire being.

"Relax and enjoy it," she whispered in a soft purr.

Bringing his hands to his sides, Bill admired the overhead swaying naked body that was bringing him to heights of pleasure. Leaning down, she focused on his eyes and kissed his lips tenderly. Bill felt his mind give in to the tantalizing and thrilling feelings that swept through every cell of his being.

Some time later, Ellie Sue settled back and sat upright on Bill's groin area. Twisting and grinding her body, she contracted and expanded around Bill in rhythmic movements that drove his feelings wild. Rolling the cheeks of her buttocks, she ground down against his testicles, causing him convulsive reactions.

Bill felt unable to control himself, or to hold himself back any longer. In heated breath, he blurted out, "I'm coming."

"No!" she cried out. But, Bill, unable to restrain his emotions, began involuntary thrusting with but one objective in mind. Feelings of passion burst forth in Bill, shattering his will and exploding a rush of fluid into Ellie Sue.

While looking at Ellie Sue and relaxing slightly, Bill became aware of love juices oozing down into his groin. With renewed emotions, she continued working her vaginal muscles around Bill's newly aroused penis until her twitching signaled Bill that she'd released her own desires. Feeling a shudder sweep through her body and seeing a contented look spread across her face, he felt her relax.

Completely satisfied, Ellie Sue lay down beside Bill, resting her head on his shoulder. He rolled her over so that she faced him and looking into her eyes, he complimented, "You ARE good."

An impish smile covered her face. "I told you I WAS," she stated in no uncertain terms and they laughed.

Bill kissed and caressed her willing body. Running his hand down onto her butt, he partially inserted one finger into her crevice and they lay silently kissing each other.

After their kissing and hugging each other. Bill withdrew his finger and Ellie Sue stretched out on the bed, rolled over into his arms, and relaxed.

A short time later, Ellie Sue sat up on the edge of the bed.

Appearing slightly embarrassed, she looked down at Bill. Then, looking away, she asked, "How long does it take for you to get your pee pee ready again?"

Running his hand down her back and stopping on her butt, he glanced down at his limp form and assured her, "Not very long."

Turning and looking at Bill, she responded, "Good. I'd like to try you again."

231

Reaching for her cigarettes on the nightstand, she asked, "Do you like to smoke after sex?"

Bill sat up next to her and remarked, "I usually smoke a pipe or cigars, but I'm fresh out."

She handed Bill a cigarette and lit it for him. While smoking, Ellie Sue looked down at Bill's penis and commented, "You've got to extend it. You come too quickly."

"I will . . . It's been a while since I've had sex. Besides, you really turned me on and the excitement was too much for me."

Finishing their cigarettes, they lay back on the bed and Ellie Sue, glancing down at Bill's feet, questioned, "You didn't take your stockings off!"

"Sorry, I'll do it now." He sat up, removed them, and lay back beside her. "Better?" he asked.

"Ummm humm," she whispered.

Bill began kissing her and inserted his finger deep into her moist vagina. Feeling her body heat increasing, Bill stimulated Ellie Sue back to urgency. Her eyes went dull. "You're making me horny," she breathed as Bill kissed her behind the ears. Straddling her body he began sucking on her breasts. Minutes later, he propped himself above her, but his penis remained uncooperative.

Eagerly Ellie Sue breathed, "I know what to do." Reaching down, she grasped his penis and stroked it, gradually increasing pressure and speed. Slowly at first, then in a rush, he felt prepared. "Put it in," Bill directed in a whisper.

Continuing to massage him, she questioned, "Put it in?"

Emotionally he requested, "Put it in!" and she complied by quickly guiding it into her hot orifice.

Bill, feeling the intense heat of her body, pushed forward.

Realizing that because of the flat position she was in on the bed, he was unable to fully enter her. Then, reaching beneath her buttocks and lifting, he pushed himself into her, to the hilt.

Ellie Sue, moaning in ecstasy, met Bill's body movements rhythm for rhythm. Moaning approval and kissing the side of Bill's face, Ellie Sue rubbed the left cheek of Bill's buttock while he kneaded both cheeks of hers.

Kissing her lips and caressing the back of her ears, he emotionally whispered, "Do you like to fuck?"

"Y-e-e-s-s," she moaned, between short breaths.

Panting and feeling the fire of passion increase Ellie Sue's contractions, Bill tried extending his time before orgasm. Shortly, Bill felt her body quiver with emotions and her legs stiffen. Clamping her feet around his ankles and holding his legs firmly to the bed and quivering, she whispered, "How is it for you?"

Increasing his thrusting, he murmured, "The best!"

"Ummmmm," she moaned while passing her fingers through his hair.

Panting and on the verge of exhaustion, Bill whispered, "You are truly the best, Ellie."

Looking down, he kissed her waiting lips. The fire that had inflamed her mind and engulfed Ellie Sue's entire body revealed itself in her eyes. Bill, looking into her face, saw the projection of serenity, as the feeling of satisfaction broadened her smile. Relaxing her grip on his thighs, she breathed deeply.

Rolling over to Ellie Sue's side, Bill slowly ran his hands along the length of her body, caressing it as he placed kisses on her face and neck.

Feeling her energy totally consumed, she breathed deeply and whispered, "You're so good at making love that I never wanted you to stop."

Seeing the fresh-fucked look on her face, he whispered, "Was it really that good for you?"

Looking into his eyes, she remained silent. Shortly afterward, she asked, "Does it mean a lot to you to know how it was for me?"

Immediately he replied, "Yes, it does."

She snuggled to him and answered, "It was wonderful. Just wonderful. It couldn't have been any better."

Totally relaxed, Ellie Sue lay back, gently stroking the hair on Bill's chest with her hand. Glancing down, she commented, "You're not circumsized."

Feeing a little embarrassed at the question, he shyly answered, "No. . . . My parents didn't believe in it."

Her eyes sparkled as she remarked, "My god, but you're big. I couldn't believe it when you entered me. You're twice the size of my ex-husband. No wonder he was so insecure."

Smiling, she gently stroked Bill's chest and spoke. "Your thing can make two of most of the men I've been with."

Pleased that she liked him, Bill silently kissed the tips of her breasts and nuzzled his nose behind her ears.

With her body limp, Ellie Sue's eyes deepened. She ran her hand over her sweaty hair, pulling it back from her eyes and in a low tone, she stated, "I guess that's the thing I miss the most about not being married. I can do without the hassles, but not having someone you care about to make love with and going to bed alone is difficult."

Bill lovingly stroked her wet hair, saying, "I know the feeling. I found it very trying when my wife died. Sometimes, being single isn't what everyone thinks it is."

Not having known before of Bill's wife's death, Ellie Sue looked into his eyes and caringly she said, "I'm sorry to hear that you lost your wife." With a sympathetic voice, she finished, "Now you've got a lot of other problems to contend with. I wish there were some way I could help you to find your friend Peter."

Bill kissed her lips tenderly, saying, "I wish you could come with me, but I guess it's my cross to bear. I'm not even sure what will happen when I find him. There may be trouble, and I wouldn't want you getting hurt."

A faraway look appeared in Bill's eyes.

Seeing this, she smiled and with her hand wiped the sweat from his face. Sighing somewhat regretfully, not knowing if she would ever see him again, she said, "You've made my night. It has been one I'll never forget."

Bill, wanting to share his innermost feelings, leaned over and after kissing Ellie Sue, he said, "I've enjoyed being with you tonight, too. You've put real meaning into my life that's been missing. . . . I really feel happy being here with you. It's like a huge weight is lifted from my heart, when I'm with you. . . . When the girls died, I felt I had died, too. And, a feeling of utter emptiness came over me so strongly that I believed it would consume all hopes of my ever being happy again."

Ellie Sue blurted out, "I have an idea. . . . It may be silly."

Then she quickly added, "No, maybe I shouldn't say anything."

Because Bill liked looking into Ellie Sue's eyes when they talked, he brushed to one side the wet curl of hair that covered her eye.

Wanting to know what she was thinking, he requested, "Please, go ahead and say what's on your mind."

"It was just a thought, but I have a girlfriend, Rosalie, who is going through a divorce. Sometimes she stays with me and helps out. . . . I thought maybe she might look after the motel for me, and I could go with you."

Surprise appeared in Bill's face. He stated, "It could be dangerous. I wouldn't want to take a chance on your being there and something happening to you. . . . I'd never forgive myself if it did."

Bolstering her case, she responded, "I don't want to lose you, now that I've found you. I want to be with you. Besides, you might need my help."

Longingly looking at her, Bill thought for a few moments, then agreeing, he said, "Okay. . . . I want to be with you, too." He hesitated, then said, "I know you're strong-willed, but you'll have to do what I ask, even if you don't agree."

Looking tenderly into Bill's eyes, she agreed, "I promise. . . . I know Rosalie will do things right, here."

Her eyes taking on a concerned look, she said, "I've been trying to help her. I know what she's going through . . . She worries about what her family and friends think about the divorce. . . . It took her a really long time to decide to go through with it."

Ellie Sue paused and looking down, she ran her fingers through the hair on Bill's chest, then continued, "She told me she had always thought she would be married for life and the fact that she took her vows to God in front of her family and friends has held her back. She didn't feel she could continue to live in the same town with them, especially because she knows a lot of people here and is worried about what they might say about her."

Pausing, Ellie Sue became aware of her unconscious twirling of Bill's chest hair around her finger. Looking at his chest, she smiled sheepishly, ran her hand slowly across it, then continued, "Her husband has a lot of friends here, too, who might side with him and cause her problems. She needed someone to talk to and we've become close."

Listening attentively, Bill understood. When he saw she'd finished talking, he spoke. "I know what you're talking about. People are always afraid of what other people will say. In my whole life, I've never had anyone come up to me and ask me how I thought they should run their life. I figure, why should I worry about what they think I should do with mine? Too many people make their decisions based upon what others think they should do and not what is best for them. . . . Since they don't have to live your life, why should they have anything to say about it?" Then he concluded, "I don't worry about what people think or say about me."

Ellie Sue's eyes brightened as she responded, "That's a good way of looking at it. Unfortunately, most people don't see it that way."

"Then it's settled," she stated. She paused and followed with, "If you can give me some time in the morning to make arrangements. I'll go with you."

Smiling, Bill responded, "Great! A few hours more or less probably won't change anything."

Shyly, Ellie Sue asked, "Can I ask you something important?"

"Sure, Ellie, what is it?"

"Will you stay with me tonight?"

Pulling her naked body against his, he answered, "The pleasure will be all mine."

Feeling a renewed interest in love-making, he kissed her lovingly as passion rose in his groin and permeated his body. He thought about how special a woman she was, and his desires rose higher. Kissing her passionately and moving his hand between her legs, he felt them fall apart in anticipation.

Chapter 10

BOSTON

IT was late in the day when Bill and Ellie Sue made their way through the streets of Boston. Many old red sandstone buildings were interspaced with new structures in a fine blend of the old with the new. Neither of them had been there before, so they took a short tour of the city to get the lay of the land. The sun still hung bright in the sky, and the heat of the sidewalks became stifling to Ellie Sue, who wasn't accustomed to the city way of life.

"Let's get a room and something to eat," Bill suggested. "Later, I'd like to see if I can locate the address where I was supposed to have lived in that other life."

Ellie Sue, sitting close beside Bill, put her hand on his leg and replied, "Good idea. But, it has to have air conditioning, or we'll be swimming in our own sweat." Then, unable to anticipate his reaction, she ventured, "I want to pay my own way. I believe a woman should earn her own money and pay her own way."

First checking the traffic, he looked at her. "You are different! And, I appreciate the offer, but I can handle it."

Determined, she insisted, "I won't have it any other way."

Glancing toward her, he agreed, "We'll split the expenses when we're through. In the meantime I'll pay the bills.

Smiling, she replied, "Agreed! . . . Thank you!"

Later that evening in their motel room, Bill picked up his atlas map of the city. Checking it for Starling Street, he couldn't find it. He examined the map over and over, but was unable to find a street by that name. Giving up in exasperation and throwing the map book into a corner, he exclaimed, "That damned hypnotist must be a hoax! I should have checked the map before we drove all the way down here on that guy's

237

whim! He must be laughing right now! . . . Really thought he put one over on me, getting me to believe in him."

Returning from the shower and clothed in a bathtowel, Ellie Sue showed her level-headedness. "You have the tape. I heard it myself. You did say Boston on it. Maybe we should check again. It could be we misunderstood the name of the street."

All of a sudden, having an inspiration, she exclaimed, "What if they changed the name or even eliminated it during construction? Before you do anything, like leave, you should go to the city hall and check with them. They might be able to help. . . . They may have old records with the name on it."

Bill's feelings of discouragement ebbed. Looking away from the wrinkled book, he sighed. "That means losing time tonight. . . . But, you could be right."

Walking over and sitting beside him, she smiled. Turning to her, he said, "It's a good thing I brought you along. You may have to think for both of us. My head is so jammed full of thoughts, it's a wonder I can think at all."

Smiling coyly, Ellie Sue, turning toward Bill, left the towel fall to the bed while saying, "It won't be entirely wasted. Believe me, I can see to that."

Teasingly, Bill suggested, "I suppose you're like all women. You'll want to go shopping."

"That's not what I had in mind. It was more like an instant replay of last night."

Beaming from ear to ear, Bill quickly responded, "Now you're talking my language."

Lying back on the bed, hands beneath her head, she suggested, "Tomorrow, if you think I might get in the way, you can drop me off at a mall, while you do your thing."

Bill responded, "That might not be a bad idea. At least at first, until I can get some idea what we have to do."

The following morning, Bill took Ellie Sue out for an early breakfast. Then, driving to the city hall, he found it didn't open until 10:00 A.M. As it was only 7:30 A.M., Bill decided to drive through the outskirts of the city, looking for the best shopping areas. Having located a few, and finding that the doors didn't open until 9:30 A.M., disgustedly Bill stated, "Seems like the entire city likes to sleep in late."

Leaning over, Ellie Sue massaged the muscles on the back of Bill's neck and smiling softly, she purred, "Try not to be so uptight, Bill.

There isn't anything we can do about it. . . . We might just as well return to the motel, unless you have something you'd rather do."

He answered, "Not really much we can do. But, you're right. We might as well go there and relax a bit, I've got a feeling it's going to be a long day." He paused, then sober-faced, he remarked wryly, "At least there's life there. We can sit in the lobby and watch all the people checking out."

Reaching under his seat, Bill produced a bottle of brandy. Ellie Sue's smile waned and stopping rubbing his neck, she kiddingly jabbed him in the ribs with her finger. "That's another habit we have to break you of."

Implying he didn't understand, he questioned, "What habit is that?"

"Overreacting, then pretending it doesn't bother you, when you know perfectly well that it's gnawing at your insides."

After taking a small nip, then setting the bottle on the seat, he answered, "Naw. It doesn't bother me. Besides, what makes you an expert on me in such a short time?"

Looking at him, then away, she remarked, "I read minds."

"Do you read lips, too? Cause if you do, read mine now." He tried to keep from smiling, but his eyes gave him away as he added, "Take a long walk off a short dock."

Lovingly she lightly jabbed him a second time. "Don't get extracited," she said, then added, "I've only been kidding. I wouldn't change anything about you. First, because I don't believe anything needs to be changed and second, I realize that no one can change another person just by thinking they can. Everyone does what's best for themselves and THERE AIN'T NO ONE going to change you but yourself."

Bill laughed a full-belly rolling laugh. "A brilliant deduction, my dear Ellie Sue."

Suddenly jerking his head to look out the side window, Bill cried out, "THERE HE IS!"

Turning to Ellie Sue and forgetting she had never seen Peter, he questioned her or maybe himself. "Did you see him? I'm sure that was him!"

Momentarily without thinking, she responded, "See who?"

"Peter. He went into the alley back there!"

"If you think it was him, you'd better check it out. . . . But be careful," she cautioned.

Excited by seeing Peter, Bill floored the gas pedal and the car roared down the street as he replied, "I'm going to!"

"What are you doing? You should have stopped back there and went in after him," Ellie Sue suggested.

Turning the corner, Bill yelled excitedly, "I'll catch him as he comes out on the next street!"

Within minutes, he was at the corner of the parallel street and found it to be one way——the wrong way. Instantly, making a decision and pulling over to the curb, leaving the motor running, and jumping out, he yelled to Ellie Sue, "Stay with the car!"

Bill began running. Having difficulties with his overhanging stomach protesting the speed he was trying to make, he panted loudly. While carefully watching the alleyway, he ran toward it. Seeing Peter emerge and look his way, Bill became excited. . . . Only then did he realize the boy wasn't Peter.

Slowing to a walk and feeling dejected and embarrassed, Bill crossed the street, walking back to the car. It was then that he realized how jumpy he was becoming. His stomach rolled, partially from the run, but mostly from the excitement of having thought the boy was Peter. Arriving at the car, Ellie Sue deduced, "It wasn't him. . . . Bill, I'm sorry. . . . I wish I knew what he looks like so I can help you."

Puffing and breathing deeply, Bill pulled himself in behind the wheel, saying, "Just having you here with me will be help enough. You can be my anchor." He looked at her concerned face and finished, "If you don't mind going through this with me."

As the car started rolling, Ellie Sue moved over and snuggling close to him, she tried to be reassuring. "No, I don't mind. . . . You're a very dear man."

Bill put his arm around her shoulders and pulled her tight to him. Suddenly he felt his stomach cramping. Unexpectedly a small rolling string of farts eased out. Looking to one side and feeling embarrassed, he rolled down the window.

Putting her hand on his knee and understanding his feelings, she said, "Don't worry about that. . . . We all do it. . . . My father once told me there was a tombstone that had inscribed on it, 'Where ere you be, Let winds blow free, For that's what caused the death of me.' "

Smiling, Bill relaxed and looking at her, he commented, "You really are something else!"

Having dropped Ellie Sue off at the Nut Island Shopping Mall, Bill went directly to the Old City Hall. While looking through old records, the clerk found that Starling Road had been renamed in the early 1930s. After his initial setback, Bill's spirits rose once more.

Driving along he glanced at the next road sign he passed. *Osceola Path*, he mentally noted. "It's in this general area," he mumbled, then cursed himself for having left the atlas maps in their motel room. *Not thinking clearly,* he thought while mentally visualizing the map book still lying in the corner where he'd thrown it.

Before long, he came upon his object of intense searching. "Outlook Road," the sign read. It was then he realized the numbering of the buildings may also have been changed, especially if the street had been relocated. Considering the possibility that the street numbers had been partially changed, he realized that it could be enough to screw him up.

Turning onto the road, he started reading the numbers, Five-thousand, nine-hundred, thirty-six. It hit him . . . they ran higher as he drove.

He cursed and muttered, "Damn. I'm going the wrong way." With that, he whipped the car into a U-turn. Mounting the curb on the far side of the street, he cursed again, "Probably put it out of alignment now, too! Lucky I'm only renting it!"

"Now we're getting somewhere!" he stated aloud as the numbers receded. After driving a mile farther, he came upon a low, two-story building with the numbers he was seeking. "Murphy Storage" a weather-worn sign over the doorway read. It looked deserted.

After parking in the front, Bill got out. He noticed that the brick building was built tight against another larger one on the left, while it had a large, overgrown, vacant lot covering the area to the right. Thoroughly searching the windows for a sign of life, Bill found none. Slowly walking through the vacant lot, he examined the building for possible entry, believing that if Peter were there, some indicators would be present.

Bill found nothing out of the ordinary along the side, as all of the windows were intact. Reaching the back he found a partially demolished enclosed porch.

Carefully, he climbed the weakened steps. Instinctively, his hand went for the butt of the gun he carried. He hesitated, wondering, *Can I use it if I have to? . . . Maybe if I only shoot him in the leg or somewhere to wound him. . . . That's what I'll have to do, if he doesn't get scared and attack when he sees it.*

Keeping his hand on the gun, Bill was careful not to make a sound as he ascended the steps and reached the door. Finding it unlocked, he noiselessly nudged it open.

Hastily looking around, he found it empty. The dust on the floor was patched with footprints, which led to a second door in the center of the wall to his right. Slowly, he crossed the softwood floor, which creaked unmercifully under his weight.

"He's going to hear me. Maybe he'll get out through another opening," Bill muttered under his breath, half-wishing that Peter would, so there wouldn't be a confrontation. Reaching the door, slowly pushing it open, and preparing for the worst possible event, he peered in. The room was empty. Pushing it all the way open, he entered.

It was then that Bill noticed an old, discarded carpet piled in a heap in the corner behind the door. Empty food cans and other garbage were strewn near the carpeting. He judged by the freshness of this litter and the footprints that it was someone's living quarters. Noting the deplorable conditions, he didn't want to believe it was Peter's. This was not like the person he'd come to know as a son.

He spoke out loud, "I hope for Peter's sake, this isn't where he's living. It's probably some booze hound or junkie."

Turning, Bill left the shed. Then, preparing himself for the ordeal of finding a hiding place where he could watch for arrivals at the house, he wandered about the vacant lot.

Realizing that it had to be close enough to be able to recognize Peter, even in the dark, a thought came to him. *If it is Peter living here, maybe he's inside the building. I'd better check that out, too.*

Returning to the first room in the porch, where the roof was partially missing, he tried the entrance door to the main building, but it was either locked or jammed tight. Rubbing the single pane of glass in the door, Bill attempted to peer in. Inside, it appeared that a couch had been pushed up behind the door. Applying pressure to the door with his shoulder, he managed to move it slightly. Unable to move it any farther, Bill returned to the grounds outside. Noticing a small, open door underneath the porch, he stooped and entered.

A pile of old boards and tires filled most of the area, but Bill saw just what he needed: a half-inch pipe laying on the ground at his feet. Returning to the main door into the building, he forced it open enough to enter.

Bill found the building to be a maze of partially empty rooms. Noting the dust on the floor was absent of tracks and the entire area had the appearance of having been a used-furniture warehouse, with many damaged items still remaining, Bill became disappointed, but he judged by the many bathrooms, with most of the fixtures removed, that it was obvious it had once been apartments. Checking over the entire remaining building area, he assured himself that no one had been in it for years.

Returning to the porch, he closed the door, but it hung up part way open. "Damn it. Everything has to be the hard way," he muttered to himself. Knowing he couldn't leave it open—a telltale sign of his presence—he did what he wanted to avoid having to do. Pushing it all the way open, he slammed it shut with a bang that rattled the windows. After finding a hiding place, Bill left the area.

Disappointed and disgusted, he picked up Ellie Sue and returned a short time later. "It will probably be disgustingly boring," Bill informed her as he parked the car in a parking lot a half-block away.

She responded, "I'm game for anything. I know it could be dangerous, but it's exciting, too. I've been getting rooted to that motel. . . . I'm awfully glad Rosalie is watching the place for me."

Bill removed the plastic bag of items he'd brought with him. "Take the car and get something to eat. Come back in about an hour, and I'll watch for you. When you get to the vacant lot, if no one has come yet, I'll show myself and you can join me."

"What are you going to eat?" Ellie Sue questioned.

"You have to ask hard questions, don't you?" he remarked.

Her eyes lit up. "I try," she answered.

Bill looked at her. "I've got the food we brought. Besides, someone has to be here in case he shows up. I wouldn't leave you alone here while I went to eat, so I'll have to brown-bag it tonight."

Pausing, Bill directed, "Go already," but she didn't move.

"No. I'm not going. I'm staying with you. If you can eat cold, I can, too," she persisted.

"I want you to get a good meal. Now get going so you can get back before it gets dark," Bill suggested.

Stubbornly she persisted, "You'll find out that I'm the kind of girl who will do just about anything. That includes staying with you now!"

Seeing that he was getting nowhere fast, he agree, "Oh, all right, stay with me. But, let's get moving," he stated while locking, then slamming the car door.

Once they were in the place he'd selected, he tried to make it as comfortable as possible for Ellie Sue. "What are those?" she asked.

"Cushions." Then pointing, he directed, "You just sit back there a little and eat what you want while I try to put a little more protection in front of us." He paused and added, "Keep an eye out for me. If you see anyone come this way, give me a nudge so I'll know." She nodded her head in agreement.

As Ellie Sue ate, she watched Bill weaving branches and twigs into open areas in the brush for protection from observation. "You do that just like the birds I've watched building their nests. Is this going to be ours?" She couldn't help teasing, even in a serious situation.

Smiling, Bill turned to her. "Some love nest, I'd say."

She smiled back. "Well, maybe we should consider it a picnic."

Bill stopped dead silent and with his hand down by his side, he motioned for her to be still. He'd noticed someone appear along the sidewalk in front of the building. Seeing him continue walking, he

243

realized it was only a passerby.

Once Bill was satisfied with his work, he lay down beside Ellie Sue and resting on his elbow, he whispered, "Have you ever handled a gun?"

Looking at him questioningly, she answered, "My dad was into them when he was alive. He taught me how to shoot rifles and pistols."

Carefully, Bill handed her the pistol. "Good! You keep it and if Peter comes, you can cover me. Don't shoot unless it's absolutely necessary. If you do have to, try to wound and not kill him."

Laying it on the ground next to her, she began to feed Bill a ham sandwich she'd made, but he found it difficult to eat while looking forward. Chuckling to herself, Ellie Sue found it comical the way Bill twisted his head to reach and get at it. Washing it down with beer, he opened his mouth for a second bite. As he was about to close his mouth on it, she jerked it away. Hearing his teeth gnash together, she couldn't help chuckling out loud.

Trying to get her to be serious, Bill turned to her disgustedly, remarking, "I can see this isn't going to work."

Seeing her grinning, he laughed with her. Her playfulness kept him from getting too uptight inside, but he knew that it could ruin any chance of catching Peter unaware. "Ellie, you've got to take this seriously. There's a time and place for everything, and this is definitely not the time or place to be fooling around."

Ellie Sue, being a natural tease, found it difficult to contain her actions and apply herself to the business at hand. But, with much effort, she decided to act appropriate to the situation. While wanting to continue teasing, but knowing that Bill was right and grinning sheepishly, she answered, "I'll behave. I promise."

After finishing their meager meal, Bill and Ellie Sue settled down to the grueling task of sitting still, while watching and waiting for the occupant of the porch to show himself.

Shortly before dusk, Bill noticed a movement in the empty lot a little to his left. Subtly he pointed it out to Ellie Sue, being careful not to attract attention. The figure crouched low as it moved from bush to bush. While watching intently and trying to distinguish whether it was Peter, Bill had doubts.

With the poor light, it was difficult to make an identity. As they watched, it became evident the person was heading for the building. Bill waited to be sure.

When the person mounted the steps and disappeared into the porch, Bill motioned to Ellie Sue to follow him. She stood up and started moving close behind. Turning to look at her and with a frown, he directed in a muffled tone, "The gun, Ellie! Get the gun!"

A sudden, embarrassed look appeared across her face as she whirled and returned for the gun. Feeling she'd let him down when he had depended on her, she realized it was better to have him find her incompetent now than to have a disaster happen later. Picking up the pistol and like a child trying to keep up with her older brother, she tiptoed until she caught up to Bill, where he was crouching behind a bush.

"Now, stay close behind me," he commanded as they started moving noiselessly from one clump of brush to another until they were at the porch steps.

Turning to look at Ellie Sue, Bill suggested in a whisper, "I'll go in. You stay here. Keep your eyes peeled and if you hear a struggle, rush in." Then giving her a stern questioning look, he whispered, "Do you think you can handle that?"

Pouting, she whispered, "Yes, master."

Easing his way up the stairs, Bill tried moving like the shadows. Wishing he hadn't been unsuccessful at losing weight and knowing the floor in the porch wouldn't belie his presence, he felt uneasy. Noting with relief the door had been left open, he made his way through it. Seeing a dim light beneath the far door and feeling he hadn't been heard as yet, Bill momentarily stood, trying to determine how to cross the room without announcing his presence.

A slight noise behind him caused him to glance over his shoulder, and he caught sight of Ellie Sue's outline silhouetted by a distant street light. She held the gun ready for action, motioning for him to proceed. A thought interrupted his thinking. *Surprise. That's it. I'll rush across the room and take him by surprise. If it turns out not to be Peter, I'll have to handle that, when the time comes*

Looking to the far door, he extended his hand to lean against the door jam and bolster his courage. A noise of metal against wood behind him caught his attention. Turning and looking to see what it was, Ellie Sue's figure presented itself making its way up the steps.

"Damned woman won't do what she's told," Bill muttered and with a burst of willpower, he darted across the room, bursting through the door, crashing it open. A sudden look of surprise arched his face. . . . The room was empty. . . . Entering it further and looking first toward a lighted battery lantern that lay beside the pile of carpeting, then checking the windows, he found them all closed.

Caught by surprise, Bill felt the weight of a body as it hurled down upon him. Shock erupted through his entire being as he struggled to escape the attacker. Catching him by the shoulder, Bill hurled himself free.

A young, emanciated rag-clad human form lay slumped, moaning on the floor. With it now appearing to be helpless, Bill studied the back of the head of the long-haired creature that had mounted such a fierce attack.

Having entered the room and now standing keenly alert, her pistol poised at the ready, Ellie Sue exclaimed, "Who is it, Bill?"

"Billll. Isss thattt youuu, Billll?" a voice ebbed from the form; it was hollow and childlike.

A vague recognition ripped at Bill's heart. "Peter. Is it really you, Peter?"

The tangled mat of hair turned, and a sign of recognition appeared then twisted into a forced smile. Bill ran over, then scooping him up into his arms, he felt a sudden release of emotions burst through his body. Shaking him into a emotional quiver, tears flooded his eyes. Brushing the long hair back, Bill looked into Peter's face momentarily without speaking.

The sight before Ellie Sue was in unbelievable contrast to what she'd imagined. She hadn't known what to expect, but now the hulk of a man she'd come to love was smitten with emotions and stood holding tightly a bundle that gave the appearance of being human. She could read the mixture of joy and sadness crawling through Bill as he stood bent kneed, hugging this pitifully helpless boy. Then, relieved that she didn't have to use it, Ellie Sue lowered the pistol and walked over to them.

Placing her hand on Bill's shoulder, she spoke, "I'm so glad we found you, Peter. Bill has been beside himself since you disappeared. Are you all right?"

A moment of silence prevailed, then Peter's forced voice, resounding as though arriving through a long tunnel, met their ears. "I'mmm . . . sorryy . . . I jumpeddd . . . you . . . , Billll. I've . . . searcheddd . . . forr youuu . . . whenn . . . I . . . coulddd thinkkk . . . clearlyyy." . . . He paused, breathing deeply. Then in a weak, dragging voice, he continued, "I don'tt . . . rememberrr . . . muchh . . . any more. I . . . have . . . all . . . tooo . . . dooo . . . tryinggg . . . tooo . . . gett . . . thruuu . . . the . . . daysss."

Fighting back emotions, Bill asked, "Do you remember anything of how you got here?"

Peter's hollow eyes turned to him. Seeing them, he was briefly reminded of the thing they'd seen in Marie and Diane's apartment. Remorse over the loss of the girls clawed at his guts as thoughts of them entered his brain.

His voice continuing to be weak, dragging, and a little distorted, Peter answered, "Noo. . . . Myy . . . body . . . hasss . . . its . . . ownn . . . thoughtsss." He paused and, breathing deeply, added, "I . . . have . . . to . . . gooo . . . alonggg . . . with . . . ittt."

Ellie Sue glanced around the room, her eyes coming to rest on the bag Peter had carried in. She walked over to it while Bill quizzed Peter. Picking it up, she looked inside. Wrinkling her nose and shaking her head in disbelief, she looked away, then carried it to Bill. Leaning over, holding the bag with the tips of her fingers to avoid contamination, she opened it to allow Bill to peer inside, saying, "Look what he's been eating."

A second flood of despair for his friend filled Bill's body. "Garbage vegetables!" he exclaimed questioningly. "Is this all you've been living on?"

Peter's voice remained shallow and distant as he answered in a hesitating voice, "That'sss . . . whatt . . . my . . . bodyyy . . . cravesss. It . . . knowss . . . I . . . wasss . . . eatinggg . . . alll . . . the . . . wrongg . . . thingsss . . . before . . . it . . . tookk . . . overr . . . controlll."

Realizing that Peter must be talking about the entity, Bill asked, "Is it in control of you now? Does it let you talk with people the way you are now?"

Appearing to have regained his breath somewhat better, Peter answered, "I . . . can . . . always . . . tell . . . when . . . it's . . . being . . . stretched . . . tight."

With his free hand, Peter reached over and took hold of his shoulder. Rubbing it, he said, "I think . . . I hurt . . . myself."

Bill looked at Ellie Sue. "We've got to get him to a hospital. He's been wasting away and possibly very dehydrated, too."

Turning to leave, she requested, "Give me the keys. I'll get the car."

Bill carried Peter out and seating him on the steps, he sat next to him. Seeing that he was about to speak, Bill covered Peter's mouth and with a fatherly smile, he said, "Save your energy, Peter. When we get some good food into you, your memory should improve. We can talk then."

Bill remained quietly with his body in a state of hyper-emotions while persistent thoughts flowed through his mind. Thoughts of the past pleasures they'd shared along with the disappointment of loss he'd suffered when Peter disappeared; the confused feelings of despair in searching for him all milled helter-skelter in Bill's mind.

The shock of disclosure upon hearing of the deaths of the girls and now, the release of pent-up emotions blocked his clear thinking. He'd forgotten the potential eruptin of danger that lurked in his friend. Now his immediate concern centered around returning him to health as quickly as possible.

Bill's wandering thoughts were interrupted by the sound of the car engine. Ellie Sue appeared at the corner of the building. "I'll help you get him into the car," she offered.

247

"Can you stand up?" Bill questioned.

"Yes. . . . I . . . can . . . make . . . it."

"I'll help you," Bill said, putting Peter's arm around his shoulder.

"You two sit in the back and I'll drive," Ellie Sue suggested.

Immediately after being admitted to the hospital, Peter was given an IV sedative. Bill and Ellie Sue returned to the Old Colony Motel.

Throwing his jacket into the corner and trying to express his feelings, Bill remarked, "That damned thing has Peter in its control. I can't figure out what it's attempting to do with him by dragging his health down like that."

Walking over to the bed, Bill sat down next to Ellie Sue, placing his chin into his hands. Placing her hand onto the back of his neck, she began to massage his tense muscles. With sympathy in her voice, she said, "I'm sorry you had to find Peter in such deplorable living conditions. I could see it was a shock to you."

"I'm thankful we found him, but I didn't expect to see him that way." Bill looked over at her and caught the expression of love in her eyes. He looked away and reflected, "There are a lot of questions unanswered. Hopefully, Peter can be of some help, if and when his memory improves."

Trying to encourage Bill, Ellie Sue suggested, "There may be some way we can find out more about you and Peter's previous life and how it relates to that other person. With the fact that Peter was here and since the address from your memory proved to be true, there may be old birth or adoption records here at the courthouse. There may even be some old people around the place you lived who might remember something."

"I've thought about looking up old records here, but it would help if I knew what I'm looking for." He turned to regard Ellie Sue, "You may be right. If there is someone who still lives around there, we might be able to narrow down our search."

Ellie Sue, smiling, reached for the buttons on Bill's shirt. With nimble fingers, she started to unbutton it. "I'm going to make you relax," she purred. "There's nothing we can do about it tonight but enjoy ourselves and we know how to do that, RIGHT?"

The following morning Bill and Ellie Sue visited Peter in the hospital. Tears came into Bill's eyes as he looked upon him in bed with the protrusions of medical items reminding him of the last time he'd seen him in a hospital. This time Peter's plight aroused a deep pity within Bill.

He knew Peter had never wanted anyone's pity. He was too independent and carefree for that.

Ellie Sue, noticing Bill's watering eyes, took his hand and squeezed it. Peter rolled his head over to look in their direction. It appeared someone had attempted to wash the grime from his hair as it lay in long entwined strings of blond and sandy brown.

Bill smiled broadly. "Hi, Pete. How are you doing this morning?"

With more strength in his voice, Peter answered, "Better. . . . The nurse said they're going to try to put some weight on me."

Bill walked over and stood by his bed. "Good. They'll have you back in shape in no time."

"But I don't want to put on any weight. I'm just right the way I am. My body wants me to be this way, so I can have a good figure."

Bill's mouth dropped open, his upper plate loosening fell with a clicking sound as it came to rest on his lower plate. Showing obvious shock, he closed his mouth and reset his upper plate before speaking, "What are you saying? I don't believe I heard you right."

"If I'm going to look pretty, I have to have a good figure," Peter said matter of factly.

Sensing the shock Peter's statement was to Bill, Ellie Sue lightly placed her hand on his shoulder. He turned to look at her. Surprise and disbelief written on his face, he was speechless. With a sly wink at Bill, being careful not to let Peter see, she advised him, "Peter probably has his reasons for the way he feels."

Still at a loss to understand, Bill turned back to Peter. "This is Ellie Sue. She's been a very good friend to me, and I know she'll be a good friend to you, too."

Ellie Sue hesitated and then extended her hand and clasped Peter's bony fingers. "I'm awfully glad to meet you, Peter. You may remember, I was with Bill last night."

"Yes, vaguely. I have trouble remembering sometimes. I'm glad to meet you."

Bill, not being sure if he should question Peter about the entity, resisted the temptation to wait until he had recovered his health. He asked, "Can you tell me anything about the control your body has over you?"

"It's strange and I don't understand it."

Bill persisted, "How do you feel when it takes over?"

"Sometimes it's in my mind. It's like I'm telling myself I'm no good for anything, that I've got to change myself entirely or no one will want to be with me. All the while, something in me is saying no." He paused and looked at Ellie Sue. "I want to be like you. You're beautiful."

"Peter, listen to me, " Bill pleaded. "You've got to resist those feelings."

With much effort, Peter pulled himself to a sitting position. "I don't always feel this way. It's the strongest when my body is in control."

Trying to instill logic in Peter, Ellie Sue interrupted, "Peter, Bill is right. You are not a woman, and you don't have to look beautiful. Besides, you're skin and bones, now. No one should be that thin."

"I've seen myself in a mirror a few times and I've wondered about it, but my body wants me to be thinner. It tells me this is the way I've got to be, if I'm going to be a woman."

Bill was determined to change his thinking immediately. "You're not a woman and will never be a woman! You've got to fight those feelings!"

Peter looked squarely at Bill. "I've been thinking of having a sex change."

In a quandary as to what he should do, Bill asked, "Do you feel that way now?"

"Yes. My BODY CRAVES it."

"Do you feel like your body is in control now? I mean, is your skin feeling like it's tight and has more than you in it?" Bill tried to imply there was another spirit in him without actually saying it.

"No. I feel all right. I'll be out of here soon." He half-smiled, "I know sometimes it's wrong, but this is the way I want to be."

Bill turned and walked a short distance away. Feeling he wanted to talk with her in private, Ellie Sue followed. Bill leaned over and whispered, "He's been brainwashed from within by that thing. We've got to find some way to free him before he has no control whatsoever."

Ellie Sue nodded her head in agreement and under her breath, she suggested, "Maybe we should leave here now and try to find out what we can in the city records."

Turning and looking back at Peter's emaciated face, Bill held back his emotions as he informed him, "We're leaving now, but we'll be back later." He paused momentarily and half-shouted, "For God's sake, Peter, please do what the doctor and nurses say! You have to eat to be healthy!"

Ellie Sue added, "Even a woman needs to be healthy."

Bill and Ellie Sue ate a late breakfast, then returned to their motel room to replay the tape recording, looking in particular for names and dates.

Bill's mind ran rampant with cluttered thoughts, mostly of Peter. He contemplated what he'd become and how, once they'd found some information, they could apply it to freeing him from the entity.

"I just don't know what we're going to be able to do for Peter," Bill reflected as he set down the new bottle of brandy from which he'd been drinking.

Ellie Sue, who had been compiling a list from the notes she'd taken from the tape, answered, "We'll take this list and question anyone in the area of that old building who looks old enough to remember anything."

"I mean about his condition. How will we be able to put the information to good use and free him from that thing? It seems so awesome. I hate to even think about it."

"We'll have to do what we can. You did say that the hypnotist back home wanted you to bring him there if you found him. We'll have to try that. Right now I'd say we concentrate on what we can do here. If we get enough information, it might help him."

Bill got an idea. "Maybe we can identify the spirit and why it's after Peter. I know we're putting all of our hopes on the possibility that it's someone from that particular life, but it was Mrs. Karsti's suggestion that I'm going on." He paused, took a drink of brandy, and added, "God rest her dear old soul."

Bill pulled the car to a stop in front of the storage building on Outlook Road and was about to get out when Ellie Sue caught his shoulder. "Better let me go alone. You smell like liquor," Ellie Sue warned. "Besides, it doesn't take more than one."

Reluctantly, Bill agreed, took a new bottle of brandy out from under his seat, and raised it to his lips.

Ellie Sue frowned. "You don't need that as a crutch."

Bill cast a sheepish look toward her. "You're taking what I said about being my anchor seriously, aren't you?"

She grinned. "You're damn right I am."

While Bill waited, he ran and reran through his mind the facts as he knew them, but they didn't present anything meaningful. Soon Ellie Sue appeared at his car window. As he rolled it down, the cool, refreshing air from the air-conditioner flowed up to cool her perspiring face. She blurted out, "There's an old woman in the house across the street who remembers the girl you were with the night of your sixteenth birthday party."

Bill appeared stunned, "I was with?" he questioned.

"Yes, you," she insisted. "In your previous life. I think you should talk with her."

Unable to contain himself, Bill's curiosity compelled him to blurt out, "What did she say?"

"She knew Ann Daget, who had a daughter by the name of Jill Daget. Does that name ring a bell?"

"Sure does. She's the girl Ed LaBark was with that night."

"And you, being Ed LaBark, didn't know that she was pregnant from that night, when he left a few weeks later and hired on an ocean-going ship."

Bill felt encouraged. "She told you that?"

"And more!" She paused and looked at Bill in a teasing way.

"Come on, woman! Spit it out!" He glared at Ellie Sue as she waited without saying a word. "I think you're enjoying this!"

Holding an impish smile, she continued, "They moved to somewhere in New York."

Bill felt excitement flood his mind. "The woman who was killed in my old home was Jill Daget!"

Bill's excitement passed to Ellie Sue. "No! Jill had a daughter born out of wedlock before they moved. Her name was Martha Daget! You told me the woman's name who was killed was Martha Daget! . . . Or is your memory suddenly failing you?"

Bill's eyes gleamed. "Well I'll be damned. Martha Daget must have been Peter in that life."

"That's the only way I can figure it."

Bill's face muscles tightened. "Could she tell you anything that would help us find out about the entity that's possessing Peter?"

Ellie Sue nodded her head. "Kind of."

Bill interrupted her. " 'Kind of'? What's that supposed to mean?"

"Jill and her daughter returned here a couple of years later, but her mother stayed in New York." She paused and, reading the look on Bill's face, continued. "Well, she said Ed LaBark's father owned the apartment building, and he gave them a place to stay. When Martha grew up, she married a tall, burly, dark-haired man. The woman didn't know his name, but she said they didn't get along. So, one night Martha left town. The woman said she heard she had gone back to New York to live with her mother."

Bill gave her his full attention. "What about her husband?"

"The woman said she felt at the time that they were married, the guy was half-crazy. Anyway, she heard some time later, that he'd been committed to an insane asylum."

Bill was ecstatic. He threw his arm out the window and pulling Ellie Sue to him, he kissed her. "Nice going, Ellie! We can check with the marriage license bureau and find his name!"

Having visited the clerk's office at the county courthouse and obtained information from old records, Ellie Sue and Bill returned to the hospital to see Peter. They chatted with him for an hour, before Bill said, with a concerned look, "Peter, I've been talking with Doctor Jacobs about taking you with us to a small town in upper New York. He wants you to remain here for a few more days in order to control your electrolytes, and then he'll release you."

Peter smiled. His voice still weak, he replied, "I'd like that. Any place would be better than this shit factory."

Watching Peter's face for resistance, Bill said, "He'll make arrangements for you to be admitted to the hospital there."

Peter's smiled vanished, his skin tightened onto his shallow cheekbones. "I feel fine. I won't need anything but to get back to eating that good food again." He paused and looked at Ellie Sue, wistfully saying, "I wish I could look like you. You're pretty."

Ellie Sue, believing the entity had some ominous reason for its vicarious use of Peter's body, didn't want to cause it to vent its wrath on Peter, if it knew they had knowledge of it. Carefully, she chose her words. "Why do you want to be a woman?"

Peter's eyes narrowed. "I'm convinced my body would be happy as a woman. It's as if it was a mistake when I was born a male. I have a feeling that my spirit has always been a female and was trapped in this body against its will." He paused, his face tensed. "It's too hard to explain. There's a driving force in me that makes me feel this way. It gets more intense when my body is in control."

Peter paused and, looking at Bill, he said, "You may think I'm crazy, but it's as though my soul is male and wants my body parts to be female so we can be both."

Bill frowned. "That's confusing. Your body is male." He paused and scratched his head before saying, "Do you mean the part in you that takes control of your body is male?"

"That's it. When it takes control, it tells me it is male, but it wants me to have a sex change, so my body parts are female."

Wheedlingly, Ellie Sue tried to dissuade him. "I'll bet you were a very handsome and masculine man with powerful muscles."

Tears welled up in Peter's eyes. "I wish I could remember the feelings I once had, but I can't. All I know is the agonizing feelings I get inside if I try to think of anything but being a beautiful brunette."

Bill's teeth suddenly clenched tight. His face whitened as he tried to whisper something to Ellie Sue without Peter overhearing it.

Turning toward him she immediately knew something was bothering him. Seeing that he was burning inside with something she took to be hatred and fear, she turned to Peter, who showed no recognition of Bill's driving emotions. She said, "I just remembered some things we have to do. We'll be back later and can talk about this then."

Broaching an emaciated smile, Peter replied, "Sure. Thanks for coming. I'll see you both later."

Bill turned without speaking and walked out. Immediately upon leaving Peter's room, Bill turned to Ellie Sue. In a frenzy, his lips white and with anger consuming him, he spit the words out. "The fucker's trying to change him into the woman he was in his previous life!"

Ellie Sue's face reflected shock at the disclosure. Putting her hand to her mouth, she exclaimed, "My God! Do you really think that's what he's trying to do?"

"At first, I was thinking he wanted to degrade him by making him into an anorexic, to break down his resistance! When he mentioned being a brunette, it hit me. He wants to resurrect his wife through Peter! We've got to get him to Dr. Meyer as quickly as possible!"

While walking toward the nurses' station, Ellie Sue asked, "You could be right, Bill." Then she added, "It could also be as you originally thought!"

Bill stopped her and looking at her intently, he said, "What do you mean? I know I'm right! . . . Once that son-of-a-bitch changes him into what his wife was, he'll probably take over another man's body and change it into who he was!"

She took his hand and squeezed it. "Relax, Bill. I just meant you're probably right on both counts! Now he's probably trying to degrade him and make him submissive. Then, when he feels the time is right, he'll change him into Martha Daget!"

Then, her face turned white. "I just had a thought."

Bill looked at her questioningly.

Her eyes narrowing, Ellie Sue continued, "What if he tries to take over your body for himself once he has Peter changed into his wife!"

Bill's face showed his determination. "If that bastard tries it with me, he'll find he's taken on more than he's bargained for!"

Ellie Sue smiled inwardly. She believed in Bill and felt he lived up to what he said. She hadn't known him long, but she knew he was the man she wanted to be with, and not temporarily until an entity took him over. She didn't want to live her life in fear that it would happen, either.

"I guess I shouldn't have said that. From what you told me, Peter was in a weakened condition when it entered him." Pausing, she looked down the hall toward Peter's room before adding, "I don't think we should wait here much longer. If we can take Peter tomorrow morning, Dr. Meyer could get started right away."

Bill looked at her and nodded agreement. "He'll have to go by ambulance in the condition he's in. I'll talk with Dr. Jacobs, but he may not understand the urgency. Even if I explain everything, he may not believe me."

"He'll have to believe you!" she exclaimed.

Bill turned and once more he started walking to the nurses' station with Ellie Sue following. "I'll see if Dr. Jacobs is here now," he said to her over his shoulder.

"Good idea."

They waited until the nurse returned from a patient's room. "Is Dr. Jacobs in the hospital?" Bill asked.

"No, but he'll be in at six-thirty this evening. Is there something I can help you with?"

"I want to talk with him personally."

"When he comes in, I'll tell him you want to see him."

"Thanks," Bill answered, then he turned to Ellie Sue, saying, "Let's go back to the motel. I've got some heavy-duty thinking to do."

That evening, Bill and Ellie Sue were waiting at the nurses' station when Dr. Jacobs arrived. Bill walked over to him and said, "Dr. Jacobs, I'd like to talk with you in private about Peter Dunn."

Nodding his head, he showed them into an office nearby. Once they were seated, he looked at Bill and spoke. "I've been told his family can't be contacted. Have you known him long?"

"We've become very good friends. That's why I'm concerned about him."

Dr. Jacobs's opinion showed his medical training. "I think he needs pyschiatric intervention. He doesn't seem to be rationalizing very well."

Bill looked at the floor as he spoke. "We'd like to move him to New York tomorrow morning."

"Right now he needs medical attention. I don't believe he should be moved until we've had a chance to run tests and get the lab reports back on his blood work."

Ellie Sue spoke up. "We understand, Dr. Jacobs, but there's more to this than you're aware of."

Bill produced a slight frown as he looked at her. He'd hoped they wouldn't have to explain. Seeing the questioning look on Dr. Jacobs's face, Bill informed him, "I called Dr. Meyer in Far Rockaway, New York. He feels we should move him as soon as possible. I suggest you call him and have him explain it to you."

Dr. Jacobs's facial muscles tightened. "It sounds serious."

"It is," Bill responded. then, reaching into his shirt pocket, he produced a piece of paper, which he handed to the doctor. "Here's his number. Please call him."

After talking with Dr. Meyer, Dr. Jacobs sat thinking momentarily before saying, "I don't know what to make of it. We've had a case where a relative felt one of our patients was possessed and they had an exorcism, but we didn't see any change in the patient." He was silent again while he considered the situation. Finally he agree. "Well, all right. We'll send him by ambulance early tomorrow morning."

Ellie Sue, concerned that time was of the utmost importance, said, "I think we should leave before that, like tonight. . . . I'm a registered nurse. . . . We can take the IVs and whatever else he needs with us. He'd be more comfortable in a car than one of those clunky ambulances, anyway."

Surprise spead across Bill's face as he turned and looked at her. "I didn't know that," he said softly.

Dr. Jacobs looked at her sternly. "It'll be risky. Are you sure you want to take that chance?"

Ellie Sue spoke to Bill. "I feel it's the best way. Peter and I can ride in the back seat, and we can hang the IV bag from a clothes bar." Pausing and looking at the doctor, she folowed with, "We'll take good care of him, you needn't worry."

"It wasn't only Peter I was concerned about." The doctor paused and, looking at Bill, he added, "We could add a sedative to the solution."

She made the decision on the spur of the moment. "Then it's settled. We'll leave right away."

Bill reflected surprise at her sudden conclusion. She turned toward him and questioned, "Is that all right with you, Bill?"

Rubbing his hands together, Bill stood silent for a moment, then he agreed.

Feeling reassured, the doctor said, "I'll call the hospital and let them know you'll be bringing him in tonight."

Bill stood up. "Thank you, doctor, for being so understanding." Then, turning to Ellie Sue, who was preparing to rise from her chair, he said, "I'll take the car and gas it up, check out of the motel, and be back in a few minutes." As he was leaving, he suggested, "You help them get Peter ready."

Later that evening, Bill and Ellie Sue with Peter were making good time along the expressway. Peter was asleep when she checked the needle inserted in his arm and said to Bill, "We may have to put a new IV bag on him soon."

Bill was in the process of placing a cigar in his mouth. After lighting it he partially turned around and answered over his shoulder, "It won't be long and we'll be there. If it runs out, it probably won't matter if he goes a few minutes without it."

"If we're that close, I guess you're right," she answered and catching a smell of the smoke, she commanded, "Put that out."

Bill complied. Then, looking in his rear-view mirrow, he chuckled to himself.

"What are you laughing about?" Ellie Sue challenged.

"It's the way you look with Peter lying there all wrapped up in the blanket, with his head in your lap. That tubing running alongside his head, with all that tangled mat of hair he has, looks like it's coming out of a rug."

Ellie Sue smiled. Then, feeling uncomfortable, she shifted her position and complained, "It hasn't been the most comfortable trip I've ever taken."

"It'll be over shortly. Then we can relax."

While looking forward at the oncoming traffic, Bill glanced into the mirror at her, then back on the road, and said, "A little nookie should fix you up in no time at all."

Ellie Sue leaned back, combing her fingers through Peter's hair. "Ummm. I could use some good lovin' all right," she breathed softly.

Peter's body started shaking under the blanket. Ellie Sue became concerned. "He's beginning to shiver. I hope he's not getting something."

Bill glanced into the mirror once more, then looked forward. "Just a little farther now," he announced. "It'll be good to get him into the hospital."

Ellie Sue became excited. "His whole body is quivering! It's almost like he's going into convulsions!"

Bill floored the gas pedal. "We'll have to take our chances on the cops!" he spit out.

Ellie Sue placed her hand on Peter's forehead to check his temperature. Quickly, she pulled it away. "Bill! There's an energy field around his head! I could feel my whole hand tingling!"

Bill checked the speedometer, which read ninety miles per hour. He quickly looked ahead, down the road. It was straight and no cars were in sight. He looked back into the mirror at Ellie Sue. A strange white mist clouded his vision. "What's happening back there?" he shouted.

"I don't know! His whole body is quaking and there's a cloud coming out of his head!" she yelled to Bill.

Suddenly Bill heard Ellie Sue scream. He glanced ahead, then into the mirror. A large shaggy head was forming from the mist.

"It's him. He's leaving Peter," Bill shouted.

The misty head floated forward into the front seat next to Bill. Instantly a half-body was beside him. Its pale green eyes glowed through thick, black, tangled hair. Bill felt the intense heat of its body only moments before it suddenly reached out and grabbed hold of the steering wheel. Struggling, Bill attempted to wrest it free and regain control. Ellie Sue, still screaming, reached forward over the seat trying to help Bill.

Using its immense strength, the creature suddenly jerked the wheel sideways, and the front wheels dug into the soft shoulder of the road.

"Bill, that tree! Watch out, we're going to hit it!" Ellie Sue screamed.

When Ellie Sue regained consciousness, she was hurting all over, and she found herself lying on the side of the road covered with a blanket. Flashing lights of police cars and an ambulance sent chills through her. A policeman, bending over her, instructed, "Lie still. You've injured your leg. It could be broken."

"What about the others in the car?" she asked excitedly.

"They're being taken to the hospital," he informed her, pointing to an ambulance, which was beginning to drive away. "We have another one coming for you. It should be here shortly. Keep your head down. We don't want you to go into shock," he advised.

Ellie Sue painfully turned her head and looked toward the car. The front end had partially climbed a large oak tree. Closing her eyes, she passed out.

When Ellie Sue came to in the hospital, she looked around anxiously for a nurse, but she didn't see one. After pushing the call button while waiting, she discovered a bandage taped to the side of her face. Beneath it, she felt a faint throbbing.

Before long a nurse's aide appeared in the doorway. "Did you need something?"

Attempting to sit, Ellie Sue pulled herself up in bed. The strain on her left leg caused it to pain. She bit her lip momentarily before asking, "How are the others who were in the car with me?"

The aide walked over to her bedside. "The boy had some slight scratches. Dr. Meyer is in with him now."

A fear swept over her. "What about Bill LaBark? How is he?"

"He must have been the one driving. They said he was thrown through the windshield when the car struck a tree."

"How is he?" Ellie Sue demanded in slight hysteria.

Taken by the suddenness of her demand, the young nurse's aide blurted out, "He died on the way here."

"No!" Ellie Sue cried out and recoiled in shock. "I don't believe you!"

Seeing her face whiten in disbelief, the aide reached over and took hold of her hand. And, with empathy in her eyes, she said softly, "I'm very sorry, Mrs. Carling. I wish it weren't true, but he didn't make it."

Ellie Sue slumped back in her bed. Her mind raced through the last thing she remembered before the accident. The ugly giant of a half-being burned in her memory. She remembered the notes she'd made during the visit with the old lady and the court records. Now their importance took on a greater meaning. Bill was more than a casual acquaintance to her. She clenched her teeth as she thought of him and how he'd given his life for a friend. "He didn't die for nothing! I'll see to that!" she mumbled with determination.

Leaning over to her, the aide asked, "What did you say?"

Her eyes burning with a deep fire from within and talking through her teeth, Ellie Sue repeated herself and added, "I've lived my life, and it's been a good one! That boy has no one else but me to help him now! I'm not ready to die, but somehow I'm going to try to help him to free himself!"

The nurses aide looked at her, puzzled. "I'm not sure I understand."

Looking at the girl and with her voice controlled by the fire within her, she mumbled, "You wouldn't!"

Then, looking away and down at the end of her bed, she calmed herself down somewhat and said, "It's too complicated to explain."

Trying to be helpful, the aide asked, "Is there someone we can contact and inform them that you're in the hospital?"

Ellie Sue tried concentrating her thoughts while the aide waited. First, she thought about her family, then her thoughts turned to Bill. She knew he would want to have his friend Jim know what had happened. *Jim will contact whoever else I want later, but now I need to talk with him,* she thought.

Slowly raising her eyes, she looked at the aide, saying, "Yes, Jim Switzer. He lives here in town."

"We'll call him for you." She turned to leave, then said, "I almost forgot. Does the boy who was with you have a family we can call?"

Ellie Sue's eyes turned downward. "No." Giving the aide Jim's phone number, she added, "Just make that call. Tell him I have to see him right away."

After the aide left, Ellie Sue lay in bed thinking about how Jim would help her think clearly and know what to do. Since he and his wife were the only ones in town who knew about Peter, she felt she had no one else to turn to.

When Jim Switzer walked into Ellie Sue's room, her eyes were red, portraying the anguish she'd been going through. Her face was moist and flushed. He and his wife rushed to her bedside. Tears erupted, cascading down her face. Gin put her arms around her and squeezed her tightly. "We rushed right over when we heard," she said in a soft, reassuring voice.

"They told us Bill died in a car crash!" Jim looked at Ellie Sue as though expecting her to tell him it wasn't true. "Can you tell us what happened?"

Taking Ellie Sue's hand, her eyes reflecting the compassion she felt, Gin interrupted, "You don't have to talk about it now. It might be better if you wait and tell us later."

Leaning over and taking a tissue, Ellie Sue dried her eyes. Looking first at Gin and then at Jim, she said, "No. I want to talk about it now. We found Peter and he's in pretty bad shape here in the hospital. He's in a room just down the hall. . . . and, he's really confused." She wiped her watering eyes and blew her nose, then continued. "That thing has been using him for its own purposes. We could see something had to be done right away or he'd be lost forever." She shifted herself in bed, then looked back at Jim, instructing, "Get me my purse. I have some notes in it I want you to keep."

Jim found Ellie Sue's purse in her bedstand and handed it to her. She removed some papers and gave them to him. "Here, you can read them. Then, see if you can make a copy and give them to Dr. Meyer. He'll need the information to help Peter. . . . Put the originals in a safe place."

Accepting them, Jim assured her, "I'll take care of it. I know Bill spent a lot of time trying to find Peter to help him get rid of the creature that's in him. If there is anything I can do for Bill, I'll do it."

Ellie Sue lost control of her feelings at the mention of Bill's name and began to cry. Jim and Gin said nothing. Her emotions reached their souls, and their faces reflected their concern for her. Patting her on the shoulder, Gin consoled her, "Go ahead and get it out of your system. It's all right to cry. We know that you and Bill grew close to each other."

Finally, Ellie Sue regained her composure and with determination, she stated, "I'm going to take over where Bill left off. Somehow, there's

260

a way to beat that thing." Turning to Jim, she added, "You have Gin to consider. I don't care about myself, but I don't want you to endanger yourself."

Jim's eyes narrowed. "Bill was a good person and friend to me. You let me decide what I should do. If you feel up to it, I'd like to know everything that happened since you and Bill left here."

Ellie Sue's eyes softened. "Okay. I'll try to tell you everything."

Chapter 11

BREAKTHRU

W HILE Ellie Sue was in the process of explaining to Jim and Gin what had happened in Boston, a slight movement to her left caught her attention. Turning herself in the bed to get a better look, her eyelids suddenly flashed wide open and her eyes bulged out forward. Her heart racing and her blood roaring through her veins, she exclaimed in disbelief, "Bill?"

He stood by the door, looking at her without speaking.

With a flurry of excitement, Ellie Sue spun around, threw her legs over the side of the bed, and sat upright, oblivious to the pain in her leg. throwing open her arms to him, tears of joy flowing freely onto her cheeks, she cried out, "I'm so happy you're alive!"

Slowly Bill walked over, put his arms around her, and squeezed her against his body. then, releasing her, he stood back. Holding her hands and speaking in a gentle voice, he said, "I can only stay a very short time."

Her expression changed to fear. "What do you mean?" Pausing, she looked at him closely. "Are you trying to tell me that you aren't alive?"

Attempting to put aside her fears, Bill said, "My physical body died in the crash. It was only through the strength of our feelings for each other that it's possible for me to be here now."

"But, Bill, I need you! Now that I found you, I've already lost you!" Ellie Sue sobbed uncontrollably. With their hearts absorbed, Jim and Gin stood mute.

"I know we've only had a very short time together, and there's nothing that can take away from us, what we've shared. . . . But, I'll have to leave soon." He paused and looking through her eyes deep into her soul, he solemnly added, "I want you to help Peter."

Ellie Sue wiped her eyes, cleared her throat, and with her eyes reflecting a newfound strength, she asked, "What can I do?"

Bill answered, "I want to explain some things to you. This knowledge may help you to make the right choices."

Although she wasn't sure what he meant, she held back her questions for fear Bill wouldn't have sufficient time to finish explaining. Blinking her eyelids, she nodded her head.

Bill looked at her squarely, saying, "That's my girl! . . . There's a physical wall of energy that separates this plane of existence from the spirit world to prevent intervention by spirits in this life. It's formed by subatomic particles vibrating at varying frequencies."

Pausing, he glanced at Jim and Gin, then back at Ellie Sue before continuing. "Some time ago, complications in this energy field were created when the alignment of the cosmos varied slightly. Even though it was only momentary, it was long enough for a few spirits to break through the barrier and invade this place of the living. The entity that entered Peter was one of those who broke through. It was because of this phenomenon that he also gained a tremendous amount of energy from the restraining wall when he escaped, so you must be careful."

Bill squeezed her hands as he cautioned her. "You remember when I told you about Peter and how he was blamed for the school burning, then the fire in the Ozark Mountains, and the death of the girls? . . . The entity caused all of these things to happen."

She nodded her head in acknowledgement, holding constant eye contact with Bill.

"Well, the quirk occurred, and the entity slipped through shortly before the school burned. He first attempted to punish Peter for the miseries he caused the entity as Martha Daget in his previous life, because she had left him, filed for a divorce, and came here. And, when she changed back to her maiden name and moved in with a man, it enraged him."

Ellie Sue was ahead of him. "The man who killed her in your home."

"Right," Bill agreed. "When her husband found out about her death, he became violent and was committed hopelessly insane. He died there." Bill paused a moment, then continued. "When he failed in his attempt to degrade or destroy Peter, the entity's vengence turned to this deceitful use of his body."

Ellie Sue became concerned. "But, Bill, what can we do against something as powerful as this evil creature is?"

"The strength of the three of you can become collective and multiply if you strengthen your belief in your abilities and pray sincerely."

Glancing at Jim and Gin, then looking back at Ellie Sue, Bill advised, "Find a priest who can perform an exorcism. . . . It is very important that the four of you work together to augment each other."

With her eyes softening and feeling Bill's deep love giving her strength, Ellie Sue squeezed his hands and whispered, "I understand that you must go, and I really do appreciate you're returning to be with me now. . . . I felt such a loss when I believed I couldn't see or talk to you ever again." She smiled softly and whispered, "I love you, Bill. I know I haven't told you before, but I do love you with all my heart and soul."

Bill closed the distance between them, put his arms around her, and, pressing her to his breast, he kissed her tenderly. Then leaning back he looked deep into her eyes. She felt a warm feeling refresh her soul. Pressing his lips to hers once more, he kissed her good-bye. "I truly love you, Suzie," he said, and the tears caused by their not being together filled his eyes.

Ellie Sue's expression changed to surprise, and words quietly flowed from her lips. "You've never called me that before!" But he was gone. Only a whisp of white mist remained momentarily, then it dissipated.

Now she knew Bill would not be with her for the rest of her life, but his returning left its mark on Ellie Sue, who turned to look at Jim and Gin. Reading their faces, she stated, "You saw him, too, didn't you?"

Jim looked at her questioning look and affirmed her statement, "Yes, he was here! You weren't seeing things!"

Jim and Gin walked over to Ellie Sue. Her eyes reflecting her renewed strength and conviction, she asked, "Do you know a priest who's performed an exorcism?"

Looking at Ellie Sue, Gin spoke, "I can ask Father Duggan if he will come. . . . I know he did at least one . . . on a young boy a few years ago."

A feeling of determination swept over Ellie Sue, and she said, "Good. Call him right now!"

Surprise crossed Gin's face. "Right now?" she questioned. Then she stated, "It's the middle of the night!"

Ellie Sue said firmly, "Yes, now. From what Bill said, the hypnotist won't be able to help Peter. I have a feeling that Bill didn't want us to wait on an exorcism."

Seeing the determination in Ellie Sue's eyes, Gin immediately agreed. "All right, but Bill did also say we are to pray hard and believe in ourselves having the power to overcome that entity."

Waving her arm toward the door, she instructed Gin, "You go and call him. Ask him to come right over! Tell him we'll explain everything when he gets here!" Then to Jim, she said, "We'll pray together here!" To Gin she said, "You can join us when you get back!"

Gin hurried from the room. Ellie Sue pushed herself to the edge of the bed. "You'll hurt your leg," Jim cautioned as he moved to help her. Carefully with his assistance, she lowered herself to the floor.

"It's only bruised," she stated as she knelt to pray. Then she advised Jim, "We'll pray out loud. Put everything you've got into it!" she implored him.

With Jim kneeling beside her, they began to pray in earnest.

Upon returning, Gin knelt beside them and joined them in praryer.

Later, they were still praying when Father Duggan arrived and without saying a word, he knelt beside them and joined in.

Finally, Jim's knees begain paining him and his shifting positions signaled a break in their prayers.

Ellie Sue, catching hold of the bed, pulled herself to her feet and spoke, "Thank you, Father, for coming here. I know it's extremey late." She paused, glanced out the window where the sunlight was beginning to become brighter, and added, "Or, should I say early in the morning."

From beneath his vestment cap, a soft smile appeared. "I understood it was urgent. I can always catch up on my sleep, but saving souls must come first."

Jim helped Ellie Sue back into bed. After finding a comfortable position and looking at the priest, she spoke, "Please, let me explain to you what we are up against."

When she'd finished, Father Duggan appeared hesitant. "I didn't know there was to be an exorcism."

Feeling a flow of conviction, Ellie Sue spoke. "Please, Father, Peter needs you now! His soul needs you before it's too late!"

Father Duggan turned to Jim. "I'd like to see the boy."

"I'll go with you. His room is right down the hall." Turning to Gin, he advised, "You stay with Ellie. We'll be right back."

With Jim leading the way, they talked softly as they walked to Peter's room.

"This is his room." Jim indicated the room with the closed door. Thinking the nurses might be caring for Peter, he knocked. Hearing no response, he pushed the door open and he entered. Through the dim sunlight, Jim glanced at Peter's bed and finding it empty his eyes quickly searched the room. Jim stood petrified. Father Duggan, stretching around him, pointed and becoming mortified, he involuntarily shouted, "Up there!"

Drifting near the ceiling, Dr. Meyer and a nurse floated while suspended inanimate, shrouded by a blue-green field of energy.

Turning on his heel in a rush, Jim's elbow caught Father Duggan in the chest, knocking him backward. Pausing but momentarily to keep the priest from falling, Jim then ran down the hall to Ellie Sue's room and burst in.

"Peter's gone!" he exclaimed, his face white with beads of sweat.

Father Duggan, following on Jim's heels, panting, presented his reddened face in the doorway. With fear he'd never known before controlling his mind, he tried desperately to settle his rapidly pumping heart. Breathing deeply while grasping the door jamb, he felt the quavering motions, hampered by his sixty plus years of age and a life of inactivity, forcing his blood through dangerously narrowed veins. Slowly, he wiped the small beads of perspiration from his brow.

Upon seeing them, Ellie Sue leaped from the bed. "I know where he's going!" she exclaimed as she caught her gown from the end of the bed. "We've got to hurry!"

Jim objected. "You stay here and tell us where he is! You're in no condition to leave!"

Showing her bull-headed determination, she shouted, "Not on your life! I'm going!"

Jim grabbed Gin by the arm and hurried her after Ellie Sue. Father Duggan hesitated. Quickly retracing his steps, Jim caught him by the shoulder. "You're coming with us!" he demanded.

Having only a slight alternative, Father Duggan resisted no further and panting, he hurried along behind them, to Jim's car.

With his radar detector on, Jim drove at breakneck speed to Boston. When they arrived, Ellie Sue directed Jim to the old storage building, which looked deserted.

"Damn it," she cursed under her breath as she opened the door to get out.

"What's the matter?" Jim inquired.

"The gun was in Bill's car. I'd feel a whole lot safer if we had it."

"From what you've told me, it wouldn't do any good!" Father Duggan remarked. Then, looking at the ground, he shook his head, wanting to leave. "I'm not sure we're going to be able to do any good against that evil spirit."

Ellie Sue limped to his side of the car and attempting to bolster his courage, she tried to be reassuring. "Bill told us we have power only when we believe and cling together. Our positive forces will magnify if we concentrate and pray."

Not wasting any time, Jim ran through the lot to the back of the building closely followed by Gin. Ellie Sue, limping in hops, tried to keep up with them. Father Duggan, with fear engulfing his face, desperately forced his perspiring body to cooperate, and he lagged somewhat behind.

Leaping the steps and rushing into the porch, Jim found it empty. Leaning against the doorway, he paused, catching his breath while he waited for the others to reach him.

Feeling mixed emotions of both relief and disappointment, then answering their questioning looks, Jim stated, "Looks like he's either not here yet or he went somewhere else."

Walking down the porch steps, Jim directed Gin, "It's almost noon. Take Ellie Sue and Father Duggan and get something to eat."

Surprise flushed Gin's face. "What about you?'

"I'm staying here in case he comes. I'll be all right." Then turning to Ellie Sue, he asked "Where did you wait with Bill?"

Showing determination in her voice, she stated, "I'm staying with you, Jim!" Then, pointing across the field to a clump of bushes, she answered, "Over there is where we waited."

Knowing he had no chance of deterring her intentions, Jim turned and she followed him walking across the lot.

Calling to them, Gin said, "I'll bring something back for the both of you."

Turning to face her, Jim said, "Okay. . . . Leave the car in the parking lot up the street, when you return."

Ellie Sue's guts tied themselves into knots and her leg throbbed as the four of them crouched in anticipation. What seemed to her like an eternity passed before, whispering in short breaths, she announced, "Someone's coming."

A figure reached the back of the building. Ellie Sue's heart jumped beneath her breast, and her blood careened through her veins as she recognized Peter.

Stopping and looking around, Peter let his gaze come to rest on where they crouched, hunching down close together. Appearing satisfied, he entered the porch. Ellie Sue turned to look at Father Duggan, who was perspiring profusely. "Are you going to be all right?" she asked.

Hesitatingly, he nodded his head and then with renewed strength, she directed, "Then let's go!"

Carefully, with Jim in the lead, they worked their way to the porch steps. Upon reaching them Jim suddenly leaped upward with inspired energy. He ran through the first room and burst into Peter's living quarters.

Caught by surprise, Peter recoiled on the carpeting like a serpent ready to spring. After having tackled him, Jim was struggling to restrain him when the others rushed in.

At the sight of the priest, Peter's eyes turned to fire in their sunken sockets. Immediately his body took on a bright red glow. This changed to a luminescent blue-green with bands of multicolored energy flowing from his head while it swelled in size. While stretching Peter's skin into a multitude of cracks, the entity burst into burning flesh.

A bolt of searing energy erupted from Peter's oversize mouth, heading for the priest who was standing, his mouth agape. Encircling his body and twisting, then compressing, it wrenched his guts into a compact ball, while spinning him into the air. His arms flailing uselessly as pain and terror flushed his face, Father Duggan hung momentarily suspended in midair. Then, spinning like a top, he was cast through the porch wall. His body passing between the fibers of material left no hole when he emerged outside and was sent sprawling unconscious to the pavement.

Ellie Sue, upon seeing him disappear into the wall, immediately dropped to her knees and began praying.

Through all of this, Gin stood mute, her frozen gaze of terror directed upon her husband, Jim.

Roaring in a raucously savage growl, the emerging beast hurled Jim across the room, where he landed in a crumpled mass of singed blood and smoldering clothing.

Knowing this to be the end for them, Ellie Sue closed her eyes, not wanting to see it happen. She prayed aloud in hysteria.

"JACK ARCHER!" a booming voice shouted.

In shocked disbelief, Ellie Sue, instantly opening her eyes, caught sight of Peter who had grown to seven feet tall, shreds of clothing remained clinging to his hairy body. Bolts of energy flashed and cracked about him. Blue-white flame spewed forth from his nose and mouth as he breathed.

"JACK ARCHER! LEAVE THAT BOY'S BODY!" the voice boomed command, and Peter turned his attention toward the origin of the voice. Ellie Sue followed his piercing eyes, in disbelief.

Bill stood a short distance to her right. "YOU DON'T BELONG HERE!" he shouted to the entity in Peter. Then, with his jaw clenched firm, Bill stood defiantly, looking at Peter with a piercing stare.

"I COMMAND YOU IN THE NAME OF THE ONE MOST HOLY TO LEAVE THAT BOY'S BODY AND RETURN TO THE OTHER SIDE!"

Peter's scarcely clothed body slumped to the floor as the entity emerged from it. A bolt of flaming energy flashed toward Bill. Passing through Bill, it struck the wall directly behind him, splintering it into burning shreds in a terrifyingly loud crash.

Gin regained her voice, and in shock she began to screech hysterically. Ellie Sue, jumping to her feet, began pulling Gin toward the steps.

Outside, she found the priest with his clothing charred, wandering around in a stupor. Blood oozed from his mouth and nose. Ellie Sue, running to him, caught him by the shoulder, shaking him. Yelling, she proclaimed, "You've got to help me get Jim and Peter out of there! They'll be burned to death!"

With an ashen-white face and his horror-stricken eyes glazed, he stared on past her. Finally he managed, "I-I-I c-can't!"

Feeling a flush of empathy-laden disgust for him, Ellie Sue rushed back into the porch. Reaching the inside porch door, she narrowly avoided Peter by coming to a screeching halt. Exerting great effort crawling, Peter reached his hand out to her.

Glancing up from looking at Peter, she caught sight of Bill, who was locked in the massive arms of the creature. Huge belts of multicolored pure energy zapped, cracked, and spit around their twisting and contorting bodies.

Through dazed eyes, Peter looked at Ellie Sue and pleaded, "Please help me to get out of here. I don't want to die."

Glancing toward where Jim had fallen, Ellie Sue saw sparks smoldering in his clothing. Frantic and pointing at Jim, she yelled to Peter, "He's going to burn to death. We've got to get him out!"

A movement behind her caused her to whirl around. It was Gin, heading for her husband. Removing her jacket and throwing it to Gin, Ellie Sue directed, "Use this to smother the fire. I'll help Peter to get out and be back to help you with Jim.

Grabbing Peter's arm and straining with every ounce of energy, she could muster, Ellie Sue half-dragged him to the outside.

Quickly, Ellie Sue returned through the billowing smoke to help Gin with Jim. Momentarily, she looked at Bill and Jack Archer's struggle, and her eyes burned from an intense light and heat, as they appeared to be consuming each other.

Turning to look toward Jim and Gin, her mouth dropped open in surprise. Another form was materializing near them. Her fear became mixed with amazement as she watched the form of a woman take shape. *Martha Daget, Jack's wife,* she caught herself thinking.

"JACK! YOU MUST RETURN WITH ME!" the woman commanded.

Standing in awe, Ellie Sue couldn't help noticing how beautiful the woman looked with her long, flowing, black hair.

"JACK!" she repeated. "THIS IS WRONG! YOU MUST LISTEN TO ME! I WANT YOU TO RETURN WITH ME!" she insisted as she moved closer to them.

Jim, attended by his wife, groaned in agony on the floor. A putrid smell of rotting vegetables, smoke, burned flesh, and ozone from the intense fire and electricity encompassing Bill and Jack, stung Ellie Sue's nostrils.

Her feet frozen to the floor, watching wide-eyes, her mouth agape, Ellie Sue became entranced by the supernatural struggle unveiling before her.

Slowly, the twisting and spinning of Bill and Jack came to a halt. The intense heat and energy they were emitting faded. Jack freed Bill and stood looking at the woman. "Martha?" he questioned in a bellowing voice.

"Yes, Jack. It's me." She spoke softly, trying to reassure him as she watched him carefully.

"Where were you all this time?" he asked, his voice somewhat calmed.

Smiling reassuringly, she stated, "On the other side waiting for you."

He continued to question her, "But, I looked for you and couldn't find you."

"My mother kept me from you because of your jealousy," she explained.

Bill remained standing close to Jack without speaking as Martha moved closer to them. When she had reached Bill, she put her hand on his arm and turning to him, she spoke in a low voice, "Now," she directed.

The combined energy of Martha and Bill formed a large linked chain and collar. One end was attached to Bill's wrist. While Jack concentrated his attention on Martha, he remained unaware as it moved snakelike up behind him.

Looking down at Martha's petite figure, Jack questioned in a guttural voice, "What did you say?"

Looking up at Jack, Ellie Sue saw the fire in his hollow eyes had diminished. Then, she heard Martha, in a controlled voice, request, "Please come back with me."

Suddenly, the collar of energy snapped itself around Jack's neck. Immediately reaching for it, he tried to break free as it clenched itself ever tighter with immense pressure. Jack struggled desperately to free himself, but it continued to choke his resistance and subdue him.

Martha directed, "Take him back quickly, Bill. They'll know what to do with him. Once you have him on the other side, he'll never be able to return."

Even as she spoke these words, Bill and Jack vanished. A whisp of white mist hung in the air momentarily, then it dissipated.

Ellie Sue struggled to speak. Then finding the words and blinking her eyes, she exclaimed, "Martha!"

The woman looked at her. Then smiling, she said, "I'm not Martha. My name is Angeline Karsti." As she spoke, her form slowly changed.

A smell of smoke caught Ellie Sue's attention. Remembering Jim, she exclaimed, "We've got to get him out of here."

Angeline raised one hand, and the fire near him was extinguished. Then she spoke, reassuringly to Gin, "Jim will be all right. There are no serious injuries."

Ellie Sue's eyes continued to blink, and her face reflected her astonishment. She asked, "How was it that you came at the right time?"

Angeline answered, "When Bill arrived on the other side, he told me what had happened. They had been checking over there to determine what spirits had broken through the energy barrier and when we told them about Jack Archer, they agreed to allow us to return here to entrap him. We knew he had absorbed great amounts of energy and that we had to cause him to expend most of it before we could succeed. Bill agreed to come first. Since we are pure energy, we each have a great deal of our own. Bill was able to draw some of Jack's energy and, thus, augment his own. When I touched Bill's sleeve, our combined strength that we put into the chair and collar was too much for Jack to break. Those on the other side assisted Bill to enable him to bring Jack back."

Ellie Sue looked in amazement at the kindly old woman who stood before her. With a sincere feeling of appreciation in her heart, Ellie Sue smiled warmly, saying, "Thank you, Mrs. Karsti. When you see Bill, tell him I'll be waiting to be with him."

"I'll do that. I know he'll be waiting for you, too."

A question entered Ellie Sue's mind as Angeline's form began disappearing. "One more thing. Why did you help Bill?" she half-yelled into the misty form.

As though blown on the wind, Angeline's voice came to her. "Because he once was my son, who died shortly after his birth."

Outside the day had become very hot. The priest was nowhere in sight, and Peter lay resting on the ground. Gin, her face covered with dusty wet streaks, appeared through the doorway with her husband. Ellie Sue, helping to support Jim, stumbled along behind.

Descending the steps and still trembling, Gin spoke. "Thank you, Ellie, for helping Him! . . . I was just completely useless in there!"

Having assisted Gin with Jim, Ellie Sue walked over, seating herself beside Peter. She wiped his dirty face. To Gin, Ellie Sue responded, "I'm glad it's finally over with. If you and Jim hadn't come here to help me, this wouldn't have happened to him. I do appreciate your help."

Gin stated, "That woman did say that Jim will be all right. Whatever she did with her arm stopped his bleeding immediately . . . and I didn't even thank her."

"I'm sure she understands . . . Let's get Jim and Peter to the hospital. . . . Get the car, I'll wait here with them," Ellie Sue said.

After a short stay in the hospital, Ellie Sue had Peter flown to Far Rockaway, New York, where she nursed him back to health, in her home.

Several months later, Ellie Sue could see that Peter was becoming restless. Before long, he approached her. "I don't want to leave you, Ellie." He paused and looked down at the floor. "It's just that I have this yearning to go back home to Boston." But she did not answer.

With her facial muscles tightening, her face drew long and she felt saddened inside, even though she'd long expected this.

With his love showing in his eyes, he said, "It's not what you might be thinking. . . . You know my family lives there, and it's been a long time since I've seen them." Pausing, Peter looked at her. Feelings of regret at leaving crept through his mind. A tear ebbed from the corner of one of her eyes. Reaching out, she came to him. He hugged her tightly, then, leaning back, he looked into her eyes and spoke, "I've grown up a lot since I left home. Now, I think I can go back and face them all."

"Yes, Peter, I believe that you can! You've become a real man, and I'm very proud of you." Then, smiling thorugh misty eyes, she added. "You don't have to worry about me. I'll be all right. You have to do what's best for yourself."

"I've hated to leave you alone, but I knew you'd understand how I feel about it. You know, I've been thinking about getting a place of my own when I get there . . . and maybe taking some night courses to finish high school, too."

Tears swelling her eyes, Ellie Sue squeezed Peter's hands, saying, "That's a wonderful idea. I know you'll do very well for yourself."

Peter was momentarily silent before saying, "I hate to think about what would have happened to me if it weren't for you." His eyes teared, "And Bill," he finished.

His mind momentarily flashed back to when he and Bill were with Marie and Diane, and he cried inwardly. "I'll never forget what you've done for me. I know there's no way to really say thank you. . . . You know I'll be back to visit."

Looking at him through tear-filled eyes, she answered, "You know you'll always be in my heart."

Peter threw his arms around Ellie Sue and hugged her. Then, standing back, he said, "I only wish Bill could be here, for you, so you won't have to be alone."

Her thoughts turned to Bill and her eyes took on a faraway look as she said, "I do, too. But, we'll be together, again!"

Looking at Peter she wiped her eyes with a tissue. Then smiling, Ellie Sue gave his hands a quick squeeze before releasing them, saying, "You are a precious person, just as Bill had told me you were."

Peter grinned. "You are something else, aren't you? It's no wonder Bill fell for you. . . . I'll miss you." He leaned over and kissed her gently. "But, I'll be back to visit."

"Good-bye, Peter . . . and take care . . . you hear? . . . . I'll miss you, too!" . . . and she found herself alone.

Later, back in Boston, Peter went directly to his parents' home. He walked in and his mother's surprised face brightened into a huge smile, as she jumped up and rushed over to him. "Oh, Peter! We've been worrying ourselves sick over you," she exclaimed. "Where have you been?"

Peter pulled her tightly to him and hugged her, with his hands clasped behind her back. Glancing over her shoulder, he saw his father rise from his upholstered chair. "Speak for yourself, woman!" he stated in no uncertain terms as he glared at Peter. Sternly he questioned, "Where you been, boy?"

As useless as it had seemed, Peter had hoped his father had changed. Glancing in his father's direction, he flippantly remarked, "We'll discuss it later."

The remark being unexpected caught his father by surprise. His chin dropped as he recoiled slightly before sinking back into his chair. Turning his attention to his mother, Peter guided her to the outside and after seating her on their porch swing, he sat down beside her.

Tears forced their way forward, then flooded down Peter's mother Delmar's face, in torrents. She spoke softly and kissed him on the cheek. "I've missed you, Peter! Why didn't you let me know that you were all right?"

Peter replied, "It's a long story. I'll tell you all about it some other time."

Then, holding back the anger she'd felt toward him for not having contacted her while he was away, she cried softly, "I'm so happy you're finally back home."

Looking into her watering eyes, he felt a feeling of guilt sweep through him as he said, "I know, Ma. I've missed you, too."

273

And, he turned away, not wanting her to see the tears welling up in his own eyes. After a few moments, he put his arm around her shoulder and gave her a squeeze. "It's sure good to be home again! . . . I love you, Mom!"

"I love you too, Son!" She kissed the side of his face.

Peter settled himself back into city living. Entering into evening courses, he worked hard to earn good grades and was determined to graduate with a GED.

One day the following spring, Peter waked past the new high school, remembering the last days he'd spent in the one that had burned. The day was warm, the sun was bright overhead, and his expectations for life were high. Shortly, he met up with Jaako and they walked along the sidewalk, idly talking.

Glancing up and looking forward, Peter noticed a girl approaching them. Although she was still some distance away, he recognized her. His mind tuned his memory banks, and he thought, *She walks like Maggie!* And, an image of her propped into his head. *Yes, that's her!* his mind shouted at him.

"There's Maggie!" Peter blurted out to Jaako as he suddenly bolted toward her. Getting within a half block of her, he involuntarily shouted, "Maggie!" Panting and running, he yelled a second time, "Maggie! Is it really you?"

Maggie couldn't help feeling hurt and angry with Peter since he hadn't gotten in contact with her, since she'd last seen him. Upon seeing him now, she recalled the many horrible times she'd cried, wanting to see him. Although she didn't know how he would, she'd expected him to get in contact with her.

Now seeing him running toward her, his face beaming his excitement, she felt a strange mixture of joy and resentment. Throwing up her hand, she signaled him, knowing that she'd have to give him a chance to explain his failure to contact her.

Excitement coursed through Maggie's body, threatening to burst her blood vessels. "Make him explain! Make him explain why he didn't contact me!" she mumbled to remind herself, trying not to let her emotions dissolve her resentments. Then, he was upon her! Grabbing hold of her waist! Raising her up high into the air! Spinning her around! She yielded to her emotions and became totally engrossed in the feelings that rushed through her body, which were accentuated by the strength of his muscles surrounding her. Then, feeling her body light back down on the pavement, she couldn't rebuff his immediate embrace. Unable to resist him, she pulled him to her and kissed him in an extended, sensuous kiss.

Finally standing back and looking at him, she exclaimed, "I can't believe it's really you!"

Being hugged by Peter brought feelings of closeness that quickly replaced all of the many doubts she'd harbored, about their possible future together.

Images of the past flashed through her mind, and a warm feeling flooded her body. He came to her, but she pushed him back and held him at arm's length, silently looking at him. Then, she heard him excitedly blurt out, "I looked for you when I came back! Sissie told me that you hadn't returned home! . . . But, she wouldn't give me your address!"

Maggie flushed with a warm happiness, which brought her a contented feeling. Taking Peter's hand and swinging it in hers, she started walking. Looking up at him, she said, "I know! . . . You know how Sissie is. I wrote to your parents a number of times, but I only received one letter back. Your mom wrote and said she didn't know where you were . . . I hated her for being so cold about it."

Stopping her and pulling her to him, he kissed her. In an apologetic tone, he said, "I was on the move and didn't stay in touch with them. I know that I should have, in case you got in touch with them, but I'd figured they wouldn't have let me know anyway. The important thing is we're together now and NO ONE will ever separate us again."

Flashing her eyes at Peter, she said, "You're going to have to tell me about all your lustful adventures."

Almost shouting, he replied, "They were hell days. Right from the beginning being without you, then things you'll never believe started happening!"

Wrinkling her nose, she suggested, "Try me! I just might believe you!"

"Someday I will, but not right now." Then, as they walked leisurely along the sidewalk, she looked up at him and said, "I truly love you, Peter. I've missed you so much, you'll never know." Then she added with determination, "We'll always be together from now on!"

"FOR SURE!" Peter's eyes sparkled as emotions flashed though him awakening dormant feelings. A broad smile spread across his face, and he said, "I have something I want to show you!" He paused, looking into her eyes. Then grinning impishly, he added, "But you'll have to be patient!"

Her eyes gleaming with excitement, she asked, "What is it?"

"I have my car around the corner! We'll have to use it to get there!"

Squealing with excitement, she exclaimed, "I'm game for anything!"

Reluctantly, Maggie agreed to be blindfolded while he drove to their destination. Then, parking the car, he ushered her out, turned her around, and removed the blindfold.

Maggie looked out onto the farmland in front of her. Recognizing it, she spun around and looked up. Her eyes climbed to the bluff, then followed the rock steps that were built into the hillside upward from the bluff beside the Natural Wall. Finally, they came to rest on a house at the top of the cliff, which Peter had built with the money Bill left him.

"Oh, Peter, I love it!" Her eyes sparkled. A huge smile crossed her garden of freckles, and her hair danced in the sun as she jumped up and down. Unable to contain her excitement, she shouted, "It's just like we talked about having! . . . I want to see it!"

Bursting into a sudden sprint, Maggie ran to the bluff and started climbing.

Peter's eyes gleamed brighter than they had for a long time. "You'll kill yourself going that way!" he cautioned. "We can drive right up to it."

Running to the car, opening the door, sliding into the seat, and slamming the door closed, Maggie exclaimed, "Then let's go!"

Shuffling her body sideways, she scooted over next to Peter as he entered. Putting his arm around her, he reached for the key, but Maggie stopped him. "Wait!" she requested. Then, she reached into her blouse pocket and produced a folded piece of paper. All a-twitter and handing it to Peter, she proclaimed, "I've waited a very long time to give this to you. I hope you like it. I wrote it when I only had you in my memory."

Peter unfolded it and read the contents.

MEMORIES

My mind has lingered in the place we knew so well,
Special to us where the waters swell;
We talked and dreamed of future plans,
Things we'd do in far-off lands;
The love we shared, ever a part,
When we gave each other our heart.

Remembering the river in my mind, now I see,
How we paint our lives in memory;
The fun we had, only few have known,
These treasures now I carry all alone.

Your smiling eyes, in my mind,
Still sparkle, dance and shine;
If ever we meet again, in time or space,
My memories will reunite me, with your precious face.

Time makes fools of mortals we,
Passing swiftly, we fail to see;
Thinking only all things will last,
Wondering what happened, when they've past.

Until someday together, we can see,
What real love is for you and me;
I'll continue relieving what used to be,
And passing my life in memory.

Peter thought about Bill and how much he would have liked Maggie, too, if he'd had a chance to get to know her. A warm and tender feeling flowed through Peter's entire being. "I love it!" he exclaimed. "I kept the other one you gave me, with me and read it until it was in shambles. Then, when it got burned, I really missed having it, but I'll keep this one with me forever!"

Peter's eyes reflected his emotions as he looked deep into Maggie's. A small tear moved from the corner of her eye and drifted down her cheek. Gently, he wiped the tear of love from her cheek and spread it across his own cheek. Holding her by the shoulders and looking at her through blurry eyes, he said, "I DO TRULY LOVE YOU, MAGGIE!"

Feeling his passion rising, with one motion, Peter pulled Maggie to him, kissing her in a long, wild, and savagely sensuous kiss.

EPILOGUE

T HE traditional fairy tale ending: "They lived happily ever after" would appear to be fitting, but life doesn't deal the cards that way.

Peter's brother continued causing him problems. Maggie and Peter married with a ceremony less than total bliss when her mother refused to attend, leaving a seed of regret deep within her soul. This festered beneath her skin, boiling toward eruption.

Upon graduation with a GED, Peter found employment prior to attending college, while they worked on creating their family. First born was a son, Roger, nicknamed Rusty, followed shortly by a daughter they named Lori.

Their lives remained shrouded in secrecy and mystery ever since . . . until? But then, that's another story!